Cause of All Causes

The Maghreb Trilogy
Book 3

By

I0618484

James Marinero

Also by James Marinero

Fiction:

Gate of Tears
(featuring Steve Baldwin)

Sicilian Channel
(The Maghreb Terror Trilogy Book 1 featuring Steve Baldwin)

Sword of Allah
(The Maghreb Terror Trilogy Book 2 featuring Steve Baldwin)

Non Fiction:

Susan's Brother

Image Credits

Cover Images: fotolia.com
Artwork: projectpdq.com

Join my Readers List and get a Free Thriller Book* at:

Marinero's skill at describing people with a few deft strokes is remarkable. The action is fast, furious and believable. This is a must read for lovers of complex geopolitical thrillers: · Lee Holz, author of The Bowin Novels

Make no mistake, our society is under threat...

In this terrorism thriller, Steve Baldwin has sailed to Crete in his search for a quiet life, still licking his wounds after a near-fatal assignment in the Red Sea. The Royal Marines had been his family, but now he tangles with Helena, a Greek waitress who is far from what she seems, so Baldwin sets sail again.

In Malta, he is coerced by MI6 into the pursuit of a psychopathic female specializing in assassinations, with whom he shares some painful, bloody history. Can he ever escape these two clever, dangerous and demanding women - one of whom he is ordered to kill?

Malta, with its Crusader history, is a key target for terrorists. Abu ben-Zhair, the cold and calculating Islamist master planner, is upping the terrorism stakes and religion is just a lever in his lust for power.

The chase - and the women - are more complex than Baldwin could ever have imagined.

*Free Books offered change from time to time and may vary from that illustrated here.

Cause of All Causes

Published by Wavecrest Publications
3 Murray Street, Llanelli
Carmarthenshire, SA15 1AQ, UK
www.wavecrestpublications.com

First Edition 2017

Copyright © James Marinero, 2016

ISBN-13: 978-0-9956410-1-3

The moral right of the author has been asserted.

With the exception of certain historical figures, events,
scientific papers and news items for which references have
been provided, all persons, organisations and events in this
novel are fictitious, and any resemblance to actual persons,
organisations or events is purely coincidental.

The paperback version is printed on paper which accords with
UK: Forest Stewardship Council™ (FSC®) Mixed Credit.
FSC® C084699

Contents

ACRONYMS (These are <u>not</u> fictional entities)

AQIM -   Al Qua'eda in the Islamic Maghreb

AIS -   Automatic identification system (AIS) – automatic
         tracking system used for collision avoidance on
         ships and by vessel traffic services (VTS)

AISI -   Agenzia Informazioni e Sicurezza Interna (Italian
         internal information and security agency)

AISE -   Agenzia Informazioni e Sicurezza Externa (Italian
         external information and security agency)

AWE-   Atomic Weapons Research Establishment,
         Aldermaston, England

BCIJ -   Central Bureau of Judicial Investigations – the
         Moroccan Secret Police

CISR -   Comitato interministeriale per la sicurezza della
         Repubblica (Italian Interministerial Committee for
         the security of the Republic)

DIS -   Dipartimento delle Informazioni per la Sicurezza
         (Italian security information department)

DRS -   Département du Renseignement et de la Sécurité or
         Department of Intelligence and Security – the
         Algerian Secret Police

GUOANBU – The Chinese Ministry of State Security - Guojia
         Anquan Bu

HMG -   Her/His Majesty's Government (UK Government)

ISIL   (so called) Islamic State of Iraq and the Levant (aka
         ISIS - Islamic State of Syria and the Levant)

NAJA -   Law Enforcement Force of Islamic Republic of Iran

PAVA - Iranian Intelligence and Public Security Police, part of NAJA

QUDS - The Quds Force - a special forces unit of Iran's Revolutionary Guards responsible for extraterritorial operations

TOR - The Onion Router – an internet mechanism for anonymising communication. TOR routes internet traffic through a free, worldwide, volunteer network consisting of more than seven thousand relays.

The Syriac compendium of knowledge known as *Ktaba d'ellat koll 'ellan*, "The Cause of all Causes", is unusual in asserting that there were three columns in the Pillars of Hercules.

According to Plato's account, the lost realm of Atlantis was situated beyond the Pillars of Hercules, in effect placing it in the realm of the Unknown.

Today we recognise only two – Jebel Musa in Morocco, and the Rock of Gibraltar.

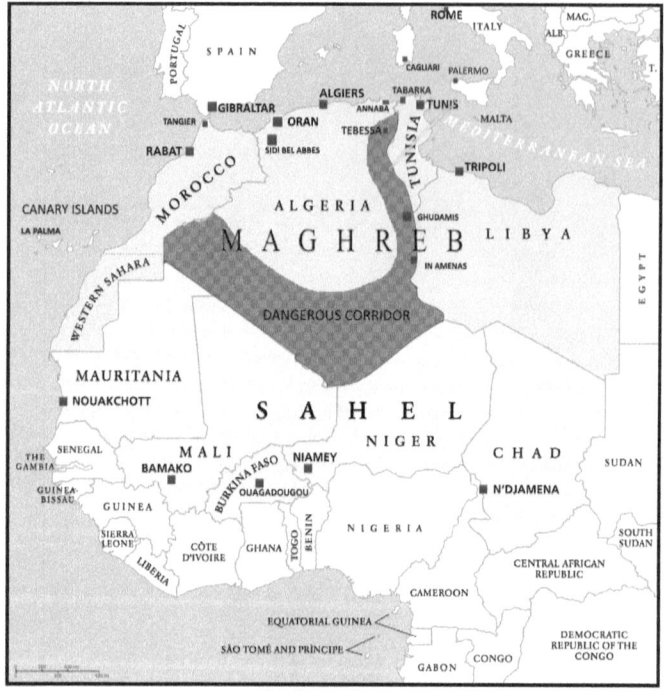

Credit: Fotolia.com

Prologue

The First Day of Ramadan, an Atlantic Island

"I think it's going to hit." The awe in Tricia's voice was clear as she spoke the words slowly and distinctly. She was looking at the ship, whilst Peter's eyes were drawn to the missile in flight.

She watched in awe as the ship quickly slowed, skewing, as more than fifty thousand tons of steel met the rock and sand less than forty feet below. It drove onwards, its outer bottom hull ripping and filling with water, then the inner skin was tearing as the ship slowed. Inside, the rigidly built containment structure remained intact, the generators continued to run and the vacuum tubes remained solid. The decks and cargo stacks held firm – insurers mandated that such ships were designed to cope with such accidents.

Fifty meters outside Spanish airspace the first two cruise missiles self-destructed as the one remaining F15 screamed overhead in a desperate attempt to evade the *Novyy Rassvet* SAM missile.

"What was that?"

Peter Gillespie peered through the binoculars at two small clouds to the east. "It sounded like explosions. Far away, though."

They didn't see the others.

Above them, the F15 launched its own missile – an AGM-88J AARGM – which turned sharply and locked on to the ship's anti-aircraft radar, passing closely by the SAM missile closing rapidly on the F15.

Peter held the binoculars. "Good God Tricia, the ship has stopped! It's only about fifty yards offshore. Maybe it's hit a rock or run into the shallows?"

From the Gillespies' vantage point the bow of the ship was clearly visible over the cliff edge and its thick cover of a banana plantation. They didn't know that the ship was hung up on an outcrop of harder igneous rock. This outcrop had been selected more than two years previously by Nassim Kateb to act as the initial conduit of the explosive shock wave. He planned that it would conduct the power of the weapon through a hard stratum into the softer rock.

In Sidi bel Abbès, the voice of Jafa Sharifi was heard on the virtual bridge of the ship.

"All parameters are within limits – laser temperature, power bank levels, mirror alignment. Fuel pellet parameters are perfect!

Above it all, ex-President Trump's cloned voice droned on. "Counting down five seconds, four, three, two, one, trigger release. I love you all!"

*

Three years previously, the Tree House Café, Rabat, Morocco

"Surely it is not possible, Nassim?"

"Surely it is, *Al-Mahdi.*"

Al-Mahdi – Abu ben-Zhair - looked out from the Tree House café in the lush Forêt Nouzhat ibn Sina, known locally as the Forêt ibn Sina Hilton. Named after a previous hotel which was now officially the Sofitel, the name 'Hilton' had stuck to the forest. To the north, beyond the eucalyptus and pine trees lay the Agdal campus of Muhammad V University in Rabat where Nassim Kateb was a professor in the Earth and Universe Sciences Department.

Anyone who looked at the two men seated in the café would assume that they were brothers. One was clearly older, but not old enough to be the other's father. Perhaps they were discussing serious family matters? However, the physical resemblance between them was entirely coincidental.

Ben-Zhair leaned back in the chair and scratched his chin. "For your idea to work, the power needed would be huge, would it not?"

"Certainly, but the target point I have suggested is, I believe, in delicate metastasis."

"Metastasis?"

"A tipping point, just one small push is all that would be needed."

6

"How small?"

"My calculations show that we would need to generate of shock of more than 6 on the Richter Scale."

"Richter Scale?"

"It is a measure of the energy released in an earthquake."

"But that is not small, surely earthquakes are huge events?"

"Yes and no. It is a matter of precise positioning to act as a trigger. I believe that there is pent-up energy there, ready to be released. Metastasis, as I said."

"This will require some thought and would require a huge investment. It would also be very complex to arrange."

"Yes, I understand, but it is an interesting possibility, yes?"

"Certainly it is an interesting idea, Nassim. I will continue to provide funds for your research for the moment, while I consider the requirements. High energy weapons are almost impossible to obtain, and I have other projects close to fruition."

"I understand, *Al-Mahdi*, but the impact would be on a global scale and out of all proportion to the energy input required. That's what metastasis offers."

"Of course, I see that, and I am grateful for your suggestion, but it is the initial trigger that is the problem. We have known each other for many years and I respect your deep knowledge of the matter. Your research should continue to explore the precise area in more detail, so that you can be certain it would work – if I could obtain a suitable initiator. I repeat – you must be certain. On that basis I will continue to fund your research."

"*Al-Mahdi*, 'certainty' would be ninety five per cent confidence in my scientific terms. I doubt that I could ever be that certain about this. It is the difference between 'likely' and 'very likely' to happen. This is not a minor experiment in a laboratory."

"Then you must find a way to make it nearly very likely! Then I will be able to decide whether it is a worthy investment."

"I will try. The research papers are on this memory stick – there is still scientific disagreement about the probability of a natural event, but with Allah's will we can change that. Thank you for continuing to fund my work, *Al-Mahdi*."

"Yes but remember, I do expect a return on my investment. Now, I must go, before the godless Moroccan secret police find me."

"Yes, it is best. Perhaps next time we will meet somewhere else?"

"Yes, if this idea of yours may become possible, then we will have to be even more careful. I will contact you in three months time. By then I want you to be certain it would work – and I may have a solution about the trigger."

"Insha'Allah"

"Insha'Allah"

Ben-Zhair stood up and walked away to his parked car, deep in thought and neglectful of his tradecraft, but it did not matter. This man, soon to be at the centre of major international events was undetected, untraced, unfollowed. Surely, this really could be earth shattering, but so much more than just an earthquake or a volcano. So much more. Nassim Kateb was certainly worth the investment if this scheme worked out. But first, the trigger design would be tested, in Rome.

His heart raced at the excitement of the prospect, and, unknown to him, the old, faulty and fake pacemaker in his chest sent out a data packet to the local Algérie Telecom mobile network, from where it wormed its way to a deeply protected Guoanbu server in Wuhan, China.

*

Before Rome

"This can't go to COBRA. It's beyond Ultra."

'C' muttered. "Obviously, Prime Minister. *Non plus ultra.*"

"What was that?"

"Nothing PM, sorry just muttering to myself."

"Besides you, me and Tweedy at AWE, how many of our people know the full details of the situation?"

"A baker's dozen – plus the Head of Middle East and North Africa Desk."

"Are they secure?"

"I may need to weed out one or two of the possible doubters of our actions."

"Weed out? How?"

"The way one usually deals with weeds, Prime Minister."

"Weed killer?"

"Precisely."

"Very well. And the new Deputy Director?"

"She knows nothing – she's only been in post a few weeks. She may have suspicions, but nothing more."

"I understand. All Blue Angel files are to be archived as Ultra Plus?"

"Yes, Prime Minister."

"Very well, let's draw a line under it."

The line dropped.

'C' could not help but be impressed. 'Hard bitch' was his view of the PM as he reviewed the files. This had been the dirtiest operation imaginable, and she had held steadfast, whatever the morality of the situation, and was continuing to tough it out. He looked down at the list.

Thirteen names. Two sets of files. All database records re-encrypted and locked with a quantum key; only two paper copies accessible – and these he would personally destroy within the next two weeks. The HR files had been purged. All that was left were eight paper career summaries in one pile. Five in the other pile and one in no man's land.

Two of the team would have fatal accidents. Two others – Stone and Gregory – were still missing. They had been with

Williams and Baldwin when the explosion had taken place in Rome, but had been well outside the blast area. The others would receive posthumous commendations and not for publication. Their cover names would go 'on the wall' – the wall that listed the names of those who had died on active service. Two of those were missing and still unaccounted for. The thirteenth file presented a conundrum.

BALDWIN, STEPHEN.

Which pile should that file be put on?

'C' scanned the latest medical reports. Amnesia. The trauma of the blow to the head had caused loss of short term memory. Events prior to the Rome disaster were apparently lost. The neurologists had tried triggering his memory with news reports, video images and audio but had not stimulated any reaction in the subject.

Baldwin's reactions were clearly those of someone with no recall of the events portrayed and the photos of the people involved. He apparently did not know Bryan Elliott, an MI6 colleague blown to pieces by Pavkovic in Tunis. Baldwin had recognised a picture of a Greek waitress from Crete, and he recognised pictures of his boat, Adèle. He had some recollection of leaving Crete for Malta and there were vague recollections of the events in Malta – these would probably be recovered in full. The period after Malta until he had awakened in the hospital appeared to be a complete blank.

The memory loss was thought to be permanent, although one could never be absolutely sure – doctors always qualified their prognoses – and Six's tame doctors even more so.

'C' locked the list of names in his safe. On balance Baldwin was very useful – capable, deniable and nowhere on the payroll - as long as the amnesia lasted. But Baldwin did suffer from an over-active conscience and a deep streak of independence – not really the profile of a cold-blooded assassin. He lacked proper respect for authority. Was it worth the risk? He sighed and shook his head. He would have to instruct Ogilvy to pay a visit to Baldwin before the final decision was made. And then, he,

'C', would have to deal with Ogilvy, the current Head of the Middle East and North Africa Desk.

*

A COBRA is the meeting forum used when the UK is subject to instances of national or regional crisis, or during events abroad with major implications for Britain.

The purpose of the COBRA committee is to co-ordinate the actions of bodies within the Government of the United Kingdom in response to the crisis. Usually, the policy regarding a particular type of crisis has been established and is held in a library of policies (and action plans) which may be subject to variation according to the circumstances.

The quorum and attendees of a UK COBRA meeting are variable depending on the nature of the particular crisis in hand. If the issue is a national rail strike, then one would not expect to see the Chief of SIS or the Chief of the Defence Staff in attendance, though the Commissioner of the Metropolitan Police and the Minister of Transport would certainly be present. Neither is the meeting necessarily held in Downing Street, but it would usually be held in Cabinet Office Briefing Room A (hence the acronym COBR[A]) in Whitehall, unless of course the Government had been moved to a secure location.

Meetings may also be virtual, particularly when held at short notice or when senior government ministers have been located outside of London.

Cobra Committee Meeting, Downing Street

Edited Meeting Transcript:

Sir William Gore, MI6:

'This matter carries the rather unfortunate code name 'Blue Angel' – a random computer selection I might say. We have information both from our own sources and the United States about the latest North Korean atomic weapon test. The radionuclide residues which have finally percolated through the subsoil and into the atmosphere have a radioactivity

signature which is typical of a fusion bomb – that is, a hydrogen bomb.

Beyond that, there is little in the sample data which is typical of a fission bomb which is the usual trigger of a hydrogen bomb. I am advised that there is no way that the test – which measured five point one on the Richter scale could have been a fusion bomb – at least with the technology as we understand it. However, the radioactivity data would definitely appear to support the claim that North Korea made about a fusion device – with qualification. I stress the phrase – 'the technology as we understand it'. The nature of the radionuclide signature is unique – it has never been seen before – it appears to be 'fusion plus'. Now, we have Jonathan Tweedy on secure video link. He is the Technical Director of the Atomic Weapons Establishment at Aldermaston. It is a briefing and he will not be taking questions.'

Jonathan Tweedy, Technical Director of the Atomic Weapons Establishment:

'The conventional hydrogen aka fusion bomb requires a fission – aka an atom bomb - as its trigger to generate the high temperatures necessary to enable atoms to fuse (classically these are deuterium and tritium which are forms of hydrogen). In the process huge amounts of energy are released.

In contrast, peaceful fusion research has been geared towards maintaining a high-temperature plasma of deuterium and tritium in a relatively steady non-critical state. This requires continuous high energy input and the output must be controllable and continuous - an atom bomb is clearly out of the question! The energy output must also be usefully greater than the input for it to make economic sense for power generation. Present experiments are achieving the holy grail of 'net energy gain', but only for microseconds.

There are many technical issues – it is a far more complex process than making a bomb. Indeed, for the last sixty years, fusion power has always been 'at least fifty years away', whereas the first hydrogen bomb was tested in 1952.

Some avenues of current fusion power research involve the use of high-energy 'pumped' lasers to produce the high temperatures required and also need a lot of electrical power to hold the hot plasma stable in an electromagnetic 'doughnut' – the so-called tokomak – a Russian word. This is a complex configuration in which to maintain the stability of a very hot plasma. The United States and, we assume, other countries have been exploring alternative methods. Of course we have one ourselves.

If the energy output is not required to be continuous as for power generation but just one big pulse - as in a bomb - then high energy input needs only to be for the briefest of intervals to create a runaway reaction. The challenges of containment - maintaining plasma stability - are greatly simplified if not removed altogether. A special fuel pellet is used in the US test configuration – for peaceful purposes of course."

"It is a mixture of deuterium and tritium – forms of hydrogen, held in a small plastic pellet.

The pellet is located in a small gold canister known as a 'hohlraum' – the German word for space – smaller than a sewing thimble, although the term is also used in the physically larger context of a conventional nuclear bomb. Then, more than a hundred lasers pump out huge quantities of energy in less than a billionth of a second with the energy focused on the fuel pellet in the hohlraum. This has been demonstrated in fusion power research at the Lawrence Livermore lab in the US – supposedly for peaceful purposes as I said although the prime directive of the Lawrence Livermore Laboratory is to enhance US national security. Of course, many would argue that energy security – and therefore peaceful nuclear power research – falls within this definition. I digress, sorry.

These are big lasers and many of them are required for just one hohlraum - delivering one point nine megajoules of energy in slightly more than a nanosecond, the lasers are rated at five hundred terawatts – that's five hundred trillion watts. That's equivalent to well over twenty thousand times the output of Dungeness nuclear power station in Kent. But it's only for a nanosecond.

One of the difficulties for a 'rogue state' or terrorist group in building a conventional atomic or fusion weapon is that some components - for example very fast-acting electrical switches for detonation - cannot easily be bought on the open market and are subject to very strict export controls – and they are not easy to make at home. And that's the least of the difficulties. Plutonium – or enriched uranium – is required. This is not easy to obtain. Then, miniaturization to produce a suitcase-size fission bomb is practically impossible for any entity other than a major state.

But with a pumped laser fusion device - 'PLFD' for short - these scarce, tightly controlled components would not be needed. The components that we envisage would be required are much more freely available, although still specialist – for example high power lasers. This would simplify the construction process. Nevertheless, some exotic materials are required but deuterium and tritium are relatively easy to obtain through university research laboratories. We believe that these weapons are feasible – I'll say no more on that – but nevertheless, the reality of a practical weaponized PLFD had been thought to be several years away.

One further and critical advantage of the PLFD is that fissile material - usually uranium 235 or plutonium - would only be required in very small - that is sub-critical amounts - to enhance the performance of such a device. Or even not at all. So, a little goes a long way – at least in theory. And, uranium 235 is much more easily obtainable than plutonium.

Another aspect of the PLFD is that it would create minimal fallout. This would make it more useful when targets are nearer to home and does not create long term radioactive no-go areas – unless it is doped with, say, cobalt. I cannot see any way that such a device could be miniaturized, but, within limits, it could be a relatively simple route to constructing a true fusion bomb, and could of course avoid the use of plutonium or enriched uranium which are difficult to produce and relatively easy to track – unless of course they obtained some from a country friendly to the terrorists..

I have a team of technical analysts still working on the sampling data from the test. We are also trying to work out if North Korea could have 'hoaxed' us by falsifying a specific radioactive signature as part of a conventional atomic weapon test. We think that this would be very difficult to achieve and is *very unlikely given also the seismographic data. That is all I am able to say at present, apart from the fact that with the exception of the North Korean aspect, there's nothing secret here – this design is all in the public domain. Sorry if I got a bit enthusiastic there – it's a very interesting development. Thank you.'*

Two months later, another Cobra Meeting, London,

There was a hubbub in the briefing room.

"Order please! Let's get on with it. I've come straight from Northolt, I'm very tired and need to get some sleep."

The Prime Minister started her report on the P5 meeting (the UN Security Council Members) to the Cobra committee in a Cabinet Office briefing room adjacent to 10 Downing Street.

"First, the latest P5 session. There is a consensus in the P5 that North Korea has very probably got a miniaturised fusion device. We know that they first claimed to have tested such a device in February 2016, but the claim was not believe at the time. By miniaturized we seem to agree that it is not a suitcase, but needing several trucks at the least to move it. So, it's not *yet* a practical proposition as a missile warhead. This information comes from the Chinese who probably know a lot more than they are letting on.

The Chinese did say that they have seismographic data from one site that supports the theory. They shared it with us.

All P5 members are pulling out all stops to pressurize the North Koreans, but sanctions have led us nowhere.

Now, this is completely unprecedented: we are *jointly* working on a plan for disarming North Korea. The Chinese have volunteered to invade and replace Dim Pong-un. Not all members were happy about that – the Chinese would obviously have access to the technology – not that they need it – we're all up to our necks in fusion bombs already. The Chinese are insistent on having a buffer state between themselves and South Korea where there are US troops. However, the plan does have the attractive elements of simplicity and low cost – to us that is.

Politically it keeps us clean, though we'd have to make a show about condemning Chinese aggression and so on, for public consumption, but that's understood by the P5. And China will insist on the new North Korean regime being Communist – in their own image. We can live with that. Japan might have an issue though, but the US would have to manage them. There would be some sabre-rattling from Tokyo. Of course, this would all be orchestrated in advance.

I have my doubts and frankly, I expect unilateral military action by the United States any day now."

If such a thing were possible, the silence intensified in the briefing room.

"That is the good news. When I was in the plane on the way back, Sir William called me. It gets worse. Much worse. Sir William, please update the committee."

He nodded.

"Prime Minister, ladies and gentlemen. In the last twenty four hours we have discovered that North Korea has shared the new fusion technology with Iran. It seems that Iran has developed a new weapons research establishment at Yazd, unknown to us or the UN Weapons Inspectors until now. Iran has been building a prototype of the new device for the last several months in an effort to circumvent the nuclear arms treaty which they signed two years ago.

Even more disturbingly, we believe that Iran has lost control of the prototype, and we have further reason to believe that it is now outside Iran. I have high confidence in this intelligence and this information is certainly not being sexed up. Naturally I cannot discuss our sources of this information.

As you would expect, we are deploying all our resources – and I do mean all – towards determining the full facts and the location of the missing nuclear technology."

He nodded to the Prime Minister who held up her hands and waved to attempt to silence the eruption of noise around the table..

"Thank you Sir William. I cannot go into sources and reasons, but we believe that the Chinese know about this nuclear technology leakage. We very much doubt that other members of the P5 do. For the moment we are not sharing this with the United States – there is simply too much risk that Tel Aviv will hear about it and then, well…you can imagine.

I'm not taking questions now, but would remind you that this is Ultra Secret. I want you to think about policy implications so far as it impacts your individual responsibilities. No discussion anywhere but here. Put nothing in writing or on your systems. This subject is not to be discussed with *any* of your staff, not even your Permanent Secretary. And don't clear your diaries – that would raise questions. Just cry off the appointments as necessary. We will reconvene at three p.m. Meeting closed. Sir William, please wait behind."

Six members of the Blue Angel quorum left the meeting.

The door was closed.

"Right, Sir William, I want you to run through again what you told me about earlier."

"Well PM, in addition to what I just told the meeting, we believe that the prototype device is in North Africa – probably Algeria - and under the control of ICIM – that is 'Islamic Caliphate in the Maghreb'.

"Good God! This is an unholy situation."

"Quite, Prime Minister."

"Algeria? Well, we can't brief them in on this although the Foreign Secretary might want to. They've already lost control of half their country."

"Agreed. It is absolutely vital that this intelligence does not leak. We cannot let anyone know that we have sources of this quality. We have certain knowledge which indicates that at least one Chinese agent is tracking the device and is tasked to take out the mastermind behind it. We have assets close to the agent – very close. I would expect the Chinese to infiltrate more agents very soon – if not already.

It is very likely that the Chinese are leaning heavily on Iran. There are indications of increased diplomatic activity and signals traffic, but we know no more than that."

"I thought we could read some of the Chinese traffic."

"We could until recently, but the cryptography war is never ending. They are continuously upgrading their encryption – and decryption - technology."

"Then how do we know all this about Blue Angel?"

"If you don't mind Prime Minister, I'd prefer not to comment. It's better that you don't know at this time."

The PM's eyebrows arched and her lips pursed – rather sexily, thought 'C'. "Very well, I understand – but if this proves to be more sexed-up intelligence data then…"

"I fully understand Prime Minister. I have the highest confidence in the source."

"And you are sure we are not being fed a line here?"

"As certain as it is possible to be. You have heard what the other P5 members have to say."

*

Threats and Claims

There had been two announcements. The first was on November 24th - Thanksgiving Day in the United States of America and the day before Black Friday, the crazy retail shopping extravaganza.

ANNOUNCEMENT
Issued by ICIM Operations Command
Dated: 24 Safar1440 A.H., 06:00 hours, Mecca time.

The IC today advises the infidel states of the world that it has miniaturised nuclear weapons in place in several major infidel cities. These weapons – the Sword of Allah - are ready to use.

We have a list of demands which we expect to be met unconditionally by the appropriate countries and organisations if use of the Sword is to be avoided. These demands must all be met by 20 Rabi al-Awwal 1440 A.H. (20th December this year). There will be No negotiation, No agreement, No truce, No dialogue. All diplomatic channels – and backchannels - are closed.

Our demands are:
1. Formal recognition of the Islamic Caliphate by the US, EU, China, Russian Federation and all other members of the G20.
2. IC Membership of the United Nations
3. Freeing of all IC prisoners worldwide
4. Withdrawal of all infidel forces from IC territories in the Levant and Maghreb
5. Abolition of the so-called State of Israel and transfer of the government to IC control

Signed: ICIM Operations Command

End

The announcement by the Islamic Caliphate in the Maghreb ('ICIM') became public simultaneously on Al Jazeera, Twitter,

Instagram, YouTube, Vimeo and 47 other websites. It took the form of a text slideshow with no audio. There was one picture included in the deck of slides – that of a '*hohlraum*' – the small but central component in a new design of nuclear fusion device originally developed in the Lawrence Livermore Laboratory, just east of San Francisco.

The next announcement was on 20th December that year, and was a final warning. The world community had failed to respond in a coherent way which was satisfactory to ICIM. The rest, as they say, is history and Rome suffered.

The Maghreb – the area stretching from Libya in the eastern Mediterranean to the Atlantic coast of Morocco and the historical base of the Barbary pirates – was now the centre of a feared regional power. The governments of Libya, Tunisia and Algeria, together with the monarchy in Morocco, were tottering as the ICIM annexed even more of their territory and spoke with nuclear power.

It was not, however, a regional power in the traditional sense. Although it held physical sway over large tracts of central and northern Africa (the so-called Dangerous Corridor), it was in essence a 'virtual power'. It exercised control through Shariah Law but that power was exercised in the minds of individual members of the populations. Outside of the Dangerous Corridor sanction against shariah lawbreakers would come in the night.

However, with no obvious geographical centre of power of ICIM, no obvious heart, there was little that the UN or the individual superpowers could do or attack. ICIM had learned from ISIS. In Syria, ISIS had set up its administrative headquarters – and that became a focus for air strikes and attack by the US Marines in the spring of 2017. ICIM's governance structure was completely dissipated and amorphous, and even simple administration tasks did not significantly rely on telecommunications. Word of mouth and written messages were adequate for most purposes. The Ottoman Empire had been run without telecommunications.

When it came to the matter of arms and terrorism projects, the use of telecoms was inevitable. ICIM could not challenge the major developed countries when it came to cryptography and worldwide networks, but it could hijack and use satellite channels for brief periods and communications bursts. It could also use multi-level combined one-time symbolic and PGP encryption which was impossible to break in a useful time horizon, even by China or the US.

But inevitably, the ICIM left footprints during its operations – and these could be tracked. However, the tracking, like the codebreaking, took too long and the hunters were always several steps behind.

The rest is history, with major attacks in Paris (a dirty conventional bomb) on Christmas Eve and Rome (a nuclear bomb) on Christmas Day .

"Well Jafa, what went wrong?"

Jafa Sharifi's face was serious as he replied to ben-Zhair using his operational code name. They were on fishing boat headed out from Rome to Cagliari in Sardinia. It was 26th December, and less than 24 hours after Rome had been attacked.

"I do not know, *Al-Mahdi*. I have looked at the news pictures from Rome. The yield was obviously less than calculated – perhaps thirty percent of what I expected. It could be that the containment area – the vault - was too deep, too well- hardened – although I cannot believe that. It could be that the fuel pellet was insufficient and we did not achieve the energy release we calculated. I am still trying to understand the shortfall in yield. Unfortunately we do not have all the data as the telemetry failed just before ignition. It may take several weeks to find the explanation."

Ben-Zhair smiled. "You are too serious, Jafa. This was a great success. The infidels now know that we have the technology and the capability – and they have no idea what is coming next. And those dogs in Iran now have Israel to worry about. We could not wish for more.

Next week we will be in Sidi Bel Abbès, preparing the final stage. Then next year the Cause of all Causes will be completed and Islam will rule more than half the world.

21

But Jafa, remember that we need all the yield and more for the Cause of All Causes to be a success. You cannot fail next time – we need a hundred percent."

"Yes *Al-Mahdi*, I understand. One hundred percent."

Ben-Zhair's phone vibrated and he glanced at the text.

"It is done Jafa. I am now effectively the Caliph of the Maghreb."

Following the events in Paris and Rome over that Christmas period, Abu ben-Zhair's Head of Security, Qasem Hamadani, had directed the team which moved swiftly to cleanse the ICIM Inner Council. It was a tightly-coordinated a strike at the precise moment that the ICIM claim of responsibility had been released under ben-Zhair's instruction.

The Islamic Caliphate *per se* had been usurped by ben-Zhair's strike at the world Christian Community.

*

A Month After Rome

The pain was like a steel band around his head. He could not move. Sounds intruded, bright light was in his eyes. It felt as if all his senses were overloaded and then, mercifully, it ended. Each time that consciousness broke through, the sensations were a little less intense. Then after three days the painful tidal ebb and flow of his sensations and consciousness started to abate. By day six he was sitting up in bed.

He could use the bathroom by himself though he felt very weak and unsteady on his feet. The door to his room was always locked.

The nurses and doctors had said little and refused to answer his questions, but they did at least smile – and ask him questions, questions to which at first he had no answer, questions like 'What is your name?', 'Where are you from?' Then they started to show him videos. A cruise liner devastated in Malta. He could remember that. Pictures - Maruška Pavkovic, Charles Tobin, Helena – or was it Ellie? The memories came back piece by piece, it seemed. A villa, a brief firefight. Then nothing.

He watched video footage of the Pope's Christmas Blessing – to a point. A nuclear bomb in the centre of Rome. His shock was apparent and captured on the room's webcam which monitored him 24 hours a day. The instruments noted the elevated heart rate and blood pressure.

On the seventh day he had a visitor, a face he recognized but could not put a name to.

"The medical team says you are doing well."

"I know you – you are erm…we met in...erm."

"Don't push it Baldwin. You are making progress."

"Where am I?"

"You are in a private clinic, in Hertfordshire."

"Why?"

"You were injured."

"How?"

"I don't know. You tell me."

"I can't remember a thing."

"The doctors say that you suffered serious head trauma. Delayed concussion and slight skull fracture – apparently it would have killed most people. Everything physical appears to work well, but you have some memory loss and you may never recover your memory of the missing period. Now, there is some bad news I'm afraid."

"What bad news? What you just told me sounds bad enough."

"It's Helena actually?"

"Helena? Helena who?"

"A Greek waitress."

"Oh, yes, yes, I seem to remember something. Dancing in Greece."

"She's dead."

"Is she? That's a pity, I think that she was fun, but that was a long time ago. Crete. Oh yes – then she showed up in Malta. Real name Ellie something, was it? Not much recall I'm afraid. She was as spook wasn't she?"

"Ellie, yes, she was killed in a car accident – in Malta. Along with Bryan Elliott. Sadly, you were the only one to survive, if you see what I mean. Came off the road at Dingli cliffs – landed on a ledge. You were very lucky." Sadder than you will ever know, thought Ogilvy, but he could now tie it all up neatly in Malta by watering the seed of these false memories that his people had planted.

There was no visible reaction from Baldwin.

"Do her parents know yet?"

"She has no parents. She was an orphan, brought up by several sets of foster parents in Bristol."

"But her father worked in the British Embassy in Athens. At least, I think that's what she said. My memory's a bit patchy."

"Is that what she told you? She certainly has – or had – the gift of persuasion and a wonderful ability to play a part. No, her natural mother was a junkie, she never knew who her father was."

Steve thought about the Greek waitress he's met, who had been – so she had said later – an Oxford graduate. "Is that what she told *you?*"

"That's what the records say."

"Then the records are wrong."

"No Baldwin, it's your memory that's wrong."

"We captured that Serb bitch – Maruška Pavkovic - didn't we?"

"Yes that is certainly true, and a fine job you all did. HMG is very grateful."

"For what it's worth. Anyway I need to get out of here and back to Adèle."

"Adèle who?"

"Adèle, my yacht, in Malta."

"Ah, yes. That will not be possible I'm afraid, not yet anyway, not until you are fully recuperated, the doctors sign you off – and I agree. And there is another reason. More bad news."

"What?"

"The Tunisian authorities have impounded your boat."

"What the fuck, Tunisia, why is she there? The last I can remember is...is...Malta.

"You tell me how she got there."

"I can't remember. You must know more than you are letting on. You must know what has happened to me over the last few weeks. Tell me."

"We only have a vague idea of where you were and what you did."

"Tell me, you bastard."

"There's no need for that attitude Baldwin I don't need to be here you know!"

"Ok, ok, sorry, must be the bang on the head."

"Perhaps. Anyway, I don't know the details - I'll look at the files and get back to you. I do know that your boat was in Malta. Now she is apparently in Tabarka – a port in Tunisia. The Tunisians would like to arrest you for illegal entry, kidnapping and murder. They claim to have strong evidence."

"You must be kidding!"

"Not at all. They are seeking extradition. We have told them that you are too ill to be moved – for now. Your passport is there on the side table – there is no entry stamp for Tunisia in it, so you must have been there illegally, if at all. Look, Baldwin, HMG do not want you going to Tunisia. It would cause too many problems."

"Right, I see now. Same old bloody story. Stitched up again! Just like the Gate of Tears."

"Gate of Tears?"

"That job in Djibouti when you landed me right in it."

"I don't know about Djibouti – before my time I'm afraid. Look Baldwin, you were very lucky to come out of this alive. However, HMG really appreciate what you did for your country in Malta. Let it rest – the doctors say you are bound to be troubled by the memory gap but you need to learn to live with it. Anyway, HMG will make reasonable funds available to cover your work, plus expenses. We might even cover the loss of your boat – even if she was insured you'd probably not get the payout. So, be a good boy, stay here and recuperate properly for a few weeks and we will sort it out. I will be in touch when the doctors are ready to sign you out. Trust me."

Ogilvy omitted to mention that the UK did not have an extradition treaty with Tunisia.

Steve glared at him as he turned and left the room then settled back on his pillows to reconcile his memories with what he had just been told by his visitor, the man he remembered from the villa. He glanced at his passport – he knew it had been doctored and that he would never be able to find the joins.

He shut his eyes and lay back, his face a mask for the video monitor in the corner of the room.

The gap in his memory was only a few hours at most. He could remember swinging across on the climbing line and smashing through the window of the bank in Rome, the frantic work in the bank vault, then being on the scooter with Ellie – Helena the multi-role Greek waitress. Then, then…nothing. Ellie dead? Car crash? Grief touched his face briefly as he turned from the camera. Whatever happened, he decided that he would not admit to knowing more than they had told him.

They had caused him enough pain already, screwing up his life
– and his body - repeatedly.

Baldwin did not know that 'C' had tagged Ellie's file as one
of the two for special treatment, but that his own would be
returned, untagged, to the Registry in the basement of Vauxhall
Cross, on Ogilvy's recommendation. It would not be destroyed.
For now.

*

A few days after Alex Ogilvy visited Baldwin in hospital,
Ellie Williams met with Ogilvy at Leo's Lebanese Grill on
Baylis Road near Waterloo Station. It was a quiet lunch hour
and they chose a corner booth, each with a view of one of the
exits. They ordered mezze and water.

"How's the arm?" Ogilvy nodded at Ellie's left arm in a
sling."

"Much better thanks. I should have this sling off next week
and then a bit of physio and I'll be as good as new."

"Good to hear, you did well. We have plans for you."

The waiter arrived with the mezze and drinks and the small
talk stopped.

"Why did you ask for this meeting Ellie?"

"Because I know the way the service works and I have a
pretty good idea what your plans are for me. Rome was a
seriously dirty operation – as dirty as could possibly be - and
there will be a clean-up in Six as surely as night follows day.
All the Noel team from Rome died in the blast – very
convenient. Baldwin has gone MIA. Tweedy in Aldermaston
must be looking over his shoulder. No doubt his team have
been read the riot act and been threatened in a dozen different
ways – but their knowledge was limited. And you of course –
are you safe, Alex?"

"Perfectly. Unassailable you might say."

Ellie looked at him and he held her gaze steadily – but he
then diverted to help himself to some falafel.

"Great mezze here, though I don't get here as often as I
should. They do grilled lamb on Thursday evenings – some say

they slaughter it themselves out at the back – they've got a halal licence. Too much information, I know, but I enjoy it."

"Cut the crap Alex! You know that if what we did gets out then it would damage HMG beyond all comprehension. We would have no friends left in Europe – and we have precious few anyway since Brexit. The damage would last for a generation – at least. The Cousins would be pissed off beyond belief and the 'special relationship' would be broken - forever. This means that HMG cannot be found out. No way. That means that both you and I are at risk, considerable risk – of the final kind. God knows how Six is going to manage the members of Cobra. They must be crapping themselves – or have they taken appropriate precautions?"

"The final stages of the op were kept very close. The idiots in Cobra don't know the half of it. Anyway, you have nothing to worry about."

"That's just the answer I would expect from someone who has already received an order about me. You will be next, as sure as shit."

Ogilvy blustered. The stolen car was waiting around the corner.

"You are as safe as houses and you'll get a commendation out of this."

"You can bet your life I'm as safe as houses. I don't know how long you think I have got, but you had better cancel any operation to neutralise me. I have taken considerable precautions and if anything happens to me then the dirty washing will be hung out to dry by Wikileaks and others. Believe me I have this covered in a dozen different ways. I just want to retire and live in peace. And I want a full pension – thirty years worth."

Ogilvy looked up, with something close to panic in his eyes.

"Thirty years – you're not entitled."

"Wrong answer, Alex!"

"Leave by the rear entrance. Now."

She looked at him.

"Goodbye Alex."

"Go find your beach Ellie."

They nodded to one another.

Ogilvy took out his smartphone and keyed the ABORT code. He had already held a similar meeting of his own with 'C'.

Ellie Williams headed through the kitchen, single-handedly pulling a black North Face beanie over her hair. She left Leo's Lebanese Grill through the kitchen, past the sous-chefs smoking outside now that the lunch rush was over. Not that there had been much of a rush - it was two weeks after the Christmas atrocities and people were still afraid of being in public places without good reason.

The tension was palpable but the sous chefs were unconcerned. Allah's Will would be Allah's Will. So they smoked and chatted as the sky threatened rain. Around them in London the stiff upper lip of the English was trembling, and behaviour was much the same in many cities across Europe even where stiff upper lips were cultural oddities.

Her right hand slid into the sling that held her left arm as she felt for the Beretta that nestled there, ready for action. She looked up and down Frazier Street and crossed the road to her waiting cab and the driver she had trusted for more than three years.

She gave him an address in Battersea and after he had dropped her off she walked around the corner and down into the Tube station. After fifteen minutes of careful de-lousing she approached the Mailboxes Unlimited storefront. She hadn't noticed a tail, but these days even good old tradecraft was not enough. Microtrackers were everywhere and while she might have strong-armed Ogilvy into a notional corner he might well have tagged her in the Grill. She trusted no-one now that Baldwin was dead, and the Six smartphone was always tracked.

She scanned her card at the Mailboxes Unlimited reader and went down into the basement to the highly secure deposit box area. Not as secure as a bank vault, but relatively discreet and very expensive, a service known to very few people and unadvertised by the company. Her thumb print opened the box and she deposited her Six phone in a metal cashbox after removing the battery. From the safety deposit box she took out her own clean Samsung model – customised for her at the cost of a month's salary.

After closing her box she went into one of the private rooms - more extra costs - and scanned herself with the custom Samsung. She was clean – within limits. There was always the possibility that she had a device embedded in here body. She'd had herself checked, but if it was as small as Maruška Pavkovic's nanochip then it would require the very latest technology to locate it – and she did not have access to that. It was some small comfort that it was unlikely that Six could have replicated the Chinese technology in the few weeks since they had first uncovered it.

She was not currently on assignment so the lost tracking signal of the Six phone would not ring any alarm bells yet. And if they did - so what? She'd fixed Ogilvy.

*

Fear

In 'Risk – The Science and Politics of Fear' (Virgin Books, 2009), Dan Gardner wrote that

'...the Bush administration's response to 9/11 was emotionally satisfying but utterly wrong-headed. Define the attacks as war and terrorists become soldiers and their organization an army.'

...this was the greatest gift Osama bin Laden has ever received. Before Bush gave it to him, he was an outlaw forced to shift his band of followers from country to country until they wound up in the deserts of Afghanistan.'

Ben-Zhair had not read those insightful words, but he understood terror as a weapon. Its purpose was not to kill, but to instil fear, and use that fear to attain political objectives.

The attack on the British cruise liner in Malta had been devised to demonstrate capability and means whilst pulling a lever of terror.

Then, having demonstrated capability and means, the ICIM threat of a nuclear attack was an opportunity for world powers to respond to a specific set of outrageous demands – which they signally failed to do. Ben-Zhair had not expected them to accede.

The atrocity in Rome was the result, with the follow through that 'no further warnings would be given.' Widespread public panic was the result – fear on a grand scale. Governments had no answers to give their publics.

During the Great Depression in the US, Franklin D Roosevelt had paraphrased Michel de Montaingne:

'The only thing we have to fear is fear itself.'

Fear was rampant in all non-Muslim societies, and the Muslim societies were themselves fearful of the response that the atrocities would attract, both economic and military.

Nuclear weapons could be used with no warning – anywhere, anytime. At least, that was the perception, and perception was all that mattered. It was one thing to remember quotations about fear, but quite another to live every day as if in a condemned cell. Nevertheless, most people just got on with their daily lives, but those with properties near significant religious sites started to move away, and property prices started to fall in city centres. Some insurers withdrew cover and compounded the downward spiral.

Abu ben-Zhair had learned much from *al-Qaeda* and other modern terrorist histories. He was now at war – asymmetric war. The enemy's opportunity to accept the demands of ICIM had been ignored. He didn't need – or want – to use terror. He wanted to destroy so that he could conquer.

It really was one sided – asymmetric, in the true sense of the word. Governments had no targets for their bombs, no country to embargo with sanctions or attack with any other kind of weapon. The European Union was collapsing rapidly as internal border controls were strengthened. The man in the street's dictum was 'Security begins at home'. Governments had to listen to their voters, so they put up the shutters.

'War is the continuation of politics by other means' was von Clausewitz's well known dictum. Ben-Zhair was ready to strike – and he did not agree with Clausewitz. Politics was irrelevant. There would be no negotiations and backchannels would remain closed.

The Cause of All Causes really could change the world.

*

The Cause of all Causes

According to some Roman sources, Hercules had to cross the mountain that was once Atlas while on his way to the garden of the Hesperides on the island of Erytheia. Instead of climbing the great mountain, Hercules used his superhuman strength to smash through it. By doing so, he connected the Atlantic Ocean to the Mediterranean Sea and formed the Strait of Gibraltar.

One part of the split mountain is Gibraltar and the other is either Monte Hacho or Jebel Musa in modern day Morocco – it is still a matter of some debate. These two masses facing each other across the Strait have since been known as the Pillars of Hercules, but the clear distinction between Monte Hacho and Jebel Musa might have given rise to the idea that there were in fact three Pillars of Hercules - as had been asserted in the Syriac compendium of knowledge known as *Ktaba d'ellat koll 'ellan*: "The Cause of all Causes".

Renaissance writings say that the pillars carried the warning '*Non plus ultra*' ("nothing further beyond"), serving as a warning to sailors and navigators to go no further. According to Plato's account, the lost realm of Atlantis was situated beyond the Pillars of Hercules, in effect placing Atlantis in the realm of the Unknown.

Abu ben-Zhair intended to make this a reality.

*

Cambridge

She could barely walk straight after leaving the Kambar club – vodka and ecstasy were not the best of mixes. Looking up she saw the black van draw smoothly to a halt at the curb a few feet ahead of her on Wheeler Street. As the side door slid back two men in balaclavas and black clothing stepped out and scooped her smoothly in through the door before she could gather her wits. She heard a gruff Scots voice "This is no night for a young lady like you to be out on the streets." The man stepped back out to collect the shoulder bag which she had dropped on the pavement. Then the side door slid shut with a solid thunk as the van pulled away. There was no traffic, and the pick-up had not been seen.

The nineteen year-old girl tried to struggle and started screaming, but strong arms held her wrists as handcuffs clicked.

A light came on as she was restrained in the seat. Facing her sat a man, about thirty years old with a pinched face. He too was dressed in black but wore no headwear. He was naturally hairless and his bald skull was shining in the light, with a small goatee proving that he was still able to grow some hair. Small circular spectacles hid his eye colour in the dim light, but from what she could see they were dark. The effect was terrifying and she looked around in desperation. There was a solid bulkhead between them and the driver's compartment and there were no windows.

"There's no way out for you, so let me get to the point."

"Let me go you bastards!"

"Kirstie Tomlinson, you are being detained under the provisions of the Counter Terrorism Act 2008 and the Counter Terrorism and Security Act of 2015 on the suspicion of committing or planning to commit acts of terrorism."

"Bollocks!"

Goatee man droned on as she rapidly came to her senses.

"I'm sure that if we went through your effects then we would be bound to find some Class 'A' substances. However, we're not interested in such peccadilloes, so sit back – we have a long drive ahead, so sit back and relax."

"I don't do drugs!"

"You were seen popping E in Kambar."

"Tonight was different – an exception."

"Exception or not, it's Class A possession." The effects of the vodka and ecstasy were wearing off rapidly and as if reading her thoughts the man held out a bottle of Evian water to her.

She nodded and he removed the lid, placing it in her outstretched handcuffed hands. She drunk deeply and after emptying the bottle she passed it back. "What's this all about? I want a solicitor."

"You'll get no legal representation until I say so. Your rights were explained to you. We are under no obligation to explain any potential charges to you. So, sit tight and shut up!"

"I need the loo."

"You're sitting on plastic. Go ahead and piss yourself. We're used to it."

"Fuck you!"

"It's funny, I anticipated more imaginative swearing from a Girton student. Something in Greek maybe – or should that be Geek? No matter, save your breath and try to get some sleep. There's a long drive ahead. Here." He placed an airplane-style sick bag on her lap, switched off the light and settled back in his seat with eyes closed.

Just over two hours later the van pulled into the driveway of the safe house off the A34 at Sutton Scotney near Winchester. The air was chill and foggy, and Kirstie started shivering violently as she was led across the driveway. She finally gave in, turned and threw up on the grass at the side of the gravel turning circle. Mr Goatee handed her a bottle of water and she rinsed her mouth then finished the bottle. Two carriage lamps lit the imposing front steps of the half-timbered Tudor style mansion in the damp pre-dawn grey. As she was led inside she noticed a discreet desk at the side of the oak-floored entrance hall. The Scotsman went over to the desk and spoke quietly to the man who was standing behind it, a holstered pistol clearly visible on his belt. Meanwhile the other man steered her up the wide main staircase, then down a carpeted corridor to the right hand side of the broad galleried landing. Mr Goatee used a swipecard as she noticed a number '7' on the door of the bedroom he gently guided her into – she was weak, tired and very frightened. Thoughts of escape were far from her mind as the vodka excess thumped in her head. "Here, let me take those cuffs off. There's a bathroom over there, and there's water and paracetamol on the nightstand. Don't think about escape. We've cameras everywhere – and Tom is an excellent shot. So, get some sleep – you've an early start."

He closed the door and she heard two solid clicks as the electronic locks engaged. She checked her shoulder bag and discovered that her smartphone had been removed from her purse.

Back in Cambridge her shared house had been raided and her housemates detained. The house was cleaned of all computer equipment and swept by a specialist anti-terrorist team. Within six hours her housemates had been released having been charged with the possession of drugs – the evidence was genuine. They had also been cautioned under the Counter Terrorism Act but vehemently denied any sort of involvement. After a night in the cells they were released.

*

Annaba

Spring in Annaba is unpredictable. On the Algerian coast and less than forty miles from the Tunisian border, the winds can be fierce from the north east, or violently northwest from the Mistral blowing down the Rhone valley and across from France. Cold either way – and cold in the early morning when it blows off the night-chilled Sahara and then warming during the day as the sun does its work.

On the morning that Nassim Kateb flew into Annaba for a short visit to his childhood home, the wind was gentle and from the west, bringing warm air up from the tropics and around Morocco. As the taxi drove from the airport, the smell of jet fuel slowly faded, and the scents of the spring plants were strong enough even to overcome the fading air freshener of the taxi.

He loved his childhood home, he loved Algeria and he so wanted to see change in the country. He had been a devout Muslim since childhood, but had hidden his fervour from a world that was becoming increasingly divided – even here in Algeria. The Islamic Caliphate had extended its control but had not yet completely usurped the Algerian government or gained control of the lush coastal strip along the Mediterranean coastline. He knew that the Caliphate would win, *Insha'Allah.*

Nassim Kateb was excited. The call from the leader - *Al-Mahdi,* Abu ben-Zhair – had come in an email, apparently innocuously worded. This was not one of the regular convocations that ben-Zhair held - this was a unique meeting and could only mean one thing – Nassim's own proposal was being enacted.

He checked into his hotel and called his mother to arrange the visit to his home outside the city of Tebessa some 100 km to the south. It would be good to see her and his sister on the following day, and he looked forward to meeting his two-year-old twin nephews for the first time.

With a dallah of hot tea and some fresh lemon, he sat at the table in his room to review his calculations and the data from the latest survey.

He could not yet be 95% certain – and never would be – but the latest analysis certainly strengthened his belief. Nature was helping. Satellite data had shown increased levels of thermal activity, measurements of radon emissions were increasing and the data from his network of magnetometers on the steep slopes of the island indicated changes deep underground. A natural event was nevertheless unlikely – these changes he had measured were not unusual but could be effective indicators of stress building in the earth's crust. It would be important to pick the best moment. He held a strong belief that God was on his side and that the timing was propitious.

*

Kateb checked carefully that he was not being followed. The checks were not obvious and if he had spotted a tail he would have aborted the meeting, in line with everything he and his fellow 'students' had been taught over many sessions with Qasem Hamadani, Head of ICIM Security and his lieutenants during their desert retreats or 'convocations' as ben-Zhair called them.

The tradecraft sessions had been a break from the brainstorming and debates about tactics for ICIM. His group was a technical group – a brains trust - which spanned a wide range of specialist capabilities, including scientific, economic, cyber and psychological asymmetric warfare. The group was entirely separate from the Inner Council of ICIM – and neither knew about the other.

It would not matter for much longer, however, as, working under ben-Zhair's instruction, Qasem Hamadani would eliminate the Inner Council immediately following the attack in Rome – still more than six months away.

After the security protocol was observed, they embraced. The café was quiet, chosen by ben-Zhair for its local patronage and discreet location – two blocks back from the Plage Saint-Cloud, in an alley just off the Rue du Congo. It also served very good coffee. Even here, alcohol was a rarity – the influence of the ICIM was having an effect. They sat in a corner booth, noting the side entrance as an alternative exit. Nassim was nervous - he was, after all, an academic to whom subterfuge and tradecraft did not come easily. He had fired a pistol and had a rudimentary knowledge of brutal self-defence, but he was not a warrior. He ordered an orange juice – even coffee was, for him, off limits,

"So, Nassim what are the results of the most recent research?"

"The signs are good, *Al-Mahdi*. Stress is building and in three to six months' time, maybe a bit longer, I think will be the optimum moment. Here, the results and my recommendations are in the report on this microdrive."

Ben-Zhair slid the small chip off the table and into a pocket. He fixed Nassim with a stare, but Nassim did not flinch. He was confident, certain of his work, sure of his results.

"Tell me what it says."

"All the established scientific indicators are showing changes which indicate optimal conditions for an event. Gases, magnetism, infra-red imagery are all good. Nevertheless, an event is unlikely – the volcano has exhibited these patterns before. The last eruption was in 1971, and before that 1949."

"Surely then, another one is due?"

"We don't know. There is no pattern. Anyway, we may be able to trigger one, although my proposal does not require a full eruption."

"That is good, but how certain are you?"

"Much more certain than I was when we last met. All the indicators for Teneguia are moving the right way. This really could work – if we have a sufficiently powerful trigger, and place it at the right point. The activity level on Mount Teide is not increasing. Teneguia and Teide are the two most active volcanoes on the African Plate – that is, apart from Kilimanjaro and others in the East African Rift area."

"No one cares about Africa. It is the potential of your plan – and this one volcano – that could change the world."

"Insha'Allah"

"Insha'Allah"

"I will need twelve weeks' notice of the optimum time - and it cannot be before May next year."

"I have no control over the timing. Only Allah has that."

"I understand. Then I will set a date. You must be sure of the position."

"I am. It is on that microdrive. I have recommended the position so that there is deep water in the approach and so that the rock will direct the pulse into the heart of the structure. It is just south of Punta de Lava. There is twenty meters of depth within fifty meters of the shore. The rock is soft, which is not ideal, but it is the optimum point."

"I think that we can provide a trigger capable of six point three on the Richter Scale, but first it will be tested. You will see it in the news in the next few months. I can say no more, but I need you to continue monitoring."

"I cannot say whether that will be enough energy."

"I understand. Does it improve your confidence?"

"It will never reach ninety five percent - there are too many variables. But yes, I feel more certain."

"You have done well, Nassim."

"Thank you *Al-Mahdi. Insha'Allah* we will change the world."

"*Insha'Allah*. Then that is all. We must leave."

They stood up and embraced, then ben-Zhair left by the side door. He smiled to himself. It was a long shot that this would work – he was not as certain as Nassim who took the trigger as a given. Rome would provide the proof.

And at Christmas that year, it did. Almost. 4.7 on the Richter Scale, plus the added bonus of small earthquake in the Apennine Hills.

*

A New Yacht

It was early February – almost two months after the Rome atrocity - before the doctors were ready to release Baldwin, although they had not told him as much. He was still struggling to balance his impatience to leave against his need to maintain their conviction that his memory loss was permanent, that everything of (and especially, *after*) the supposed car crash was beyond his recall. Indeed, he really wished he had no memory of those events in Rome. He had been subject to countless MRI scans and other tests. The wound on his skull had healed leaving a scar which was almost invisible, even under his closely cropped hair.

He was in his room at the clinic, after lunch, browsing on his laptop, having started his search for a new boat, wondering if he would ever get the money together, despite what Ogilvy had said. The morning had been filled, as was the pattern, with test after test - endless pictures, shapes, questionnaires, quizzes, ink blots. This had gone on for over a month now. They had said that his was a unique case, and he knew that once or twice he had nearly given the game away and been caught out on a memory test.

There was a capable-looking guard outside his room twenty four hours a day, although he had no plans to leave – he had to play this straight. The guards were rotated regularly and he had failed to strike up any sort of rapport with any of them. He was out of cash and without a home, a plight typical of so many ex-servicemen. At least he had money coming from HMG, although government promises had so often turned out to be empty.

He thought of Adèle, moored in Tunisia and probably under guard. She'd served him well, with over 40,000 miles under her keel. He was sad, but it was not a major loss given the offer from Ogilvy. He'd lost about $1000 – his emergency fund – in a small safe in the bilges, welded to the keel. And then there were his two Sigs and spare ammunition in the waste oil drum. Someone would find them eventually. He looked up - a knock at his door. A visitor.

There was little pre-amble as he slipped into his persona.

"Hello Baldwin. I'm from Six. The name's Stevenson."

"Fuck off."

"I was told that those would be your first words. It seems the knock on the head didn't do quite enough damage."

"Fuck off."

"Yes, well whether you like it or not you are going to hear me out. Or you are going to an anonymous prison for the rest of your life – that is if you don't have an accident first."

"The last visitor from Six – I can't remember his name, but I'd met him in Malta – came here and told me that HMG was grateful for my services and I'd get payment, not a string of threats."

"People move on, policies change. Your earlier visitor is no longer with us. He had a breakdown as a result of the exotic substances he enjoyed during his leisure. Permanent damage, and such a great shame. So, here I am. A new broom as they say."

"Sweeping up shit."

"You could put it that way, if that's how you see yourself."

"Fuck off."

"I can see that I'm not getting through to you, but I'll give it one more try. Firstly, you will get money for your boat. I guarantee that, but God only knows why HMG are bothering. But before that I have some work for you – for which we will pay."

"How many times have I heard that? Is the shit too smelly for your new broom?"

"Far from it. I'm making the offer because you are uniquely qualified. You remember Maruška Pavkovic, I know, from your debriefing. We captured her."

"You mean *I* captured her, in Malta. Then you let her run. I don't know what happened after that – I was in a car accident."

"Yes, but what you don't know is that we later re-captured her."

"Where?"

"That's irrelevant now. What is relevant is that after recapture she escaped captivity on *HMS Bulwark*. At sea, thirty miles off Tunisia. She is missing, unaccounted for."

Baldwin shook his head.

"What?" said Stevenson.

"You lot really are a bunch of amateurs, losing a prisoner off a warship at sea. If she's not on the ship she's in the sea. Anyway you can track her can't you? At least you could, the last I remember, though thirty miles is a bit of a swim."

"Agreed. But we believe that she didn't go into the sea, and there has been no tracking signal – we disabled that when she was in the sick bay on the ship. Our Navy boys have infra-red in their helicopters that can pick out a cigarette butt two hours after it has been thrown overboard. And believe me, the captain of *Bulwark* really did have a vested interest in finding her – and didn't. He's probably playing golf now. We practically pulled the ship apart."

"So?"

"I need you to confirm that she is dead..."

"What, without a body?"

"...or alive."

"I'll think about it."

"My time is valuable and I can't waste it. Your time is – well, it's not your own. Right now it's mine. I'm going to see if I can find a decent cup of coffee. I'll be ten minutes – I want your answer then. Here, you will need to sign this. Then we can see about providing you with money for a boat and payment for your services. You do realise that there is only one answer don't you?"

*

Baldwin was pacing the room when Stevenson returned.

"Where did *Bulwark* dock next after she escaped?"

Stevenson picked up the papers off the desk. Baldwin's signature was on the bottom. A re-signed copy of the Official Secrets Act and a contract of employment with a shipping company, salary 'to be agreed'.

"Gibraltar."

"That's not legal, you know."

"What, docking at Gibraltar?"

"That contract."

"It'll do."

"And salary?"

"Shall we say three thousand pounds a month?"

"No, we shall *not* say that. That's only what a troop leader gets these days. Five thousand a month."

"You don't have much choice you know."

"Yes I do, but you don't see it."

It didn't matter to Stevenson. It wasn't his money and there was only one job he needed Baldwin for. He could let him have this small apparent win, though he would have gone a lot higher. He sighed grudgingly. "Very well."

"And compensation for my boat?"

"Let's be clear, neither of us knows how your boat got to Tabarka. You were engaged by us in Malta. We owe you no compensation for anything."

"Now wait a minute, you just said…"

"Nothing about compensation. HMG will make an ex-gratia payment for services rendered including your work in Djibouti – although you were not even on our books. Here."

Stevenson passed an envelope to Baldwin.

He opened it and slipped out a bank account statement headed 'Lombard Odier Darier Hentsch Private Bank Limited'. Its address was in Gibraltar, and the account holder was 'Steven Baldwin'. The account was in credit.

"One hundred k? That's not half enough. It might cover my boat, but nothing else."

"That's it, that's all you'll get, there's no more. Full and final settlement up to today. We have a fair idea of what your boat was worth, so don't push it too far – and remember we don't know how it got there, so why should HMG pay compensation? If you don't want the one hundred k we can easily siphon it back out."

Baldwin glared at Stevenson, but the other man had his measure. "Thanks but I'll hang on to it for now. I'll need documents and a company credit card, the usual if I'm to be a credible gopher."

Stevenson passed his attaché case to Steve. "It's all ready. You will be travelling as a representative of the Chatham Maritime Services company if anybody asks. Everything you need is in there. There's a BA boarding card for Gibraltar – you are on the next flight from Heathrow tomorrow morning. There's also a phone and a tablet PC – make sure you know how they work – there is a special manual which only you can access. It already has your thumbprint and retina scans encoded. You will also need them to access your bank account.

The pin codes are in the case which opens with your thumbprint – just here. If you open it the regular way using the devil's code – 666 and 666 on each lock – then the bottom compartment is concealed. You will be busy this evening."

"You people are something else."

"You are rather 'over a barrel' as they say, but there is the *ex-gratia* payment after all. One of my people will pick you up and take you to the airport in the morning.

Until then you will stay here – it's much tidier that way, don't you think? We will deliver some clothes and personal items this evening. I do hope that this will be the start of an effective working relationship. You report only to me – daily at least. If you need any resources, or technical access then ask. Come on Baldwin, look on the bright side. It's not a bad deal, really."

"You are not in *my* shoes. So, why Gibraltar?"

"*Bulwark* docked there two weeks ago. For the purposes of the investigation on Government and Royal Navy premises and ships you are Steven Baldwin, a Chief Petty Officer attached to the Royal Navy Police, Special Investigation Branch. You'll find a warrant card in the case. No need for a uniform. That should get you anywhere on *Bulwark.*"

"Where is she now?"

"Still in Gibraltar for another week. Waiting for a new Captain as I said. There's been a murder. Rather gruesome, but it fits a known MO which Interpol has been tracking."

"Maruška Pavkovic?"

"That's very astute of you. I like to think it's her, though others disagree. She's a new project for me. You will find the reports on your tablet in the case."

"I'm not a bloody detective! Ellie Williams had me playing that game in Malta."

"No, but you're learning. Some people in London think you have a good brain and that you did a good job – but you'll have to prove it to me."

"You must be bloody desperate."

"Not really. You know Pavkovic and always seem to find a way to track her down."

"She may be dead."

"Perhaps, GCHQ is still listening for her chip signature – at least for a couple more weeks. Have a look round, read the reports. You may come up with an answer. There's more. Two crew went missing from *Bulwark* at Gib, just after she docked. One was later found dead in the harbour. It looks like natural causes – drowning after a bellyful of beer. The other seaman is still AWOL. The curious aspect is that they both had some contact with Pavkovic – in fact, the one who is still missing guarded her on the ship.

Anyway, you'll find my contact details under 'Barbary' in the smartphone."

"Barbary, as in ape?"

"Exactly – and don't forget that I live up to that name."

The door closed.

Baldwin knew that there was little prospect of recovering his boat Adèle from Tabarka – the Tunisian coast near the Algerian border was actively patrolled and Adèle could barely make 7½ knots – much too slow even to outrun a fishing boat. And that was even if he could get into Tabarka and aboard her. Without proper papers – false papers - too many things could go wrong. Still, the future did not look too bad with £100K in the bank. Was there a catch?

It was time to move on – and to find Helena. He'd met her as Helena, a waitress, but still hadn't got used to using what she said was her real name - Ellie. He'd tried to remember the last time he'd seen her. The last memory was on the scooter in Rome on Christmas Day. Until that moment his memory was virtually intact – as far as he knew. He smiled to himself as he remembered Rumsfeld's twisted quote and realising that there might be unknowns he didn't know about – or memories he didn't know he had forgotten.

46

He moved to the desk and opened the new tablet PC, fired it up and checked the smartphone. Then he went to the bathroom cabinet and found a box of assorted wound plasters and stuck a couple over the front and rear camera lenses of the tablet pc and phone. He waved two fingers at the cameras in the room then settled down to read the contents of the attaché case.

His mind drifted back to Stevenson and the day ahead as he checked the documents. At least he was not travelling under an alias – the idea of being a 'secret agent' would not sit comfortably with his nature.

Then, he spent half an hour online changing the various pin codes and moving some of the funds into his British bank account. After that he located the .pdf manuals for the smartphone and laptop and started to skim them.

Suddenly he snapped up straight. He'd fallen asleep and it was dark outside, the clock showed 6.30 and his heart was racing, his skin clammy. His brain had an image – or series of discontinuous images, as if a video was playing and jumping frames. It was vivid. Rome, walking across the street with Helena to the Café Abyssinia in Ostia Antica, both Flynn Gregory and Elias Stone ahead, pistols at the ready. They were heading round the back of the café. Yes, it had been Christmas Day. Then, gunshots and he was diving through the broken window, Helena following, more shots, a Russian F1 grenade rolling across the floor towards them. Then, blackness.

Unlike a dream, the memories were strengthening and not fading as he thought of them and worked at them like a tongue working at a piece of meat lodged in his teeth. Then he caught the smell of strong coffee mixed with cordite sharp in his nostrils and his mind flashed back, flickering over more images - a dead body, a split second and his own thrust forward to grasp the grenade and another half second gone as he pushed it under the body and rolled away, another split second, another frame and then nothing.

He had no recall of the muffled crump followed by the wet thump of the shrapnel-riddled body dropping back to the floor after the dead proprietor's amputated hand and heavy gold wristwatch had struck his head.

Then, the door of his room burst open and a nurse rushed in, responding to his wireless vital signs monitor.

He looked at her, trying to come round from the dream and the new memories he had experienced.

"Are you alright Mr. Baldwin?"

"Yes, I'm fine thanks June. I er...just nodded off at the desk and...er... had a nightmare about this evening's meal."

"Very funny. Let me just quickly check you."

Just then a doctor entered.

"What happened?"

"I dozed off at the desk and slipped off the chair – that must have triggered the heart rate monitor."

"Did you bump your head?"

"No."

"You're sweating."

"Must be the heating."

"No new memories?" The doctor examined Baldwin's eyes and then the scar on his head.

"Nothing at all. You know it all. I still can't remember the car crash."

"Ok, I'll make a note in your file to that effect. You seem to be fine."

"Yes, I am."

As the doctor left, Baldwin turned to the nurse.

"Anyway, June, what's for supper?"

"Lasagne, followed by tapioca pudding."

"Jesus, that's worse than my nightmare!"

"Behave yourself, you're leaving tomorrow."

"Yes, and you haven't done anything nurses are supposed to do for wounded soldiers. At least we've still got tonight."

"I'm just going off duty and home to my husband. So dream on, soldier – and don't fall out of bed!"

They laughed and as she closed the door Baldwin cursed. He checked that the tablet was on and started to look for a new boat, wondering what other memories might be buried in his head, wondering what had happened to Helena. Was she still alive – and if so, where?"

*

The Interview

A loud bell rang and she struggled to wake up, emerging from one nightmare into another. "Be ready in fifteen minutes" the voice announced. "Fuck you whoever you are." She couldn't face the toast and coffee that had appeared on her nightstand. She ran for the bathroom.

The Scot and Mr Goatee were in the bedroom when she emerged from the bathroom. Frightened, disoriented and with a ghastly hangover, Kirstie was handcuffed again and led along the corridor by Mr Goatee into a bare, white-walled room with a plain deal table and two chairs facing one another – all were bolted to the floor. On the table were two bottles of water and two plastic glasses. She could see several camera pods in the corners of the ceiling.

"What the fuck is going on?"

"I'm sure that you can guess. Someone will be along shortly to take your statement."

"Statement? I've got nothing to say!"

Mr Goatee locked one handcuff to a steel ring on the table and left the room without another word.

Less than five minutes later two men entered.

"Hello Kirstie."

She glared at the well-dressed man – a plain, tailored designer suit covered an open-necked check shirt with wide collars, set off by black loafers. He reminded her too much of the father she hated – seemingly approachable and inoffensive, except that her father had been nothing like that underneath the polished exterior.

"My name is Robert" the smooth man said as he took the seat opposite and placed a thin buff folder on the table. He studied the plain young woman who sat across the table. Adorned with a piercing in her right eyebrow, a ring in her left nostril and a stud in her navel she was not the most alluring of females. She was still dressed in her nightclub gear and it seemed that she hadn't made much effort in that department either.

Meanwhile the other man stood near the door. He was dressed in an off the peg grey suit with plain Oxford shoes and a non-descript blue tie set off against a plain white shirt. Kirstie remained silent as Robert spoke.

"We know exactly what you have done. It was a very clever piece of work - inspired, even, one might say. I also know that you are going to fail at Girton – in fact you only narrowly scraped your first year. It seems such a shame when you really are *so* talented."

"Yeh, well why are you holding me then? I haven't been involved in any terrorism! Let me get back to my studies."

"Kirstie, I haven't got time to waste. I can resolve the issues at Girton College and offer you a good career with the technology that you love. The alternative is an assured and secret conviction under the Counter Terrorism and Security Act followed by a *very* long prison sentence."

"But I haven't done anything!"

"You can deny all you like, but we have the evidence." Robert Grey nodded at the buff folder.

"Prove it!"

"You probably think you've been clever, but I can show you your own footprints. But before I do you must sign the Official Secrets Act."

"No way."

Robert sighed. "Kirstie, it's time you got real."

"My parents will be looking for me."

"No they will not. You have lost touch with your father in Gerrard's Cross – you positively loathe him in fact – and your mother died three months ago from breast cancer. You are an only child. I'm not a psychologist but all these factors have probably compromised your academic career and certainly pushed you towards drink and drugs."

"I don't do drugs! How do you know all this?"

"I can't tell you that." He opened the folder and slid a copy of the Signature Page of the Official Secrets Act across the table. Then he took out a fountain pen from the inside pocket of his jacket and placed it on the form. "Your choice – believe me, this is no joke and I don't have time to waste!"

"Tell me *one* thing that would convince me that you have any proof at all."

"Bude."

"Bude?"

"Yes, as in Cornwall."

Kirstie picked up the pen with her tattooed left hand, unscrewed the top and signed her name.

"Date it please."

She scowled as she inserted the date.

"Interesting tattoo you have there. One three seven."

"Yeh well, it makes the world go round."

"Indeed, a pure number, related to the fine-structure constant of quantum electrodynamics."

Kirstie looked at him, the first glimmer of respect in her eye.

"Yeh, well."

"Just remember that I bite back too."

Instinctively she looked at the back of her right hand, where the word IByteBak was floridly tattooed.

"It's an old one."

"Maybe, but indelible."

"I don't like it any more. I'm going to have it lasered one day."

"That's the problem with rash decisions we make when we are young. Some cannot be undone. You could wear a glove like Michael Jackson did. The tattoo would still be there, though."

Kirstie looked at him thoughtfully, the meaning not lost on her. Grey stood up.

"Right, Dave, please remove the young lady's handcuffs. Kirstie, I suggest you take a shower and then you'll find some of your clothes in the bedroom. Don't look surprised – we've cleared your flat. It's *all* evidence. You will not be going back there. We'll meet again in half an hour, so get a move on."

"Hey, wait, you can't do that!"

"We can and we did. You're with us now – on probation, shall we say, as an employee of GCHQ. And do try and eat some breakfast – it will help get rid of that hangover. Listen carefully, Kirstie, I'll spell it out. We *need you* and we need you thinking clearly as soon as possible. I'll tell you more in the car – and I have a few questions for you."

Kirstie looked at him, but could find no more words to express the confusion she felt at having 'joined the enemy' – and got out of jail.

"Dave, we leave in one hour's time – let's say nine thirty. Nine thirty Kirstie – be ready."

*

Ellie Goes Black

Baldwin dead? She still couldn't believe it. She had been concussed by the explosion in the café in Rome on Christmas Day when the table shielding her had toppled on her, then she had regained consciousness briefly when the other two agents, Gregory and Stone - both wounded - had dragged her and Steve outside as the café had started to burn. In hospital Alex Ogilvy had told her that Baldwin was dead and that Gregory and Stone had disappeared.

She replayed the memories over and over, but they never changed and the pain did not subside. From their first meeting in Crete, the cruise along the coast in Baldwin's yacht, making love in the sun, Malta, Tunisia as man and wife, the final frantic hunt for 'Sword of Allah' in Rome - the memories were vivid, the pain of them intense.

As she waited for the train in the miserable drizzle of Crawley station, she sobbed quietly, realising that she was in no state to attend a job interview. Then, there was a tap on her shoulder and a firm grip held her right elbow, the other hand on her shoulder held her down on the bench.

"Don't do anything stupid, Ellie. If I'd wanted you dead you'd have been under that last train. Let's just go and have a coffee in the Lemon Tree over there."

"Let me go! I have a train to catch, Alex."

"There's another one in fifteen minutes."

She looked at him, her eyes wide, still moist.

"Surely you're not surprised? I've known your every movement since we had lunch that day. Forget the job interview – there are plenty more like that about. Besides, you're in no fit state to tell anyone how clever and capable you are. They wouldn't believe you – but I know the truth."

He changed his grip and steered her gently towards the coffee shop. They ordered and then sat on a bench outside. The drizzle was not blowing in on this side and there was a brightening in the sky to the west, but the vista was miserable and her outlook no better.

"I've got a job for you."

53

"I don't want a fucking job from you, you tosser!" The venom was apparent in the hiss of her sibilants as she spat out the words. "Leave me the fuck alone!"

Ogilvy ignored the TV language.

"Come on, Ellie, I've never done anything to you to deserve that, have I?"

She stared at him and shook her head.

"But you know the people we worked for, they don't piss about. Still waiting for that pension payoff cheque? It's been delayed."

A look of alarm spread across her face.

"Oh, don't worry, you'll get it."

"Get stuffed Alex!"

"Baldwin is alive."

"How bloody low will you stoop, you bastard?"

"I kid you not. He's alive. Here, look."

Ogilvy held out his smartphone which showed a clip of Baldwin at the desk in his hospital room.

"Heathrow, yesterday."

She studied the footage and re-played it. "

"Don't worry, it's not his doppelganger. It really is him, and he's working for us."

"Pull the other one. Exactly what do you take me for?"

"A smart and clever woman, one of the best. That's what. Listen Ellie, after the fracas in Rome and your failed lifting of ben-Zhair, 'C' had to batten the hatches down – tightly. And I mean tightly. You were told Baldwin was dead, and he was told you were dead. You'd been too close to be properly professional, though we can see now that it was effective and had its uses for the operation. I was in the firing line too. That Wikileaks stunt you pulled on me – well, I'd already put that move on 'C' myself. That's the game. And both Gregory and Stone are still MIA. We have our concerns."

"Where is Baldwin?"

"Right now, he's packing for Gibraltar, with a bad case of amnesia. Or so he leads us to believe – he's been making a decent fist of it actually. He'll make a good operative, but we want him to stay honest. That's where you come in."

"Me?"

"Yes. He's working off the books, and we want you to join him on the same terms. He'll need you for the current operation. And we need to know if his memory loss is real?"

"So, I spy on him and if his memory loss is an act then you'll terminate him? Well I've got news for you – what goes for me goes for him. Wikileaks squared – if he's really alive he's under my protection, as of now."

"Should I be surprised?"

"I guess not – you always were the wily one."

"You and me both – that's why we're with Six – or were. We're in a sideshow now."

"Anyway what operation are you referring to?"

"Blue Angel is not over – although Baldwin doesn't know that. Right now he's trying to find Pavkovic."

"Maruška Pavkovic? But she's in one of our clinics isn't she?"

"No. She vanished off one of His Majesty's ships, in the middle of the Mediterranean. We have reason to believe that she is still alive – and has been to Gibraltar. Baldwin is there to track her."

"Fucking hell."

"Quite, if not a little unladylike."

"Is that nanochip still operational?"

"We think that we disabled it when she was in the hospital on the ship, but she disappeared before we completed the tests."

"Still, if you know she was in Gib then there's a chance that Cheltenham could find it – as they did in Tunisia?"

"They're on the case."

"What about Jacob, the techie we worked with in Tunisia – and Rome?" Her face fell as the memory and its implications returned.

"Just atoms in the Rome atmosphere, I'm afraid. And Blue Angel has been rebranded – it's now Red Cedar. All Blue Angel files have been expunged. I didn't tell you that."

"Really?"

"'C' had to tell the politicos 'yes'. Which he did, after copying them over to 'Red Cedar'. You do see that I'm trusting you, don't you? You know almost everything."

"Almost being the operative word – it's what you may be holding back that bothers me."

"Nothing of real consequence, believe me."

Ellie was lost in thought as her phone sounded.

"That's a text with an address. Meet me there tomorrow evening, seven p.m. Usual precautions."

"I'm not sure that my usual precautions will be good enough. You found me. How?"

"Because I'm in the Magic Circle."

"What's that?"

"Just a metaphor. It means that I have trade secrets."

"That's not much help to me is it?"

"Don't worry Ellie – your usual precautions will be adequate, I'm sure. There will be a room booked for you tomorrow night in town. Pack ready to catch the Gibraltar flight on Saturday morning. If you're in, that is."

"Oh I'm in alright. Except, it seems, the Magic Circle."

"That can wait. You've got the room next to Baldwin in the Rock Hotel. Just one more minor matter – I'm dead to the world - I died of a drug overdose."

"So you're off the books as well?"

He nodded, almost imperceptibly.

"But don't you have a family?"

"I had a wife, we were childless – not that it's any of your business. Time for a change, suits me well."

"You must be a really heartless bastard."

"I'll take that as a compliment and yes, that certainly helps. It's why I'm good at my job."

"How far does this go?"

"You don't need to know, but we're a small team."

"Are we legal?"

"That's a bit of a grey area, actually."

"But there's obviously funding for the operation."

"Indeed. Money is not a problem. Money is fungible, but passports and cover stories, technical equipment, access to GCHQ – well, that's a bit more tricky to organise – it takes time and planning."

She held his penetrating stare, saying nothing, waiting. Let him fill the silence, she thought.

"Trust is essential. And now you have to trust me. None of this is for Baldwin's ears, yet. We'll tell him - all in good time. Only you and 'C' know the truth. And don't try to contact Baldwin yet. You can surprise him on Saturday."

She looked up at him, her anger rising as he stood up, but he read her well.

"This is a shitty business Ellie, but someone has to run it. Sleep well tonight." He stooped to kiss her on the cheek and turned.

"How do I know that this is legit – you could be..."

But it was lost in the sound of the next train to Victoria Station slowing to a gentle stop. She wasn't sure whether to smile or rant. Why were there so many bloody secrets?

She looked at Ogilvy. Friday night. The bar was busy but the table in the corner was discreet and their conversation lost in the general din. Despite her best efforts, Ogilvy had tracked her down to her low-rent retreat in Crawley and then the train station. She'd been sure she was clean, but obviously the technology was improving. She had slipped up somewhere, but that was past now - there was a spring in her step, and she had even put some makeup on.

"As this is off the books – for now – there's only so much support we can provide at the moment. There's a phone and tablet in the case, and some cover papers, passport, credit card etc."

With his foot he pushed the case across under the table.

"What I don't understand Alex, is why this is all off the books?"

"Orders from the PM. Too many leaks in Cobra. We think that we have a Five mole on the team. 'C' is even doubting Six itself."

"But why?"

"Your guess *etcetera*. We're keeping this tighter than a duck's rear end – the post-Booth paranoia is rampant."

Anthony Booth had been Ogilvy's predecessor on the Africa and Middle East Desk. In line for the Deputy DG's job he had been uncovered as a Chinese mole the previous year, following the Gate of Tears incident, which almost led to a war between NATO and China. As far as the public was aware, Booth had died from coronary disease. His treachery had been too serious to become public knowledge at least until the 30 year seal on his file had expired.

Ogilvy omitted to mention to Ellie that the Prime Minister's order to keep the Rome operation completely secret, even from the Italians, was a matter of great sensitivity. Arguably the failed attempt to obtain the 'Sword of Allah' weapon for the UK had so far cost almost eight thousand lives – still rising - and many thousands more were expecting an early death from radioactive contamination.

Even worse, the United Nations was still wringing its hands in the face of the open and ongoing threat by ICIM to use the weapon again. The UN was impotent and its very existence was under threat. The former president, Trump, had even threatened to expel it from US soil, ignoring the niceties of international sovereign territory law.

*

Maruška's Escape

After her capture in Tunisia by Baldwin and Ellie Williams, Maruška Pavkovic had been held in the brig on *HMS Bulwark* after treatment in the hospital ward. She could remember little between her car crash outside Tunis caused by that bastard Baldwin, and waking up on the ship. Her arm had been broken and she knew that she had been drugged, but she remembered nothing about the clandestine night boat trip in a Special Boat Services RIB that *Bulwark* had sent in to the beach just north of Cape Carthage. The sea had been rough and the beach extraction hazardous in the surf – she had been pulled off a small rubber dinghy wrapped in a survival suit and strapped to a folding stretcher

Her fractured arm was still in a sling and she wore a thin collar designed to jam transmissions to and from the nanochip buried in her body near the C6 vertebra – or so the doctor had told her. As such she was safe from any possible interference by Wan Chuntao, her controller in the Guoanbu.

It had been four days since her capture and she knew that it could not be long before she was moved off the ship. The British wanted the technology that was embedded in her – and they wanted knowledge of her recent operations. She was headed for England.

Andjela Karanovic aka Muaruška Pavkovic sat and pondered her future, shaping it slowly in her mind, visualizing escape and how it could be achieved, although many years before she had made preparations for such an event.

She anticipated helicopter extraction or docking of *Bulwark*, possibly in Catania, but more probably Malta or Gibraltar. Escape from a helicopter or plane would be almost impossible without a lot of help – and she had none - yet. She had to act quickly, when it was unexpected and thought by her captors to be very unlikely. That is, she had to do it with a fractured arm and no resources, from within a prison cell on a ship.

This was yet another challenge – she had faced many in her life and had overcome them, coming a long way from that young Serbian girl who had watched her family being killed by

Muslims, so long ago. Working her way up through the ranks of the Serbian warlord Srecko Vidovic's organisation, she had left behind her real identity of Andjela Karanovic, assuming that of her lesbian lover Maruška Pavkovic, groomed for the purpose and then killed. She had also left behind her life with the SNP - *Sedam Nogu Pauk* – the Seven Legged Spider. The SNP was Vidovic's gang of Serbian paramilitaries, which had competed with Arkan's Tigers for the title of the most ruthless and extreme of the irregular Serbs.

After the war in Bosnia-Herzegovina, Vidovic had transformed the SNP into a seven-legged organised crime outfit, which Andjela had been running for him after he had moved to South America to escape an international arrest warrant (and to open a new drug smuggling channel). Respected and feared in equal measure by the small army of Vidovic's killers, she had taken over the SNP and Vidovic had been killed in captivity in Colombia. She had expanded SNP operations further – and then disappeared overnight.

Running a commercial operation – legal or illegal – was not for her. Nothing thrilled her as much as being close up to the kill after a hunt, feeling the fear of the target, enjoying the visceral process of terminating life. She had first experienced that thrill as a teenager, avenging the deaths of her family. Now, she killed and tortured for money and for pleasure - for pleasure as Senka, her alter ego. Hatred of men had been burned into her as she had watched her mother being raped. Sex for Maruška was a tool, a bait, and it worked equally well against women as well as men. As Senka, she avenged, and she enjoyed.

As she sat on the bed in the cell, she looked forward to rewarding herself for her escape from *Bulwark*, feeling herself moisten at her many memories as Senka. There would be more. She worked the memories around in her mind as she started doing what came naturally - manipulating her captors, unknowingly reversing the Stockholm Syndrome, building a relationship and dependency between captive and captor. She might be incarcerated, but her guards were susceptible, and, unwittingly, her captives. During their rotating watches, they were captivated by her mystery, by the danger she represented and by the raw sexuality which they glimpsed in her presence. There were just two naval ratings and the Sergeant at Arms who checked her every hour, and the Master at Arms and ship's Doctor checked her twice daily, although she could only remember the last few days. There were also a couple of technical geeks who checked her collar and waved scanning wands over her, recording data on a tablet.

Apart from the inconvenience of the arm she felt strong and ready.

*

Everybody had their price and she had prepared well for captivity – and escape.

As far a she could tell, four days had passed since she had been taken aboard *HMS Bulwark* and she still didn't understand why she had not yet been moved off the ship. She had no idea where the ship was and what it was doing. Perhaps it was to do with the nanochip in her neck – at sea she was well away from mobile phone masts? Then why the jamming collar? Whatever the reason, she felt the need to act very soon.

It was now shortly before 04:00 hrs on what she thought was the fifth day (working from the pattern of the meals she had received) and she had heard some guard discuss 'going to Gib'. There was always a light on in her cell, and she knew that the Sergeant at Arms would shortly be checking her through the observation hole in the door in the next few minutes. She was not considered a suicide risk and they had not put any electronic tags on her. The SAA came and went and was replaced by a senior rating who would take the next four hour watch. He had other things to do, and would check her every hour or so. She lay back on her cot, restricted in her movements by the plastic casing that held her broken arm in place. With her left hand she pulled open the trousers she had been given to wear – the ship carried a stock of women's clothing which was used to clothe refugees picked up in the ongoing exodus from Libya. She put her hand inside the plain white undergarment and started to stroke herself and moan. She pretended that she didn't notice the leading seaman open the observation cover, but carried on with her act at a steadily rising tempo. Then she stopped abruptly and threw her head to one side, feigning frustration.

Then she heard his voice. It was Carl Halborg – the weak one who used bravado as a smokescreen to hide his inadequacy.

"What's the matter love?" Frustration is it? What you need is a good length."

Her reply was spoken quietly.

"Say that again, I didn't hear you."

"I said *yes*, I do need a good length and I can't even use my fingers properly."

"Well, the Royal Navy has just what you need, right here."

"Men are all talk! No man has ever been able to satisfy me, so go back to your chair and your sleep, sailor."

"I bet I could give you what you need."

"How many times have I heard that from a man? Empty fucking promises is all I ever hear – and empty trousers."

"Of course, I'd have to put handcuffs on you so you wouldn't escape."

"I love handcuffs, but this plastic arm sling would be a problem - and anyway we'd be caught."

"We wouldn't be caught, we could make it a quickie. I know the routine around here on this watch. I run this area."

She wriggled on the cot, trying to remove her panties.

"Come on then, let's do it, now."

"I just need to shut the watertight door and wedge it."

"Be quick Carl, I'm desperate."

Carl Halborg knew that he had maybe half an hour as he turned the wheel and the watertight door clamped shut. He took a fire axe off its retainer and wedged it in the wheel. His thought processes were now below his belt.

The cuffs were in the drawer of the metal desk of the guard's office. He scrabbled around and found the keys for the cuffs, then moved back to the second cell where Maruška waited. The first cell was empty – the rating who had caused trouble ashore in the Gibraltar bar had been cleared out that morning after a session with the Master at Arms.

Carl Halborg keyed in the code for the cell door lock and it opened. She was waiting, her panties beside her on the bed.

"Come on Carl. Let me have it. I like it rough."

And so he did.

It was quick and unpractised, but she seemed satisfied as he zipped himself up and looked furtively at his watch.

"Thank you Carl that was just what I needed."

He looked at her. There were no visible marks. No woman had ever thanked him before. In fact, he usually paid for the performance.

"It was a pleasure, we could have done with more time though."

"And you could have been a bit rougher." She smiled at him. This man was a real fool. "You know, we could go a long way together."

"Are you mad? You're in a holding cell on one of the King's ships. You're classified as a Category A risk."

"Then why did you fuck me?"

"Because I like you. And because I could. Maybe they've got you all wrong."

"They usually do. Listen, I can help you if you can help me."

Despite the conspiratorial whisper, she desperately wanted to kill this man, slowly and she fought down the revulsion of the recent act, putting it out of her mind, letting her cold calculation take charge.

"And what makes you think I need help?"

"Just a feeling. As I said, we could go a long way together. You probably wonder what you'll do when you leave the Navy, don't you? Well I have a bank account with almost a hundred thousand euros in it. Or at least, I did. That was five years ago. It's probably grown a bit since then. It can be yours if you help me."

"You must think I'm really fucking stupid."

"No I don't. Think about it – one hundred thousand euros, you could sign off now. Or, of course I could just report what just happened."

"You fucking stupid bitch. They wouldn't believe you anyway."

He moved towards her as she sat on the edge of the cot and raised his right fist, but she was too fast, even with her arm in a sling. Her bare right foot caught him in the genitals and he doubled over with a groan.

"Now *you* are being stupid. I can be rough too, you know? So, just stop and think. You didn't use a condom and you've probably given me some sailor's disease. I've got the evidence right inside me Why make life difficult? I just offered you more than a hundred thousand euros. I have a plan, so get some paper and I will give you the details of the account. Then you can decide. But I haven't got long – they will move me from here very soon I think. I have an idea what you will need to do."

They didn't move her and the ship continued its patrol for two more days before being ordered to Gibraltar.

*

Halborg's watch ended at 08:00. He went to his berth and pulled the curtain across while he thought about his options. His testicles still ached - he had been really suckered and he had to find a way out. He would need help.

Naval policy had evolved as the organisation sought to recruit and retain the best – but sometimes 'the best' was a moveable feast. As a leading seaman he was allowed 15 minutes a week for emails and web access when the ship was at sea and not locked down. The bandwidth wasn't great, but for his immediate needs it was enough.

He logged on to his account in the ship's leisure network and check the time he had left for the week. Then he opened the iPad browser and located the Geneva bank's site. Using the credentials she had given him he worked through the complex login procedure, with one name and two levels of password and a challenge question.

It worked like a dream, and the account opened. There it was, in the name of Mademoiselle Broussard. Account credit €117,131. He looked again and snapped a screenshot with his smartphone, then quickly logged out and cleared the browser history.

Shit! This was for real.

Who could he ask for help? How much would they want? His mind was racing and he couldn't sleep. She had him over a barrel, for sure, but helping her escape from a Royal Navy ship at *sea*? That was crazy. The last he'd heard they were thirty miles north of Tunisia and headed for Gibraltar.

*

The Hunt

Nuclear weapons left radionucleide traces, but the core of the weapon in Rome left no pieces of bomb timer, no 'bomb maker's design fingerprint', nothing at all beyond atoms and exotic chemical compounds.

The task of the hunters had to be based on intelligence, and few countries had any. The UK was closest to the truth, and China was in the hunt. Iran knew some details of the bomb's design and source, as did North Korea, but sharing of information with these countries was not politically possible – not even through back channels.

The international search was beyond anything that intelligence services had ever mounted, with the P5 countries setting up a joint task force and sharing information to an unprecedented degree. It was almost an 'open-book' arrangement – almost, that is, because the United Kingdom did not share everything. The part of MI6 in the Rome disaster was known to very few people, and the files had been buried.

Alex Ogilvy and Ellie Williams knew the crucial elements of the story. David Stevenson, the officer known as Barbary was Ogilvy's replacement and 'C's go-between, but his knowledge was limited.

There was doubt as to whether Steven Baldwin had any recall of events after the capture and subsequent release of Pavkovic in Malta, and he was being watched very carefully – out on licence, one might say.

Two other officers, Elias Stone and Flynn Gregory had been at ground zero in Rome, but had been despatched to Ostia Antica with Williams and Baldwin before the detonation occurred. They were in the know, but missing in action and *not* presumed dead – until proven.

'C' – Sir William Gore - held the most information including the precious knowledge of the UK Prime Minister's deep involvement and specific orders.

And, of course, by extension, the UK Prime Minister herself knew the core secrets – and wanted them to stay secret.

As the hunt for the key players in ICIM continued, the UK Cobra meetings were held weekly through February unless there were significant developments. All UK building planning applications over the previous two years were being vetted. The construction sites and completed buildings were physically checked for unusual specifications – the Rome bomb had been installed in a new bank building, the International Commercial Bank of Iran.

At the Atomic Weapons Establishment at Aldermaston in Berkshire, a special team had been set up by the Director, Jonathan Tweedy, to analyse the fallout from the Rome explosion and attempt to reverse-engineer the bomb's design. It was thought that the initial assumption of a design based on the seed research at the US Lawrence Livermore Lab was correct, and component back-tracking was underway. This information was not being shared with the P5 Joint Ops Team.

China already suspected the North Korean link – and their Northern Wind task force in the Guoanbu knew that Abu ben-Zhair was the driving force. He had been their agent until going rogue before the earlier Malta cruise liner atrocity when the Queen Katherine had been destroyed.

The fact that ICIM had publicly announced that it had more of the weapons was a matter of great concern to governments and the public. In Russia and China, and in common with all leading western countries, security levels were unprecedented.

The dirty bomb explosion outside Notre Dame Cathedral in Paris on Christmas Eve, twelve hours before the Rome catastrophe, had not been forgotten either. The French DGSE had some small success in identifying the dead bombers, but the trail stopped there, although the cobalt 60 that had been used was known to have originated in a reactor in Pakistan. The ICIM had claimed responsibility for that Paris bomb, and the deaths of almost two hundred congregants and Christmas revellers passing by the cathedral. An unknown number would become casualties and have shortened lives due to Cobalt 60 ingestion.

The US President had extended his sympathies to both Italy and France, and had offered US help in tracking the terrorists. For domestic consumption he rammed home the message that he had been right to ban immigration from Muslim countries. At the same time the US had launched the largest ever intelligence thrust to locate the weapons source and controllers of the Sword of Allah, a search even bigger than there had been for Osama bin Laden.

*

Kirstie had never 'done cars', but she recognised the Jaguar as being similar to one her father had owned, and she quickly shut off the painful memory. So, she did not appreciate that the plain blue Jaguar was low on its wheels and heavily armoured. Neither did she notice that there was a tail car in attendance. As the Jaguar pulled out of the mansion's entrance, Grey closed the partition and isolated the rear seats. Within two minutes they were back on the A34 and heading north for the M4. 'Dave' held to the speed limit.

"Right Kirstie, let's get down to business. We know what you did, but I want you to tell me in your own words. Start at Bude."

"You're bluffing, Bude means nothing to me."

"Kirstie, don't be tiresome. We've been through all this. You've read all the Snowden leaks, I know that. I know that you hacked Level 3 Communications – the people who use the Apollo transatlantic fibre optic cable." Kirstie's eyes opened wide as Grey continued "Yes – the one that comes ashore in Widemouth Bay near Bude. And there are three others you've worked on."

"Well it's not right that GCHQ should tap into all these cables. There has to be some sort of privacy."

"So, you're on the side of terrorists then and it's ok for you to tap them?"

"It's not as simple as that."

"But it is, Kirstie, it is. Whether you like it or not, you are involved in the fight. You now work for GCHQ – and I expect you to become a star consultant for us. I know you have the capability to come up with unique approaches to our problems - and the skills to make them work."

Kirstie's eyes opened. She had never thought of herself as a consultant. Her Dad was a consultant, albeit a psychologist. That was different. This was tech, her tech.

"Show me some ID."

"Now that's the first sensible thing you've said." He took a card on a neck cord from his pocket.

"It just says Robert Grey."

"What do you expect? My full details in plain English? The vital data is embedded there, in that chip, RFID."

"It proves nothing."

"Here, use your phone. Google me and check the picture. Unfortunately there are some things I can't keep hidden."

She went to voice control on Samsung and requested the search. She examined the picture carefully.

"Deputy Director. OK, I believe you – for now. But I do know that these things can be fixed."

"Good, now can we please move on?" He took her phone back off her and removed the battery. "Can't be too careful in this business. We'll give you a special phone later. Anyway, there really is no time to lose – believe me, many lives may depend on *you*..." her eyes widened yet again "– yes, Kirstie, *you*. So please let's not waste any more time."

During the next 15 minutes, she outlined her hack into Level 3 Communications and how that led her back to the control switches for the Apollo North cable link – and she applied the same techniques to the other 3 fibre optic cable links that came ashore in Widemouth Bay: TAT-8, TAT-14 and Yellow/AC2.

"It's public knowledge UK telecoms companies are forced to co-operate in your operation to tap the data and 'tee' it to GCHQ Bude. You've got them by the balls - they have to operate under secret warrants forcing them to allow GCHQ access to the cables."

"I cannot possibly comment."

"Come on, get real, Mr Grey. Edward Snowden opened Pandora's Box. Don't you read The Guardian or Wikipedia?"

"Don't believe everything you read. There's a lot of fake news about. And don't get any ideas young lady, or you'll be in handcuffs before you know it. You're on licence and will be for the foreseeable future. And your passport is invalid until I say so."

Kirstie scowled. "Yeh well anyway, you make it so easy for hackers. I also hacked the switches of the Apollo South cable…"

"The one which came ashore in…" Grey paused thinking better of any disclosure.

"Yes, Lannion in Brittany, France, as if you didn't know."

In GCHQ Cheltenham, four senior network specialists were sitting around a meeting room table listening to the conversation being relayed from the car on the M4 – at least, those parts of the conversation that Grey did not mute from them. There was a gasp at the latest revelation.

In another room at Cheltenham, Grey's superior, Timothy Kaye, shook his head in disbelief at the girl's revelations.

"So then I worked back from the data switches and was able to tee off some of the data."

"But that's impossible! It's all hard wired fibre optic."

"Yeh, I wondered about that. And no, it's not impossible. The switch monitoring software has a data analyser tap for performance measurement. It's only narrow bandwidth – less than a hundred channels - but it works. That's over copper – I think."

Grey's face paled as Kirstie continued. "What I was really interested in was the most secure content. That was in the TAT-14 cable – you know, the one that the NSA says is critical to US security?"

Grey groaned inwardly. "Why?"

"Because I thought I would try to de-crypt the data."

"But surely you know that is practically impossible."

"Maybe. I assumed RSA encryption based on prime number pairs."

"That's a fair assumption."

"Everyone knows that the number of prime numbers is infinite – Euclid proved that 2,300 years ago. And the largest known prime number – as of yesterday, when I last checked – had 22,338,618 digits. Base a key on the product of any two large prime numbers and you have a key which would take forever to break using today's fastest computers even though one number – the public key – is known. Quantum computers will be able to break that encryption fairly quickly."

"That's a very long way away." But not so far away, thought Grey. "And by then we'll have quantum encryption."

"Maybe, maybe not. Anyway, I couldn't get through to your quantum computers – but I got close."

Grey did not flinch, but there was more reaction in Cheltenham and another listener left the meeting room.

"I'd written a screen-saver as a project and it was selling quite well to students, mainly, all around the world. The trick was I'd embedded analysis code in the screensavers. A bit like SETI – the search for extra-terrestrial life? Except that users didn't even know I was using their systems to analyse signals.

"Yes, I know about SETI."

"I couldn't use your quantum gear, so I had to go for quantity not quality. Still too slow though."

Kirstie reached for the bottle of water and took a mouthful.

"Then I had a bit of a breakthrough, which is why I was out celebrating – only last night was it? God it seems like a year ago. So, I'd been parsing the traffic samples and my program picked up a pattern with some of the data. It turns out that the data with the pattern was of Chinese origin – the US was copying raw Chinese satellite signals data and piping it through to you, via Bude. And of course you were piping data back - data sharing you call it, playing fast and loose with private telephone calls and emails.

I analysed the pattern and wondered why it was there. It was like a fingerprint but there were about a thousand – as of yesterday and still counting. Give me my smartphone and I can check now if you like?"

"Let's leave that for later - please carry on."

"OK. I think that the Chinese were lazy and in a hurry. They had used some code off the web – there's plenty available and it's common practice not to re-invent the wheel. It came from a legitimate Italian security company, The Hacking Team, you know?"

"Yes, the good guys they call themselves - they specialise in offensive security - and they have themselves been hacked."

"Exactly. So, the Chinese built this specific sub-routine into their system – the latest version. What they didn't realise was that there was some additional tricky embedded code which the Hacking Team had disguised because they were pissed off with their code being nicked. The Chinese must have seen it in the source but somehow it got through their testing – and into live use." Kirstie continued to astonish Grey and the few remaining Cheltenham listeners.

'Not bloody likely' thought Grey. "You haven't by any chance done any work for the Hacking Team, have you?"

"Erm…Not exactly, no, no. So, following on from that, I looked at the Hacking Team code and reverse engineered it." Kirstie's hesitation was barely noticeable, but enough for Grey to detect and he let her continue uninterrupted. "All that the fingerprint does is provide an upper bound – as a factor of ten - within which the private key lies. And there is no corresponding public key in the signal"

"So that narrows down the private key search a lot?"

Kirstie's face lit up "Exactamente!" and then it fell. "But that was only the start. Then I couldn't believe my luck. The idiots used the Chinese Remainder theorem – ironic really."

"So…?"

"So, it's known to be open to a side-channel attack. Stupid really, even the credit card companies stopped using this years ago. Then it got really interesting, because the US includes the metadata of the source Chinese satellite - with the time and location etc. - from which they nicked the Chinese signal. I thought, well give it a try, you know?

So, I think each signal target – embassies I guessed - uses its own public key which is not transmitted in the data exchange. Maybe it's even unchanged. I got so far then hit the power wall."

By now the meeting room in Cheltenham was down to two people.

Grey knew that earlier UK and US – and presumably Russian – attempts had some modest success in attacking Chinese cryptography. There was a cryptographic arms race under way and to be in the front demanded leadership in quantum computing technology. The pressure on the GCHQ budget was huge – and now the nascent optical computing technology was also demanding resources.

"But I still need more teraflops than I can harness over the web."

"We have that computing power for you Kirstie – way beyond even petaflops. Now, I want you back working on this before close of play today. But first you have to do the GCHQ induction and security briefing. We have to be very rigid and structured in these matters."

"To stop people like me getting access?"

"Precisely."

"Fat chance!"

They both laughed as the car stopped at the security gate at GCHQ Cheltenham, where the meeting room was by now empty.

"We're here."

Then she realised that he'd told her nothing – and she'd told him everything. Almost.

*

After her induction, Kirstie was introduced to her immediate superior, Seamus Kilpatrick. Seamus had been recruited from Queens University, Belfast, several years before after coming to the attention of GCHQ. He'd been an outstanding student, gaining a 2:1 honours degree in computer science, with the prospect of a Ph.D. research offer. Then, GCHQ had caught him hacking into the systems of the Irish State south of the border. A full-blown Ulsterman, he'd been trying to learn about Irish policy with regard to its border with the UK – which was about to become an EU frontier. Innocent enough, but illegal. He'd progressed rapidly at GCHQ and become a section leader.

Within a day of her initial induction (there were many more induction courses to come), Kirstie was working in a sanitized environment with highly restricted access. Her focus was on the Chinese traffic she'd worked on that very week, but now she had more computing power available – but only after two levels of authorisation. The bean counters had decreed that time on the quantum machines was to be costed at £47 per millisecond of machine time. Over a year that added up to a budget of £1.5 billion for quantum computing machine time alone. To justify access to the machines there had to be a costed machine time application which put a notional value on particular projects – in other words, what's the value of discovering a secret?

That was the formal procedure, but the exigencies of national security often short-circuited the procedure. Seamus handled the applications for machine time and in regard to Kirstie's work he had a direct line to Robert Grey.

Kirstie had been there just twelve days when she sat again in front of Robert Grey, with Seamus Kilpatrick alongside her. With them sat Leanne Billings, their department manager. Less than two weeks had passed since Kirstie's induction and already Seamus and Kirstie had slept together – strictly against the rules. Today, though, their secret was safe, though Leanne was beginning to notice their artificial body language when together.

"So if I understand your report correctly, one specific set of Chinese signals traffic has been broken, and it relates to one satellite channel and one sending organisation – the Guoanbu."

"Yes, sir, whatever that may be."

"Come on Kirstie, don't waste time. We know you checked it on line."

The sheepish look on her face told Grey that he's guessed correctly.

"It's good work."

"Thank you. I didn't get much sleep."

"I can see that from the project log."

"The work you have already done will continue under Seamus, but I'm going to move you into an operational team which will monitor these specific signals – it will widen your experience during your probationary period. Seamus will introduce you to your new team this afternoon. Keep up the good work."

Grey picked up the phone to the Director.

"Robert."

"Gareth. We've broken some Chinese signals. It's very specific to one comms channel and is Guoanbu material. It apparently relates to management of field agents. We're currently seeing a lot of traffic with an 'Agent 29'. We're backtracking through the data now, but it seems she's operational in Gibraltar and Spain, and has been in Tunisia and Malta."

"Thanks for keeping me in the loop. You'd better let 'C' know. Sorry, I've got a budget committee meeting about to start. Let's catch up with a round of golf on Sunday? Call my PA and get something in the diary will you."

"Of course. I hope that the meeting goes well."

"That would be a first for a budget meeting. I was going to call you later anyway. Is there any sign of the quantum computing hardware budget coming under control? It's not on the agenda today, but I'll need a heads up by Monday."

"It's still proving difficult. We're upgrading continuously, but costs are not falling. There's good news on running costs though as the thermal efficiency is going up in leaps and bounds. I'll have some numbers for you by Monday."

"We do need to get a grip on it. I'll look forward to the golf. Goodbye."

Robert Grey called 'C' to brief him on the Guoanbu signals.

"My concern, Sir William, is that this seemed to be just a little too easy. There were errors in the coding algorithm and some sloppy work. It's a very specific set of signals. So, I have concerns that..."

"...that this was deliberate and that they want us to know."

"Precisely."

"And if we tip our hand and act on the content, then they will have some measure of our capability – both in monitoring and decryption. That's the old Enigma problem – knowing secrets that you cannot act on."

"The signals are going through our analysts now, but they are specific field agent communications. Our systems are throwing up compound search matches with Malta, Tunisia,

Rome and Gibraltar. What's really set us going though is a name and a photograph – Abu ben-Zhair."

Grey did not know about Red Cedar and Sir William maintained a level tone, despite a frisson of excitement - he still loved the thrill of the chase.

"That sounds like good work, Robert. Send me what you've got and we'll take a look at it."

"Will do. You'll get the report and data before lunch." As if reading 'C''s thoughts, he continued "I've set up a monitoring team to track these signals."

"Good, let's run with it while we can – if you've got the resources, of course. I'll look at the signals with a pinch of salt, though."

Grey smiled to himself as the line dropped. They had both been around the block a few times. 'C' didn't look at anything unless there was a very good reason. So, there was a black op on. Maybe he'd dig a little more himself?

*

The Rock Hotel, Gibraltar

This was all new to Baldwin. Operating under a cover was not his style. He was a plain and straightforward guy from a Portsmouth fishing family. He had arrived on the morning flight and taken a taxi to the Rock Hotel. Signing the hotel register had almost given him away. To whom, he wondered? He was still Steven Baldwin even if he worked for Chatham Maritime Services.

He opened the mini bar and took out a Peroni beer. What the fuck, he thought. Expenses - this was a whole new world for him. Well, he was a supposedly a company representative, he had a cover to maintain, a front to present. And he had a home to find.

During the two and a half hours flight time from London he had checked over the shortlist of yachts he'd drawn up the night before – a much more interesting pastime than reading computer manuals. But first he would have to make a start on the hunt for Maruška Pavkovic - and wonder about Helena.

Once he had got through the security barrier on his tablet computer, he opened the document entitled '*HMS Bulwark – Missing Person Report*', Classification:Ultra.

There was little of substance to read – just the fact that Maruška Pavkovic had been treated in the ship's hospital, her arm set in a plastic sling. There was a mention of a special neck brace, and a footnote explaining that it had been fitted to neutralise the effects of an embedded nanochip and to prevent external communication to and from the device.

He nodded, recalling the interrogation in the villa in Malta.

After treatment in the ship's hospital she had been moved to a cell in the ship's brig. Two days later she had vanished.

Her disappearance had been sometime between 2 and 4 a.m. Steve nodded to himself – the graveyard watch which runs from midnight to 4 a.m. - was a low point in the body's daily rhythm, guards would be struggling to stay awake. A good time for an escape. She had not been shackled, but her arm was in a sling.

The locks on the door were controlled by a key pad. The cell was checked every two hours – she had not been considered to be a suicide risk. The obvious escape routes – the door and the air conditioning – showed no signs of tampering.

The ship had been searched thoroughly three times using different search teams and even dogs. That was no small task on a ship of 20,000 tons and almost 600 feet in length. Baldwin knew the ship – he had spent some time aboard her when he was in the Royal Marines on a training exercise – and during the Gate of Tears operation.

The guards responsible for Pavkovic had been thoroughly interrogated without any explanation being uncovered. They were not suspected of complicity. Nevertheless she had escaped. Baldwin opened another beer and thought about the facts – and the stories. Historically, it was not at all unusual for sailors to smuggle women aboard ships and hide them, despite the superstition about women bringing bad luck. Some prostitutes had crossed oceans on Navy ships – but that had been a long time ago. But the reverse – an escape? Without thinking about it, he raised the bottle in a silent toast.

'Got to hand it to her' he thought, 'but I'll kill her.'

*

Steve had finished reading the police report of the murder. The killing had raised quite a stir, as a murder in Gibraltar was a rare event. Other salacious aspects had brought it to the front pages of British newspapers.

The man's body had been found by tourists, apparently the day after his death, just five days ago. Harry Calthorpe was an ex-pat British citizen who had retired early to Gibraltar three years previously after his wife had died from ovarian cancer. He'd been a solicitor in a Bedford practice and his wife had been wealthy in her own right. There were children in Australia and California. Baldwin doubted that they knew about their father's dark secret.

There were other reports – Interpol reports – with details of other deaths all over Europe and even in Moscow. There was a link to a spreadsheet and Baldwin clicked to open it.

Across the top were over forty columns, each one representing a specific aspect of a death. Baldwin scanned it quickly – gender, cause of death, location of body, straight/gay/lesbian, toxicology and so on. It was a simple summary only. There was an accompanying pie chart which made it clear that there was a high degree of commonality between many of the murders. There was also a note that the gender of the victims was apparently random.

Clearly, this search had been going on for some time. There was one death per row, and over twenty rows. Harry Calthorpe was on the last row. He had last been seen in a club known as 'Charlie's Hole in T'Wall', very popular with sailors – whatever their persuasion. In fact, Baldwin himself had been to that club when he was in the Royal Marines and HMS Manchester had paid a visit on the way back from a mission in Libya.

He stood up, and stretched his arms, wondering why he and not an ace detective, was reading these files. He walked over and opened the balcony doors, letting the warm late afternoon air flood the room. The view was stunning. The day was not yet done - the sun was still an hour above the mountains of Andalucia to the west across the Bay of Algeciras. The ferries to and from the Spanish enclave of Ceuta on the African coast were cutting up the Bay, which held almost twenty ships at anchor, many 'bunkering' – loading up with duty free fuel oil. Steve decided to walk down to the Marina Bay marina to look at the boats and clear his mind. There was also a boat there that had caught his eye on a broker's list – many sailing dreams ended in Gibraltar, but someone's broken dream was another's opportunity. He liked that.

*

The stroll down the hill took about thirty minutes – he would be out running the route the next morning. When he'd been in the RM his troop had run up the Rock. At two and a half miles with a climb of 1,100 feet it was a tough run and the Gibraltar Rock Race was now an annual event. He crossed the North Bastion and headed towards the marina area. The yacht broker's office was shut and so Steve walked across to the marina entrance. There was a wooden footbridge to the jetty. As he crossed it Steve looked up at the *Sunborn Gibraltar*, a floating hotel/casino, ex-cruise ship, seemingly bolted to the quay with huge hydraulic rams. There was a security gate into the marina, with a guard on duty. Steve would have to talk his way in.

"How did you know I'd been in the forces?"

Steve nodded at the guard's bare arms – short sleeves were the order of the day even at this time of year.

"Ah, right, the tatts – dead giveaway."

It turned out that the guard, Liam O'Neill, lived on his boat and had stopped in Gibraltar to top up his funds before heading into the Mediterranean.

Liam was from Northern Ireland and a proud Ulsterman – that is, until Brexit caused the border issues.

Shaven headed and stocky, he sported a gold earring and a nose which had not been set quite straight. He was only missing one tooth in his broad grin. However, he was clean-shaven and his security guard's uniform was immaculate and the shine on his shoes would pass a Coldstream Guards inspection parade.

Liam was happy to prattle on with his life story, but Steve didn't give much away about himself.

"I knew nothing about yachts but the idea came to me one evening when I was at my wits' end, walking down at Ravenglass harbour – we lived up there as my wife was from Lancaster. Anyway she had found another bloke while I was on a tour overseas and she took me for everything. I did give the new guy a hiding though!

I hit the bottle for a bit but then saw sense. So, I bought myself a small boat and learned as I went along – and I love it. I'll stay here another few months and then move on when I've got enough cash for the next leg – I'll be heading for Greece. These days I don't see the kids much but they still keep in touch. They think it's cool that their dad lives on a boat. Maybe next year they'll come out and stay with me for a few days - if their bitch of a mother lets them, of course."

Greece brought back some memories for Steve – he'd wounded Maruška there.

"I did a bit of crewing work in Greece. Crete was ok too." Steve's mind flashed back to one of the best weeks of his life, sailing in Crete with Ellie – or Helena the waitress as she then was."

"Anyway, Liam, I'm looking for '*Dream On Two.*'"

"Ah yes, *Dream on Two*. She's on Delta pontoon. Just follow the main gangway there."

Steve ducked in fright as a Royal Air Force F35 fighter took off from the runway just 200 yards away, its engines on afterburner as it turned sharply to the left in a steep climb so as not to cross into Spain's air space.

"Bloody hell!"

"You get used to it, though it's usually Ryanair or BA. Things have been hotting up here."

Liam let him through the gate as another fighter rattled the windows of the hugely expensive flats overlooking the marina.

Steve found the boat on the end berth of Delta pontoon. '*Dream On II*' looked tired after a prolonged period in the hot sun. However, her sails were well covered and that was a good sign – at least somebody still cared and knew what they were about. He didn't know her recent history, but 'Reason for Selling: Owner's change of plans' usually meant that the lady of the family (probably the second judging by the name) had decided that the dream of sailing around the world ended at Gibraltar. Some couple didn't get that far, with their dream ending in northern Spain or even France after bad luck with the weather and a challenging offshore passage across the Bay of Biscay. Steve pulled out his mobile phone and took a few shots of areas that need attention. '*Dream On II*' was well outside his budget even after a recent price reduction, but any problem pictures could be used to see how soft the pricing was before he inspected her. The cost of a survey would be significant and would be the last step before a final offer.

He spent another half hour wandering around the marina then headed for the gate. The sun was now behind the Andalucian hills and he was looking forward to a beer. The walk around the marina had been an escape, but now he remembered that the evening was to be spent re-reading the files on the murder – and on Maruška's escape.

"Thanks for letting me through. I might see you tomorrow."

"Sure, I'll be here. Is she what you are looking for then?"

"Yes, fits the bill I think on first glance but I need to talk to the broker and arrange a lookover. But she's way out of my budget."

"Yeh, more expensive than women - I should know. I've had a few since my wife buggered off."

"Tell me about it. Women are just ships passing in the night - I'm sticking to boats."

Liam's Ulster burr rolled on. "For what it's worth most of the yachts here sell way below asking price. I was thinking – I know of someone who has a boat coming up for sale – might do you nicely, though she is steel – and she's in Morocco. British reg though. He had to go back to the States – cancer I think - and I heard he's in a hospice. His wife took a shine to me when they were here for a month, but I'm staying well away from that. She still emails me every couple of weeks, getting saucier all the time. I think she fancies a bit of rough and the poor bugger's not dead yet. She's not a bad looker though."

"What colour is she?"

"White of course. Oh – you meant the boat? Yeh, sorry I got a bit carried away there. It's the Irish blarney in me. The boat is white too."

"Steel's no problem, but maybe Morocco is."

"Morocco shouldn't be too much of a problem. Marina Smir is only twenty five miles from here. They're civilized there and the Islamists haven't got a hold at this end in the North. The south is a different story though. Tell you what, I'll see if I can get you some details. All I can remember is that she's about forty feet long, well looked after. She's ketch rigged. I can't remember her name even though she was moored alongside me."

"Sounds good Liam. I might see you tomorrow then."

"Ok – maybe we can have a beer?"

"You're on."

"Wait, I might have it here." Liam pulled out his smartphone and scrolled down his emails. "Yes, here it is...*dream about you every night...da de da...I will have to sell Rubaiyat when Theo's estate is sorted. Maybe we can meet then...*"

"*Rubaiyat?*"

"Yes here, look. You might find some info on the web."

Liam held out the phone and Steve glanced at the email, taking in the name of the boat and trying to ignore the explicit picture below the text.

"Too much info Liam."

"See what I mean?"

Steve headed through the North Bastion wondering whether he could face a beer with Liam and followed the zig-zag streets climbing upwards towards the Rock Hotel. He had worked under fire with many men – and a few women – and had learned to judge people quickly, learning to go with his gut feel – and it rarely let him down. Steve got the feeling that Liam would be a good guy to have at his side in a tight spot, although he didn't know why the thought had come into his head. Whether he could put up with the prattle was quite another matter, although he knew that such people could often be cold, controlled and focused under fire.

*

Back in his room he showered and checked himself in the mirror - his new beard was almost presentable, and he decided to stick with it. The day's report to Barbary would have to wait – there was little to say beyond the fact that he had read the files. He could pad it out with details of the in-flight breakfast and the weather in Gibraltar, but doubted that Barbary would appreciate it.

As he dried himself he wondered what he should wear. *'What the fuck would a rep from Chatham Marine Services wear on a Saturday night in Gibraltar?'*

Best bib and tucker, that's what. He would be out to pick up a woman. Steve rummaged through the clothing he had been given in a case. *'What the hell?'* Tasselled loafers. *No way.*

'White trousers?' *No way – too much like naval uniform – but no choice.* He settled on a polo shirt and then noticed that the shirt had a logo and 'Chatham Marine Services' embroidered on its left breast. He threw it back in the case and picked up a pink short-sleeved cotton shirt and grimaced. *'That'll do'.* He took the cheap Rolex copy diver's style watch from his case and slipped the metal bracelet over his wrist. That was about the only thing that he felt comfortable with – even if it was a copy.

'Yeh, that's me alright' laughing as he looked at himself in the mirror. *'What a plonker.'*

He checked around the room, picking up his smartphone and key card. Then he noticed the small hotel envelope on the floor near the door. It must have been put there when he was showering. The note inside was brief, written in an elegant flowing hand.

> *'Meet me in the Lounge Bar downstairs at 7.30 for an aperitif?'*

There was no signature.

Intrigued, he looked at his watch - 7.45 p.m. He would be late, but as he didn't know who he was meeting it hardly mattered. Tough on them –whoever.

*

Steve strolled in to the Lounge Bar of the Rock Hotel. The furnishings were mostly white, with strangely-shaped wing-back chairs and low glass-topped coffee table with eight or so high chairs around a rectangular-shaped cocktail bar. The cocktail hour was in full swing, even in the twenty first century.

What had once been a critical strategic outpost of the British Empire was now a focus of the internet gambling industry – and it showed. Although there were many tourists, the conversations from the locals (who were clearly identifiable by tan and tucker) were smattered with gambling parlance, site hits, odds setting and even that afternoon's English Premier

League results which were critical in the weekly sports betting cycle.

Steve wandered through the bar. No one looked at him, no one approached him. He strolled out through one of the French doors on to the terrace.

It was the view from the Wisteria Terrace that drew people to the Lounge Bar, as well as the famed floral fragrances.

Steve knew nothing of this as he gazed out.

The coast of North Africa was visible in the twilight with the lights from the Spanish enclave at Ceuta sharp and clear, and the lights from villages on the flanks of Jebel Musa twinkling as the cooling air rolled down the mountain. He could see the navigation lights of ships moving through the Strait, as they had done for centuries. Down below were the garish lights of two cruise ships at the terminal, and the lights of Algeciras across the Bay. Drifting up from the city below was a mixture of music – from African drumming to Arabian themes blended with pop.

Then there was a laugh – a female laugh – and heads turned seeking out the source of the sound. Steve turned. A woman was walking towards him.

Steve stood and stared, his mouth opening and closing soundlessly. Then her lips met his. He knew that taste, that embrace – and much more. She drew away and placed her finger over his lips, shaking her head and pulling him to a corner table where there was a gin and tonic and a beer waiting.

The clientele shrugged and went back to their G&Ts and chatter about next month's Cheltenham festival.

Steve looked at her, staring into her obsidian eyes, his eyes questioning, remembering dancing with her in Crete, the chase from Malta to Tunisia and the finale in Rome. He stood, dazed. Her finger went to her lips. "Shh, drink your beer. Yes, it is me."

She stood back from him and looked up and down his wiry body remembering the scars both physical and emotional – at least, those which he had exposed to her. His close cropped reddish hair was flecked with grey and his brown eyes were buried in a narrow, angular face set off by a nose which betrayed a history of fighting. His medium height frame was set in a stance ready for movement and action.

"Where on earth did you get those clothes?"

"They came with the territory. I'm a sales rep now, as if you didn't know."

"Someone has a sense of humour."

"The Ape."

"Ah yes, of course. I do like the beard though."

They laughed awkwardly, and then she got serious. "Come on let's sit down – we've got some catching up to do."

"No. First you've got some explaining to do."

"Later." She reached across the table but Steve withdrew his hand.

In the few minutes it took them to finish their drinks not a word was said by Steve as Helena tried chip away at his defences. Steve's emotions were in turmoil, raging at what he thought must have been a deception, through to happiness in the extreme – and back. Then Helena stood up. She reached again for his hand, but he ignored the gesture as he followed her out of the bar.

*

The silence continued while they waited for the elevator. It was empty. The doors closed and Helena pushed the button for the fourth floor.

"What the hell Helena. You've been playing me for a berk. I thought you were dead!"

"I didn't play you for a berk! And until two days ago I was sure that *you* were dead! That's what they told me. The only fun was seeing your face in the bar just now. I didn't have to do it that way, but what the hell - we've got to laugh sometime. And those clothes."

"Cover, they told me."

"Idiots, it just doesn't work for you."

The elevator chimed.

"Come on – my room is this way – next to yours."

*

Steve opened the mini bar and found a miniature of Bell's scotch, and mixed a gin and tonic for Helena as she opened the door onto the balcony and dusted off the chairs. She turned on the wall screen and found a hard-rock station, then turned it up.

He stepped outside and passed her the drink.

"How come you like hard rock all of a sudden?"

"Walls have ears. And I've always liked hard rock."

"Fair enough, then we should be ok out here?"

"It's the best we can do right now."

"What about talking in the shower?"

"I thought you'd never ask. Let's save it for afterwards shall we?"

"I didn't bloody mean it."

"Look Steve. I didn't fucking set this up right. We've both been played, so let's play our own game shall we?"

"I lost the boat you know – seems I was in Tunisia. She's been impounded."

"You – we – were in Tunisia alright. I can tell you the whole story."

"Are you supposed to?"

"No, I'm under orders not to, but fuck them, it's our game now."

"How do they explain the car crash in Malta then?"

"The story is that it happened, and we both survived, though Bryan didn't. In reality, he was killed by a bomb in Tunisia when we were there. That's the truth of it."

"OK Ellie, but try to see it from my perspective. They may doubt that I lost my memory, so they put you in to check me out. How can I trust you?"

"Yes, I understand that might be difficult. But why didn't they just bury you?"

"There's something in my memory that they want?"

"It's possible, though I don't know what that could be – we were together right through to the end of the Rome job. I know as much as you."

"I wouldn't know that – memory loss, remember."

His face was deadly serious and she knew that there was a big gap between them.

"It's up to you to decide Steve."

"And I'll decide later. Let's play it by ear shall we? What I don't understand is why they put us together again?"

"They want us to find Pavkovic. It's simple. I'm the beauty and the brains, and you are the brawn."

"Thanks for that. Let me remind you that I was the one who figured out how to pin her down in Malta. So much for GCHQ."

"Lighten up Steve, everyone who matters knows that. I think it could have been a lot worse."

"What do you mean, worse?"

"I know the way they work and think at Six, and they are as sharp as they come. You do know that we are working off the books?" Steve nodded. "They lost a whole team in the Rome disaster. It was a major cock up – and there are still some unaccounted for. Stone and Gregory for example."

"Who? I don't remember anything about Rome. My last memories are of Malta."

"Fine, stick to your story. Amnesia – a special case. I don't know what the truth is – only you know that, but they could have buried us both."

Steve downed the remains of his scotch and mixed another round.

"So, what's your take on Maruška's disappearance?"

"Have you read the files?"

"Yes, and I have my theories."

"She was certifiable all along, but I reckon now that she's found another gear. Doesn't care, maybe thinks she can't be caught."

"Or she wants to be caught."

"That doesn't make sense."

"It does – there are plenty of cases where multiple murderers want to get caught – buried guilt drives them to make mistakes."

"Where did you get that daft idea?"

"It's not daft, it's psychology."

"I thought English was your thing."

"It was – but I did a joint English/Psychology degree."

"Really. And how are your parents?"

"What do you mean?"

"You heard me."

"I've told you about my parents."

"Yes, and Ogilvy told me your mother was a junkie in Bristol, that you were brought up in care."

"He would have done. As I said Rome was a major balls-up. The files have been cleaned up and they've created alternative histories to cover the trail."

"You've got an answer for everything."

"It's the truth. Look Steve, I can see you are bitter and suspicious. Paranoia is healthy in our profession. I should know – Ogilvy had lined me up for the mortuary in St Thomas's. For Christ's sake, you are a soldier! Get your act together man!"

"A Royal Marine actually – or I was. I am not a spy or a bloody detective!"

"Then let's focus on our target and do the job! So what's your theory?"

Steve looked at his watch. "You are right. Focus on the target. My theory will keep for now. Come on, we're going out on the town. There's a bar I want to take you to."

"What?"

"Believe me, it's part of the investigation."

"But you can't go out in those clothes. And those shoes – God where did they come from?"

"Just watch me – they're perfect cover. As for the shoes – ask your boss – he arranged all this. And you, haven't you got anything a bit more flashy, something that shows your chest off a bit more?"

"What, like a black lacy bra?"

"Yes, and say a white T shirt over it? Just the job."

"I'd better go and change then."

"Don't hang about – the bar shuts at five a.m. - or it did when I last went there."

*

Walking down the hill Steve told Helena about the recipe for JC cocktails, for which the bar was renowned. It was unique to Gibraltar, known as a JC and not a Joan or John Collins.

"You love gin, so this should suit you down to the ground. A proper JC comes in a long glass and consists of a measure of gin, a dash of angostura bitters and a splash of lime or lemon juice topped up with a splash of lemonade. Posh places put sugar round the glass. We drunk it in pint glasses."

"That sounds like a hellish drink."

"It is, and it's the bitters that give you the hangover – but the Rock Run the next morning would sort that out."

It was almost 10 p.m. when they arrived at Castle Street.

"So that's why we're here!"

Helena looked up at the tattered pegboard sign. Charles's Hole in T'Wall bar was all action.

"Yes, Calthorpe was last seen here."

They squeezed into a corner seat with their JCs.

"I'll tell you what I know. First off, not everyone here is straight."

"Funnily enough I got that feeling when we came in."

"Yes, the sailor's motto: Sleep on your back because if you don't then somebody else will."

Ellie rolled her eyes. "Droll in the extreme!"

"Anyway, the bar has always been the Royal Navy's number one drinking place. It's said that almost without exception every member of the Royal Navy for the last forty years has had a skinful here. If you haven't been to Charlies then you haven't been to Gib. Charles was always on the lookout for 'fresh meat'. And that Boxer dog of his - there are some stories I couldn't even begin to repeat. I'm going to chat to Alicia the barmaid – don't move. I need to do this alone."

Helena was unaccustomed to the reaction she felt as she watched the barmaid's eyes light up before she gave Steve a long kiss. History? She wondered.

The chat went on for a few minutes and then Steve returned when there was a whistle and the barmaid turned to serve a customer.

"You certainly are a man of mystery!"

"Not really. I'll tell you the story one day - I certainly didn't give her one if that's what you're thinking. I just asked her what she knew about the guy who was killed, whether there was anything she remembered after making her statement to the police."

"And…"

"She said there was a tranny in here on the night he went missing - someone she hadn't seen before. Gib's a small place. The sailors come and go, but all the trannys and drag queens are well known – so Alicia said."

"So you think Calthorpe was a gay?"

"Or bi- or whatever. It doesn't matter does it – this was where he was last seen?"

"Do you really think Pavkovic is still alive?"

"I don't *know*, but my gut says yes."

"So, where do we start?"

"We just did and *I* continue tomorrow by meeting the Jaunty on *Bulwark.*"

"Jaunty?"

"The Master at Arms – he is responsible for security and discipline aboard the ship. You can't come."

"Want to bet?"

"What do you mean? You know nothing about the Royal Navy."

"Maybe, but I am a civilian on special detachment to the Special Investigations Branch, as of yesterday."

"The SIB? Bloody hell, will this never end?"

"Face it Steve, you're stuck with me, like it or not."

"Another JC?"

"No, thanks. We need clear heads tomorrow…" she smiled "– and it would be nice to get an early night."

"I've still got to send a report to Barbary. What shall I say – checked out the main gay bar in Gib?"

"You could try 'met partner and exchanged notes and theories and …'"

"Blah blah blah."

As they laughed and enjoyed the moment, the hubbub in the bar changed in note. Angry voices were raised, followed by some cheering, and then the fighting started and a glass flew overhead, smashing against the centuries old wall behind them.

"Okay, it's time to leave. We'll do The Donkey's Flip Flop another night."

He pulled her arm and they pushed their way around the edge of the throng as another glass shattered.

"What's the Donkey's Flip-Flop?"

"Another well-known Navy watering hole, not really a place for ladies, but dragons *are* acceptable."

"Dragons?"

"Yes. I'm not explaining that – you can look that one up for yourself."

*

After a few days rest in a discreet hotel, Maruška Pavkovic had crossed the border from Gibraltar and was now in Andalucia in Spain, across the bay from Gibraltar.

The escape from the ship had been difficult. Four days hidden in an air conditioning duct had stiffened her joints, but regular food supplied by Carl Halborg had kept her going and isometric exercises kept her muscles in tone – more or less. It was the boredom that had nearly killed her. She had heard the ship being searched several times but she had remained undetected in her corner of the aircon ducting, wrapped in a foil survival blanket and invisible to the bots with thermal imaging equipment that had been used to access the seemingly unreachable places. Sniffer dogs had been used, but no one had thought to check the ducting. Even if they had, a small trace of best Moroccan hashish which Halborg had available had been left inside the first ceiling panel. That would excite the dogs but not raise suspicions.

Her waste had been bagged and sealed in plastic bags which she hid inside a second survival blanket. It was a grim existence, but she had lived through worse as a teenager during the war in Bosnia.

On the fourth day the ship docked in Gibraltar, and it was time to move. Halborg was in too deep now and if his involvement was ever discovered then he would spend the rest of his life in a naval prison. She had no worries on that account, and anyway there was still DNA evidence to be found, evidence which she had carefully secreted on the night it had happened, in a corner which would probably not be cleaned for some time.

Spirited to the stern of the ship well after midnight, she had dropped over the rail at the ship's dock and splashed into the dark water wearing a buoyancy aid and a velcro arm sling, towing a waterproof pouch with cash. She wasn't sure whether the directions she had been given should be believed and it was a slow backstroke journey keeping the rising moon directly in sight.

This was an ideal opportunity for Halborg to get rid of her, but the fishing boat had been waiting as arranged outside the *cordon sanitaire* of 50 meters to seaward of the ship. The fishing boat had been challenged by a Ministry of Defence Police guard boat which had nearly run over her, but the fisherman was a regular, well known to them and not suspected of smuggling.

No words had been spoken as she was hauled aboard and handed a towel, a track suit and some trainers, just as she had specified to Halborg. She still wore the jamming collar but knew that it was probably dead after the swim and it certainly was after she got the Gibraltar fisherman to remove the lock with a bolt cropper and it joined all the other detritus at the bottom of the Bay of Algeciras.

Halborg had done well, being surprisingly resourceful, earning his money and making the arrangements through the network of people who lived below the radar in such a port. He had emptied her 'ransom' bank account but that had been expected. Her 'carrot' had been enough.

"I have other bank accounts. We can have a great time together when you leave the Navy. Maybe the Caribbean? And besides, you want my body even more now – and I want yours, I ache for it Carl. No man has satisfied me as much as you have. And I can do things for you that no other woman has done before – I promise you that." That statement was certainly true. Men could be really blind and stupid, led by their dicks and dying because of them. She had suggested a repertoire – and he had listened intently, drooling like a stupid dog. However, there were some things in her repertoire that she kept secret – for now.

The money was a small price to pay, and anyway she recovered most of it two days later when he gave her the details of his own accounts before she made the final cut and he bled out. The rest of the money – five thousand euros – had gone to one of Halborg's shipmates. She would get that back too.

The fishing boat turned slowly and the fisherman, Jo-Jo Garcia, opened the throttles. Within five minutes they were rounding the North Mole and turning into Marina Bay. It was next to the airport runway which jutted out into Algeciras Bay, busy with ships even that late at night – shipping is a twenty four by seven business. It was at that moment that the nanochip in her neck woke up and locked on to Jo-Jo's mobile phone signal. Then, a coded message packet started to worm its way through the Gibtelecom network servers and on to its ultimate destination in China.

After the boat was moored, they stepped ashore and the fisherman walked alone to the security gate, stopping to chat with Liam O'Neill, the security guard. They occasionally drunk together in one of the local pubs - Jo-Jo Garcia was a rough diamond and into all sorts of dubious dealings – unproven, of course – and his stories were always entertaining.

"Something for supper Liam, fresh tonight."

Garcia handed a plastic bag to O'Neill. As he looked at the small tuna, Maruška slipped by unnoticed.

"That's great Jo-Jo. I'll buy you a beer on Friday."

"Can't do Friday" he winked at Liam "things to do – my wife has gone to see her sister in England. She's away for two whole weeks. The peace is wonderful."

"While the cat's away…"

"Exactly!"

"I'll look forward to it."

And with that he slipped away to meet Maruška and lead her to his small house near the North Bastion.

As they walked, Jo-Jo explained that his wife was away in England and that she was welcome to stay in his home for a few days and there would be no charge. She got the message and when they got back to his house he opened a bottle of Johnny Walker Black Label whisky. It was nothing special but it had been a while since she'd drunk alcohol and after the swim the sensation was pleasant. What came next was not so pleasant but she did what had to be done expertly and quickly – he was soon asleep and snoring in one of the chairs.

*

She was awake, ready and dressed the next morning when Jo-Jo brought her a coffee just before six a.m.

"You must leave now, before it gets light."

"Of course. Show me the way.

He turned to leave the room and she followed then pushed him hard on the back of the neck as he reached the top of the stairway.

"What…"

He tumbled forward in a near-somersault and she heard bones break and a slow fading groan. When she reached him there was frothy blood coming from his mouth with shallow, laboured breathing and one of his ears was seeping a straw coloured fluid.

She found some paper towel, went back upstairs carefully wiped the room. She quickly checked the bed for hairs and then made it up. It might be enough – she'd have to take a chance about skin flakes – it would almost certainly be assumed to have been an accident. She finished her coffee and washed the cup in the small galley kitchen and checked Jo-Jo again. He was dead.

A quick search revealed a wad of Euros and plus some Gibraltar sterling and some credit cards in a wallet in his pockets and a mobile phone on the kitchen table along with the house keys. She left some of the cash and pocketed the rest of the wad.

In Wuhan, it was mid-afternoon and Wan Chuntao was drinking tea. The Northern Wind team had been working through hacked systems trying to trace possible bomb components, very much akin to what GCHQ in Cheltenham had been working on, as had the NSA and DIA in the US, the FSB and GRU in Moscow and innumerable other intelligence agencies of lesser capability. Her tablet PC chimed gently and a pop-up appeared 'Location Notification: Agent 29'. She launched her Agent Management Screen and tapped on the 'Location' icon. This brought up a map which auto-zoomed in to Gibraltar where the network signal had originated and had been attached to the nanochip's data packet. She refreshed the screen and the coordinates remained unchanged – it was not good to prod an agent on the move – a car accident and a lost agent could be the result. Another ten seconds and still no change. She checked the local time – just after 6 am and tapped the icon for 'Prompt Agent'.

As Maruška opened the rear of Jo-Jo's phone to remove the SIM card there was a sudden pulse of pain in her neck. Too late. She cursed and the phone slipped through her fingers and clattered to the floor. After more than a month, she had forgotten how severe the pain could be.

'*Jebati!*'

Even if Jo-Jo had been alive he would not have understood the Serbian for 'fuck!'

She was in Chuntao's control again.

Jo-Jo's keys were on the table but she found a spare key on a hook in the kitchen and locked the door as she left. The sky was lightening above in the false dawn, but the city on the west side of the Rock was in darkness. The street cleaners and early joggers were already out and about. She bought a coffee and a croissant at a café and walked around the town getting her bearings and checking the shops. Two hours later she had bought a burner phone and called Chuntao from outside the King's Bastion Leisure Centre.

Wan Chuntao had assumed that the nanochip had failed and was surprised that it had apparently come to life again. At least she now had her agent back. Nevertheless the anger in her voice was clear.

"Where have you been?"

"I was captured by the British and held on a ship, but I escaped."

"How did they capture you?"

"In a car crash. They knew where I was."

"How?"

"I don't know, but I think it's your clever technology. They seem to know how it works."

"Why are you in Gibraltar?"

"Because that's where the ship docked and where I escaped."

"Are you injured?"

"I broke my arm – it is still healing."

"You need to get back to work. Quickly. I will arrange documents and a secure cellphone. Do you remember the name Abu ben-Zhair?"

"Of course."

"Well he is still a target. We believe that he is in Morocco.'

"I have never been to Morocco. Do you not have other agents there?"

"Do what you are told! Do not use this phone again. Buy another. Use them once only until you receive one from us. Call me in twelve hours' time."

The line dropped and Maruška swore. The initial thrill of the double game she had played with the British in Malta had been invigorating, the risk intense and the satisfaction immense. Now, reality hit her. She had committed to the Chinese again, and it was killing her.

She shook her head, cursing quietly, and started to jog towards the shops. After twenty yards she stopped, groaning at the pain in her arm. She would need another sling and painkillers. She would need a lot more for the meet with Carl Halborg to 'plan their future'. It was set for the following evening when he had shore leave. What an idiot he was.

In Wuhan, Wan Chuntao was fretting. There was no Chinese consulate in Gibraltar, so the use of diplomatic baggage to move papers and equipment would be impossible. She would have to rely on another channel. She checked the list of embassies and consulates in Gibraltar. There were no obvious friends, unless she could lean on Thailand. Since the death of the King in 2016, political tension had built and it was likely that China would have some influence there. She clicked on the icon for Northern Wind Two – her superior.

97

"I need to move a diplomatic bag into Gibraltar, urgently. We have no embassy there, but Thailand does. Would that be possible?"

"I will find out. How urgent and where from?"

"Within twenty four hours, from our London Embassy would be the easiest – it is a direct flight from there to Gibraltar."

"Make sure that London is ready with what you need. I will check if it can be done."

The meeting with Carl Halborg had been brief, despite her arm.

She had moved hotels regularly, paying in cash. The swim along the coast north from Gibraltar had been slow, but the water had been warm and she took her time crossing the invisible border in the sea.

*

Abu ben-Zhair

As with some other European countries, colonialism had left a bitter aftertaste and even today the Algerian Arabic ghettoes in France are places of hopelessness and raise xenophobic and racist feelings in some French people.

The problems are manifest and the outcomes dreadful as terrorist atrocities continue across France today.

In Algeria itself, a whole generation grew up with a legacy that stimulated many to associate themselves with groups such as Al Qaeda and ISIS - and to try to re-establish Shariah Law and a return to the old ways.

Abu ben-Zhair was one of that generation.

*

The six year-old boy had woken to the sound of shouting and his mother's wailing. He could hear the rough wooden door being smashed down and then heard shouts in French. He recognised the language as that of legionnaires, but he understood little. There was commotion and the sound of breaking furniture. He heard men on the flat roof above him. Then the door to the room in which he slept was thrown open and two legionnaires burst in, with torches.

'Il n'est pas ici' one said as they turned his bed over and scattered his possessions, trampling the rug and dragging him out into the family room where a legionnaire had broken a paraffin lamp over the wrecked table with a rug thrown on it. The trooper took out an old brass cigarette lighter which reflected the flame as he struck it in the dark room and set the fire.

His mother was outside, wailing as the soldiers removed her clothes, exposing her shame. There was no sign of anyone else beyond the legionnaires. The village remained almost silent bar the roaring and spitting as the flames took hold and he heard the dry wood of the poor furniture crackling wickedly. The air pockets expanded and burst the cellulose fibres, feeding the eager fire and sending sparks up through the fallen roof. He was tied to a camel.

Abu ben-Zhair's father had learned to fight, to shoot and had received a modicum of education. He had skirmished with the Foreign Legion and learned to stay cool in the heat of a firefight.

Now, as a man, Abu ben-Zhair's legacy was to fight on, but on a much larger scale than that of his father. He was not fighting for the liberation of Algeria. He was fighting for the Muslim religion itself on a world-wide scale. He was not a 'spectre' as his father and grandfather had been, his name was known to the leading intelligence agencies since the bombing of the *Queen Katherine* cruise liner in Grand Harbour, Malta. It had been publicised and the UK had put a reward of £1 million on his head.

Ghudamis is a town in Libya near the conjunction of the Libyan, Tunisian and Algerian borders. Today the N53 route which heads south for Tassili N'Ajjer National Park, a World Heritage site, becomes the N1 onwards to Tamanrasset. This is classical French Foreign Legion country. To the south lies the Aïr Country of Fort Zinderneuf where Algeria meets Niger and Mali - the setting for the novel Beau Geste.

The people of this region are Tuareg – an ancient nomadic tribe who inhabit central Africa and pay little heed to borders. They are classified as a Berber tribe and their DNA extends across much of North Africa. Tough and warlike, many were hired by Muammar Gadhafi to form his elite 'presidential guard' in Libya.

Just south of Ghudamis lies the village of Deb Deb.

The night that Le Capitaine Moitessier and his platoon visited Deb Deb is not forgotten there, even more than seventy years later. The legacy of that night in that poor village lived on in the emotions of Abu ben-Zhair, in the stories his father had told him and in his very genes.

*

Abu ben-Zhair was in many ways like his father and grandfather, but the need for more change in Algeria was driving him in his own way. He had enjoyed the privileged education as a child of a senior government official, including attending university overseas in Moscow. Later he had spent time in Beijing when China was starting to turn outwards and see the world as a pool of resources for its use – and Africa was ripe for development. In Algeria, the Islamists in the form of the GIA had been causing problems within major terrorist acts against tourists and the government alike. Eventually, a form of co-existence was established between the Government and the extremists. This continued through the so-called Arab Spring which had led to the liberalisation of Tunisia and Egypt, and major civil war in Syria.

This was the story of the real Abu ben-Zhair, the story of the man whose body had been fed to pigs on a farm outside Beijing, the story that had been absorbed, learned and lived since that day by another Algerian man, a man who carried a malfunctioning pacemaker in his chest, a pacemaker that connected him to his Chinese masters.

*

In Wuhan, eight weeks before the Rome attack, The Chinese had set up the 'Northern Wind' team, tasked to find the nuclear weapon stolen from Iran – and the person behind it. Highly secret, the team reported directly to the President and General Secretary, roles which had now been merged in an effort to drive China forward.

Accordingly, the final decision was made at the highest level of the Chinese Government. A list of names was prepared by the man known as Northern Wind One, six floors below ground in the Tenth Bureau of the Guojia Anquan Bu – the 'Guoanbu' – the Ministry of State Security in Wuhan, the capital of Hubei province.

Chinese intelligence networks, both human and electronic, are vast, highly capable and effective. They continue to exercise themselves in cyberwarfare, diplomatic and industrial espionage against other countries. The agency known as 'Guoanbu' has over 100,000 agents worldwide operating not only out of embassies and consulates, but out of Chinese takeaway restaurants, bazaars and larger businesses. They were hooked into universities and anti-government groups, business networks – virtually every type of social, political and economic organisation worldwide. They also had their black teams, operating against the more serious dissenters.

The list was narrowed down and three members of the Northern Wind Team were each given a name to research. Unprecedented access was granted to other systems within the Chinese intelligence community, ordered directly by the General Secretary without a reason being given. Full cooperation was guaranteed.

Northern Wind Five - Wan Chuntao - was given the name Abu ben-Zhair. He was thought to be the most likely candidate, having been linked to the recent Malta atrocity. His file in Beijing indicated a 'high degree of strategic vision and extreme levels of personal ambition, supported by outstanding leadership capability." That is why he had been selected many years before to participate unknowingly in an experiment with electronic surveillance and tracking technology – and to take the name and place of another man.

Wan Chuntao scrolled down the screen, reading the file to which she had just been given access. A man, an Algerian, had been fitted with one of the first production nanochips, almost twenty years previously when he had been a graduate student in Beijing. At that time the design was very basic – it was far from being a nanochip in size and was embedded in a heart pacemaker. The first batch of one hundred had been produced and implanted in a cohort of foreign students over a period of two years. The implantations had taken placed when they had been hospitalized following regular health checks which had uncovered seemingly irregular heart rhythms. The students were very happy to have first class treatment at one of China's leading hospitals, and most eventually forgot that they carried pacemakers – they were never recalled for battery changes.

The early microchips embedded in the pacemakers had been relatively simple, able to detect a mobile phone network and send a location signal, date and transmission number. There was no GPS functionality and the 'prod' – the nerve impulse connection such as was used to direct Maruška Pavkovic – had not been developed at that time.

The later generations of the design had been shrunk in size and embedded near the spine, invisible to all the then available scanning technology at airports and in hospitals.

As a part of the long-term strategy this man had replaced the real ben-Zhair, adopting his identity almost completely. Now, before the Malta ship bombing, he had apparently 'gone rogue', failing to communicate with his handler. However, there were some tracks to follow.

Ben-Zhair's file contained a link to the 'pacemaker' datastream which had been very intermittent. The signal serial numbers showed that only about 10% of transmissions had got through, if sent at all. Recent data had a couple of hundred records with position signals from a wide range of places. Chuntao clicked a link to a mapping function, entered a timeframe – to narrow down to the last 12 months - and pressed the 'animate' button.

As she had watched, the map slowly built up the tracks ben-Zhair had followed. The data was incomplete and intermediate locations might not have been recorded at all. He had been very active and mobile – within the previous 12 months there had been signals from widely spaced locations across Europe, North Africa and the Near East, including Paris, Rabat, Sid bel Abbès, Kabul, Rome, London, Malta, Tunisia and Algeria.

Then, Wan Chuntao had instructed Maruška Pavkovic to travel to Tunisia, find the nuclear weapon and terminate ben-Zhair. The mission had failed. Pavkovic had gone off the grid. The last data burst from ben-Zhair's aged and apparently faulty pacemaker had once again been from Rome.

Wan Chuntao read the latest analyst's report on the Malta and Rome attacks. The summary said:

'Such a series of events of this complexity would have required funding and assistance by a State-level entity or individuals of such wealth that there are less than twenty worldwide.'

Reading further, it became apparent that the author held the terrorist planner in a high degree of awe, and Wan Chuntao could not help but feel the same way.

Sidi bel Abbès

The ancient city of Sidi be Abbès is home to some 600,000 people, about 40 miles from the Mediterranean Sea and south of the major Algerian port of Oran. Ben-Zhair's master control centre had been no more than a lights-out data centre during the 'Sword of Allah' attack. Construction of the site in the hills to the south west of the city had started five years previously and three years before the 'Sword of Allah' was actually used.

The campus had been generously endowed by a Saudi Arabian Prince, Sheikh Khalifa ibn Abu Bakr. Supposedly a radio astronomy observatory and physics campus run by the University of Oran – there actually were researchers working there – the control centre had been expanded slowly as concealed facilities had been brought to secret life under the observatory complex, accessed via a separate track and tunnel. The University research cover was perfect and it was in a country which was now the natural home for the Islamic Caliphate in the Maghreb.

As the man known by some as Abu ben-Zhair sat in the rear of the car driving up the long mountain access road on one of his rare visits to the control bunker in Sid Bel Abbes, he reviewed his plan to make it the centre of cyberwarfare operations for his group. That phase would come after the completion of the 'Cause of All Causes' project. With its heart torn out, the West would no longer be important. Then his attention would turn to Russia and the East.

In Russia, Vladimir Putin had set up the APT28 group of hackers, also known as Fancy Bear. Their 2015 cyber attack on the French TV Network 'TV5Monde' had been claimed by the 'Cyber Caliphate' and it irritated ben-Zhair that APT28 should have adopted an Islamic identity. There would be a reckoning – he would see to it.

Despite his access to nuclear technology his group of scientific specialists had been adamant that cyber warfare was the war of the future, with drones and unmanned ships deployed to do any killing that was necessary after the hackers had remotely destroyed a country's technical infrastructure -

from food supply logistics, water, power and communications – even to cars and refrigerators. These were all being connected to the 'IOT' – the internet of things as western companies invented new technologies to solve problems that they had invented. They were fools. They had opened doors into every home in the West.

That was the future. Ben-Zhair re-focused on the 'Cause of All Causes' which would be the last major overt weapons use that the world would see.

In his master control centre deep under the Radio Astronomy campus, there was a room which was being specially configured, superficially to look like the bridge of a ship. When finished it would be much more than a ship simulator, it would be at the leading edge of virtual reality. From there, the ship would be controlled.

His own chosen operational name '*Al-Mahdi*' – 'the guided one' – might have been selected during a moment of vanity, but the new name – '*Al-Rasul*' - chosen for the ship in Yanbu, Saudi Arabia, was as well suited to the ship, as '*Al-Mahdi*' was to him.

Ben-Zhair was not a religious man, but he used religion as a tool, a lever to motivate and energise, and to that extent he had to espouse religious views. Despite his deeply hidden atheism, he was moved that morning to wonder if it was indeed Allah's will that had brought him to this point, where he could, almost literally move the world.

Was he really 'The Guided One'? He did not believe that he was in the full religious sense, but the ship would surely be 'The Messenger'.

*

Maruška Roams

After Wan Chuntao had located her, Maruška changed her plan. It was easier to call on Chuntao's resources, but she always had a plan 'B'. In a small backroom upstairs in Jo-Jo's house she found an aging PC on a rickety desk and started it up. Five minutes later an email was on its way to a small store in Paris. It cost her a thousand euros a year for the service which she rarely used, but when she did it was worth every cent. The owner, Marcel Lefevre (if that was his real name), held one parcel in her name.

Securely boxed and taped with the name Marie Kirouac on it, the parcel contained a steel cash box with a combination lock. Inside the cask box was a Kimber Ultra Carry II, finished in satin silver and mounted in a 3 inch speed paddle holster, together with a spare clip, a box of .45 ACP ammunition and a cleaning kit, all in a Ziploc bag with two silica gel sachets. Under the gun was a French passport in the name of Marie Kirouac along with a small black leather purse containing two special credit cards, some receipts and a French driving licence. There was also a bundle of 5,000 US dollars and a phone with 3 SIM cards. All were up to date. The final item was a knife with a 20cm ceramic blade in a sheath. In bubble wrap, it was all a tight fit and the box did not rattle.

Marcel prepared an address label in accordance with the email instructions and within two hours the package was logged as collected by UPS and *en-route* to Algeciras for next day delivery to a Mlle. Francoise Herbeville. This was her insurance package. It was simple, quick and effective – as long as it stayed within the borders of the EU.

The problem of Carl Halborg had been easily solved.

She had bought some waste bags and duct tape and bagged Jo-Jo's body as it was beginning to smell, badly. There was nowhere obvious to hide it so she just stuffed it behind the sofa and covered the bag with a blanket.

With new clothes and makeup and some low-power reading spectacles she transformed her appearance. Carl had met her during his Wednesday night shore leave as arranged on the phone, but hadn't recognised her at first. Although he had arranged her pickup from the sea, he'd done it through a friend of a friend in Gibraltar, and hadn't really expected to see her alive again. After some drinks and a promise, he had readily come back with her to Jo-Jo's home. Two hours later he had bled out on the bed after a very painful experience and a deep shock.

Then, she sat on the sofa and made the call to the London number which asked for a pin and then connected to Wan Chuntao in Wuhan via an anonymiser and a satellite uplink in the Chinese embassy in London.

"It is organised. The package will arrive in the Thailand Embassy in Gibraltar tomorrow morning. You will go there at five minutes before noon exactly and ask to speak to Chai Charoen Yildiz. The protocol will be:

'I am Chai Charoen Yildiz'

'That is an interesting name you have'

'Yes, it means Triumphant Star'

He will give you an attaché case. He knows nothing of the contents. Do you understand?"

"Yes."

"Then repeat the protocol to me now."

Maruška was word perfect.

"Your cover will be that of a French journalist."

"Again?"

"Yes, it's easiest. Now, we must deal with Abu ben-Zhair."

*

Early the next morning she locked up Jo-Jo's house, and with her new clothes and travel case she strolled to the Continental Hotel on Engineer's Lane where she had reserved a room. She showered and did her floor exercise then headed out for breakfast.

At precisely five minutes before noon she rang the bell at 120 Main Street. The brass plaque said that it was a Consulate.

There was a tap on her arm and she turned sharply to see a short dark haired man, obviously oriental and dressed in a well-cut lightweight suit, with a plain tie and a coat of arms visible. He carried a burgundy coloured attaché case in his right hand and there appeared to be a thin steel chain through the handle, disappearing up his sleeve.

"I am Chai Charoen Yildiz."

Just as the consulate door opened their security protocol was completed and Chai turned away. Maruška followed him into a waiting taxi.

There was shout from the consulate, but she did not look back.

He didn't speak as the taxi moved away from the kerb. She could see that the attaché case had what she assumed to be the Thai Royal Coat of Arms in gold embossed in it, with the legend 'Diplomatic Baggage' below it. Chai Choren took a key from a chain around his neck and opened the case. Inside was a slightly smaller, thinner black case which he handed to Maruška. He re-locked the case and in good English told the driver to stop. He looked at Maruška. "You leave now."

As she climbed out of the cab, she heard the diplomatic messenger say "Airport please."

The afternoon would be occupied by a shopping expedition and a fitness session with particular focus on the muscles of her weakened arm. The next morning she would cross the border into Spain to collect the UPS package.

Back at the Hotel Emile she opened the small case and laid out the contents and checked them. Satisfied, she called the hotel desk and said that her plans had changed and that she would be staying another week.

Then she turned on the wallscreen and found the CNN channel. The Rome disaster was still the leading news item, more than three months after the event. An international task force had been organised to search out the perpetrators who were believed to have been based in Algeria. A NATO task force was assembling to patrol the Mediterranean and ostensibly pressurise the Algerian government. The UN was wringing its hands uselessly, as usual.

There were reports of increased naval activity off the coast of North Korea. The incredible possibility of joint naval exercises involving the US, Russian and Chinese fleets in the area was being openly discussed, and tension between Israel and Iran was increasing dangerously.

She watched the analysis for a while, wondering about the man who had planned it, full of professional admiration. This was a man to be admired not only for the organisation of such a complex attack, but for its absolutely cold-blooded and merciless execution. This was a man worthy of her talents and she relished the chase to come. But first she needed a lead, a pointer, some indication as to where she might pick up his trail, the trail she had lost in Tunisia.

The Chinese tablet was fully charged and she fired it up, waiting while it checked two of her fingerprints and a retinal scan. She checked the new smartphone and read the public key she would need to access the encrypted files on the tablet.

Within five minutes she knew that ben-Zhair's last known location was Port Said but that data was almost three weeks old. A text from Chuntao instructed her to wait in Gibraltar pending a further update.

At that moment, less than half a mile away a man by the name of Harry Calthorpe was reading the Daily Telegraph and enjoying a coffee. In less than twenty four hours their timelines would intersect, and Calthorpe's would end.

Maruška locked the essentials in her room safe and headed out of the hotel. Within ten minutes she had paid off the cab and was queuing at the Spanish border. The wait was almost an hour but once through immigration and customs she picked up a Spanish cab to the Aura Hotel in Algeciras where she had pre-booked a room online. At the desk the receptionist was a pleasant and talkative man of about thirty five and obvious African extraction. She checked in as Françoise Herbeville, a French journalist. Speaking passable French, the desk clerk asked about her current assignment. She explained that she was researching people smuggling from North Africa and asked if he knew anything that could be of help to her. His manner changed immediately to one of brusque efficiency and he quickly handed her the keycard. The UPS delivery had not arrived so after checking her room she strolled around the tired dock area to look for lunch, eventually settling for some tapas and an Estrella beer at a local café obviously focused on the dock trade.

When she returned to the hotel Aura the UPS parcel was waiting. She paid two weeks in advance for the room and after removing the documents from the steel cashbox in the parcel she repackaged it and asked the receptionist to place it in the hotel safe. Then she locked her room and headed back to her Gibraltar hotel. The border delays were even worse than they had been in the morning.

The early evening would be spent shopping – and then she would go partying - and treat herself. Although she didn't know it, the result would be another row added to an Interpol spreadsheet.

*

Nassim Kateb

Was it Allah's will that had brought Nassim Kateb to ben-Zhair? Kateb was a brilliant and quietly devout research student when, purely by chance it seemed, they had met in a café in Algiers. During the meeting, which followed a set pattern, ben-Zhair had discovered that Kateb's family had been persecuted during the time when France was the colonial power in Algeria.

Ben-Zhair had sponsored Kateb's further education (including a year in Paris as a visiting lecturer), and had also invested in the futures of several similar students he had met. Even if they worked in esoteric areas of the arts and sciences, these were devout Muslims who impressed him and who he thought he could use at some time in the future of the ICIM as he envisioned it. At that time ben-Zhair had no conception of Kateb's research subject area. It didn't matter. They shared a very jaundiced view of France and the French, and an enthusiasm for change in Algeria – without being too obvious about it. Kateb was a devout, though not zealous, Muslim.

After earning his doctorate at the University of Algiers, Kateb had published several well-reviewed research papers. Then he left Algeria to take up a post as a lecturer in Tectonics and Geomorphology in the University of Rabat, Morocco.

During his time in Algiers, the physical focus of his research had been the active earthquake region of northern Algeria and Morocco, where earthquakes as large as 6.3 on the Richter Scale are not uncommon. Then, when he moved to Rabat he shifted his earthquake research focus to Western Morocco and the offshore islands.

His appointment had been carefully vetted by the Moroccan educational and government authorities, and a file had been opened on him by the BCIJ – the Moroccan secret police. This was normal, and his appointment raised no eyebrows. Indeed, there was no reason to doubt his motives or purpose – they were, it appeared, purely academic. His attendance at the mosque was regular but not zealous and he was not one to leave his desk or his students to pray during the academic day. This was as ben-Zhair had required of him.

"There are many ways to serve Allah" he had been told when ben-Zhair first provided funds. "I am working towards building a Caliphate in the Maghreb, and I expect you to help in its future. Do your work, do it well and do it honestly. Then, occasionally, come to join us and share our vision. I will tell you when and where."

So, two or three times every year, Nassim Kateb along with several other similar advisors had visited ben-Zhair to spend a few days discussing politics and revolution in the changing, asymmetric world of international terrorism. These interludes had been passed in various farms and old villas and gradually inducted the attendees into a secret way of life, a shared vision and a clear purpose. They also learned how to handle weapons and the basics of unarmed combat. At one special session ben-Zhair had addressed the assembled group. They were sat out in the open under some palm trees at an old farm, near the town of Medea, some 50 miles south of Algiers. It was hot day and the air was dry, the view down the valley one of lush greenery following the spring rains.

"After the first attack, I want to show a pattern of increasing escalation in the power and sophistication of our attacks. We must show the highest levels of technical sophistication, capability, reach and logistical expertise. Only that way will our vision of a Caliphate be feared and respected by world powers. Besides the Great Satan and his running dogs, I include Saudi Arabia and Iran, as well as Russia and China.

I ask you all to consider these requirements and at our next meeting propose projects. No matter how unusual or demanding your ideas might be, they will be considered. Just think how outlandish the idea was that two airliners could be stolen and used to destroy the twin towers of US capitalism. It can be done."

It was during these sessions that the considerable assembled brainpower conceived of the attack on the British cruise liner *'Queen Katherine'*. However, the subsequent 'Sword of Allah' attack had been ben-Zhair's own idea and he had not shared it with the group – it had been a huge step up from what the world had seen before.

113

At a later meeting that Nassim Kateb had proposed his idea. At that time there was no obvious way that it could be implemented, but it was there, waiting for the right moment.

And so, two years later, ben-Zhair had held his brief meeting with Kateb in the Tree House Café in Rabat and the 'Cause of All Causes' was initiated.

*

The 'Yanbu Explorer'

The Saudi Arabian shipping company had been set up under the auspices of Sheikh Khalifa.

Wealthy beyond what most people could conceive of, Sheikh Khalifa ibn Abu Bakr was a distant cousin of the Saudi royal family. His closest relatives were more than usually devout Sunni Muslims of the Wahhabi sect, more observant of Shariah law than was usual in the higher echelons of Saudi society. Their observance was more than external, more than what was necessary for meeting the norms of Saudi society. It was internal, genuinely held and based on deep conviction. It was dangerous.

Most of the Saudi ruling clan were, in common with the rest of the human race – or at least those who professed to being religious - hypocritical when it came to religion. Alcohol was enjoyed in secret, but sexual vices were less the norm amongst males – after all, the faith permitted polygamy.

As far as the common man was concerned, Shariah law was strictly enforced in Saudi Arabia with 157 beheadings in 2015. Stoning women to death for adultery was unusual, although such sentences were still passed and nearly always commuted. Amputations as a punishment for theft were everyday occurrences.

The Saudi prince with dollars to burn by the billion was not interested in business. Money had little value in his eyes – other than as a tool to enable him to achieve those things which he thought were important in the world – and those revolved mainly around religion. That included the war against Satan in whatever form he took, whether as the United States, the Shia State of Iran or tyrants such as Assad in Syria. The Prince had even provided very discreet support to Osama bin-Laden, Al-Qaeda and the Taliban, and latterly to a range of terrorist organisations which were aligned with the Sunni interpretation of Islam and the Wahabi sect in particular.

The major Western countries knew about Saudi support for Islamist terrorists and that they had provided huge funds to IS in its war against Assad in Syria. The problem was that Saudi buying power in the arms - and other lucrative markets – was huge. They controlled vast amounts of oil reserves and at a blink they could seriously damage the Western economic model. The West bought the oil, Saudi Arabia spent the petrodollars on arms and consumer goods, on building huge leisure complexes to attract tourists and take more western money. And so the money continued to go round and round, with a small but very useful percentage finding its way to Islamist terrorists. After all, Saudi Arabia was the guardian of Mecca – it had responsibilities to Islam and to the legacy of Muhammad.

Ben-Zhair knew that the funding he received was only a small portion of Sheikh Khalifa's *zakat*. The *'zakat'* – Islam's Shariah Law expectation that every true Muslim should devote 2.5% of his earnings to good causes – amounted to more than $200 million per annum for Sheikh Khalifa.

And so, the Prince Khalifa amused himself funding wars and projects which took his fancy – and they were always 'good causes'. He circumvented the problems of money laundering and funds transfer by making use of the *hawala* money transfer mechanism. To prime the process and prevent the obvious imbalance he had a personal yacht built, as did all Saudi princes. This yacht was not conspicuously large when compared to those of his cousins, but it was large enough to occasionally transport a ton or two of gold from Saudi Arabia to other countries where it would percolate out through soukhs and other outlets and so fund his projects. This method was below the radar of the Western security services and impossible to track.

Sheikh Khalifa was not the only such patron of Islamist terrorism in Saudi Arabia, but he was the one whose funds had enabled ben-Zhair to acquire the Sword of Allah.

Now, in the port of Yanbu on the Red Sea, his funds were being used by ben-Zhair and the Islamic Caliphate in the Maghreb to re-fit a container ship. This ship – the Yanbu Explorer - was formerly known as 'MSC Venezuela' and supposedly broken up – that is, scrapped. Now registered in Saudi Arabia, she was of 'Supramax' size, although a container ship and not a bulk carrier.

The typical deadweight of a Supramax ship is 50-60,000 tons and when fully loaded they need about 13 meters (40 feet) of water to float. Having less than 13 meters draught was a key requirement for the 'Cause of All Causes' to succeed.

Ben-Zhair and Jafa Sharifi planned that she would carry some cargo containers but her critical cargo would be concealed in a special, strengthened housing running almost half the length of the ship, mounted in a carefully constructed tunnel passing through all the holds and into a sealed space near the bow. The after or rearmost hold space would house high-power krypton-fluoride lasers. These would direct a coherent set of laser beams through the high-vacuum tunnel, to be focused on to a target in the forward hold. This was all to be constructed in heavy gauge stainless steel and would be capable – with suitable pumps – of being maintained at near zero pressure – the highest of vacuums. It would also be at the lowest of temperatures, close to absolute zero. The basic design – the 'Sword of Allah' - would have been tested in Rome before the ship put to sea..

The target for the lasers was a marble-sized plastic pellet containing a mixture of the radioactive gases deuterium and tritium, within a small gold cylinder no larger than a sewing thimble which had originated in North Korea before being sold to Iran – from where two of the pellets and two *hohlraums* been stolen by ben-Zhair's agents.

These central components of the cargo were already in secure cryogenic storage in Yanbu, and other, larger components were *en-route* from Germany.

Because the ship was being refitted she would have to pass a survey before she could put to sea. The design changes could be argued as being a new approach to strengthening, to prevent the ship 'hogging' – bending lengthwise – in a long, high ocean storm swell. Hogging had been a recognised problem in the past, leading to some major ship losses – such as the MV *'Derbyshire'* during Typhoon Orchid in the South China Sea, with the loss of her crew of 42 and two wives of the crew. Nevertheless the design of the changes to the *Yanbu Explorer* might be questioned for a container ship and so the surveyors would have to be bought off. Qasem Hamdami (ben-Zhair's

117

Head of Security) was a resourceful man backed by the practically limitless funding of the Sheikh. The surveyors would be fixed, either by using a carrot or a stick and maybe even both.

The meeting was held out in the desert, away from the prying eyes and the active ears of the Saudi Secret Police – the Mabahith.

"And so, brothers, are we able to meet the May timetable?"

Hamadani and Sharifi looked at one another. Although they were both Iranian – and in the minority of Sunni Muslims of that country - they had not known each other during the period when Sharifi was working to simplify the design of the North Korean nuclear weapon which Iran had bought. When the weapon had been stolen from Iran, Hamadani was the Major General in command of the Saberin Takavar Battalion of the Iranian Army Special Forces responsible for weapon security – and responsible for stealing the relatively small components out of the country. It was at that time that they had met because Hamadani was also responsible for smuggling Sharifi and four senior technicians out of Iran.

Hamadani spoke first. "I believe so, *Al-Mahdi*. The construction work is being supervised by Gamal al-Nasri, a ship surveyor who is devout and loyal, though of course he knows nothing of the weapon. He believes what the naval architect has said about strengthening the ship. Work is proceeding according to plan, and the ship will be ready on time – by the end of February. That should give Jafa enough time to install the weapon. "

Ben-Zhair turned to look at Jafa Sharifi, the Technical Director and master architect of the weapon.

"And you, Sharifi?"

"The nuclear fuel pellet and *hohlraum* are in storage nearby, maintained at a temperature close to absolute zero and in near total vacuum as required. The last cargo of Siemens High Capacity Fast Discharge Capacitors will be here within two weeks, and the last of the forty krypton fluoride lasers, two weeks after that. All these items are arriving in multiple shipments to avoid suspicion – they are unusual here in Yanbu, even in Saudi Arabia itself. However, sourcing the equipment has been much more difficult as we believe our enemies may be trying to track it. Some of the items have been made the subject of export controls."

"Yes, I know – Qasem has briefed me. Somehow it seems that the dogs have an idea of our design. They have learned from the Sword of Allah attack. They are on our trail for sure."

"Yes, *Al-Mahdi*, for sure. On the other hand we learned a lot during the Rome installation and expect the process to be much quicker this time, even though it is in a ship. Some of the work can even be done when we are at sea.

We have a shipment of twenty generators arriving next week in several batches. Each is of two megawatts and is in a standard shipping container. They will be carried as deck cargo and be used to charge the capacitors in Hold Number Three of the ship and provide an additional power supply for the lasers when the weapon is detonated. To maintain the very low temperature required to keep the pellet stable there will be two tanks of compressed helium in TEUs."

"TEUs? What is that?"

"'Twenty foot equivalents' – it is a shipping term which indicates the size of a shipping container, although most are forty feet – that is, two TEUs each. The *'Explorer'* is capable of carrying four thousand five hundred TEUs. Much more than what we need, but it is the length of the ship that is important for the weapon."

"That is good. You have both done well. You are great servants of Allah."

"May he be praised. *Al-Mahdi*, there is also some other news. I have solved the problem of the reduced weapon yield in Rome. Nassim Kateb was a great help in finding the answer – he believes that the ancient deposits of rubble and refuse which are extensive under the city, along with the alluvial deposits – that is, river stones and sand - had acted as a sponge, soaking up some of the ground-wave energy, while a section of harder rock structure under one of the Seven Hills had acted as a lens – focusing some of the energy to trigger the small earthquake which we did not expect."

"No, but it was a gift from Allah, may he be praised."

"For sure, *Al-Mahdi*. Perhaps the four point seven magnitude in Rome would be a great enough magnitude for the 'Cause of All Causes' to succeed. We know that the rock is soft at the target point. It could be a problem."

"Soft rock? Nassim is quite confident. He has taken much care to choose the exact impact point, and the ship has been chosen carefully so that it can get in close enough. You, Jafa, have to make certain that the weapon yield is one hundred percent."

"I understand, *Al-Mahdi*. This time I am increasing the number of lasers and storage capacitors, to maximise the yield of the weapon."

"You have over-run the agreed costs - they have escalated hugely and I have had to request more funding from our sponsor. It should not be a problem as he is delighted with what happened in Rome – but his expectations have increased as well. So, can you meet the final date for installation?"

"We are on track at the moment, and do not anticipate any major difficulties, but the virtual reality ship control system is still untested. We will install the control systems and do the testing when the ship is underway, but that is not ideal."

"But it is necessary." Hamadani interjected "The surveyors may not certify the ship if there are changes to its control systems which use unapproved equipment. We have to install them at sea. All the equipment will be loaded in cargo containers in Hold Four. Jafa has assured us that we will only have to connect them into the ship's upgraded bridge controls. The camera systems and satellite links will not be an issue for the surveyors and are being installed now. These are normal."

"Good. Time is short. I have planned four weeks for the ship to make the voyage, although we should not need all that. We will take you, Sharifi, and the crew off the ship once we have passed *Jabal Ṭāriq* - the Rock of Gibraltar. From there on the ship will be controlled from Sidi bel Abbès using the VR. The technicians there already have the navigational charts of the target area and are building a computer model. They will be able to test the approach course and speed and simulate the final moments.

We *must* detonate the weapon on the first day of Ramadan – as you know this year that falls on the fifteenth of May. That will be a message from Allah - and the ship will be the messenger."

"*Al-Mahdi*, why do we need the VR system – why can we not use suicide martyrs?"

"Very well Jafa, you can lead the team."

"But I did not want to be there myself *Al-Mahdi.*"

"Why not, Jafa? It would be a great honour would it not?"

"But I am a scientist, *al-Mahdi*"

"Jafa, we have been through this before. We will not use suicide martyrs, not even you. As I have told you, we need to demonstrate mastery of technology – not only nuclear weapons – as if that isn't enough – but electronics, control and communications. They will discover that we have access to satellites links and can fight them on whatever territory they choose. They will be certain that they cannot defend themselves against us."

"Except conventional war – ISIS failed in Syria, *Al-Mahdi*."

"Yes, but conventional war is not the future for us, or them. Cyberwar is."

"But this VR adds more complexity – and technical risk."

"Jafa, you have shown that you can make a nuclear bomb work. Surely the VR control is not too much for you? If so tell me now!"

"Not at all, *Al-Mahdi*. It is just another link in the chain – but every link has the potential to fail."

"Then see that it does not!"

"Of course, *Al-Mahdi*. It has passed final testing. Jamal Sawfeek is an electronics genius. He was the top student in his year at MIT. His team are exceptional."

"I am becoming impatient with this discussion Jafa! The virtual reality bridge *must* work."

Cyberwarfare was the future, and assembling Jawal's team had cost almost a ton of the Prince's gold. The eight technicians in Jawal's team at Sid Bel Abbès – figuratively, every one of them a 'rocket scientist' *summa cum laude* – ranged across cryptography, electronics, satellite technology, infrastructure systems and communications. Registered as

121

graduate physics students at the University of Oran, they had gone to ground, literally, in the hidden bunker beneath the Radio Astronomy facility. Jamal's team would eventually be backed up by two more levels of technical operational cells across the world's major countries as the next phase of ben-Zhair's strategy unfolded. Ben-Zhair knew that the hunters were closing in – obtaining the capacitors, pumps and lasers for the nuclear weapons left too many data trails which could not all be swept over. Of course the core of the weapon – the deuterium-tritium fuel pellet – was now impossible to obtain. He'd already used one of the two stolen from Iran, and the second one would be used within days, *Insh'Allah.*

Jafa Sharifi's technology was becoming redundant, and the Cause of all Causes would be the nuclear swansong. Jafa would soon be yesterday's man. It would then be time to move the battlefield.

He nodded almost imperceptibly at Qasem Hamadani. The message was received and understood.

After the meeting, ben-Zhair headed to the airport to board the private jet for the flight to his meeting on the other side of the Arabian Peninsula. The flight to the private airfield in the artificial desert oasis, home of Sheikh Khalifa ibn Abu Bakr would take less than an hour.

As he sat back in the air-conditioned limousine with an outside temperature touching 42°C, he went over the details of what Hamadani and Sharifi had told him. Together with the latest monitoring data from Nassim Kateb in Rabat, there was every chance of success. The name 'Cause of All Causes' was indeed well chosen, because the chain of cause and effect would reach a long way, half way around the world and more.

*

Al Hofuf

Sheikh Khalifa ibn Abu Bakr lived in an ancient palace near the oasis city of Al Hofuf, on the eastern side of the Saudi Arabian peninsula.

As the Gulfstream lined up for its final approach to the private airstrip, ben-Zhair could see limitless acres of date palms below him. The area was said to be the largest date producing area in the world, noted also for its soukhs and palaces. The one drawback was the smell of petroleum which drifted down the forty five miles from the Al Jubail refinery complex and industrial area when the wind was from the north.

Parts of the Sheikh's palace were indeed ancient, but that would have been difficult to prove without an extensive archaeological dig. History had given way to ostentation and despite the employment of leading interior designers, it would never feature in a magazine – unless the focus was on 'what not to do' to a palace when you have unlimited money. Undoubtedly the influence of the Sheikh's wives had some impact on the result. Limitless wealth does not always square up with good taste.

The palace itself had been in the Sheikh's family for many generations, the family's wealth being founded on date production – the kholas variety in particular. Caramel flavoured when cured, it is the variety most often eaten with coffee, and the Sheikh's estates produced the best of the best, obtainable only in the most exclusive shops in the largest cities.

Ben-Zhair knew that Sheikh Khalifa would offer him the choice selection of the year's crop when they took coffee, and that was a problem. The traditional fare of a Saudi desert feast, including the sheep eyes and other unmentionable delicacies, was not an issue but Ben-Zhair hated dates. He hated the texture, he hated the sweetness and he hated the seeds in his teeth. Nevertheless he would have to smile, swallow the dates and enjoy the two day visit, wasting precious time in the Sheikh's private mosque and observing the prayer rituals.

'Wadi-bashing' in luxurious SUVs would be on the schedule, together with a camel race and some falconry. In fact the, full panoply of Saudi culture – including traditional music which was an acquired taste that had failed to impress ben-Zhair. At least there would be some female companionship after dark – another aspect of Saudi culture. Arabic hospitality was generous, but ben-Zhair could do without most of it.

Sheikh Khalifa was a conundrum to ben-Zhair. He was a Saudi prince through-and-through, and yet he was devout almost to an extreme. Nevertheless he was the banker, and over the two days of the visit, less than fifteen minutes would be spent on business – and millions of dollars would change hands, figuratively.

At their last meeting, the Sheikh had rejoiced over the success of the Rome attack and confirmed further funding for equipping the ship at Yanbu, and completion of the complex operation. However, at this meeting ben-Zhair expected the Sheikh to press for more details of the 'Cause of All Causes' plan. He was reluctant to give much more away than the general outline that he had already provided.

In particular, the precise geography was known only to him and to Nassim Kateb in Rabat - and he wanted it to stay that way. The complexity of the operation was huge and the security risks significant. He had almost been caught in Rome and he had yet to establish how the British had found and tracked him. There would be others, without a doubt as world governments were in a panic since the Rome attack. Paranoia was good for his survival.

As the plane sank along its glide path to the runway, he reflected on his position as the Caliph of ICIM. He maintained a very low personal profile whereas on the other hand ICIM had a huge profile but was really a 'virtual state' – almost like Roman Catholicism, but without a 'Rome'. Both were driven by a fear of hell and damnation. The geographical heartland of ICIM was the interior of Algeria – the Dangerous Corridor – which continued to grow and spread towards the Mediterranean coast. Roman Catholicism had the Vatican State – and churches around the world. His churches were virtual – hidden websites and chatrooms where teams of expert online recruiters worked 24/7 to build his secret army. His technical team had worked hard to ensure that the CIA, NSA, MI6, FSB and myriad other intelligence agencies could not penetrate his recruiting channels, whether they use fake personnel or technical means. Ben-Zhair could afford – and bought – the best brains in the business. He had even bought a company specializing in on-line security. Ben-Zhair smiled at the thought as he saw his reflection in the window of the Gulfstream. This meeting would be an ordeal, but it was vital for the Cause of All Causes to succeed.

A series of bumps brought him back to the moment as the plane touched down in the hot, thin and turbulent desert air and taxied to the air-conditioned hangar where the stretched limousine was waiting for the short ride to the palace.

*

Mediterranean Voyage

Finally, the *'Yanbu Explorer'* was ready. All the paperwork was in place, duly stamped and signed, the survey completed and the insurers happy. The Yanbu Commercial Port Director General authorised her departure, set for the morning tide on 2nd April.

In charge was Captain Hussein Hindawi, with a minimal team of officers and Filipino crew, sufficient to meet the legal minimum requirements. Also aboard were the key senior members of ben-Zhair's team: Qasem Hamadani, Jafa Sharifi and his technicians. They were backed up by some junior engineers and a security team under Hamadani's control.

On the morning of departure the wind was from the east and blowing strongly as it carried sand from the interior of the Saudi Arabian peninsula and the smell of the oil and gas industry across the dockside and out into the Red Sea.

According to the documents file with the Customs Authority, the *'Yanbu Explorer'* would head up the Red Sea and through the Suez Canal. The short voyage to Suez was uneventful and the ship passed through the Canal without incident.

Ben-Zhair joined the ship in Bur Sa'Id (Port Said) where the Canal met the Mediterranean. Then the *Yanbu Explorer* headed just north of west at 17 knots, through the Eastern Mediterranean basin.

Some 58 hours later, and 947 miles from Port Said, she dropped anchor just before midnight on the Hurd Bank about fifteen miles off the east cost of Malta. There, she would be outside of territorial jurisdiction while final alignment work, tests and checks were carried out on her deadly cargo.

The anchorage was busy as was usual in this time of world economic depression. The shipping trade was depressed and since 2015 had been in the doldrums. Following the disaster in Rome there had been a further loss in confidence in world markets and international trade. So, ships anchored here where the costs were minimal and waited for orders from their owners to tell them where to collect their next cargo. These were the lucky ships. Many less economic vessels were being scrapped every year, driven up onto beaches in India and Bangladesh where armies of workers swarmed over them, tearing them apart as ants would a much larger dead insect. It was a fate that the *'Yanbu Explorer'* had only narrowly escaped under her previous ownership.

During the voyage from Yanbu in Saudi Arabia the work had been unceasing. The weather had helped – although there had been little wind the April heat was not oppressive and the sea mirror-like. At anchor off Malta the work continued unabated.

On deck, the twenty huge electricity generators – each in a 2 TEU package - were connected together to supply the ranks of capacitors in Hold 4. The generators were fuelled up and tested and then the capacitors brought up to full charge and checked once the heavy cables – each as thick as a man's arm and of a precisely measured length - had been installed and connected. The lasers and their control and telemetry systems were installed, configured and tested.

One shipping container held an array of drones. These had been obtained on the black arms market and had been transhipped from a Libyan freighter when the *'Yanbu Explorer'* was north of Benghazi in Libya – yet another consignment marked as 'farm machinery'. The drones were armed and tested with their remote control from the bunker at Sidi bel-Abbès fully operational. A second container had also been transhipped off Libya.

This one contained six *Novyy Rassvet* anti-aircraft missiles – the latest in Russian short range SAM technology. The container had been 'liberated' from a Russian forward position in the Crimea and shipped across the Red Sea, its tracking devices disabled. The 'lost' container had provided a substantial pension fund for a Russian logistics general before his theft had been uncovered and he had been shot. The container was accompanied by two Russian missile operators, Yuri Koslov and Alexie Stepanov.

Completely self-contained, the missiles could be fired remotely through the top of the special container. They were practically unstoppable, with infra-red and radar guidance built in, together with remote optical override. An AI system automatically changed guidance modes following the heuristic model which had been built up over hundreds of test firings on the Russian ranges with human optical guidance. Chaff, flares, radar spoofing – it could beat all the known de-lousing technology.

The remote links to the control room at Sidi Bel Abbès were enabled and tested – as far as was possible with live missiles. The Russians pronounced themselves satisfied with the ship-board tests and the ship's launch took them ashore to Valetta with two of Qasem Hamdani's security team. From Malta the four would travel by ferry to Oran via Spain, thence to Sid Bel Abbès for the final control set-up and testing.

At the Hurd Bank anchorage the weather remained kind and the spring storms stayed away. The area could be very rough when the north easterly Gregale wind drove the sea from Greece until it reached the shallows of the Hurd Bank and shortened in length, growing in height. The calm seas greatly simplified the final alignment of the big lenses which were needed to focus the laser beams onto the thimble of gold and radioactive fuel – the core of the nuclear fusion bomb.

On the evening of the fourteenth day at the anchorage, ben-Zhair assembled Hamadani and his lieutenants together with Sharifi and his senior technicians in the wardroom, one deck below the bridge. The ship's captain, Hussein Hindawi was also present.

Ben-Zhair spoke, quietly, as the rays of the sun setting over Malta to the west filtered in through the windows.

"We are on the verge of making history. Nothing like this mission has ever been attempted before. Since I came aboard, I have watched you all work with devotion to the cause – 'the Cause of All Causes' as I have named it.

Jafa has reported that the technical work is finished on the weapon. We know that the design works – we proved that with the 'Sword of Allah' – itself an incredible achievement. Now, this weapon is ready – I say the weapon, but it is only a trigger as some of you already know." Sharifi and Hamadani nodded silently as they looked at him.

"The real weapon is the earth itself, and what we will achieve at the start of Ramadan will still be remembered in a thousand years time.

Captain Hindawi assures me that the ship is ready for the final voyage. Tomorrow we will leave here to head west for *Jabal Ṭāriq* as we test the final system – that of the control of the ship using virtual reality. Wars of the future will be fought at a distance with cyberwarfare, drones and robots. Just as the 'Sword of Allah' was a test for this, so will this mission test out systems for the next five years, when we will attack Russia and the East.

Tonight we head west and we will all leave the ship once it has passed *Jabal Ṭāriq* and is out of the Strait - we will go ashore near Tangier. From there on, the ship will be controlled from our bunker at Sidi Bel Abbès to its final destination.

You have all done well, and will be rewarded well – here on earth. And of course, Allah will reward you in heaven. So, go now and prepare for the final leg. May Allah be with us!"

*

'Rubaiyat'

"What I don't understand is how Spain can defend its claim to Gibraltar when it has two enclaves in North Africa. It's bloody hypocritical. Ceuta is just like mainland Spain, though I've never been to Mellilla."

"That's politics for you. Anyway, you can't talk – remember when the Royal Marines invaded Spain – 2004, was it?

"Don't remind me! Luckily that wasn't my troop that stormed up the beach on the wrong side of the border. GPS and all – and they still got it wrong. That troop commander was a real plonker. It was certainly not our most illustrious moment."

"It's a strange world alright."

"Well I've seen enough of it. I just want to get back to sea. There's just the small matter of Maruška to deal with first. And I need a boat to live on."

Ellie met Steve's eyes. "*We* need a boat to live on."

"Agreed, point taken."

"And I can always contribute, you know. Equipment, running expenses. I do have savings you know."

"Let's just take it a step at a time Ellie – I'm an independent bloke. Sharing a bunk is a big stretch for me."

It was noon on Wednesday. Steve was sipping his beer on the high speed ferry across the Strait from Algeciras to Ceuta, travelling at almost 40 knots, cut across the wake of a ship which was butting into a fresh westerly wind. The ferry juddered and the beer froth surged and coated his upper lip, splashing up his nose. He spluttered and they laughed. "It looks like you are out of practice."

Sunday morning had been spent on *HMS Bulwark*. They arrived at the dock gate a few minutes before 9 a.m. where their credentials were carefully scrutinised by a naval guard who ticked off their names on a list and opened the gate. Another armed guard appeared and accompanied them along the quay to *Bulwark's* gangway. The morning was bright and an easterly breeze was sending gusts around the Rock.

They had called ahead and were met at the top of the gangway by Chief Petty Officer Drew McAllister. The First Officer had sent his apologies that would be unable to meet them – not surprising in the circumstances.

The CPO was a stocky, hard looking man about six feet tall. What little red hair remained was close-cropped and his cauliflower ears betrayed an interest in either boxing or rugby, embellished by the application of years of naval discipline in bars around the world. Hard drink had probably done the rest - he looked about forty five years old, but Steve knew from the file that he was only thirty eight.

McAllister looked them both up and down then checked their IDs himself.

"So, you've come to check us out? You'll be the fourth lot to do that. Let's go to my mess and we can talk there." He was bristling, confronted with a shortened career and reduced pension - as the Master at Arms of *Bulwark* he had been in charge of Maruška's security.

He strode off briskly, with Steve and Helena in his wake. When they arrived at the mess and sat down the others there requested permission to leave, which McAllister granted. There was no offer of tea or coffee – Steve knew this to be a grave breach of mess etiquette and it set the tone for the session.

McAllister's story was pretty much exactly what Steve and Helena had read in the files - *"Now you see her, now you don't."*

"And what about the missing seaman – one of your team wasn't he?"

"Carl Halborg. Yes. Not my choice of bloke, mind you. Foisted on me - that's the way the Navy is these days."

"Did he have a bad disciplinary record?"

"Not really. He was just a cocky, lazy bastard. I'd warned him a few times – unofficially."

Steve knew that this meant that McAllister had got physical with Halborg, trying to keep a clean official sheet for his team.

"Do you think he was involved in her disappearance?"

"No."

"But he was one of the guards."

"Yes, and the answer is the same."

"His mobile phone?"

"He probably had one."

There was a note in the file that his number had been tracked through his family and a list of calls leading up to his disappearance. One number has been that of a paygo Gibtelecom phone, with only one call in the Gibtelecom logfile.

Ellie glanced at the file. The other seaman and the Sergeant-at-Arms had been interviewed several times – by experts. There was nothing to be gained by going through the process again.

"OK. What about the dead seaman?"

"What about him? Drowned, belly full of beer – it happens."

"Not often, surely?"

"It happens."

"Chief Petty Officer, should we make a note that you were uncooperative?"

McAllister turned to Helena.

"I don't give a shit what you write. I've answered all your questions. Anyway, I'm done here - I'll be pensioned off next month."

His bitterness was evident – he was just another of Maruška's collateral casualties. He stood up.

Then Steve stood up and they stood eyeball to eyeball. "Sit down McAllister – I haven't finished yet."

"Piss off. You can't give me orders! You don't outrank me."

"But *I* can, and I'll have *you* put in irons if you don't watch it."

Ellie slid a warrant card across the mess table.

'Commander Ellen Williams, Royal Navy Police, Special Investigations Branch.'

McAllister's picked up the card and his eyes popped. His body stiffened and he saluted.

"Begging your pardon, Ma'am. I didn't know. It was not on your ID card."

"There's a lot you don't know. Now sit *down*, Chief Petty Officer or you will be on a charge yourself for not properly checking visitor IDs."

"Aye, Aye Ma'am!"

With the pecking order now firmly established, Steve continued, almost as surprised as McAllister. "Now, tell us about the drowned rating."

"It's in the file already. Able Seaman David Howells. He was in the Donkey's Flip Flop with his mates, Wednesday night. Said he was going to the head – that was just after ten p.m. they said. That was the last they saw of him. The MOD Police guardboat fished him out of the water the next morning, just inside the South Mole."

"Did he know Halborg?"

"It's a small ship. Three hundred and twenty five crew. I don't know if they drank together if that's what you mean. Howells was an electronics specialist. They wouldn't normally come into contact on a day-to-day basis."

Steve checked the file in front of him. The question had been asked before. No known association.

"And his phone?"

"He probably had one, but we didn't find it."

The earlier investigation had been thorough – the file showed AB Howells's mobile phone number and an explained call from a Gibtelecom paygo sim – except that the ID of the unit itself was Spanish. Gibraltar was a small city and the team had located the shop which had supplied the Gibtelecom burner phone and SIM cards, but the search for the Spanish phone had dead-ended. It was a stolen unit. The store assistants could not recall the person who had bought the unit and the cards.

Steve looked at Ellie and they nodded.

"Very well CPO, let's go and look at the holding cell."

The interview had gone as expected – besides some basic fact-checking and orientation there was no point in rehashing what expert investigators had already done thoroughly.

Three decks down they came to the secure area where the holding cells were located.

"This is the cell she was held in."

McAllister punched in the key code and opened the door. Simple – steel walls, a basin and head – toilet – and a cot. The bedding was still in place.

Steve and Ellie entered while McAllister waited outside, then Steve spoke. "Has it been cleaned or disturbed since she disappeared?"

"No, I was ordered to keep it sealed."

"And the SOC team, what did they find?"

"SOC? What's that?"

"Scene of Crime unit."

It was Ellie's turn to be surprised. Steve had read the files and knew what was in them – and what should have been, but wasn't.

"It's not the scene of a crime."

"How do you know if it hasn't been checked?"

"But she just disappeared."

"Seemingly impossible, and still unexplained. Probably magic then – or did King Neptune sneak in at night and abduct her?"

McAllister glowered at Steve and stopped himself before the retort had fully formed.

Another puzzle. Why had there been no SOC team? Probably just crossed line between London, the Navy and the local police. Cockup usually beat conspiracy when explanations were sought.

Steve turned to Ellie. "Ma'am, with your permission I think that we should get the cell checked."

"Agreed." She turned to CPO McAllister who hovered outside the cell door, his growing discomfort evidenced by a sheen of sweat on his brow. "This cell is to be secured until it has been examined by an SOC team. Is that clear, Chief Petty Officer?"

"Aye, Aye Ma'am."

"And the SOC team will want a list of all the people who have been in this cell in the last month" chipped Steve.

"I will arrange it, Sir." It seemed that Baldwin suddenly outranked McAllister.

"Then that will be all, Chief Petty Officer. Please give our regards to the First Officer. You may show us off the ship."

They signed out at the dock gate and strolled in the rapidly heating morning air towards the town.

"Let's get a coffee somewhere."

"Aye, Aye, Ma'am."

"Piss off Steve!"

"And you wonder why I find it hard to believe everything you say? Why didn't you take the lead from the off?"

"Because I like to let you take charge. It did work though – he was completely wrong-footed when he saw my card. Admit it."

"Why not tell me beforehand?"

"I didn't think it was necessary. It's only a bloody cover anyway. Come on, I'm having a double shot espresso."

They took a table out of the sun, looking out at the street. A Carnival Cruises ship had tied up just before dawn. It had disgorged hordes of bargain-hungry tourists to clog the streets, take the funicular up the rock and give the local pickpockets a welcome infusion of income and the sun plenty of white skin to work on.

"Anyway Steve, what's with all that SOC stuff. Are you Sherlock Holmes now?"

"It's your fault."

"My fault? How do you work that out?"

"Back in Malta you assigned Bryan Elliot to watch me and help in the search for Charles Tobin."

"Yes, Bryan was a good bloke."

"And an ex-monkey – a redcap, military police. He taught me a lot in a very short time. Plus, of course, I read. I've spent a lot of time at sea and at anchor over the past few years and read tons of books I've picked up along the way. Crime fiction and the like - whatever turned up in dock offices and marinas."

"I'll report into Barbary and tell him to pull some strings to get the local SOC team in. What do you think they'll find?"

"I doubt they'll find anything – but finding nothing ticks a box, establishes fact."

"Jesus, now you do sound like Sherlock Holmes."

Steve smiled and the tension notched down.

"So, what's the plan for the rest of the day, Commander?"

"Sightseeing I guess, though I'm not supposed to socialise with the lower deck people."

"Touché. Now, have you got running gear?"

"Why?"

"You can't visit Gibraltar without doing the Rock Run."

"You must be joking!"

"No, I'm doing it – and so should you. It's only a shade over two miles – plus a thousand feet vertically. A leader should set an example."

"Where did you get that idea?"

"Management 101 – another book I read."

"I'd better go shopping then – it's duty free here."

"Ok, then I'd better allow another three hours. I'll catch up on some sleep."

She punched his arm as Steve stood up and paid for the coffee.

*

They gently tilted forward in their seats as the ferry started to reduce speed for its final approach to Ceuta harbour. Earlier that morning they had crossed the border from Gibraltar to Spain then taken a cab round the bay to the ferry terminal in Algeciras. The trip across the Strait to the Spanish enclave of Ceuta was only 35 minutes, but the whole journey had taken hours. Now they would need to take a cab south to the border with Morocco and then a cab on the other side to the Marina Smir a few more miles to the south, where '*Rubaiyat*' was moored.

"So, you think this boat is worth seeing?"

"Yes, it's promising - on paper at least. Liam – the security guard at the marina – knows it and says that the owner, Theo Sylverne, was a careful skipper. He was very fussy. Now he's dead his wife wants shot of it quickly. She even sent a copy of his 'to-do' list for the boat. She hasn't yet listed it with a broker so I might cut out the middle man and get a bargain. The asking price is already good anyway – it's not easy to sell a boat lying in Morocco and she would have had to bring it back to Gib.

I've got my doubts though. It's a Bruce Roberts design – not usually to my taste. But this one is the Mauritius class which is much easier on my eye than his other designs."

Steve pointed to the particulars of *Rubaiyat* which Sara Sylverne had sent him. '*Rubaiyat*' - what kind of a name is that?"

"It's quite erudite actually."

"Erudite? What the hell is that?"

"It means 'Of great learning'. '*The Rubaiyat of Omar Khayyám*' is the title that Edward FitzGerald gave to his translation of a selection of poems, originally written in Persian. Omar Khayyám, who wrote them, was a polymath - a scientist, writer and poet."

He looked at her and she braced herself. "You lost me there...for a moment I had forgotten your Oxford education." Steve's doubts about Helena's background were a constant irritant between them.

"I'll ignore that."

"Sorry - you know I really do want to believe you."

"You know the truth about me – I've bloody told you and I'm tired of repeating it. My mother was *Greek* and *not* a junkie. Anyway the word *rubaiyat* actually means a collection of four line poems – quatrains."

"Whatever you say. Let's see her first anyway – but I don't believe in changing a boat's name, even if it is named after a poem."

"You're not superstitious are you? I can't believe it!"

"No, I'm not superstitious at all. It's just that I don't believe in changing a boat's name."

"Why ever not?"

"It's just, well just that..."

With that the ferry's siren sounded one blast for a turn to starboard and reduced speed to a crawl as it approached the entrance to the harbour at Ceuta and another ferry came out. They stood up and walked out to watch the approach to the ferry berth.

In his bag Steve had a letter from the dead owner's wife, Sara Sylverne, appointing them as skipper and crew and authorising them to move the boat to Gibraltar. Attached to the email letter was a copy of the receipt for payment of the marina fees. Hopefully that would satisfy the authorities.

Earlier, he had phoned Sara Sylverne in Annapolis to make the unusual arrangements, which she had only agreed to provided that Liam O'Neill accompanied them. Steve and Ellie would give the boat a good look-over and if it passed first muster then Liam would come across on the ferry to accompany them to Gibraltar.

Steve would get a chance to sail the vessel and judge her, before committing to a haulout and survey before making a final offer.

*

"It's Barbary." Helena looked at Steve and he nodded as she walked along the marina quay, her smartphone to her ear. The cab had dropped them at the marina entrance and they were headed for the office to collect the keys to '*Rubaiyat*'. He walked on, looking at the collections of vessels – even including a square rigger flying the Swedish ensign and he could see the name '*Gunilla*' on her deckhouse. There was a party of apparently Swedish schoolchildren being marshalled and led aboard.

She caught him up, breathless.

"He asked why you hadn't been in touch for a couple of days."

"What did you say?"

"Just that you were waiting for the report from the SOC team."

"Thanks."

"He said that I'm to order you to switch your phone on."

"I'm surprised they can't do that remotely."

"They can, but not without a battery. Try to toe the line on this, Steve."

"Ok, I'll do it when we get back."

"That's another thing – it's a Six phone – you must carry it with you – the technology is custom."

"I guess he asked what we were doing in Morocco?"

"Yes. I told him that we were taking a day off while we were waiting for the SOC report."

"I'll bet he loved that."

"Oh yes, he certainly did. Quote 'Get your fucking arses back to Gibraltar now'."

"Bugger him."

"There's a problem. It seems that GCHQ has had difficulty with the sniffer code they put in the Gib phone network servers."

"Let me guess – they used the old version, the one that screwed up in Malta?"

"I don't know the details, but Barbary says it's sorted now. He did not sound happy."

"Does he ever? That's great, over a week of listening lost. If she's alive she's probably over the border by now – it would be much easier to hide in Spain. The whole bloody point was that she was in a small known geographical area and we could pin her down. That's why it worked in Malta."

"Well they are loading the sniffer code onto the local servers in the Spanish networks as well. It sounds as if there's been a bit of a row about it all. Anyway, we still don't know if she *is* alive."

"I'd bet my life on it. Come on, there are more important things - let's go look at *'Rubaiyat'*."

*

After half an hour while the marina dockmaster checked their papers and called the owner's widow Sara Sylverne in Annapolis, they waited another half hour while the immigration police checked everything again. Then they were finally given the keys after depositing their passports with the office. As they walked around the dock to the main access pontoon, Helena slipped her arm through Steve's.

"I can't believe it!"

Right there in front of them, there was a camel on the pontoon.

"Well, we're certainly in Africa."

"Yeh, the smell is something else."

They walked carefully around the front of the camel, and could see that it was saddled for tourists, with its ornate tooled leatherwork polished to perfection. Steve nodded to the camelmaster – a mistake.

The Berber launched into a sales pitch in broken German. Steve replied in Arabic and the man shrugged, smiling.

"What did you tell him?"

"Not today thank you, my wife has a sensitive nose."

Two pontoons further along they came to '*Rubaiyat*'. Even though the early spring daylight light was starting to fade as the sun sank behind Jebel Musa, Steve could tell that the yacht had been well looked after. There were no rust stains on her paintwork and the varnish work was recent – the dockmaster had said that the boatyard was being paid for *guardiennage*- that is, keeping an eye on the mooring lines, checking the bilges and generally maintaining her. That was a good indicator of a caring owner – even if he was dead.

"We'll give her a quick look over inside and then I'll call Liam if it all looks positive. Then we'll get some dinner at that French restaurant we saw on the way in."

"*La Relais de Paris*? You're on – it looks like my kind of place."

"Expensive you mean?"

"No, expenses – there's a big difference."

"I can do that then. Come on, let's open her up."

Steve hauled himself aboard at the shrouds and the yacht barely heeled. "She's certainly stiffer than Adèle."

"What does stiff mean?"

"I thought you were a Greek fisherman's daughter?"

"Don't start that again, Steve. It was a serious question. And anyway, Greek fishermen probably had a different name for it."

"Well, stiff means that the boat doesn't heel – that is, *tip* - easily. It can mean that she is more comfortable to sail."

"Oh, I see. Greek fishermen use a different phrase."

"I bet they do. What is it?"

"Actually, I can't remember right now…Come, on, I want to see the galley."

As he helped Helena climb over the guardrails she could see the sadness in his face, his mouth turned down, his eyes dark shadows. He had been through many scrapes with Adèle and she realised how much that the boat had meant to him.

"Come on darling, we've got to move on. Maybe *'Rubaiyat'* will be *our* yacht. Remember my plan, what we talked about in Tunisia."

"Tunisia? I don't remember that."

"Still a blank?"

"Yes, a total blank. I do remember that in Malta you talked about getting out of the service."

"Yes, I did – and we can do that together once this operation is over."

"You've never called me darling before."

"I did. Once."

"I don't remember it."

"It seems there's a lot you don't remember."

"Maybe there is."

Steve turned the key in the double doors and opened up. "I'll see if I can find the battery switch and put some lighting on."

*

Two hours later they were seated at a corner table in *La Relais*, with a bottle of Moroccan red wine on the table, the menus open in front of them. Helena's smartphone vibrated gently on the table. They glanced at it. She put her finger on the print reader and it opened.

"It's a text from Barbary.'Why still in Morocco? Did you read the SOC report?'"

"Ignore it. Let's eat first and talk about *'Rubaiyat'*."

"No, let's just have a quick look, get the business out of the way and then we can enjoy the rest of the evening." Helena opened her shoulder bag and took out her tablet.

"It won't work - there's no wifi here."

"I've got a satellite connection. You have too if you bothered to read the manual."

"And if I'd brought my tablet."

"Yes, true. Listen Steve, you really do need to start taking this a bit more seriously. If you don't access your tablet and

141

phone every twenty four hours then it will wipe itself and brick the custom electronics."

"Forty eight hours."

"What?"

"There's a setting, the wipedown and bricking can be changed to a maximum of forty eight hours. It seems that you haven't read the manual either."

"Mine's an older model." She pulled a face as Steve smirked. "What, don't you believe me?"

"Maybe. But you do tell some good stories."

"Leave it out Steve. Anyway, let's get this op done and dusted and then we can head off wherever we like."

"That's the problem – these bastards always find me and find a new way to manipulate me. There doesn't seem to be a way out."

"You took the money, willingly."

"Yes, don't I just know it? Anyway, they took Adèle – or someone did."

"And we found each other again – that wouldn't have happened without Ogilvy and Barbary."

"Ogilvy? He's supposed to be on this op isn't he? What's he up to?"

"I don't know. Here we go."

As she opened the SOC report Steve topped up the glasses. "Come around this side of the table and we can read it together."

The SOC team had been thorough – of that there was no doubt.

"Look, here are the Key Findings."

Traces of semen mixed with female vaginal secretions found in location 3, see picture 22. DNA in secretions matches that of cell occupant (data on file).

Semen DNA not on UK DNA database, but match found to that of Leading Rate Carl Halborg, HMS Bulwark (retrieved from Naval DNA records).

Female DNA matches samples retrieved from 5 (five) different homicide locations in Europe.

"Why would they have his DNA on file?"

"Standard practice in the forces in case of death in action for ID confirmation. He's a leading seaman in the Navy police – look he was one of her guards."

Helena flipped to picture #22. She shook her head.

"What?"

"There's no way that the sample location is accidental – they would have had the cot upside down to get it there."

"And it's bolted down anyway, so it doesn't slide about at sea."

"But why would they do that?"

"You mean *she*, don't you?"

"Yes, I think I do."

"She's been busy too. At least five separate homicide sites."

"I'd better call Barbary now. I'm going outside."

"Do you need me?"

"No, just go easy on the wine ok?"

Steve winked at her as she turned for the door.

The bottle was empty when she reappeared fifteen minutes later, but the two glasses on the table were still full. "It's my turn now. I have to phone Liam and give him the go-ahead for tomorrow."

"With what? You don't have a phone."

Steve held up a paygo phone and smiled.

"Where did you get that?"

"In Gib, a few days ago."

"You old dog!"

"I love you too – now order me some mezze starters and a lamb tagine. Better get another bottle of that Syrocco Syrah too - I'm quite taken with this Moroccan stuff."

"Before you call Liam, we might need to rethink tonight."

"Why?"

"GCHQ got a sniff of Maruška's chip signature on the Gibtelecom servers. It went to a number in London – after that they don't know where."

"So, she is alive. I knew it."

"Yes, and Barbary is jumping up and down."

"And swinging from the trees no doubt."

"Very funny. We've got to get back to Gib – now."

"Bugger Barbary – I'm having the lamb tagine first."

"But if she uses that phone again then they'll have her position. We need to move."

"How? The last ferry has gone – the next one is at oh seven thirty tomorrow. You'd better get hold of Barbary and tell him to get *Bulwark* to send a RIB over to Ceuta – we can get there by midnight depending on any border holdups, but anything coming from Gib by sea is going to be questioned – the Spanish are very touchy about it, and it's much worse now they are upping the ante over their sovereignty claim on the Rock. Or, Barbary can send a stealth boat in to a beach near here, though he'll probably see that as too risky. Neither is a great option."

"I'll call him now."

"And I'll order a lamb tagine. What about you?"

"Make it two."

*

The moon was in its third quarter and showing a halo which presaged rain. It was well up in the sky as they walked back, nodding to the patrolling security guard as they stepped on to the main pontoon. The camel had gone.

"That lamb tagine was great, so tender. I don't know what the secret is – I've never been much of a cook. I guess that's not a good thing for a woman to admit."

"I love cooking. Because I live alone on the boat – or I did when I had one – and there's only so much I can do to amuse myself - so I cook and I read. It's quite a challenge with limited space, two rings and an oven. I don't have a proper tagine cooker though. Maybe I'll buy one here. You first – careful now, you're a bit wobbly."

"I'm okay, but I don't think we should have had that second bottle of wine." Helena held on to the two shrouds as she pulled herself up and over the guardrails on to the deck of *'Rubaiyat'*.

Down below, Steve put the kettle on. "Only coffee here – and dried milk if you want it."

"I'll pass thanks, I need to get my head down. Just as well Barbary decided not to send a boat over. I'll set my phone for three a.m. Let's hope the cab is here on time for us. The roads should be clear – shouldn't take more than two hours to the ferry terminal, allowing for border control."

"You go ahead. I'm just going to check out a few things while I've got the chance."

In fact, the roads were busy with vegetable trucks hauling produce and there was a queue of trucks waiting to cross the border. There had been no one on duty in the office, so Steve had given the boat keys to the security guard. At least the taxi had been on time picking them up and they made the ferry with fifteen minutes to spare.

The sun was just breaking the horizon to their right as the high speed ferry '*Ceuta Jet*' accelerated past the pierhead and out of the harbour at Ceuta with its imposing bronze statue of Hercules pushing the Pillars apart.

The breeze was still in the east and the early morning fishermen were out in force, making the most of the calm sea. They sat sipping their coffees as the vessel started to thread its way through the incessant shipping in the Strait.

"I don't like the look of that sky."

"Why?"

"It's filling from the west – see that cloud formation there?"

Helena followed Steve's hand as it pointed northwest..

"What does it mean?"

"I think there's a deep depression to the north – there'll probably be a Mistral forming in the Gulf of Lyon, and we'll get a westerly gale here."

"Well, at least we'll be in a hotel tonight. Did you get any sleep at all last night?"

"No, I just wanted to check the state of the bilges and engine and take a few photos while I had the chance. I didn't get a chance to check the electronics and radar."

"And?"

"She looks good – obviously well looked-after. The hull paint was good with no signs of corrosion. The engine looked well-maintained though without running it I can't really tell. I think that she's pretty good order for a boat of that age. I will need to do a bit more research about the design – what other owners think, how well they sail and behave at sea. But it looks good and I think I'll move ahead with it. What did *you* think?"

"The boat had a good feel and I slept like a baby, even if it was only four hours, but aren't you moving a bit quickly? You've only looked at this one."

"And one in Gibraltar *'Dream On II'* – before you turned up."

"Oh, you didn't tell me about that. What's the hurry anyway?"

"I've lost Adèle so I don't have a home, and anyway life is too short. No point in hanging about. Anyway, how many women do you think I should meet before I decide on you?"

"When you meet the right one you'll know."

"Well I already did – and the same for the boat."

She smiled. "I do like the interior – the red upholstery goes well with the light wood finish."

"It's cedar. I wanted your general impression about the boat – upholstery can easily be changed. You should know – you once told me that your father was a fisherman."

"I told you a lot of things back in Crete – it went with the job, you know that. Can't you just let it go Steve? You know what the bloody truth is - I learned about boats on a summer job! I'm getting a bit tired of the sarcasm. Make your bloody mind up about me." They simmered in silence as the ferry lined up its approach into the Bay of Algeciras.

"I have, and I'm sorry. The wine last night probably hasn't helped, but I do feel that the right boat and the right woman are both within reach."

"Maybe, let's wait and see what develops."

"Fine. Now, I really would appreciate your opinion about *Rubaiyat.*"

"Well she's much more spacious than Adèle was, and there's a proper shower. The galley has three rings so that should make you a happier cook. She might sail a little faster although she's got a ketch rig – but doesn't that make her easier to handle?"

"Yes it does in theory."

"Hang on –it must be Barbary."

Helena put her phone to her ear.

"Williams, yes who else has my fingerprint to answer? Yes, yes, I understand. We should be back in Gib in a couple of hours…Yes, yes…we have to take a taxi from the ferry terminal and cross the border back into Gibraltar…Okay, I'll call you then…yes he will have his phone turned on."

She shook her head as she put the phone in her jacket pocket.

"We've got to get a move on – they've picked up her signal again and triangulated to a hotel in Engineer's Lane – the Continental. She's in Gibraltar."

A thousand miles to the east, off Malta, the *'Yanbu Explorer'* had just weighed anchor and was heading northwest into a freshening Mistral.

Two hours later Steve and Helena were back in the Rock Hotel with the TV turned on and earbuds in their ears, on a conference call with Barbary.

"First, locate her and then stay on her tail. You already have microtags in your kit - you will need to get a couple onto her clothing or gear somehow. I doubt that she will be using an ordinary paygo phone much longer. We have one conversation recorded on that phone six hours ago and the decryption has just come through. The Chinese *must* have plans to re-equip her, and then we'll never read the traffic this side of Christmas. She is still tasked with finding ben-Zhair. I'm sure you remember him."

"Who's ben-Zhair?"

"Don't fuck about Baldwin, I'm on to you."

"For Christ's sake, I haven't a clue who you are talking about."

Helena was staring at Baldwin and shaking her head, still in doubt. "I'll update Baldwin on this, Sir, offline."

"Fine, but remember the limits I laid down, Williams – don't deviate from them."

She avoided Steve's look as Barbary continued.

"Ben-Zhair is the key. We know he organised the Malta bombing and the Rome disaster. He's running ICIM and as you know they claim to have more of the same weapons. She is our *only* route to him – and the technology - at the moment. God knows how the Chinese are tracking him."

"The same way they track Maruška?"

"Maybe, but if so why do they need her?"

"To terminate him?"

"If they really had a bead on him he'd be dead by now. Maruška would be out of the game. One more thing, this op will be going over to local control. You will be met."

Their tablets blanked and their ears were filled with white noise.

"So, Ellie, what the hell is all this about '*filling me in, and strict limits*'? '*I've told you the truth*' you said this morning. "

"Not now Steve, let's get over to Engineer's Lane."

"What, without a plan?"

"We can talk as we go. And for what it's worth, what about you telling the truth? I just don't believe that you don't remember anything about Tunisia and Rome. Isn't it time you were straight with me? We need to get this sorted or there's no future for us – at all."

There was knock at the door.

*

"It's my room, I'll answer" she whispered as she pulled her pistol from under the pillow. Steve grabbed a knife from their discarded room service brunch and stepped into the shower room, cursing that he'd been too casual and too careless, leaving his pistol hidden in his own room.

"Just coming – who is it?"

"Red, Red Cedar. Remember me?"

She opened the door, holding her gun behind her back.

The bearded man in dark glasses wore a panama hat and an off-white lightweight tropical suit. He looked like a typical English senior civil servant abroad – yet he was somehow familiar.

"What the hell, Ogilvy?"

He nodded and stepped in and she closed the door.

"You might have called first."

"What, and spoil the surprise."

"I thought you were dead!" Steve had stepped back into the room.

"Well, I'm not, as you can see. And I thought you had amnesia!"

"I do."

"Good act old boy, but we're not buying it. Right, Barabary said you'd be met, so here I am. I'll be running the show here. What's the latest?"

"We're just getting ready to head over to the Continental Hotel."

"This is going to be tricky – she knows all of us – and you Baldwin especially. So, I'm going."

"I thought that you were running the show, not going active?"

"Yes and no. Give me the tags. That's an order."

Helena took her turn. "Christ Alex, this is crazy. You've been behind a desk for years so stop playing the boy scout. At least let us back you up. Anyway, you can't go dressed like that?"

"Why not?"

"Well, because you look like an idiot – you stand out too much."

"Rubbish! There were two other guys in the plane dressed just like this. This is Gibraltar, not the Costa Blanca. I'm hiding in plain view."

Helena sighed. It was hopeless, but he did have a point – the species known as Colonial Man could still be seen in Gibraltar.

*

"That's a bloody gruesome ending."

Helena pushed her coffee away. She and Steve were discussing the Scene of Crime and autopsy reports in the Steve's room at the Rock hotel. Ogilvy had not yet returned from his scouting mission.

"I can see why the murder came up on our radar – it's got a lot in common with what was done to Tobin in Malta. He would have ended up like Calthorpe if we hadn't got there in time."

"Maybe – she wanted to come over to us, remember, and Tobin's knowledge was the key."

"If it was her – I mean, could she be responsible for all these deaths – there's more than twenty on that MO spreadsheet?"

"I'm convinced it's her. There are five DNA matches."

"Five or twenty, it doesn't matter, this spreadsheet is incidental to our mission."

"The local CID theory is that Calthorpe was tortured and killed at the Battery."

"It just seems pointless. What could he have known that warranted torture like that?"

"I don't believe that he knew anything. I think that it was just his bad luck to run in to her in that club. She's a psychopath. Calthorpe's murder is a blind alley – you only have to read through the spreadsheet - most of the victims were picked up in LBGT clubs. Interpol have been tracking this for a few years and there is very high confidence that a single individual is responsible. They have done a retro-check of the DNA and what we now know to be Pavkovic's matched several samples – but only we know that it also matches the sample from *Bulwark*."

"So Calthorpe is totally irrelevant?"

"Yes, but I hope that Ogilvy doesn't send us off on that track. It would be a waste of time. We know she's here on the Rock – or was, at least until a few hours ago. I think that he's in danger of underestimating her."

"You really are starting to sound like a detective."

"Well I'm not a bloody detective. I'm just looking at the facts. Come on, let's get ready."

"For what?"

"We'll do the Rock Run and visit the scene of the crime, though I think it's a waste of time."

An hour later they were at the Spur Battery where Calthorpe's body had been found in an old ammunition bunker. It lay at the end of a potholed and neglected track more than a thousand feet above the Mediterranean. Constructed in

Victorian times, its 9.2" gun had a range of almost 30,000 yards - able to hit targets in North Africa and anywhere within the Strait itself with its 380 pound shells. The gun (and thirteen others dotted around the Rock) had all been removed, with the gun at the Spur Battery lasting until the 1970s. The emplacement itself had been vandalized. Calthorpe had been immobilised and tortured before bleeding to death.

"This is a hell of a lonely place to die."

"Yes. Getting here has nearly killed *me* as well, but what a view!"

"Almost worth the run."

"Almost."

Jebel Musa was twenty miles away across the Strait and unusually clear in the morning sun. Several ships were transiting the Strait, the waters sparkling like a sheet of silver criss-crossed with wakes. For more than two centuries traders and invaders had used this ancient gateway, and the Rock itself had endured innumerable sieges. It wasn't really a rock anymore. It was more like a honeycomb having been riddled by tunnelling over the centuries, right up to World War II. It's tunnels were now a significant tourist attraction.

"So there had to have been a car, but Calthorpe didn't have one."

"The local police didn't come up with anything when they checked hire cars, but I'm guessing they were not looking for a woman. A penis stuffed in the mouth is not a typical female MO."

"Are you sure about that?"

"Well, maybe not."

"London will be able to get at the hire car companies' data – unless it was a back street hire. I'll get on to Barbary."

*

Maruška slowed as she approached the front door of the Emile Hotel and turned away, crossing to a café on the other side of Engineer's Lane and taking a window seat. She ordered a cappuccino, and checked her smartphone. There was an MMS from the pincam in her room showing a picture of a man in a

Panama hat searching her room. She cursed, recognising him from her interrogation in Malta. She paid for her coffee and waited. Ten minutes later she saw Ogilvy emerge nonchalantly and stroll in the direction of the Grand Battery.

She had a score to settle, but Gibraltar was a small place. Why was he here? It was too strong a coincidence – it must be related to her escape from *Bulwark*. More to the point, how had they found her?

She took out her Chinese smartphone and switched it on. The app showed over sixty mobile phone signals within 20 meters. She threw some coins on the table and headed out, walking briskly to catch up with Ogilvy checking her phone constantly as she dodged through the crowds. They passed the Continental Hotel and joined Main Street. Gradually, she reduced the range setting on the app as she closed with Ogilvy and when she was within five meters of him there were only three mobiles showing on the app, and only one was British. She hit dial on the British number and ducked into a shop doorway. Ogilvy stopped and pulled out his phone. She cut the call before he could answer. 'Got it' she smiled. She watched in the shop window as Ogilvy looked around. He had not been taking any security precautions – not even withholding caller ID. Now he set off at a brisk pace retracing his steps. Maruška moved right into the shop and turned away from the door. After five minutes of browsing and buying a hat and dark glasses she left the shop, found a taxi and headed straight to the border with Spain.

*

'Yanbu Explorer' Heads West

The riding lights of more than twenty ships sparkled around them in the pre-dawn light as the Chief Engineer and his team started the huge 36 megawatt engine. Each of its eight cylinders produced over 4,000 horsepower and the engine itself weighed in at over 2,000 tons. The ship trembled. At the bow an able-seaman supervised the windlass as the 9 ton anchor was brought aboard. He was unaware – like all the Filipino seamen - that this would be his final voyage. The operational language of the ship was English, but the serious business was conducted in Arabic – and the crewmen had been recruited on the basis that they did not speak Arabic - a simple security precaution which ben-Zhair had specified to Qasem Hamandani and Captain Hindawi.

The sky was clear though the western sky was streaked with high cloud and the cold easterly wind was light and the sea slight as the huge two feet long links of the anchor chain clanked into the chain locker. The wind would change – a Mistral was on the way.

On the bridge, Captain Hindawi turned from his computer to ben-Zhair. "The weather forecast is not good. A deep depression is moving in to central Europe. We can expect a strong Mistral."

"So, what does that mean? Is it a problem?"

"We can expect very strong north-westerly winds – maybe even storm force at this time of year. The sea will become very rough."

"Can we go around it?"

"No. We have to go through it. I will route us north of Malta today and we will stay close to the coast of Sicily. Then we will head towards Sardinia which will provide some shelter, but by this time tomorrow we will be fully exposed when we turn southwest for the next seven hundred miles to the Strait of Gibraltar. That leg will take us almost two days."

"You *must* stay on schedule."

"A Mistral could blow for a week so we have to go through it. It will be not be a problem – these ships are built to maintain a strict timetable on six-week voyages from China to Europe. But the seas may be very rough."

"Jafa, what do you think?"

"It should not be a problem *Al-Mahdi*. The containment tube for the laser beam was designed to be at least as strong as the ship. The focusing lens mountings are as rigid as we could make them. If there is an alignment problem I will be able to correct them if we have some calm seas later."

"Will we have any calm seas, Captain?"

"Perhaps. It is likely that the wind through the Strait will be westerly – and probably a strong gale blowing against us, but it may be calm enough on the eastern side of the Rock. The problem is the sea will be too deep to anchor – unless we go into Gibraltar's territorial waters, but we could just drift and hold station if the conditions are suitable. We could also anchor in the Bay of Algeciras, on the Spanish side, but I do not think that the weather will change much in the next three days. Once we get through the Strait the wind and sea should become more comfortable."

"And the Moroccan side?"

"A similar problem there, with very gusty winds coming over *Jebel Musa.*"

"Very well. I would prefer us to stay out of territorial waters of any country now at this final stage. Let us begin – but we must keep to the schedule at all costs."

"I will see to it, *Al-Mahdi*."

"Good. I am going to my cabin."

The foredeck crew raised his handheld radio. "Bridge, foredeck. Anchor is inboard and locked off."

Captin Hindawi raise his handset "Foredeck, bridge. Roger that. Return to crew room."

"Aye, Aye, foredeck out."

Ben-Zhair closed his cabin door and sighed. He was well enough now, at the anchorage. The leg from Port Said had been peaceful enough, but he was not a good sailor and anticipated three days of miserable seasickness. The prospect of better weather and calmer seas on the other side of the Strait was of no comfort to him – he would have left the ship by then. He took two anti-seasickness pills and washed them down with some orange juice. He brightened at the thought of the catastrophe he had planned and prepared for, and the impact that the Cause of All Causes would have on the world. Success was so near.

The morning passed relatively peacefully as the ship drove forward at 17 knots through the Sicilian Channel into an increasing wind and ominously blackening sky, skirting the dangerous shallows of Banco Terrible. The sea was short and becoming increasingly choppy and an entry in the ship's log noted '*lightning in sight to the north, over Sicily*'. The Greco-Roman temples on the hilltop at Agrigento were clearly visible, but not of any interest to the Filipino watchkeeper. Just after noon, the ship cleared Cabo Granitola at the south west of Sicily, and Captain Hindawi ordered a slight change of course setting her head for Cape Teuladah at the southernmost point of Sardinia almost exactly two hundred miles away.

At the change of watch at 16:00 hours, Hindawi's neat script in the log noted:
Ground speed 16 knots. True wind speed 37 knots. Sea: NW state 6.
A written log was still a legal requirement, although totally unnecessary as automated voyage logging was now the norm, complete with bridge voice recorders, but Hindawi enjoyed the old formality of the handwriting and the careful choice of words. Much about him was very conservative and traditional, but he zealously believed in ben-Zhair's vision of the future and the worldwide change to come. The old ways were the best, he thought as he signed the page with a flourish.

The ship shuddered as she pushed steadily forward into the seas, now averaging 20 feet high – and still growing. The bridge windows, almost 80 feet above the sea, were running with spray as he handed over control to the first officer, Maajid Naqvi.

In his cabin on the deck below, ben-Zhair was vomiting into his toilet bowl. He prayed fervently to an Allah he did not believe in to be relieved of the misery of his seasickness and then washed the bilious taste out of his mouth with a mouthful of Bells whisky. His muscles strained yet again to empty an already empty stomach and he fell back onto his berth, groaning in abject misery.

It was dark well before sunset as the black sky continued to lower and the ship buffeted onwards into the gathering storm. The radar tracked two other ships within 10 miles and the AIS identified one crossing ahead as a ferry headed for Cagliari. The powerful lighthouse on Marettimo, the westernmost of the Egadi Islands, was invisible just fifteen miles to the north. First Officer Maajid Naqvi sat back in his padded seat and cursed as his coffee slopped over his trousers and he considered the prospect of a miserable night ahead. There would be little relief once the ship altered course for the Strait of Gibraltar – the seas would be on the beam and the ship would be rolling like a drunken pig.

The watches changed and the ship butted onwards into the still growing seas. By midnight the wind had steadied at 46 knots with severe gusting, but by now the seas – averaging almost 25 feet high - had stopped growing as they approached the lee of Sardinia. The wind held fast in the northwest, just off the ship's starboard bow and the corkscrewing motion was seriously sick-making.

Captain Hindawi came back on for the graveyard watch from midnight to 04:00 as the ship was due south of Cagliari. He decided to hold their present course which would take them under the lee of Menorca, over 200 miles away. On deck, there were only two layers of containers – the ship was not heavily loaded and the most precious cargo was in the holds. He switched on the decklights and looked forward through the bridge windows, then called the bosun and instructed him to send two men to check the container fastenings. It was a dangerous job as the seas swept down the sidedecks, and although the seamen had harnesses and hard hats on a wave could still sweep them into the steelwork and result in fractured limbs.

An hour later the bosun reported that all was well and the decklights were switched off. Hindawi cursed the schedule – they should have been sheltering in the lee of Sardinia, not driving forward into the maelstrom. She was a good ship, but he felt sure that Jafa Sharifi would have alignment work to do when they reached calmer seas.

Before coming on watch, the captain had checked on ben-Zhair himself. His condition had stabilised and he had manged to swallow some chicken soup which the cook had provided. Jafa Sharifi was asleep and seemed unaffected by the motion, but all his senior technical team were suffering to various degrees. The cook had been delegated to keep an eye on them.

Qasem Hamadani appeared on the bridge just after midnight. He too seemed unaffected though one of his security team – Iqbal – was severely ill.

"It is a problem Qasem. Seasickness can be dangerous if it is prolonged. The cook and his assistant are making sure they take fluids and they have all been given tablets."

"Jafa is well – the dog is playing computer games - but his technical men will need time to recover before he can make any final adjustments to the equipment."

In fact, in the 'technical cabin' as it had been called, the vacuum and temperature status of the weapon containment vessel was being monitored continuously, and so far no alarms had been triggered on Jafa Sharifi's 'games' console.

"How long will it take them to recover?"

"Maybe six hours, once the seas subside – but there is no prospect of that until we are south of the Balearic Islands – maybe another twelve hours. I am altering course to take us closer. It will add distance – and time. Already we have had to slow down to fourteen knots."

"I thought you said that this ship can go through any weather?"

"It can provided we do not expect too much of her and are sensible about speed and the danger of high seas. We can make up time later when the weather is better."

Qasem's feet slid and he almost fell, his mug of coffee spilling.

"I hope so. This is very uncomfortable. The ship is rolling so much, I wonder if she will capsize."

"You worry too much Qasem. There is no danger of capsize."

"I will try to talk to *Al-Mahdi* about the schedule, but he is very ill."

"Yes, he is being checked every hour. We will make up the schedule – don't worry about it."

*

A New Home

After the visit to *HMS Bulwark*, the search for Maruška started to drag. Ellie kept Barbary in the loop, but there was a sense of frustration at the London end. Steve had been chafing at the bit for a couple of days and his attention had been on the possible purchase of *Rubaiyat*.

"I've talked to Liam – he's free tomorrow to crew. I want to move ahead with the purchase. We could go across to Smir this evening and bring *Rubaiyat* back here tomorrow for a survey later in the week. Sailing across will be a good sea trial. What do you think?"

"Seems like you've decided. It would have been nice to be consulted."

"I am consulting you – I want you to come along too!"

"You'll have to clear it with the owner, won't you?"

"Yes, I've already sent an email and she's ok with it as long as I pick up the costs. The problem is we'll have to haul her out over the border in La Linea for the survey - there are no suitable facilities here in Gib. Fortunately she's a US boat so the Spaniards shouldn't play silly buggers. They're not keen on Brits now given the diplomatic situation."

"OK, I'm up for it. I need a change – I've seen enough of Gib to last me a lifetime."

"Right, I'll confirm with Liam. Pack your toothbrush. We should be in Marina Smir by late tomorrow evening."

*

"How did you sleep?"

"Not as well as you. That double berth is a killer for me, but you were out for the count."

"Yes, I've got a good feeling about this boat." Steve rubbed his head and winced. "Barring my head, that is."

Ellie giggled as she remembered Steve hitting his head on a bulkhead during their passion the previous night, after another lamb tagine at the *Relais*. She sat up in the berth as Steve passed her a coffee.

159

"Come on, get your arse in gear – we've got a busy morning ahead. I want to be ready to go when Liam arrives, with just the formalities in the office to do. I hate bloody bureaucrats."

"They have a job to do."

"Yes, but efficiency isn't a big thing with them. Come on, get out into the fresh air – it's a lovely morning."

"Is that fresh bread I smell?"

"Yes, I nipped over to the boulangerie. One of the better relics of the French colonisation. By the way, use the forward heads – the aft heads has a problem. I'll empty it later."

"Fine, I was used to bucket and chuck it on my father's boats – but I'm not emptying yours! You've put me right off breakfast!"

After breakfast, while they were waiting for Liam Steve checked the engine and batteries, and that the electronic instruments worked. There was a problem with the radar linkage to the GPS chartplotter, but the forecast was for good visibility and anyway it was too early in the year for sea fog. Meanwhile Ellie removed the sail covers before they familiarised themselves with the sails and rigging.

The engine test at the mooring went well and the steering seemed to be operational.

"Is there anything else to check, Steve?"

"Just the pumps. We'll run a hosepipe into the bilges. Anyway it's hardly an ocean voyage today, just a trial sail. No more than twenty five miles across the Strait to Gibraltar. The ocean trip will start next week."

Ellie's head snapped up to meet Steve's deadpan face.

"Next week?"

"Oh, so you are listening to me then?"

"For a second there I thought that you were serious!"

"Yes, maybe a week is ambitious. Let's say ten days?" He winked. "Where the hell has Liam got to?"

"Probably a border delay. I'll put the coffee on."

Just after 11 am Steve had a text from Liam saying that he had crossed the border into Morocco and would be with them in half an hour. The paperwork was tedious and took a couple of hours involving yet another telephone call to Sara Sylverne in Annapolis and an email exchange. The Moroccan authorities were polite but very careful – and very slow.

Although Liam had arrived in Ceuta on the 9 a.m. ferry it was after lunch before they had completed the formal paperwork and moved off the pontoon at Marina Smir.

They slowly edged out of the harbour, following the narrow buoyed channel through the silted-up entrance. Once outside the harbour they headed just east of north under engine for half an hour at cruising speed. Steve pronounced himself satisfied.

"So far, so good. I'm not a lover of Perkins engines – they were designed for tractors and seem to suffer oil leak problems, but this one looks fine so far. Oil pressure is good and water temperature is coming up to 82C. It sounds good, too, there's plenty of cooling water and no vibration from the sterngear as far as I can tell. Ellie, take the wheel and hold this course – I'm just going to look at the engine and check the stern gland. Ellie, open the engine up to full power – that's two thousand revs on that dial there. Liam, keep a sharp lookout for fishing pot markers, I'll only be a few minutes."

Rubaiyat powered ahead and within five minutes Steve returned to the cockpit. "'A OK' down there, she *has* been well looked after. Right, let's bring her up to the wind and raise the mainsail. No reefs – let's see what she can do. I'll take the wheel now, Ellie."

The wind was gusty from the west, rolling down from the mountains, as Liam and Ellie hoisted the fully battened mainsail. Steve brought her back on course and stopped the engine.

"The main sets well - nice shape, Steve."

"Yes Liam, and the cloth looks in good nick too. Three – no, up to four knots now under the main, and the wind is what – four to five? Not bad for a Bruce Roberts."

"I told you she was a good 'un, Steve."

"You certainly did that Liam. Are you on commission or what?"

"Well, there is an offer – more in kind, shall we say – but I'm not biting."

"Enough said, you already told me the dirty details. We've a way to go yet. Let's get the genoa set and then we'll look at the mizzen. Ellie, you take the furling line and Liam, you handle the sheet."

Less than a minute later the genoa unfurled smoothly and Liam hardened in the sheet. *Rubaiyat* surged forward as the genoa powered up.

"These electric winches are something else, Steve."

"Maybe, but I don't like them. They're just something else to go wrong *and* you've got to rely on batteries. Sea water and electric motors don't go well together. I might replace them."

"Hey not so fast! I might have an opinion you know. Let's give them a good try out first. You, Mr Muscle, are not getting any younger but can always use the handle with them and do it the hard way."

"Yes, Ellie, and the exercise is good for *your* arms and shoulders too."

"Anyway, you haven't bought the boat yet, but it sounds like you are half way there already."

Rubaiyat heeled to a gust of wind. "Look – six and a half knots – seven plus in the gusts. Genoa looks good. She's easy on the wheel too – hardly any weather helm. Let's see if the mizzen affects that. Here, take the wheel, Ellie, see what you think. There's plenty of depth close in to Punta Almina, but keep an eye out for the Ceuta ferries and traffic coming up the eastbound shipping lane. Come on Liam, let's get the mizzen up."

Ten minutes later Steve and Liam returned to the cockpit.

"Steve, look, there's a tanker there coming up – AIS says she's doing fourteen knots. I'm going to hold my course. We're touching eight knots in the gusts and should clear her with a CPA of half a mile."

"I'm impressed, yes hold your course. Liam, I put the 'Q' flag on the chart table – can you fish it out and hoist it?"

"Aye, aye Cap'n!"

"Alright, Liam, you can cut that crap right now you sarky bastard!""

Steve looked at the stern where the Stars and Stripes was streaming in the fresh westerly wind.

"I've never sailed under the US flag before."

Then there was a bump as *Rubaiyat* dipped and a sea slammed against her weather bow. Steve instinctively ducked, but the cockpit shelter kept the sheet of spray at bay. "Now that's one feature I *do* like!"

Ellie looked at Steve. He was clearly enjoying himself, and she could see that he was sold on *Rubaiyat.* "Anyone for a cuppa?"

"There isn't any aboard and I forgot to bring some."

"Well I didn't. Didn't you know that an English lady *never* travels without her tea bags. There's even fresh milk."

"Now you're talking. Count me in, builder's tea, no sugar."

"Right Liam, tea all round then."

*

"Scotch?"

"Go ahead, Liam" Steve nodded.

Ellie shook her head. "Not in my tea, thanks."

It was just after sunset and they were sitting in the Cockpit of *Rubaiyat* in Sheppards Marina, lying alongside the jetty and under the bow of the *Sunborn Gibraltar* floating casino hotel.

"I thought that the customs people would never stop. I've never seen such a rummage."

"Maybe it's because I was aboard?"

"Why should you make it different, Liam?"

"There's a bit of history on my record from a couple of years back – nothing serious."

"Bloody hell! What was it?"

"Just one spliff, here in Gib. Anyway, they are very sensitive about any vessels coming from Morocco."

"Thanks for letting me know – they could have confiscated *Rubaiyat.*"

"At least it would not have been yours to lose."

"That's no fucking consolation."

"Well, how thoroughly did *you* check her over before we left Morocco? The owners might have had some stuff aboard."

Steve cursed – he'd forgotten to check the obvious. "I didn't look for any stuff like that."

"Well, there you go."

Steve grimaced and swore.

"Still, Steve, all's well that ends well."

Ellie moved in to change the subject. "So, what's your conclusion about *Rubaiyat*?"

"I'm happy with what I've seen. Let's go ahead and arrange a survey. We'll probably have to go to La Linea to haul her out."

"You want me to have a word with Sara – I could tell her that you have some reservations etc, set her up to expect a low offer – subject to survey of course?"

"No thanks, stay well away, Liam. You've given me enough surprises for one day."

"Fair enough, just trying to be helpful." He drained the last of his whisky-laced tea as he stood up. "It's still my day off, so I'm heading to the bar. Are you two coming along?"

Ellie shook her head "I'll pass thanks. You go along if you want to Steve."

"No thanks, I've got too much to do here. And I need to hunt down a surveyor."

"Now that is something I can help you with – surveyors are back and fore here all the time. I'll text you some details. I'm not sure about La Linea though – the Spanish are getting awkward about Brits even though it's only less than half a mile across the border."

"Don't forget she's a US vessel."

"Ah yes, that should be ok then – I'll send you some contacts. Do you want my help to move her to La Linea?"

"No thanks, we should be fine. Here, Liam, before you go." Steve passed an envelope across. "Expenses."

"Cheers Steve, Ellie. I'll see you around then."

"And Liam – thanks for the steer. *Rubaiyat* looks just the job for us."

"My pleasure. I hope you'll be able to do a deal with Sara Sylverne."

Three weeks later the formal parts of the process were more or less complete – the survey and purchase of *Rubaiyat* had gone smoothly although there was some paperwork outstanding from the Registry in Cardiff.

Steve had lost no time in moving aboard – and Ellie had followed within a couple of days, forsaking the comfort of the Rock Hotel. "I might as well start getting used to it."

"Well, at least the hull is sound and the rigging good. I'm much happier now we've seen her out of the water.

"I think we did pretty well on the deal and we have a new home."

Steve looked up at Ellie as she corrected herself "I mean *you* did pretty well. I did offer to chip in, remember. And it will be *our* home."

"Yes, and I appreciate the offer. Helping with expenses is more than I expected."

"At least this waiting around is giving us time to get her shipshape."

*

East of the Rock

It was almost exactly 65 hours after weighing anchor that the *Yanbu Explorer* slowed almost to a stop at the pre-set waypoint, 12 miles east northeast of Europa Point – almost the southernmost point of Gibraltar and just outside the country's territorial jurisdiction. The ship had logged 1,029 nautical miles and averaged slightly less than 14 knots since leaving the Hurd Bank off Malta. Captain Hindawi checked the depth sounder. It showed 693 meters – about 2,000 feet - as expected. One hour before midnight he ordered 'dead slow' on the engines and set the autopilot to hold the ship head to wind. The wind was now slightly south of west and blowing at about 20 knots. Further south it was a full gale, the wind funnelled between the Pillars of Hercules and sending a swell north-eastwards to the ship. The swell was short and barely moved the vessel.

Thirty hours earlier they had come under the lee of Menorca and turned southwest to pass the Balearic Islands and head down to the south-eastern corner of Spain. The effect of the wind and seas had moderated progressively and even ben-Zhair had started to recover by the time they entered the traffic separation scheme off Cabo de Gata, with Gibraltar 150 miles ahead. To the northwest lay the Spanish mainland where the Costa del Sol became the Costa Blanca, just 5 miles away.

By midnight ben-Zhair had managed to eat some solid food and was no longer taking re-hydration drinks, although he remained severely debilitated. Just after ten o'clock in the evening as they approached Gibraltar, he called a meeting in the wardroom to review the status of the ship and weapon.

"*Al-Mahdi*, my team has reviewed the weapon status. As expected we will have to adjust the lens and laser alignment. Everything else is satisfactory – fuel pellet, temperature, vacuum pressure and power supply, although we have not re-tested the generators yet."

"Captain, I am worried that the alignment might change again during the leg from here to the target point – it's nearly two thousand kilometers of ocean isn't it?"

"*Al-Mahdi*, I cannot speak for the stability of the equipment, but the weather forecast for the leg down the coast of North Africa is good – typical for this time of year. I think we can expect four or five days – at least – of winds from the north of about twenty knots. The ship will be travelling with the wind and swell astern, more or less, and there will also be some current. It will be easy on the ship. It's about 780 nautical miles – which the ship should cover in less than forty eight hours."

"After the last two days I want to be extra careful. So, Jafa, your team must stay aboard to ensure that all the systems are working as they should. I will arrange for them to be taken off when we are within 100 miles of the target."

"But *Al-Mahdi*, it will not be possible to make any adjustments in the open ocean."

There was silence for several seconds, finally broken by ben-Zhair.

"Captain, is there anywhere we can anchor, in shelter when the ship arrives?"

"Very probably, but that would be within territorial waters – the Canary Islands belong to Spain. Permission would be required. I will re-check the charts as I am not familiar with the islands. We can do as we have done here – not anchor, but stay in the lee of an island, However, it is likely that there will be some swell. The weather forecast shows that conditions will be settled and with Allah's help I can find a suitable area."

"Very well, check the charts and let me know your conclusion. I think that we must make any adjustments here as planned anyway. It has been a very rough passage and if the laser alignment adjustments needed are only minor then we may be confident of the next leg. Jafa, can we not monitor the alignment remotely?"

"We can, but there was a problem with the software. We did not use it in Rome as the installation was static. That is why I do not know the full extent of any problem at this moment."

"Why have you not corrected the software?"

"I have *Al-Mahdi* – I finished the amendments last night. Although we can adjust the lens alignment remotely, the sensors must be re-calibrated. That means we have to open the containment tube and then after re-calibration we must pump down to near zero vacuum again – that will take about twelve hours. It can be done when the ship is underway, remotely."

"By Allah, there is too much to go wrong here. For sure your technical team will have to stay aboard for the last leg to the target area, perhaps you as well."

"Whatever is required *Al-Mahdi*" replied Jafa, hiding his reluctance well, but not convincing ben-Zhair.

"Then you had better get started now on making sure that the weapon is perfectly prepared. How long do you need?"

"Perhaps eight to ten hours."

"Captain, how will that affect our schedule?"

"We still have half a day in hand if the target timing of five p.m. on the fifteenth of May is to be achieved."

"Very well. We cannot afford any further delays at all. The accursed weather has caused enough problems. Jafa – you will have no sleep tonight."

Jafa nodded silently as Ben-Zhair glanced at the clock on the wardroom bulkhead. "We will meet again at six a.m. Jafa, if there are any problems you must call me immediately."

As they stood to leave the wardroom ben-Zhair turned to Qasem Hamadani. "Come to my cabin Qasem, I want to discuss some details with you. Oh, by the way Captain, did the crew carry out those small tasks I requested?"

"Yes *Al-Mahdi*. It is all done. The ship's automatic identification system has been turned off. Also, the deck crew lowered staging over the stern and completed the painting an hour ago under floodlights. The name of the ship now reads *'Al-Rasul'*, registered in the holiest city of Mecca."

Ben-Zhair smiled and nodded then left the bridge with Hamadani.

*

From the ship Jafa Sharifi called Jamal Sawfeek in the command bunker in Sid Bel Abbès.

"Yes Jafa, it is all done. The transmitter has been built and tested. It is programmed ready for use. Also, the VR bridge is ready for operation – I made the final changes to the software myself."

"Indeed that is good news Jamal. What about the North Korean satellite channels?"

"They know we are using their satellite but they cannot control it any longer – they cannot even shut the satellite down. It is now our satellite - we have complete command and control and I am changing its orbit as planned. The fools used a stolen US design and so they suspect a trapdoor in the software."

Jamal heard the chuckle in Jafa's voice. "Perfect!"

"Yes, it was a real challenge but I am sure that Allah is on our side."

"Surely he is. We will join you there hopefully within thirty six hours."

"I look forward to it – and the First Day of Ramadan."

*

Barbary had flown in to Gibraltar on the BA flight that morning. As they sat in the Waterfront Cafe he ranted about the Spanish sabre rattling over the Rock and the border with Spain. Steve and Ellie were bemused – Stevenson had obviously had a very early glass - or two - on the flight.

"Right, let's get down to business." He glanced around the café and, satisfied that they were suitably unobserved, he started.

"This is the way I see it. We have monitored occasional data from Pavkovic's embedded nanochip, but she is moving around a lot since she put Ogilvy out of action. We still have no idea what has happened to Ogilvy, but we have to assume the worst. We still cannot read Pavkovic's comms with the Chinese – the buggers are still staying ahead of GCHQ's cryptographers, despite the billions we've poured into computing resources for them. The NSA and the rest of the Cousins seem to be making even less headway as far as we know, and 'C' is not convinced that they are telling us all that they do know.

You tell me that Calthorpe is a dead end – just something that this crazy Serb woman does for fun. Well, that may be so, but I'm sure it wasn't ordered by the Chinese.

The biggest problem is that Abu ben-Zhair seems to have disappeared since she lost him in Tunisia."

Barbary looked at Steve, but there was no flicker of recognition. Baldwin's amnesia was still an open question.

"However, there is some good news – the information and data that the Noel team sent back from Rome has given us a great insight into the weapon that they used."

There was still no reaction from Baldwin, despite his having been in the same building as the weapon in Rome. Barbary looked hard again at Baldwin.

"What now?"

"Nothing Baldwin. Just thinking. Anyway, we know what some of the specialised components were and we have been tracking all sales from the manufacturers. ICIM have implied in their announcements that they have several weapons of this type, but I, for one, find that hard to believe. Although 'C' is driving this angle hard, all the sales of the components – lasers, capacitors and so on – seem to be legitimate. It looks like a dead end.

However, we are looking back even further in time – it is possible that the equipment was sourced much earlier and is in storage. Special vacuum pumps were used in what we believe was the design of the Rome weapon and before the Rome attack one of the vacuum pump manufacturers received a request for spare nitrile 'O' rings – whatever they are - to be shipped to Vienna. From there we believe it went to Rome. The purchase order for the parts included the original equipment serial number. That matched a vacuum pump sent to the University of Algeria – one which never arrived – and, it seems, was never even ordered by them. So, we're looking further back in the suppliers' sales records, and paying close attention to Algerian universities. Unfortunately getting information out of Algerian systems is very difficult."

"So, what do you want us to do? We're sitting on our arses here waiting for a lead on Maruška. It's been over three weeks now without any progress. We might as well get on with life."

"Yes, I heard that you'd bought a yacht. That could be a distraction."

"It's your bloody assignment that's a distraction."

"Don't forget Baldwin that HMG are paying you to find this Serbian woman!"

"Boys, boys, simmer down will you? This is not getting us anywhere." She looked at Barbary. "Don't forget that Steve figured out how she'd escaped from the ship – he was the one who put two and two together. Then we know she killed that Jo-Jo fisherman and Calthorpe, but now she has gone to ground. We're not really involved in this ICIM hunt."

"No, you are wrong there Ellie. We do know that she is hunting ben-Zhair."

Steve looked across the table.

"Who is this ben-Zhair you keep mentioning? Was he the bloke behind the ship attack in Malta?"

Another stare from Barbary as he seemed to make a decision.

"OK, Baldwin, let's cut the crap. Amnesia? The jury's out on that, but I am authorising Ellie here to fill you in on the background – there was no car accident in Malta. You head injury occurred in Rome. You were at ground zero less than an hour before it all went tits up in Rome. So was Miss Williams here. She will bring you up to date later. Ben Zhair was behind the Rome – and Paris – bombs."

They stopped and looked across the café as the barman turned up the television sound to full volume just as Barbary's phone chirped. He glanced at the screen and his eyes widened as the blonde female CNN newscaster spoke, taking on her most serious tone:

'We interrupt this programme with a special news flash. The terrorist organisation known as ICIM which claimed responsibility for the terrorist atrocity in Rome last Christmas has just issued a statement which says, and I quote:

'*Following the events of the past year during which our martyrs have carried out missions in Malta, Paris and Rome, the decadent and corrupt countries of the East and West have ignored the demands which we made. We are now moving to the next phase of our campaign which will cause devastation on a global scale.*

There was to be no compromise or discussion about our demands and we made that absolutely clear. Yet the so called world leaders sought to negotiate – an act of extreme foolishness which has cost thousands of lives – and will now cost millions more lives. We do not exaggerate. You know that we have the weapons, with the capacity and intent to use them – as we have already done and indeed as we shall in the future.

We do not hide behind our women and children because we need no shields. However, all those who support the governments of those corrupt so-called 'developed' countries are legitimate targets and there is no hiding from our weapons. Therefore we urge them to rise up against their impotent governments and reject their useless policies.

Allah offers a way forward for all. Al-Rasul is on its way.

The statement is signed by ICIM Operational Command.'

At that point the news producer cut across to CNN's diplomatic and military analysts for comment.

Stevenson spoke quietly to Steve and Ellie, his eyes hard and piercing, his tone of voice grave as he checked his smartphone. "I have to go now – there's a military plane waiting for me at the airport. I'll update you when I'm on the plane. We may have a lead – and God knows we bloody well need one right now. Don't leave Gibraltar."

With that, Stevenson slammed his Panama hat on his head and strode out.

"Bastard."

"What now Steve?"

"He said that lunch was his call. I'm not paying."

"Expenses, Steve. I'll sort it. Then we'll head back to *Rubaiyat*."

"Christ only knows what will happen next. I think we need to get to sea."

"There's no chance of that – we're under orders. And anyway, *Rubaiyat* isn't ready, you said so yourself."

"When a storm is coming, it's better for a ship to be well away from land."

"Really?"

"Yes, it's an old seaman's proverb."

*

The Banana Hotel

The Hotel Hacienda de Abajo was a 17th-century villa on a former sugar plantation in the centre of Tazacorte, two kilometers from the coast on the northwest coast of the island of La Palma. The ornate, antiques-filled rooms were well-appointed, many with terraces which look out onto the banana plantations.

"I expected a better view than this! All I can see is banana trees."

"Look, the sea is just visible there – beyond the end of the plantation."

"Yes, I see it – just. I should have known as much. The brochure said that there was a banana museum at the end of the road."

"Never mind, we'll make the most of it. At least it's a beautiful building – and all these antiques!"

"I did wonder when I saw the website - 'adults only' it said. I can see why now, the furniture must be worth a fortune. Anyway, you're a bit past the usual 'adults only' holidays."

"Hey, speak for yourself!"

They laughed.

"Don't know about you, but I'm ready for a gin and tonic. I hope they do them here - I'm not into banana cocktails."

Peter Gillespie and Trish, his wife, had flown in to the airport late that morning on the Binter flight from Tenerife which followed the four hour haul from Gatwick and a two hour wait for the inter-island connection. It was a late spring break to celebrate Peter's retirement from the local authority's housing department in Horsham. They had visited Gran Canaria, Tenerife and the eastern island of Lanzarote several times during their thirty years of marriage, and were now taking the opportunity to satisfy a long-held yearning to have a walking holiday on the island.

At the airport south of the island's capital, Santa Cruz de La Palma, they'd picked up a hire car and climbed through the mist to the ridge of the island, disappointed at the weather. But, as they got to the pass at the top, the sky opened up as they descended the mountain into the microclimate of Tazacorte. Pine trees and lava became banana plantations and the temperature climbed.

In their room, with gin and tonics at hand, they discussed the plan for the next day aiming to look around the town and unwind after their delayed flight. Then, over the next week they intended to visit the high point of the island at Los Muchachos, above the clouds, where the astronomical observatories were, then down into the Caldera de Taburiente, the vast caldera of the old volcano.

A visit to a vineyard, the capital and the south of the island were also on the schedule over the next week, as well as trip to the lava fields.

They went down to the bar and ordered another round of drinks, sitting delicately on an antique sofa.

Peter had his guide book open.

"Did you know that this town is built on a lava flow?"

"Really?"

"Yes, the volcano erupted and formed a caldera, and we're on the lava flow. There have been seven eruptions on the island since the Spanish first landed way back in the 1400's. The last was in 1971. We can walk on the recent volcanos."

"That sounds like a plan. That's one good walk every day, plus the trip to Santa Cruz."

"Right then, I'll download all the walks into my smartphone."

"It's taking the fun out of it. Do you remember when we were students and all we had was survey maps and a compass?"

"Yes, too well. Sleeping in a tent. We must have been crazy."

"Just young and unlearned. It had its moments though." She winked at him.

"I thought you said I was past it!"

"Well we are on holiday…"

They clinked their glasses and asked for a menu.

Back in their room after dinner, Peter turned the television on to watch the late news headlines. He found CNN and gasped as he saw the ticker run across the bottom of the screen. *'ICIM promises more nuclear catastrophe'*.

"Christ almighty! What a nightmare."

"Well darling, don't worry, we're safe here – an island in the Atlantic with only bananas as an economic target."

*

After completing the final adjustments, Sharifi met with ben-Zhair and Captain Hindawi. "We have completed the work – the alignment was close. It seems that the storm had little effect. The design of the structure was solid and well-constructed. The shipyard did well."

"It was your design, Jafa, let us credit you with that. It is good news and you have completed the checking in only three hours. Captain Hindawi - let us proceed immediately."

"As you wish, *Al-Mahdi*. I have checked the charts and weather forecast and I am sure we can find suitable sheltered water off the island of La Palma for any final checks and adjustments."

"Outside Spanish waters?"

"Yes, as you required. The swell will be less than two meters. I have marked the waypoint on the chart."

"And how close to the final target is this 'waypoint'?"

"Within fifteen miles – less than one hour's steaming at our service speed."

"That is good, let us get underway." The captain nodded and then turned to the bridge radio and spoke to the Gibraltar Vessel Traffic Service operator. He advised the VTS that the ship was about to proceed westwards through the Strait, but was careful to use the call sign of *'Yanbu Explorer'*.

"What are you doing Hindawi, telling them about us?"

"It is mandatory, *Al*-Mahdi. If we do not report to them then they will send a patrol boat to intercept us."

"By Allah, these dogs want to know everything!"

"That is the way of the world now."

Hindawi called for the First Officer who appeared within minutes to take the watch. "Maajid, the ship is yours. We are cleared west through the Strait. Call me when we have exited the Traffic Separation Scheme and are at the waypoint I have set, off Cape Espartel. We have to meet a fishing boat and unload some passengers. We should be there at about oh-three-thirty." He nodded to ben-Zhair, and left the bridge for his cabin.

The ship rolled again and ben-Zhair ran to the wing door of the bridge, to vomit down over the lower deck. He cursed and spat. At that moment the stress on his body awoke the faulty pacemaker transmitter which sent out a data packet – the first for many days. At the limits of reception it was picked up by a Gibtel cellphone mast and wormed its way onward to China. Wiping his mouth ben-Zhair turned back into the bridge to find a glass of water and some tissue.

"Allah please spare me. I hate this accursed sea-sickness – I thought I was over it. I should not have drunk that chicken soup." He faced Jafa Sharifi. "Jafa, your team must stay aboard until the ship is close to the target so that we are sure about the weapon. Qasem has arranged a fishing boat to take them off after they have finished the checks. I will need you in the control bunker with me at Sidi Bel Abbès."

"But they will be in direct sight of the explosion."

"Do not worry – we will wait for them to get well clear before we move the ship to the target. Will twenty five miles be enough?"

"That is the minimum."

"Then it shall be. Maajid , the First Officer will also be with you. Now, try to get some sleep – you have worked all night and done well."

At 03:00 the regular ship's Filipino crew members were assembled near the lee rail aft alongside the lifeboat. Quasem Hamadani spoke.

"I have brought you all together here because there has been a change of plan."

He turned and nodded to Iqbal Masood head of his security detail, stepping aside as Iqbal brought the black Heckler and Koch MP5 round from behind his back. It was almost invisible in the weak deck lighting. Before the five crewmen realised what was happening Iqbal had stitched across them with one slow sweep of the machine pistol, expertly controlling its tendency to kick upwards. He stepped forward to the bodies and put a head shot into the two that were still groaning.

"Why waste more bullets – they are going into the sea anyway?"

"Professional neatness, Qasem. Just tidying up."

Qasem smiled and nodded, holding the weapon as Iqbal heaved the bodies over the taffrail and into the boiling wake of the ship.

"One more thing Iqbal, as we discussed."

Qasem nodded at the lifeboat and Iqbal raised his MP5.

Captain Hindawi appeared on the bridge at 03:15. A ship's captain's ear is attuned to the sounds of his ship and his body to the vibrations it makes. A change of wind or sea will wake a captain, even an unfamiliar sound. He checked the compass heading and barometer. The ship was now on a south-westerly heading with the light of Cape Espartel in Morocco 12 miles away on the port beam, its white light clearly flashing four times every twenty seconds. The wind had eased and was in the northwest, with a long swell. The *Al-Rasul* had an uncomfortable slow corkscrew motion as it ploughed forward at 16 knots. Ben-Zhair was looking green again even in the subdued red night lighting of the bridge, and talking quietly to Qasem Hamadani at the other side of the bridge. Maajid, the First Officer turned. "Good morning Captain."

"Good morning, Maajid. Where is our watchkeeper?"

"Captain, I was about to call you when it happened. I expect *Al-Mahdi* will explain."

Ben-Zhair moved carefully across the bridgedeck from handhold to handhold as the ship rolled.

"Ah, Captain, good morning."

"Good morning *Al-Mahdi*. I thought I heard gunshots."

"Yes, you did. Some of our crew left the ship early – a security precaution. We are waiting for the fishing boat to meet the rest of us and take us ashore – except of course for Jafa's three technicians. As we discussed, Maajid will also stay to control the ship until you are at the control centre and can take over. It is almost three hundred miles overland from Tangier and we should be there within eighteen hours of leaving the ship."

Hindawi nodded grimly. Such events were not unexpected. He knew that he himself would be indispensable in the ship's virtual reality bridge underground in Sidi Bel Abbès. But after that?

"Captain, we have a radar contact at the rendezvous point – that should be the fishing boat."

"Good, Maajid . Start to reduce speed, and maintain radio silence until the last moments. We will turn into the swell. It will not be an easy manoeuvre in this sea. We will use the pilot's door, a ladder and a scrambling net. As we have no crew you will have to go down and rig it. *Al-Mahdi*, he will need assistance."

"I understand. Qasem – have Iqbal and Hossein assist Maajid, and then call Jafa and his team to the bridge."

Twenty minutes later they were at the rendezvous.

Jafa's team had been briefed about what was expected and the plan for the final hours of the voyage. Ben-Zhair had given one of his rousing speeches and additional bonuses had been promised. They had been told that a fast launch would collect them twenty five miles away from the target and that they would be halfway to Morocco before the detonation.

*

179

May 13th

"Good morning Prime Minister."

"Is it, Sir William? It seems pretty grim to me after digesting that ICIM statement. The media are going wild. Drafting a response that carries any credibility seems to be beyond the wits of the Press Office."

'C' nodded and took a deep breath. It didn't take an intuitive genius to see that this was going to be a difficult meeting. There was no concerted or sensible response from the UK or the international community in general to the threats of ICIM. The PM had clearly not slept. 'C' looked at her face as she shuffled the papers on her desk and realised that what had been carefully disguised feathering around her eyes two years ago had since evolved into very hard crows' feet – with no attempt at concealment. The Merkel look was in.

"How in hell can we deal with these ICIM bastards? They present no targets so we can't bomb them; they do not respond to overtures so we can't talk to them; they do not use banking or commercial systems so we can't sanction them. They have a dreadful capacity to deliver what they say they will, so a media onslaught hasn't worked and the public now believes every word of every statement they make. And apart from their so-called Caliph, ben-Zhair – a spectre more like - we know nothing about their people. How does he run such an organisation, how can he control huge swathes of several countries?"

"If I can coin a phrase Ma'am, 'the word in the soukhs' is that he is revered by many almost as a god. He is undoubtedly an expert organiser and administrator, and the tribes seem to relish the way he has us by the proverbials, so to speak. There was an interesting analysis in 'Time' last week."

"I didn't see it in my press digest."

"It was written by one of my people actually. Surely the FO would have briefed the Cabinet?"

"I'm beginning to wonder about the FO. A few things are not right there."

Sir William's look was quizzical - it was unlike the PM to talk out of school. Still, she had changed the reporting line several months previously, taking the responsibility for MI6 away from the Foreign Office. That had been an unprecedented move and was why he, 'C', was now talking directly to the Prime Minister and not to the Foreign Secretary.

"Well, Ma'am, they don't seem to have got back to an even keel since that attack by the Callisto hackers."

"They've never been on an even keel. Sometimes I think I have to lead the Foreign Secretary by the nose."

"Now there's a thought!"

"Sorry, I didn't catch that."

"Nothing Ma'am, just thinking aloud."

"Let's get back to the point shall we, Sir William?"

"Well, ben-Zhair simply annexes local administration and power structures. He appoints local 'sultans' to implement policy. Police Forces are impotent and penetrated by his followers, and the armed forces are controlled in the same way. Unlike ISIS, his application of Shariah Law is somewhat relaxed – in name only one might say, but those administrators and local officials who do not toe his line – well, they lose their feet, literally.

He relies extensively on word of mouth communications. We haven't yet identified his electronic communications channels and this is a high priority for us.

In many ways, however, he is demonstrating what the most successful sultans of the Ottoman Empire did. He is both beneficent and munificent, using power and money seemingly in the public good."

"Isn't that what politics is about?"

'C' raised his eyebrows.

"You're cynical, 'C'. Anyway that's a much better analysis than the FO gave me."

"Yes, I saw that. It was unimaginative to say the least, with respect, Ma'am."

"Yes, well, imagination should not be used for diplomacy."

"But it has its place in finding solutions and defining strategy."

"I'll grant you that. Anyway The FO seems to be making progress with Iran. Teheran has said that they will provide the names of some possible technical personnel which their intelligence services have uncovered."

"Yes but how long will that take to work through the FO? Anyway, I believe that what they want in exchange is not acceptable to the US."

"The FO suggested that ICIM might be acting as a proxy for North Korea, acting out Dim Pong-un's fantasies – with his support?"

"I think that is in itself a Foreign Office fantasy, Prime Minister. I do not give it any credibility."

"Maybe." The PM took a deep breath as 'C' reflected that she was doing a remarkably good job in these unprecedented circumstances with the challenges that Brexit had raised and ICIM seemingly threatening another nuclear catastrophe.

"Well, 'C', I'm running out of time. What is this urgent latest information you mentioned?"

"Sorry Prime Minister, I digressed. We have some news since we last discussed this yesterday with the full Cobra. This update is for your ears only."

He paused and looked at her, waiting. Then she nodded. "Continue."

"The tracking of possible components has led us to Yanbu, in Saudi Arabia. We think now that several batches of krypton fluoride lasers were shipped there, along with vacuum pumps and industrial capacitors. As you, and very few other people know, Prime Minister, we actually have video from our Noel team of such capacitors installed in Rome before the explosion there – that is our one substantial technical clue. We have sources in Yanbu who are trying to dig deeper into the details, but the Saudis are being notoriously secretive – more so than usual. My instinct tells me that this goes high up in the Saudi Royal Family but it is no more – at the moment – than a gut feel."

The Prime Minister's eyebrows rose in surprise.

"But surely they would be mad to be involved with such crimes? For one thing, if they damage the western economies then the demand for their oil will go down?"

"Perhaps. But the price would go up. The US has a clear energy security strategy which will eventually see them stop buying Middle Eastern oil. It may be that the Saudis are looking beyond that?"

"That doesn't make sense to me at all. I will speak to the Chancellor and Foreign Secretary and find out whether they have prepared any analyses."

'C' cleared his throat gently.

"Don't worry 'C', I understand – I will wrap the question in such a way as to avoid any possible linkage to this emergency. Let's move on."

"The text of the statement from ICIM…"

"So called ICIM!"

'C' winced invisibly. She was on a hobby horse of hers.

"Of course Prime Minister, that is taken for granted."

"Not by me – and it should not be by you or anyone else in Government for that matter. Bush gave them too much credibility by declaring war on them. They are worse than vermin.

'C' rode the storm and continued "The text of the statement from ICIM mentions *'Al-Rasul'*. It is Arabic for 'the messenger'.

"You told us that yesterday."

"Yes, Prime Minister, but there is more today." This was becoming tiresome. God knows how her husband must feel. "If I may continue, Ma'am…?"

"Of course."

"We have been tracking all recent online mentions of *Al-Rasul* prior to the announcement – working backwards in time. We now believe that the words refer to a ship."

"A ship? Wasn't that a scenario we considered prior to the Rome atrocity?"

"Exactly, but events led us elsewhere. As it happened the previous weapon was installed in a supposed bank building. But what if this one was in a ship, the *Al-Rasul*? It could go virtually anywhere in the world – Rotterdam, New York, San Francisco, Southampton. I emphasise that we should not yet jump to conclusions about a ship - at the moment we have no indication that it is a ship but might I suggest that increased surveillance of shipping arriving in UK waters would be advisable, discreetly of course. A major drugs consignment might be a suitable reason for such increased activity."

"Of course. There is a certain black logic there." The Prime Minister made a note on her yellow legal pad as she nodded to 'C'.

"Currently, there is no ship registered as the '*Al-Rasul*', but that means nothing as countries which offer flags of convenience for ships – such as Liberia – are almost prehistoric with their record keeping systems. Technically, the ship would have to be registered before it could be granted permission to enter a country's territorial waters – certainly to get into a port such as Rotterdam or Southampton."

"That's a lot of 'if's'."

"And just one of a dozen aspects we are analysing. However, the phrase has been clearly used – it must have a specific meaning."

"Why would they give us a clue?"

"A good question. Perhaps what they plan is even so monstrous that they want it to be stopped?"

The PM looked across her desk at him, her greying brown eyebrows raised in question.

"Yes Prime Minister, that *is* thin, but it's a possibility that our psychological profiling people postulated. On the other hand, ben-Zhair may believe that what he has planned cannot be stopped and they are laughing at us, so to speak. My people are attempting to see if there are any links between the phrase '*Al-Rasul*' and the port of Yanbu in Saudi Arabia, but they have drawn a blank so far. We are also tracing shipping which has recently left Yanbu."

"And what of the Chinese involvement and the escape of their agent from a Royal Navy ship? Didn't the Chinese have a handle on ben-Zhair?"

'C' winced and this time it was visible. It had been an embarrassing event and he was mightily relieved that the Royal Navy had been responsible for that fiasco. The First Lord of the Admiralty had since announced his early retirement, citing health issues.

"Ma'am, after their agent went to ground - last seen in Gibraltar – we believe that she killed one of our erm...contractors. We receive intermittent signals from Gibraltar and Spanish telecoms masts so she is still in the region. However, we cannot as yet pin her down and GCHQ cannot read the signals traffic yet, but they are working hard on it. May I respectfully remind you that this operation is off the books."

"Of course. I will ensure that it is erased from the audio recording."

'And I'll bloody well make sure that it is' thought 'C' as the Prime Minister nodded, accepting use of the address 'Ma'am'. This form of address had been reserved for the British Queen, but now with the King in place, this term was being used in the most senior government levels to address the Prime Minister. It had been used 'tongue in cheek' at first, but was now bordering on sycophancy.

"Once you have more details of this ship idea of yours, Sir William, I will consider whether to share it with Cobra – or whether we should try to capture the ship."

"Prime Minister, I will keep you fully updated, only via the red smartphone I have provided you. I am confident of its security."

*

"Good evening Robert."

"'C'"

"To what do I owe the honour of this late call? Good news I hope?"

"Yes, a breakthrough!"

The excitement in the voice of the Deputy Director of GCHQ, Robert Grey was plain to hear.

"In what regard my dear chap?"

"We're reading some Chinese signals and voice traffic almost real time again."

"But I thought their latest cryoptographic code was unbreakable - at least that what you tell me about our own systems."

"That is what the world thinks, and in most cases they are right. But just as the Germans were over-confident about Enigma, it seems that the Chinese have been less than totally rigorous in their application of modern techniques. Or should I say, they have outsmarted themselves?"

"That sounds like good news, but how secure are *we*?"

"Totally secure – we would not have done something as basically silly as they have done. And it's down to one person here - a nineteen year-old Cambridge computing graduate - a real genius who didn't fancy the academic world. She's a very bright but misguided young lady."

"How did she get access to signals in the first place?"

"She hacked one of our data pipes."

"I thought you said that we were secure?"

"We are *now*. She'd found a way in and was taking a range of data – including the XKeyscore feed from the US NSA into our Tempora system."

"'Tempora' as in Edward Snowden?"

"Exactly. That hack was her undoing. We eventually found her and watched her work on line. Anyway, we offered her a deal – prison for a very long time, or a smart house and high profile project down here at Cheltenham, with a summer house at GCHQ Bude."

"Sounds expensive."

"Well, you know the true value of a breakthrough like this. Blow the budgets."

"KOFIOC."

"What's that again? "Go fuck…?"

"No, no. K-O-F-I-O-C. 'Knowledge our foundation, Information our currency."

"This is all very fascinating Robert, and if I understand you correctly, we can now read Chinese signals?"

"Only those that use this particular version of the encryption. The sub-routine provides a kind of digital 'fingerprint' which our new employee identified. It was linked to the encryption key. That narrowed down the key pairings considerably. Of course she now uses our quantum computers – we don't want this stuff out on the internet. And it's quicker."

"Well, let's keep that very close to our chests shall we? Now, exactly what Chinese traffic are you reading?"

"At the moment their new version is being trialled in the Guoanbu. We're reading pretty much everything - voice and data - as they roll out this version."

"It sounds too easy."

"Perhaps it is. The signals seem to be linked to an 'Agent 29'. It does seem like a schoolboy slip on their side. Anyway, we have what you want – intercepts. The latest should be piping through to your team now."

"Perfect. Thanks for the call Robert and well done. You'd better look after that young lady very well."

"We shall, Sir William, very well indeed – she's quite a prodigy. Enjoy the rest of your evening."

*

After the hazardous disembarkation off Cape Espartel, the fishing boat headed back eastward, following the international shipping lane just off Morocco. Ben-Zhair and Qasem Hamadani had kept the change of plan secret from the others until the last moment – and even the fishing boat captain - as ben-Zhair was concerned about security.

The original plan had been for ben-Zhair and his team to step ashore in the pre-dawn light in the ancient fishing port of Tangier and use a fish truck to get to a loosely-patrolled border area for the crossing into Algeria.

There is antagonism between Algeria and Morocco with the border having been formally closed since 1994 with an estimated cost to the Moroccan economy of some US$2 billion a year. Nevertheless, the border is porous – the people are, after all, tribal and families are spread across the land. But a porous border was not a risk that ben-Zhair would countenance - the journey for ben-Zhair and his terrorist team across land to Sidi Bel Abbès would have been almost impossible. The BCIJ – the Moroccan secret police - were deeply embedded in Moroccan society and informers were widespread. He could have arranged things differently, but as much as he hated being at sea the thought of leaving the *Al-Rasul* before she had cleared the Strait of Gibraltar was not acceptable to him.

And so, three hours after they had left the *Al-Rasul,* they transferred from the fishing boat to a fast motor yacht in the Mediterranean some twenty five miles to the east of Ceuta. The motor yacht was owned by a senior member of the Algerian government who knew (or thought he knew) ben-Zhair from way back. There would be risks going ashore in Algeria, but the identity of the vessel would smooth the way. With a fresh westerly breeze and swell the voyage turned out to be more comfortable than ben-Zhair had expected and helped, no doubt, by the fact that the vessel was fitted with stabilisers. It would take them less than ten hours to complete the 220 miles to Oran and would be dark when they arrived. Then it would take just an hour or so to reach the control bunker.

As the fishing boat headed back west towards Tangier, there was an explosion in the engine room which took out a meter square section of the steel hull. The fishing boat sank within seconds without a Mayday message. Ten minutes later the hull and its crew settled 1,000 meters down on the bottom of the Mediterranean Sea. There were no survivors.

Offshore, the *Al-Rasul* continued on her way, heading southwest for La Palma, 710 miles away – about 45 hours steaming at her normal service speed.

In China, Wan Chuntao looked at the data. The display had shown ben-Zhair's latest location to be little more than twelve miles off the coast of Gibraltar. She did not know about the worldwide ship AIS system, so she ordered a data search to match the coordinates with any others in the Chinese data centres. It was a vast search, but within two hours the matches came through. The most recent was from the AIS database which held records of all ships worldwide. For the largest ships this data was recorded every minute as it was transmitted to satellites.

The cross reference of the location of the data burst from ben-Zhair was for a ship called the *Yanbu Explorer.* Chuntao checked the status of Maruška on her screen – the bio data indicated that she was sleeping. She touched the 'Prompt' icon and a pulse woke Agent 29 immediately.

The transfer of the team to the bunker at Sidi Bel Abbès went without hitch and ben-Zhair immediately established contact with the *Al-Rasul*. The voyage was proceeding as planned, and they started to exercise the VR ship control system under Captain Hindawi's guidance, with First Officer Maajid providing live feedback from the ship. The drones and the SAM missile system were checked and Jafa Sharifi conferred with the shipboard technicians, confirming his remote instrumentation. All was well with the weapon below.

There were less than thirty hours to go.

*

May 14th

"Look Ellie, it's been five bloody weeks and not a sniff of Maruška or Ogilvy. We're well and truly ready for sea now. I'm ready to cast off, Canaries next stop – maybe even Rabat on the way depending on the weather."

"Steve, you may be chafing at the bit but we can't move without Barbary's say-so."

"He can bugger off. He hasn't come up with anything at all."

"At least we're being paid."

"Yeh? I checked my bank this morning and nothing has come in for the last month. I reckon we're being strung along. He'll probably say 'no work no pay'"

"I'll just check my bank then."

Ellie turned her tablet on and logged in to one of her bank accounts.

"You're right – I haven't received a payment either. The bastards."

"Ahoy there! Good morning both."

Steve and Ellie turned and looked at the figure alongside on the marina pontoon. He was unrecognisable against the glare of the morning sun behind him, but the voice was unmistakable.

"It's you! Talk of the devil!"

"Yes, it's me, but there's no other answer to that is there, whoever I am? I thought I'd drop in and see how the lovebirds are getting on. May I?"

"Sure, step aboard - but take your shoes off first – I don't want you marking the deck."

Barbary climbed down onto the side deck then down into the cockpit.

Ellie and Steve held their grim silence.

"How long were you waiting there?"

"Long enough. Did I hear you mention the Canary Islands? You really should be more discreet – you never know who might be listening. I'd really have expected better from you, Ellie."

She glared at him as he continued with his sarcasm.

"I thought I better bring your paypackets. You surely didn't expect a bank transfer did you, for a *mission noir*?"

"You put money in my account before. Why not now?"

"Things have changed." Stevenson slid two envelopes across the cockpit table. "Cash, but naturally we deducted tax and national insurance first."

"And whose pocket did that go into then?"

"Tut, tut, Steve, you do have a suspicious mind. I certainly do wish that it had gone into my retirement fund, but it's all kosher. We can't have any accounting errors at HMG, can we?"

"They didn't pay for Djibouti?"

Come on now, that's done and dusted – you and both agreed it."

Stevenson looked around. "Nice yacht. I take it you will not be claiming for expenses at the Rock Hotel then?"

"Get to the bloody point – if there is one."

"Oh yes, there certainly is. Our missing friend Alex, your local controller. Sadly, he's turned up." Stevenson nodded across the Bay. "His decomposed body is in a mortuary over in Algeciras."

"Christ! How? When?"

"I wish I knew. Cause of death is yet to be determined for certain. He was fished out of the Algeciras fishing dock six days ago. Pure luck that we found out, given that the Spaniards are so anti-Brit. It seems that no-one can do without Europol - that at least has been immune to the effects of Brexit."

"You're sure it's him?"

"Oh, we're sure alright. Head or no head the DNA ties up."

"He was headless?"

"Oh yes. He had been decapitated – and not accidentally. The Spanish coroner says that it was the cause of death, but we'd like to do our own post mortem."

Steve looked grim as Ellie put her hand to her mouth and shook her head.

"There's more. Our friends in Cheltenham have got a fix on that Serbian lady who we believe may be responsible for Alex's demise. We think that she is still close-by in Spain with orders to cross to Algeria immediately and head for a town called Sidi Bel Abbès. She will be on a ferry from Almeria to Oran – that's the nearest route to Algeciras."

"Not through Morocco?"

"A difficult trip overland – the Algerian border is closed and it's two hundred miles overland from Ceuta to actually reach the border. There's good motorway from Algeciras to Almeria – an easy trip. We can't exclude Morocco, though. You leave this afternoon. We think that she's already left for Almeria.

"Now hang on mate. You expect us to go into Algeria at the drop of a hat. What about visas and paperwork?"

"Oh, don't worry about all that. Your papers are in those envelopes – along with a marriage certificate and two rings – which I want returned."

Barbary smiled as Steve and Ellie looked up in surprise.

"Yes, I thought I'd make it official. These Muslims can be funny about such things. It's perfect cover and it's not as if you don't like each other is it?

Steve shook his head, a grim look on his face.

"What's the matter Baldwin? The ink's hardly dry on the certificate and you're having second thoughts?"

Ellie looked at Steve "Well it's good to know how you really feel!"

"Ouch - your first marital spat! Right, let's get down to business. Your transport is being readied now, in the stern dock of *HMS Bulwark*. She's still in port, but will be leaving at sixteen hundred – with you both aboard. Early tomorrow morning you'll be put ashore on a beach to the west of Oran. It's a bit irregular but we need to get a step ahead of Pavkovic and the ferry timings are all wrong for that. So, familiarise yourself with your official itinerary and cover stories – honeymoon couple, second time around etc. It's all in those packs. Your story is now on your phones and secure. It will delete itself at midnight. So learn it and practice it together. I'll be staying in the Rock Hotel – come to my room at three this afternoon and I'll expand the briefing and deal with any questions. Then I'll take you to the ship."

*

On *Bulwark*, the late afternoon was taken up with an equipment briefing. A seaman had led then down to the internal stern dock. Steve looked at the sleek pointed stealth boat on chocks. He'd last ridden one almost two years before when he'd gone ashore to investigate the presence of Chinese Dong Feng 21D carrier-buster missiles in the Yemen. He shook his head as he thought of the dangers of that mission. Ellie picked up the nuance. "What, Steve?"

"Nothing, just some memories – another mission, another place and time."

The seaman nodded to the Petty Officer who saluted Steve and Ellie informally. He was dressed in black from head to foot. "Petty Officer Briggs, at your disposal. I'm in charge of Logistics down here. Don't tell me your names." Steve and Ellie raised their hands in acknowledgement. Briggs too had seen Steve's glance. "And no, we'll not be using the stealth launch tonight. Sea conditions are ideal for our latest baby."

"All your gear is in these two bags on the bench here – you'd better check it carefully."

Ellie held up her phone. "I don't go anywhere without this. We're under orders to carry them."

"If that's your service phone then ok, sorry. Here are your motor cycle helmets – special issue – more Kevlar which should stop a pistol round at close range, automatic night vision – both IR and starlight, boosted Bluetooth comms, plus satcomms. Headcams too of course. Online web access, satnav, Google Earth. We've trained the AI with your voiceprints, just talk and the helmet will obey. I think they nicked the code from Amazon Alexa Supreme. Yours is addressed as Anthony, and yours, Miss, as Cleopatra."

Steve shook his head in disbelief as Ellie started to open the sports bag. They had both brought some personal clothing and toiletries – they were, after all, to be a British couple on honeymoon.

The bags were innocuous and they repacked them, including the torches and some camping items. Although the feminist movement was strong in Algeria, Ellie had brought a couple of hijabs to cover her head and some lightweight cotton trousers. Keeping a low profile would be important. Steve checked the bag containing the small tent and simple cooking utensils. There was another bag holding water bottles and a first aid kit. There were some basic provisions as might be expected – and all appeared to be Algerian in origin. There was nothing for anyone to be suspicious about.

"We're fine – all the gear looks OK, thanks. I bet you had some fun getting hold of some of this stuff."

"It was a complete nightmare. The bikes came in on a special flight this morning. They are the genuine article from the tour company – or at least, they were."

"You did well, thanks."

Ellie smirked at Barbary's lack of imagination in designating them as the Tiger team.

"I don't know much about this op, but I think you'll need all the help you can get."

"That's for sure" Steve replied, looking dubiously at Ellie. PO Briggs continued his briefing.

"The gear packs on the back of the bikes in the paniers. You're ok with this model? Each has standard built-in GPS navigation. Completely legit, but we've added a transmit module, so your people can track you from – well, wherever they are. My lads fixed the GPS history as well, showing the route you took came from Oran to the beach where you go ashore."

Steve and Ellie knew that any enquiries would show that they had been genuine passengers on the ferry to Oran from Almeria, though much deeper digging would give the game away. More data was being fixed as they spoke.

"Looks good to me, though I haven't ridden this model before" Ellie chipped in. Steve just nodded, looking at the pair of Triumph Tiger motorcycles, liberally coated with dust, the engines ticking quietly as they cooled. Their honeymoon was purportedly a motorcycle tour organised by Endless Horizons, a specialist UK travel agency. There were many such tours available and Barbary had ensured that all documents and vehicle details were genuine – at least, the databases had been fixed – or so he had told them.

"The bikes will be warmed up ready – you can try them here on the dockside – in fact, I'd recommend it. But there is a speed limit" he winked. "We've dusted them a bit – not genuine Algerian sand, sorry, but the best we could get in time. We've done what we can to make them quieter – some changes to the mufflers. Your weapons and other gear, including trackers and some extra tools, are concealed here. There's extra first aid gear too – morphine and adrenaline injectors, field dressings, meth tabs – the usual field stuff. Just operate the catch like this. There's an interlock hidden here, for safety."

As Briggs held the interlock button and moved the disguised catch, the bottom of the panier dropped down to reveal a padded box.

"Both bikes are the same. The weapons are Sig Sauer P228 with 20 round mags in the right hand panier base. There's also an ounce of C4. The detonators are in the left hand panier base along with a smoke grenade, satellite tracker.

Briggs handed them helmets and gloves.

"Thanks for that, Briggs."

"You're welcome. One more thing – there's a lot of secret gear here so if you need to lose the bikes – or someone nicks them - then please destroy them. The helmets too. There's a button here." Briggs lifted the seat" Lift the red flap and hold the button down for five seconds and then you've got two minutes to get clear. It will be a big bang. Or, you can use your key fob. Open it up and hold both these buttons down for five seconds. Range is about half a mile or so. Or, let us know and we can do it for you with satcomms."

"And the helmets?"

Briggs laughed. "Don't worry they are not on the same circuit."

"Jesus, Briggs, that makes me feel so much better."

He shrugged. "If you need to destroy them then talk to them -'Anthony. I wish to destroy this helmet.' The AI is programmed with both the names, and voiceprints, just in case."

"Clever."

"We do what we can. It's the Navy motto – *'Si vis pacem, para bellum'.* "

Steve looked blank then Ellie spoke "If you wish for peace, prepare for war. Latin."

"And I thought *parabellum* was a bullet."

Briggs watched the interplay then broke in "I think we've got your boot sizes right, but you'd better check them for comfort – we have spares."

"You thought of everything" Ellie said.

"We try to, miss. You'll be on the front line after all. All ok?"

"They're fine thanks."

"There's always bunion plasters in the first aid kits."

They laughed.

"Come on, let's familiarise you with the bikes."

Briggs went over to a control panel and threw a switch. Orange lights started flashing and a beeping sound was audible around the dock. Steve and Ellie mounted the Tigers and did a couple of circuits. Some seamen at the dock stopped to watch and when the try-out ended a few minutes later there was a rousing cheer.

HMS Bulwark had slipped her lines just before 17:00 hours and headed out into the Strait. There had been a delay due to Spanish awkwardness over an apparently disabled tanker. Such muscle flexing was becoming more and more frequent. It was almost exactly 200 miles to the beach and that would take eleven hours even pushing above her service speed of 18 knots. That would be after first light – and not good for their purposes.

"Maybe they can squeeze a bit more out of her?" Ellie suggested in response to Steve's concerns.

"Maybe. I don't understand why they didn't use a helo."

"There's still time – they have them aboard don't they?"

"Yes. Barbary's briefings left a lot of gaps."

"You could have asked him."

"My brain is not as sharp as yours, I'm just expendable muscle."

"Far from it, and don't pull the 'poor me' line, Steve. It doesn't work."

It was just before midnight and they were on the side deck just aft of the bridge, watching the shipping pass in the traffic lanes. Gibraltar had dropped below the horizon a couple of hours previously. Dinner had been in their cramped cabin - supposedly designed for eight troopers. Neither of them could sleep.

"And by the way, what was that about Ramadan? That's Muslim fasting isn't it?"

Steve looked at the sky. "Yeh, and lots more besides. It took me back to the Yemen – and Libya. Ramadan is the name of the month. It's in our 'May' this year and starts with the new moon. Tomorrow."

"So?"

"Orthodox Muslims get really stressed and edgy, but it can work both ways. We'll just have to be very careful bikers. And trigger fingers could be very itchy. Bear it in mind."

"I will. Why do you keep track of all this Muslim stuff?"

"I don't know really. My Dad taught me about the moon and tides. And there was the Yemen. Come on, let's try and get some sleep."

It was 02:30 when a steward called them with strong hot English tea. "Breakfast?"

"Just some toast please."

"Make that two" added Steve.

Twenty minutes later they were guided down through the ship's labyrinthine interior to the stern dock.

A Royal Marine officer greeted them.

"Good morning. I'm Captain Davies and I will be your guide for this tour."

Ellie shook her head – the levity was not appreciated.

Steve did a double take as he recognised Davies – he'd been a Second Lieutenant in 4 Assault Squadron when Steve had left the Marines.

Davies nodded – there was no sign of recognition – he was keeping it thoroughly professional. He shook Steve's hand first, then Ellie's.

197

"You can put your desert boots on once you're aboard. Follow me. All the rest of the kit is aboard and stowed" He led the way along *Bulwark's* dock.

"That's a new one on me, Captain."

"Yes, this baby came into service last year. She's a much modified LCAC/L. Big enough to take a troop – and this one is super quiet, a real stealth job with tuned fan blades. She's just the ticket tonight – there's hardly any sea so she'll run straight up the beach at the RV point. Sixty knots in and out, with a bit more in reserve."

"The older ones topped out at 34 knots."

"Yes sir, as I said, this one is much modified and that includes twin turbines and tuned fans. No clunky diesels."

They looked at the dull camouflaged hovercraft sitting on the dockside then walked up the ramp as the seamen wheeled the bikes aboard and chocked them securely.

After putting their boots on they strapped in across the cabin from Davies and three marines. The compact turbine engines of the hovercraft spun up as the interior dock lights dimmed and the rear dock gate of *HMS Bulwark* opened. In the dim red light of the instruments they watched as the pilot slipped the craft slowly sideways off the dockside and down a ramp into the dock and then gently steered her out onto the Mediterranean Sea as *Bulwark* continued eastwards at 18 knots.

Davies passed them headsets and they put them on.

"We're behind schedule to we'll leave *Bulwark* early – we can make up the time in this. It's forty two miles to the landing beach just south of Cape Figalo – that will only take us about thirty minutes with the westerly wind behind us. What little tide there is here is ebbing, so we'll drop you just above the tideline on wet sand. There's no moon, so it will be tricky for you."

"Ramadan" said Steve.

"What?"

"Nothing, sorry. Carry on Captain. And you don't need to call me sir – I was never an officer."

"OK, but I am sure you are a gentleman."

Ellie sniggered – the officer had certain way about him that appealed to her. Davies rolled on regardless.

"We are allowing sixty seconds to de-bark you. My lads will have night vision headsets and will get the bikes off onto the sand, then you're on your own. The bikes are warmed up and the keys are in place. Passengers, please leave the complimentary headsets here." Davies smiled at them and the tension eased a notch as they settled back for the smooth ride over a slight westerly swell.

"Three minutes to beach" came the quiet voice over their headcomms units.

"Principals, put your motor cycle helmets on – I believe that they have auto night vision built in."

"Get ready team. Follow the drill I outlined. Bikes off first, principals next."

Davies nodded as he thumbed his headset.

"Pilot says the IR scan shows a clear beach"

"One minute to ramp down!"

"Good luck both. I don't know what your exfiltration plans are, but if it's us and here, you know the ropes now. And, Sir, watch that ankle."

So, Davies had remembered. Steve nodded in the dimly lit compartment "Thanks for the ride, Captain."

The craft began to slow quickly from 60 knots using air brakes, crossing the slight surf smoothly, and then they felt it tilt as it met the gradient of the beach. It slowed gently to a stop, sinking easily on to the sand.

Then the ramp went down and there was urgent, efficient activity. They gave Davies the thumbs-up and climbed on to their Tigers. During the final briefing with Barbary, they had studied Google Earth satellite images of the beach and picked out a site. The bikes moved smoothly across up the beach as the hovercraft rose on her cushion, turned and headed downbeach and out to *Bulwark*. The land breeze had set in and was bringing chill air down from the mountains inland.

They were on their own. Ellie had done all the courses, but this insertion was first. The track behind the dunes came up clearly in their night vision and they slowly picked their way along in the darkness to the spot they'd programmed in the satnav.

"Right, we've got an hour or so before dawn, let's get some sleep."

Ellie shivered as she unrolled her sleeping bag on the grass to the side of the sandy track and sprinkled insect repellent around its perimeter. "I hope this works for scorpions."

"Just keep your boots on."

Then within five minutes she was asleep.

Steve crawled out of his sleeping bag and sat against a rock, far too wired to sleep. The coming day would test them both.

*

"'C?"

"Red Cedar."

"Noted. There is no one in my office. One moment – alright, the diffuser is now on. What information do you have?"

"Prime Minister, GCHQ has just broken the latest Chinese signals traffic with the Chinese agent Maruška Pavkovic."

"The one who escaped from a Royal navy warship?"

"The very same. It seems that she is crossing from Morocco into Algeria as we speak, heading for what the Chinese call 'a control bunker' near Oran. Supposedly on university premises. I have people on her trail now. This must remain completely deniable and I would advise against any related discussions with the Algerian Government – or anyone else in your own government for that matter, particularly the Foreign Office."

"Red Cedar is secure, Sir William, don't fret."

"With respect Ma'am, it's my job to fret."

*

Two hours later the Prime Minister completed PMQs – Prime Minister's Questions – in the House of Commons. The Opposition Leader had been feeble yet again and she had scored several good points. As she headed back to Downing Street the new smartphone chimed through her almost invisible earpiece. She moved away from the waiting gaggle of

200

parliamentary reporters and headed into the Members washrooms, waving away her entourage.

"I cannot speak now, just brief me."

"Very well. Prime Minister. We have strong intelligence data – humint – that the suspect equipment we have been tracking was fitted to a ship called the '*Yanbu Explorer*'. In Yanbu – that's a major Saudi port – she underwent significant structural work to strengthen her. The surveyor's report was easily accessible and I am advised by a specialist that the strengthening alterations were 'unusual' for a ship of this type. Also, some heavy equipment was fitted internally – we believe this to be Siemens industrial capacitors and those specialised vacuum pumps we have been monitoring. The ship left Yanbu ten days ago. Her cargo included high-power industrial generators.

AIS – that's ship tracking data – shows that she anchored off Malta for several days where some crew left the ship. She then moved west, close to Gibraltar. After that she seems to have disappeared – at least we have no data from her. We are attempting to analyse satellite images but frankly that is a 'needle in a haystack' job even if any images do exist. The maritime authorities in Gibraltar have no information, other than a Vessel Traffic Service Report. That is all for now Ma'am."

"Thank you. Goodbye."

Back in Downing Street the Prime Minister sat down and pushed aside her lunch. What idiot had put *jamon* on her plate? Spanish food was definitely off her menu.

*

Ellie was still asleep and the sky in the east was lightening in the false dawn as Steve checked his satnav. It was thirty miles to Oran for a crow – but they were headed inland. They would follow secondary roads as far as possible – the W18 through Ain el Arbaa then down to Hammam Bou Hadjar. The main N95 would then lead them to Sidi Bel Abbès via Tessala.

He shook Ellie a few minutes before dawn. "Sweet dreams?"

"Yes, I was married to a sailor and we sailed into the sunset. At least some of that *is* true. My first morning as a married woman and I don't get breakfast in bed?"

"Married, my arse. Come on, go dig your hole or whatever you do and then let's look for somewhere for breakfast *en route*."

"Hang on, I need to check my phone. Did you get anything come in on yours?"

"Zilch. You're the leader here."

"Sounds like the right recipe for a successful marriage."

"In your dreams!"

"It was in my dreams – so that *must* be a good omen. OK, look, here we go. 'Pavkovic on Red BMW motorcycle currently on Almeria to Oran ferry, ETA Oran 13:45. Sidi Bel Abbès – University of Oran Radio Astronomy Observatory confirmed as MP destination. Confirm your ETA.'"

And London has loaded my phone some panoramic shots of Sebkha d'Oran, the long lake south of Oran which we supposedly visited yesterday."

"Sounds like it's worth a visit" Steve remarked as he walked to his bike and checked the GPS. "Clever stuff - the coordinates for the observatory have already downloaded from London. Our route is set up. It makes me feel like a puppet on a string. It's about seventy kilometers – allowing for a stop etc. as we *are* tourists, allow three hours. Tell him six."

"Why so long?"

"Well Mrs Baldwin, it's a beautiful morning and we haven't finished here yet. Our first night as a married couple has just passed - I have certain expectations you know."

"That's nice, Steve – I had been wondering if you'd get round to it. But first I do need to dig a hole in the sand."

"Oh thanks, Ellie, now you have put me right off!"

"And I thought marines were tough."

*

They stopped for croissants and coffee at a café in Ain el Arbaa. Ellie had received a call from Barbary as they were driving. They were on a flat, straight section of the secondary road riding alongside one another when Ellie updated Steve. "Barbary wanted to know why we were going to take six hours."

"And…?"

"I told him you'd had a puncture and needed a new tyre."

"Good thinking."

"The bastard said 'as long as it's not marital bliss that's delayed you. He says that Pavkovic has come off the morning ferry from Almeria. She'll get to Sidi before us."

"Presumably tracking her through the ferry databases?"

"I suppose so."

"She'll be armed?"

"She wouldn't carry weapons on the ferry would she?"

"Maybe she'll kill a cop for his weapons. She's that type."

"That would be too risky, surely?"

"She seems to live for risk."

*

Maruška slowed the hired BMW G650 X Country and pulled off the N2A main road just outside El Kerma. The side road was highlighted on her GPS screen with a flashing destination point a kilometre ahead. The white Peugeot SUV was waiting and as she approached a short fat man climbed out of the driver's seat, placing a sports bag on the trackside. He raised his arm in acknowledgement, got back into the Honda and drove off just as she reached the bag.

She was surprised at the choice of pistol the Chinese consulate had provided, but then they would not want any linkage to the home country. She had not handled a Caracal before and looked dubiously at the pistol manufactured in Abu Dhabi. She checked the contents carefully, ejected the magazine of the Caracal F and checked the pistol carefully before reinserting the magazine and ensuring a round was chambered. She'd heard of them and knew that they had been approved for the German Armed Forces.

The Czech vz-61 Skorpion was less of a surprise and made her smile as she remembered happier days with a Skorpion back in Serbia. That particular one she'd called *Tata* – the Serb diminutive for Father – in memory of the father she had seen brutally murdered by the Muslims. After zipping the bag she swung it over her shoulder and munched on a falafel wrap, throwing the remains aside as she turned back on to the N2A and with a wheelie accelerated the motorcycle towards Sidi Bel Abbès.

*

Barbary's voice was clear in their helmets.

"She's been told to make a stop *en route*, up a side road. That would have been about fifteen minutes ago. The message was very brief."

"So, we assume she's now armed?"

"I think that would be wise. However, she's no longer to be your immediate concern - unless she gets in your way. Things have moved on. You have her destination coordinates. Get there as quickly as possible."

"What's there?"

"Abu ben-Zhair, and we now believe he's controlling a nuclear weapon on a ship."

"Hell's bells…"

"Yes, with less than three hours before it reaches its target."

"Why don't you call in the Algerian army?"

"Just fucking follow orders and get on with it!"

"What, with two pistols and a couple of smoke grenades?"

"Improvise! That's why we've tasked you with this, you're the best we've got."

The line dropped.

Steve voiced Ellie's thoughts. "The bastard! That was a real bullshit compliment."

*

The Prime Minister opened the emergency Cobra meeting, which was being held online.

"Sir William, please brief us on the latest developments".

"Prime Minister, colleagues. We have solid intelligence that ICIM has installed a nuclear weapon on a ship known as the *Yanbu Explorer*. We believe that the work was done in Yanbu, a Saudi Arabian port." 'C' watched as Robert Samuels rolled his eyes realising that major problems loomed for the Foreign Office. There was shocked silence around the table as a stock image of the *MSC Venezuela* as she had once been, was shown on the wallscreens and touchpads. "There are several hundred of this type of ship all around the world. This particular ship has disappeared. She contacted Gibraltar Vessel Traffic Service as she passed through the Strait of Gibraltar into the Atlantic early yesterday after being anchored off Gibraltar where her AIS transmissions stopped. Everything points to a terrorist atrocity in a major port – which could be anywhere in the world – except, obviously in the Mediterranean.

You may be aware that the First Day of Ramadan is on the fifteenth of May." The murmurs and intakes of breath were audible. Yes – tomorrow. We know that ICIM is strong on symbolism and messages – and they used the term *Al-Rasul* in their latest pronouncement.

We know her maximum speed and that gives us the potential range of targets by the end of that first day of Ramadan. On that basis, she could have covered almost two thousand miles. Therefore, all of the UK and western Europe ports are in range. If the fifteenth of May is not the erm…critical… date, then she could be headed anywhere. For example, New York would be within five days steaming. Thank you Prime Minister."

"Thank you Sir William. Foreign Secretary, please draft a letter to all European leaders – those with access to the sea – informing them of a possible shipboard terrorist threat and details of the ship. Nothing more – 'C' will have to approve the text. I want the communication to be made at the highest level. I will speak to the US President myself."

*

James Marinero

The First Day of Ramadan

There was consternation in the White House. The President was in session with his National Security Advisor and the Secretary of State.

"What the hell is going on, Alan?"

"The State Department has received a formal protest from the North Koreans, following that Tweet they put out, which I believe you saw. They are accusing us of interfering with one of their communications satellites, Kwangmyŏngsŏng-7. We call it Lodestar-7, Mr President."

The President turned to the NSA, General George Schmidt.

"What about it, George?"

"It's not us Mr President. It's the first of their comms satellites, actually based on one of our designs. It's not that we haven't tried to get in to it. It could be Putin or the Chinese – maybe even the Brits."

"Is there some secret agency I shouldn't know about? Are you just saying that so's I can deny it, to protect me?"

"Certainly not Mr President. It's a geostationary satellite…" The President raised his eyebrows in question "– that means it doesn't move relative to the earth's surface. But its orbit can be changed to a different part of the surface. This satellite has moved from Central Asia to the Middle East. That will probably have used all its manoeuvring fuel reserves."

"Right, I'm going to fire a Tweet back to that headcase in Pyongyang. Maybe that crazy bastard is playing another of his games. Then I'll speak to Putin and then to what's his name in Beijing. I'd better call London too. Keep me updated."

The Secretary of State and the National Security Advisor left the Oval Office as the call came in from London, pre-empting the President's intention.

Within five minutes the US President was convening a meeting in the Situation Room.

Under ground in Sid Bel Abbès, Ben-Zhair looked at the wall clock. Three hours to go. "Right Jafa, you can start to execute the plan as you did in Rome."

206

"Plan initiated, *al-Mahdi.* Jamal activate the AIS transmission system."

"AIS systems has been activated."

And so the final hours unfolded.

Worldwide, ships transmit their position, speed and course (read from a GPS) and other data (including destination port) automatically on a VHF radio frequency. This is AIS – the Automatic Identification System. Larger ships also transmit this information via satellites. The transmissions are picked up by ships and land stations within range (up to about 50 miles). Satellite signals are relayed to land stations. These build up a real-time picture of shipping movements worldwide. Maritime authorities also broadcast data which creates 'virtual navigation marks' on ships' AIS displays. For example this is used to mark out traffic lanes in congested areas. In certain circumstances, such as in piracy areas, ships may turn the system off. Anyone can enquire on shipping at the site www.marinetraffic.com.

Modifying an AIS transmitter was a simple electronics project for a technician such as Jamal Sawfeek and his team.

"Prime Minster, I explained earlier that there was no ship registered in the name of *Al-Rasul*. Well, I have just been informed that the worldwide shipping Automatic Identification System is registering the name *Al-Rasul.*"

"At last, a breakthrough!"

"Not quite Ma'am. There are now more than thirty ships showing the name *Al-Rasul* on the AIS system. The system is being spoofed."

"Spoofed?"

"Being fed false data."

"We are urgently trying to clean the data, but each position signal actually corresponds with a real ship – which is also transmitting its legitimate data. The various ships have destinations which include Tilbury, Portsmouth, Southampton, Liverpool, Le Havre, Hamburg, Lisbon, Gothenburg New York, Miami, Norfolk – that's in Virginia – a major US naval base. Thirty or so in total, and all within a few hours of their destinations."

"But you said that the US ports were out of range?"

"We still have to double check the data."

"I take that for granted. So, do we assume that one of those ships has a weapon aboard?"

"Yes Ma'am. We should be able to eliminate many of them fairly quickly, depending on where they sailed from. We are also looking for 'the unusual' in their history – and which one is most like the *Yanbu Explorer*."

"That's some small comfort."

"Indeed Prime Minister. There's one more complication – the core worldwide AIS database which holds the ship data…"

The PM held up her right hand, exasperated.

"Don't tell me – It's been hacked."

"Correct. There are backups but they have also been hacked – they were online. There may be physically discrete backups."

"My God, is nothing immune from ben-Zhair?"

'C' pursed his lips in thought.

"They do seem to be eminently capable, Ma'am. I have instigated increased security on our own systems and advised all government data heads of the increased risk of intrusion. GCHQ advise me that there is no more we can do security wise, other than shut down our systems."

"My God. Huge cybersecurity budgets and we still get hacked. And what's all this about a communications satellite? I just spoke to President Deck in Camp David and he asked if we'd moved a North Korean satellite!"

"Yes Ma'am. I saw the Tweet from North Korea. Pyongyang may be playing some sort of mad mind game again. We certainly have not interfered with their satellite. That is, to the best of my knowledge."

"Well, things changed when I told the President about the *Yanbu Explorer* and possible linkage to *Al-Rasul*."

'C' glanced at his tablet. "Ma'am, there is more information coming in on the ship. GCHQ has now accessed secure backup AIS data and my teams have eliminated most of the false ship reports – for example those headed for Yokohama and for San Francisco – which wouldn't fit what we believe the likely timeline is since the *Yanbu Explorer* left Gibraltar. We are now down to a shortlist of four, but one in particular stands out. The physical characteristics match. She is approaching the Canary Islands. However, there is no obvious target there."

"Then why her?"

"I can only speculate that there is a big port there – Las Palmas. However, on her present course she is headed for the island of La Palma – that's about three hours at her current speed."

"But why would they advertise her position?"

"To cock a snook at us, to let us know that they are untouchable. Echoes of Moriarty, I think."

"Very well. I'm calling a COBRA in fifteen minutes time. The meeting will continue in full session until this matter is resolved – one way or the other. Keep me updated."

"Yes, 'C'?" All eyes turned to Sir William Gore.

"Prime Minister. One of our more intuitive analysts has come up with the notion that they could be targeting a geological fault in the island of La Palma."

"That sounds very fanciful. Why on earth would they do that?"

"It's an earthquake zone, Ma'am."

"But surely not many people live on the island?"

"Agreed Ma'am, the analyst is researching it further as we speak. We can see no other reason, unless of course they want to minimise the loss of life."

"In that case they could have exploded it in the middle of the English Channel! It doesn't fit their style. How certain are you that this is the correct target and that it has the weapon aboard."

"One hundred and ten percent, Ma'am."

"General?"

"We could take out the ship, Prime Minister, but even flying supersonic the RAF and RN have no planes that could get there in time."

"So, exactly what are you proposing, General, given that the US usually takes the lead in such matters and we can't get there in time?"

The Prime Minister's question was addressed to General Mike Rushby GCB, CBE, ADC, the current Chief of the Defence Staff.

"Well, Ma'am, as far as we know the US has no assets that are within less flying time than ours. We suspect that they do have free electron lasers mounted in satellites although they have never shared that information with us. We believe that they would be deployed to attack other satellites – Russian, Chinese and North Korean primarily. Our analysts do not believe that they are capable of destroying a surface target.

Spain has a wing of F18s within flying time but I doubt that they are up to much – our sources at the Gando airbase in Gran Canaria are telling us that only three are operational.

We have an SAS troop on *Bulwark* in Gibraltar, but no suitable aircraft to hand. Even if we had them, interdiction using the SAS would take too long. I believe that the only feasible option is cruise missiles.

We have a Trafalgar Class nuclear fleet submarine, *HMS Triumph,* on patrol to the west of the Strait of Gibraltar. I have put her on standby. She can have Tomahawk missiles in flight within six minutes of my command. Conventional warheads of course."

"How many would it take?"

"I would say four – two in the first wave and then two to clean up two minutes later. That's two tons of high explosive – more than enough to finish the ship."

"Trump used sixty to hit a Syrian airbase, if I remember correctly."

"Yes, Prime Minister, but the base was a much bigger target and was operational again within three hours – and it was fifty nine missiles, actually. It's not an exact science."

She glared at him - being corrected in 'public' was not appreciated.

He cleared his throat. "Yes, Ma'am, well, erm... the ship will be a moving target but we can update the Tomahawk target coordinates, real time via satellite, within limits. We can't use the Harpoon anti-ship missiles because they only have a fifty mile range. Despite the limitations, four Tomahawks should be enough."

"How many Tomahawks does she carry?"

"Ten, Ma'am."

"Yes, Foreign Secretary."

"Ma'am – it goes without saying that we would need Spain's agreement for such action."

"Naturally. General?"

"Ma'am, we could launch now and then destroy the missiles in flight if Spain has a political objection, before they reach Spain's territorial waters in the Canary Islands. The missile flying time from Triumph to the target is at least an hour – seventy two minutes to be precise."

"That's a good suggestion." The Prime Minister looked around the table. "Right, General, go ahead and give the launch order – and use all ten missiles – no half measures in this case. If they don't work then at least we've done all we can."

"Very well, Ma'am."

"My fail-safe order is to destroy them immediately before they cross into Spanish waters, unless I order otherwise."

"Very well, Prime Minister."

Rushby's fingers moved nimbly over his touchpad.

"I have given the order Ma'am. We will use a programmed spread with real-time retargeting."

"Now, let's deal with the politics. We do need to update the US President of the potential new threat to the US. I will leave to call him now. Meeting adjourned for ten minutes. In the meantime, please stay here. We will have to wait this out."

The excited chatter hushed when the Prime Minister returned and called the meeting back to order.

"I have spoken to the President of the United States and explained the situation as we understand it, and the actions we have so far undertaken. He is conferring now with the National Security Council. We do not know as yet whether they can take any timely action" She glanced at the London wall clock "– after all, it looks like we have less than half an hour left." She acknowledged the General's raised hand. "Yes General?"

"Ma'am, the target ship has just altered course and is headed directly for the west coast of La Palma at eighteen knots. The first of the Tomahawks is twenty seven minutes from the target. The ship will be inside Spanish waters before the missiles arrive."

*

The Final Minutes

Just twelve miles off Cape Trafalgar, the Spanish fishermen jumped in astonishment as they heard a huge roar. Less than a mile away, a Tomahawk IV cruise missile had ignited its engine as it rose out of the sea. They turned and watched the plume as the missile, launched from *HMS Triumph,* the last of the British *Trafalgar* Class nuclear submarines, turned onto a south-westerly course as it arced upwards. It would take just over an hour to reach the *Al-Rasul.*

Then, another roar as a second Tomahawk climbed out of its plume of water.

The Tomahawk was a land attack cruise missile, and its use against a ship was an act of desperation not yet authorised by the Spanish government. Its target coordinates could be updated in-flight and there was a recently fitted option of visual targeting during the final run-in.

Fifty meters below the surface *HMS Triumph* opened torpedo tubes numbers 3 and 4, and two minutes later the excited fishermen on the surface watched another two plumes rise into the air.

The display continued intermittently until the last of the Tomahawks had been launched. By then, one of the younger crew on the tuna fishing boat had activated the Periscope app on his smartphone. The tuna would have to wait - but the world would not.

"Ma'am."

"Yes, 'C'."

"Our media monitors are reporting that a Spanish TV station has picked up some real time footage of our Tomahawk launches off Cape Trafalgar – apparently taken from a Spanish fishing vessel."

"Oh bugger, that's unfortunate. Right, I'd better call the Spanish PM now, before he calls me. I'll do it here. This will certainly make his day."

The Cabinet Secretary placed a swiftly scribbled briefing sheet in front of the Prime Minister.

"Good afternoon, Prime Minister Perez."

"Buenos tardes, Prime Minister. I was about to call you to discuss the launching of missiles near the coast of Spain. I have just spoken to the Presidents of the United States and of Russia and both deny any knowledge of such activity, although they have monitored the launches."

"I understand Prime Minister, and will explain. This is a brief call to inform you that we have just uncovered an imminent terrorist threat to your island of La Palma and have put actions in place to assist and protect your country. We believe that the ICIM intends to attack the west coast of the island using a large explosive device on a ship known as the *Al-Rasul* which is at the moment just outside your territorial waters. We have launched ten Cruise missiles from one of our submarines in international waters to attack the ship. We believe that the terrorist attack on your country will take place within one hour. I am requesting your urgent permission to attack the ship when it is within your waters, using the missiles which we have launched. Our Defence Ministry is sending the data through now."

"I cannot give that permission immediately. This information is a lot to analyse. I will discuss it with my advisors and respond as soon as possible."

"Mr Prime Minister, I must stress the shortage of time. Our missiles are due to strike within thirty minutes. I emphasise that these missiles have conventional warheads – they are not nuclear."

"That may be, but permission is not granted. If you do not hear from me in time then you must destroy those missiles before they cross into Spanish air space. I must say that I am extremely disappointed by this late call – the matter should have been discussed before the launch. Spain considers this to be a very serious breach of diplomatic relations and agreed NATO defence protocols."

"Prime Minister Perez, we have only just discovered the threat. This is a terrorism matter and as such we believe that it falls outside the scope of NATO treaties. Also, if I may remind you, there is as yet still no agreement as to UK defence assistance to the EEC – those matters are still under discussion. In fact, they have stalled over the matter of Spain's groundless claim on the territory of Gibraltar."

"That is not correct! Wait - yes, yes. Prime Minister, Spain has advanced ground attack aircraft within ten minutes flying time of the island. We will deal with this matter ourselves. Goodbye."

The line closed as the UK Prime Minister muttered her goodbyes.

"Well, you all heard that. I had to stretch a few points there, but he wouldn't buy it. General Rushby – prepare to destroy those cruise missiles – but *only* at the last moment."

"Yes Ma'am."

In response to a discreet bleep, the Prime Minister looked at her touch screen. 'C' was messaging her across the table. Her eyes widened as she scanned the information. Yes, it would have to be shared.

"I believe that 'C' has an update for us. Sir William, if you please."

The Fred Olsen fast ferry 'Bonanza Express' from Morro Jable in Fuertaventura to Las Palmas, Gran Canaria was four miles from the outer breakwater at Las Palmas, running at 38 knots, when the off-course alarm started to squawk repeatedly on the bridge. Two miles – three minutes - and just on their starboard bow was a bulk carrier approaching the anchorage outside the harbour. 'Bonanza Express' was obliged to give way to the other ship but had veered off course as the autopilot lost control.

The First Officer quickly took command and manually corrected the course calling for a seaman to take the wheel – in reality a small joystick. He reduced speed and called for the Engineer to trace the problem. The engineer reported that the backup GPS feeds were also dead.

The Captain came to the bridge having heard the alarm. The situation was under control and there was no emergency. He spoke to the first officer.

"Esteban, call the office in Las Palmas and tell them we'll need engineers if we are not to lose time in the turnaround."

"I will do it now." He moved to pick up the VHF radio handset just as it came to life with the warning warble.

"Sécurité, sécurité, sécurité. All ships, all ships, all ships, this is Las Palmas port radio, Las Palmas port radio. Urgent navigational warning. All GPS transmissions in the Canary Islands area are non- operational, repeat, GPS transmissions are non-operational. I will repeat the navigational warning."

"Esteban, you needn't call the office. There must be a naval exercise underway. Did they give us any warning?"

"There has been nothing about naval exercises on the Navtex today, captain. Wait, there is a message coming through now. Yes, it is confirmed. GPS unreliable. Message is timed at 16.20 hours."

"Very well. Our autopilot is now taking a gyro compass feed, is it?"

"Yes, captain."

"You'd better get the paper charts out then. It will be good practice for you."

"But the pilot will be boarding in a few minutes – he will not need a chart."

"Who knows what might happen next. Let's be professional."

Some older ships navigating through the island chain were forced to use traditional navigational methods and there were no collisions or groundings – bar one, and that would be deliberate.

In her office at 10 Downing Street, the British Prime Minster looked at the Red Cedar logo on her smartphone. She looked at her Chief of Staff. "Please leave the room. I have to take a call."

She turned on the diffuser.

"'C'?"

"Prime Minster, we have agents approaching what we believe is ben-Zhair's control bunker in Algeria."

"Good news at last 'C'. I hope that they will be able to stop this attack."

"I hope so too Ma'am. We shall do our very best."

'C' cut the call.

*

At the Bunker

The guard collapsed in silence, his throat cut back to the vertebrae. Maruška dragged him aside and moved quietly forward, wiping her knife on the brush and tucking it into its sheath behind her back. The gravel track stopped at a camouflaged roller steel shutter and a keypad. As she placed a line of c4 down the side of the door, she cursed in pain. Chuntao. Then another pulse of pain in the back of her neck.

Moving away from the gate she took out her phone, swearing as the speed dial bounced through the Chinese communications satellite. Wan Chuntao answered almost immediately.

As they followed the stony trail, they could see the white buildings of the University research campus on top of the hill ahead, but the GPS led them off the road and up a side track. Maruška's progress had slowed and her last known position was still a quarter of a mile ahead. Two hundred yards short of the fix they stopped and concealed their motorcycles. The afternoon heat was oppressive and there was little wind to relieve it as they moved slowly forward at the side of the track. The track was well used – and recently too, Steve noted. The brush was clear over a width of at least eight feet and broken twigs were fresh.

"This is her last known position – less than two minutes ago. We need to go very carefully now."

Keeping off the track, they continued to pick their way carefully through the acacia bushes and other scrub.

Ellie motioned to Steve who was on the other side of the track. "Look, here's her bike" she whispered.

The motorcycle was hidden behind some scrub. The perfumes of thyme and eucalyptus were heady in the air. Ellie shook her head at Steve.

"What?" he whispered.

"I'm allergic to eucalyptus."

"Really?" She nodded.

218

"You'd better wait here then."

"No way."

"You'll give us away."

"Don't worry, I'll be ok."

"This is a fine time to tell me."

She shrugged. "It didn't come up before."

Steve shook his head then put his finger to his lips as they looked around. He touched the exhaust and winced. He didn't need to say anything. Ellie nodded. They took out their pistols and released the safety catches as they moved carefully through the brush at the side of the gravel trail. Moving ahead even more slowly for fifty or so paces and a few yards apart, Steve signalled a stop - he had found the guard. They heard a voice.

Steve looked at Ellie and dragged her to the floor, his eyes wide. 'Maruška' he mouthed to Ellie. Her eyes widened as she had the presence of mind to take out her smartphone and in hope switch it to record. The satellite signal would go live to GCHQ – and by extension, Barbary.

Maruška was speaking quietly but the anger in her voice was plain.

"You want me to withdraw, operation cancelled? I cannot believe this. Do not kill the target? I am about to enter the bunker to terminate ben-Zhair."

There was a break, then Maruška's voice again.

Steve motioned Ellie deeper into the brush. Then, his head snapped back in surprise. He could see Maruška less than six feet away, seated on a rock.

"China thinks it is in their interest?"

There was some swearing which Steve thought to be in Serbo-Croat.

"Understood. I will withdraw. And fuck you Chuntao, leave me alone. I have done enough for you. I am retiring."

Ellie turned and covered her nose as the smell of eucalyptus triggered a sneeze. It was muted and stifled but a second one followed. Maruška's head jerked up and her Caracal pistol swung round in an arc as she dropped to the floor.

Steve slithered quickly away from Ellie and waited as Maruška moved sideways at a crouch. It was 50/50 which way she went, but her movement was towards Steve's side. He picked up a handful of gravel and tossed it out, further away from Ellie. Maruška raised her head but was much too old a hand to fall for that diversion and swung her gun hand the other way as she started to move. Through the brush Steve glimpsed the pistol. A clear shot was there for him, but he passed up on it. As much as he wanted her dead, this was not his way.

"Psst."

She turned her head and pulled the trigger twice, but Steve was already moving as he heard the payload go into the bush to his left. What was Ellie doing?

The brush was thicker here but the thorns made movement difficult – and noisy – but it worked both ways. His arms were scratched and then his shirt tore on an acacia bush. With any luck Maruška would not realise that Ellie was behind her - or should be by now. He stopped, waited and listened. Not a sound. Then, the crack of a dry twig away to his right. Ellie or Maruška? There were some more sounds and then a gunshot – but whose gun? He moved quickly towards the sound of scuffling and swearing. There they were in an open area of bare flat rock. Maruška was astride Ellie on the ground and they were wresting with Maruška's pistol.

"Hey!"

Maruška looked up in surprise at the sound of Steve's voice and that was enough for Ellie. As Steve ran at them Ellie rolled, using her leverage on the pistol to exploit her opponent's loss of balance. But it was too little too late. The gun went off and there was a cry from Ellie.

Steve swung his Sig upward but Maruška reacted almost instantly. Up on her feet, she leaned back, rotating on the ball of one foot while the other kicked the gun out of Steve's hand before he could bring it to bear.

"So, it's you again you bastard. This time I finish you both." Her arms were spread for balance and she started to bring her pistol back into play, adjusting her stance. To her side, Ellie was able to roll, swivel and kick at Maruška's left leg, crying out in pain as she did so. Steve closed in, grasping the gun as he head butted Maruška, the nose splintering and spurting blood, but she rode the pain and brought her knee up.

Steve twisted away, still holding her gun and they rolled into the bushes.

As they struggled Steve broke her hold on the pistol. It fell into a crevice between some rocks as she dug her nails into one of his ears and tore at it. Grunting, he relaxed his grip slightly in surprise as she rolled aside and pulled a knife from behind her back, up on her feet like a cat and attacking him without hesitation. She danced like a ballerina, feinting and lunging as he was forced to move backwards. She feinted again but he stood his ground this time and turned, grasping her arm, the knife cutting across his lower rib cage as he turned it aside. Pulling her T shirt and holding her knife hand he fell back to the ground dragging her onto the soles of his feet and, using her momentum, throwing her over him. It was an old wrestling move and it worked. She arced in the air and landed awkwardly with a thud – and a crack. There was a groan followed by a long sigh.

He scrambled to his feet but Maruška was not moving.

"Ellie?"

"I'm OK, Steve. It's not serious. Check her first."

He found his Sig. Maruška was motionless as he moved carefully towards her, his finger on the trigger.

As he moved close, her eyes opened and she looked at him. There was a lot of blood from her broken nose, running down across her throat and the ants had already found it on the ground. The faint sign of a smile appeared on her face and a single tear slid from her left eye. A kiss formed on her lips - and then her jaw tightened and her lips tightened into a thin line as her eyes became an empty, lifeless stare and their blue sheen faded. Steve checked for a pulse in her throat. She was dead. A small track of blood was now visible running down the rock under her head and the ants had found that, too.

He rolled her over – her skull was punctured. Blood and straw-coloured fluid oozed out.

"Should have worn a helmet on that bike."

"What was that Steve?"

"Nothing, just talking to myself."

His feeling was one he had never felt before – a major anti-climax, a disappointment, tinged with sadness. In Djibouti he had come very close to making love to this woman – and to killing her. He'd tracked her and fought her and there had undoubtedly been a degree of mutual respect. Now he'd done it, he'd finally beaten her. She was a vicious psychopath with countless dreadful murders to her credit. So, why did he feel sad?

He heard a groan and turned to the other woman in his life – the only woman now. Ellie was obviously shaken and in pain. She had put her belt around her leg as a precaution. "It's only a flesh wound!" She laughed quietly, nervously betraying the onset of shock.

"Roll over." Steve cut away the rear of her thin cotton trousers on the left leg. There was a nasty exit wound. "I think it chipped the bone – you're lucky it didn't hit an artery. You need a hospital – no time to waste."

"Not yet I don't - I'm not bleeding heavily am I? We've still got a job to finish. I can at least cover your back. Anyway, there' no debate – I'm pulling rank. You go in, flush them out and I'll wait here for the duck shoot. Let's be clear Steve – you have no choice in this matter."

"We could walk away."

"No, you could walk away – I'm staying. And that would be the end of *us*."

"I fucking knew it was a mistake to have a woman tagging along. They always complicate things on the front line!"

"Make your mind up Steve!"

"You're right about the bleeding. I can see that there's no point in arguing with you. I'll get the first aid kit from my bike."

Ten minutes later and Ellie had downed some paracetamol as Steve was tying off the wound dressing.

"They put some strong antibiotics and pain killers in the weapons kit. Take these tabs if the pain gets too bad. I've put antibiotic powder on the wound and packed it. Here, put your helmet on and keep it on. It's bullet proof."

"Thanks, that's a comfort. Will the comms work?"

"I doubt it – depends how far in the tunnel goes – if it is a tunnel. I'll be keeping radio silence as I go in."

"OK."

"Right, I've got to get through that gate, but first let's check the weapons and I'll see if Maruška had anything of use to us – the guard too. It seems that there's no time to lose. Any sign of the backup yet?"

Ellie looked at her smartphone.

"Nothing. I wouldn't bet on anyone showing. Barbary is playing this very tight."

Steve shook his head in resignation. "That's par for the course. I'll get the rest of the stuff from the bikes."

Steve got a sleeping bag and water from the bike and swung the tool bag over his shoulder, then headed back to Ellie. "It's warm but you can still get shock. Let's get you behind those rocks there where you will have clear sight of the entrance from cover. Put the sleeping bag around your shoulders. Here's the guard's Uzi, and spare mag. You take our Sigs and I'll use Maruška's weapons. I found Maruška's smartphone."

"Don't do anything with it – London needs it. Don't even try to unlock the screen or it will probably self-destruct."

"Don't worry – you can look after it."

Ellie's smartphone chirped and she read the text.

"Barbary. They've broken the latest Chinese signals to Maruška. I need to call him now."

Steve checked the GPS coordinates and went over to examine the entrance to the bunker. It was off to one side of the track which meandered onwards around the base of the hill. There was a steel door wide enough for a small truck. It was painted with camouflage bushes and a rock – good enough to disguise it from thirty feet away. There was a touchpad on the left hand side of the portal but Steve could see no obvious alarm beams or cameras. He shook his head and returned to Ellie's hide.

"I've told him about Maruška, he just said 'good'. We don't know what's this place is, but Maruška was told that ben-Zhair is here. She was told to kill everyone here and destroy the installation as quickly as possible. London has put two and two together and believe that this is the technical control centre for ICIM ops. It's the first day of Ramadan and Barbary thinks that is significant."

"I doubt that we've got the punch to destroy this site - a few ounces of C4 and that's it. I'll just have to find ben-Zhair and the critical bits."

"They are picking up encrypted traffic with a North Korean satellite – from this location. The orders for us are the same as for Maruška. London will not involve the Algerians."

"That's fucking typical. We are deniable, we don't know what or how many of who are in there – even if we could get past the entrance – there's a print reader and who knows what else there. We don't have any serious demolition charges. I'll just pull my Superman suit on!"

Ellie looked at him. "There's always an air vent."

"Yeh, right, in the films."

"And this." She held out her smartphone. "Here. See this icon? Press the icon and put it against the touchpad front first. An electromagnet will hold it in place. If it bleeps then it is engaged and our computers in Cheltenham or wherever will analyse the circuit. They may be able to unlock it remotely. Your phone should work the same way."

"And if the door is booby-trapped?"

"Light the blue touchpaper and stand well back."

"James-fucking-Bond."

Steve checked his weapon again and crossed the track to the entrance shutter. The phone clamped itself and bleeped as Steve sprinted for the hide.

"How long do we wait?"

"I've no idea, but the sun goes down in about three hours."

"You'll be in hospital by then."

Ellie smiled at him and stroked his chin. "The beard suited you."

"Don't change the subject! What about that satellite signal – there will be an antenna somewhere."

Ellie pointed. Over the bushes they could see the main buildings of the university research centre on top of the hill. One building was topped by a multitude of aerials.

"Scrub that then." Steve shook his head. "Fucking hell. Maruška dead. I thought it would be different, I planned the moment, I wanted to look into her eyes when I killed her, to remind her of my pals – Bryan and Tom and the others. It all happened so quickly – and yet when I had a clear shot I just couldn't take it."

"It's best you didn't – the way it ended was best – you were fighting for your – and my – life. It says a lot about you Steve, it's something I admire and love. And we can draw a line under that spreadsheet too. One more thing – Barbary asked us to cut out a microchip from Maruška's neck. He sent an x-ray of her neck – they took it on *Bulwark*." Ellie held up the phone.

"He must be fucking joking. Pass me a brush and I'll stick it up my arse so I can sweep up the desert sand while I'm doing neck surgery on a dead body."

"Yes, I think we'll pass on that one – operational priorities prevented it."

"Here's a picture of ben-Zhair on my phone."

Steve looked at Ellie's smartphone. "That's the picture I saw in Tunisia. He's probably changed his appearance by now. Don't worry, I'll find him."

"It should be on your phone by now."

There was a rumble. "Looks like a go!" The tunnel shutter was rising slowly and Steve started to move. He put his motor cycle helmet on and slung the Skorpion over his shoulder.

"Steve!" Ellie whispered.

"What now?"

"Swap pistols with me – this one from the guard has a Maglite."

"The helmet has night vision."

"And if it fails?"

"Good point."

"One more thing..."

"What now?"

"Be careful. *Rubaiyat* is waiting for us in Gibraltar."

He shrugged and moved away, then turned back.

"Just make sure you shoot straight – and not me. The RV is here, one hour. If I'm not back get the hell out." With that he was gone. Ellie rechecked her weapons and settled back to wait. He jogged to the entrance of the tunnel. It was unlit and he moved slowly down the gravel incline of the tunnel. Ellie shook her head. 'What the fuck, neck surgery on dead Maruška?'

*

Underground in Wuhan Province, Wan Chuntao was awoken from her sleep by an alarm on the smartphone next to her bed. There was an automated text from the Agent Management System. It stated that a signal from Agent 29's nanochip indicated cessation of all vital signs and that the chip was losing power.

Chuntao shook her head and pulled the blanket back over her body. No action required.

*

First Officer Maajid Naqqvi checked the electronic charts and the radar. Seemingly there was no vessel at the rendezvous point which was now just five miles ahead, a dozen miles northwest of La Palma. The *Al-Rasul* was now under the control of Captain Hindawi, almost a thousand miles away underground in Sidi Bel Abbès. The control system seemed to working faultlessly. Maajid had listened as the technical team spoke to Jafa Sharifi over the remote link and confirmed the weapon status.

"Fuel pellet status?" - "Hohlraum temperature, stability, vacuum status and pellet radioactive emission confirmed satisfactory."

"Plutonium tracer?" - "Temperature, stability and radioactive emission confirmed within limits."

"Helium Status?" - "Confirm temperature minus two seven four point three degrees K. Pressure within limits."

"Laser Combining Mirrors" – "All confirmed stable. No vibration."

"Laser alignment stability?" – "Steady, very low vibration well within tolerance. Krypton fluoride pressure stable. Pre-heating circuits operational."

"Laser temperatures?" - "All within tolerance. Number Seven close to tolerance limit. Drifting back towards optimal."

"Capacitor Charge status?"- "Fully charged. Number seven is zero point one percent below maximum. Eight hundred kilojoules available from capacitor bank. Within tolerance."

"Vacuum status?" - "Zero point five times ten to the minus twelve pascals. Within tolerance."

"Cameras?" - "All operational."

"Internet links?" - "Data rate maximum."

"Backup generator status?" - "Fully operational. Auto-tested in the last 30 minutes. They will come on line in two minutes."

Then the ship altered course, following the twelve mile limit round the island and heading south – away from the rendezvous point.

The First Officer spoke and his words came over the remote bridge comms in the bunker.

"Captain, the ship is turning away from the rendezvous point."

Ben-Zhair spoke in reply. "Yes, Maajid. Unfortunately we were unable to arrange a vessel to take you off, so the ship is now under remote autopilot control and heading for the target."

At that moment the three nuclear technicians came up the companionway ladder and into the bridge. "Why is the ship turning, Maajid?"

Maajid held up his hand for quiet as ben-Zhair continued.

"You and the others will be great martyrs for the Cause of All Causes. It is time for you to pray – regrettably we can do nothing to help you now."

The technicians stared, speechless.

"But you can slow the ship and we will wait for a fishing boat to take us off!"

"That is impossible. The countdown has started and events are irreversible – everything is under pre-programmed control."

"Captain Hindawi, please help us."

"Maajid, I am sorry I can do nothing. It is written."

The clamour from the bridge subsided as the technicians left, to try to disable the weapon.

Ben-Zhair spoke again. "Maajid, tell the others that there is nothing they can do. All systems are now locked down. The result is inevitable. It is time for you all to make your peace with Allah and prepare for paradise. You will surely know nothing of the final moment, except for glory. Accept your fate as it is written. Your names will live forever. May Allah be with you."

Maajid picked up the primary VHF handset and keyed the microphone.

"Mayday, Mayday, Mayday. This is the *Al-Rasul*, *Al Rasul*, *Al-Rasul*. Mayday, mayday, mayday." As he continued with the mayday message protocol he glanced at the set and saw that there was no transmit light. He moved the switches and flicking the red cover aside selected the DSC automatic distress option. Dead.

He picked up one of the several hand-held VHF sets from the charging racks. Dead.

Cursing, he ran from the bridge to the captain's quarters, to where he knew the anti-piracy panic button was located - the system carried by major ships worldwide. He opened the drawer in the desk and stared in disbelief at the cut wiring and smashed button.

He slid the wall panel aside and taking his key he opened the gun cabinet. It was empty.

Was there nothing he could do?

He ran down to the technical control room. The technicians were in heated debate. Sharif Ghazali, the most senior, spoke.

"Maajid, we can do nothing. Everything is locked down. Can you disable the ship – perhaps the steering or engine?"

"To what purpose? You have said you can do nothing, so the weapon will explode, will it not?"

"Yes, surely. What about the lifeboat?"

"Why did I not think of that? Quickly, follow me."

They ran to the aft deck where the enclosed orange lifeboat sat on steeply-angled launching rails and there was a collective groan as they saw where Iqbal had emptied the magazine of the MP5. The pattern of holes resembled a smiley, but the magazine had obviously emptied without the eyes being completed.

"May Allah help us! What shall we do Maajid , we do not have much time – maybe half an hour?"

"I have an idea. Perhaps we can move the containers. What do they hold?"

"Generators, pressurised helium and other equipment. But they are all locked. We could use a torch to burn our way in."

"It will take too long – and anyway we cannot get down to the workshop to get the cutting gear. Wait, perhaps they have not thought of everything."

Maajid ran forward as the ship headed onward, turning as he ran. The *Al-Rasul* was just twelve miles from the target and headed due east crossing into the territorial waters of the Spanish Canary Islands.

*

Peter and Tricia Gillespie sat at the roadside high above the village of El Remo, with banana plantations stretching southward along the rock shelf above the Atlantic Ocean to the end of the island, some six miles away. Even though it was mid-May the sea temperature was nudging twenty degrees and to their north there were tourists and locals on the few beaches.

Walking the vent holes along the Cumbre Vieja volcanic ridge which forms the spine of the south of the island had taken them six hours, and now they were resting and having some coffee and banana cake at one of the *miradores* – the lookout points built for tourists on the LP2 highway.

"I don't know what's wrong with the GPS on this tablet. The smartphone is playing up too."

"You and your navigation."

"Well, you've got to admit that it was interesting to go back to the map to navigate."

"It's only been off for an hour. Anyway, all the paths are marked so it's easy. I just found it very tiring, that's all. My ankle couldn't have taken much more. It's never been right since I twisted it in Switzerland. I'm just glad that this is the last walk of the holiday."

"And you said I was past it!"

"Well, last night you proved me wrong."

"Glad to oblige."

"Yes, that was certainly something to remember."

229

"The children would blanche if they knew what we got up to."

It was late afternoon, and offshore they could see the white water which indicated the wind acceleration zone, though they were unaware of its nature. All the Canary Islands disturb the regular 15-20 knots north/north-easterly wind. These winds are generally called the trades, although the trade winds proper start much further south of the islands.

All the islands have 'wind shadows' – and the opposite – acceleration zones where the wind is funnelled and intensified. Sailors know about them – they are described in pilot books - and are not usually severe though they must be treated with respect.

"What's that ship doing?"

Tricia pointed as Peter put his binoculars to his eyes.

"I don't know. It's very close in and seems to be heading directly for the coast. It's moving quite fast."

He could see that the ship was now in the wind shadow, in the calm water nearer the shore. Its bow wave was plain to see.

"There must be a harbour here."

"I can't see one, and there's nothing on the map – just a bay called Puerto Naos – but that's a few miles away. Here, have a look. I can't see anything down below us. Maybe they are going to anchor."

Over the ridge of Cumbre Vieja behind Peter and Tricia, to the east and south of the island, there was the regular shipping and air traffic as well as two charter yachts, well reefed, which were having a brisk sail through the acceleration zone. The yachts were just south of Punta Fuencaliente with its lighthouse and farm of fast-spinning wind generators. The crew were looking forward to rounding the point and getting into the wind shadow after the bumpy crossing. And then the beers when they reached the marina at Tazacorte, some 13 miles up the coast.

At that same time the Naviera Armas ferry *Volcán de Taburiente* from Tenerife to Santa Cruz de La Palma was halfway through her trip, about twenty five miles to the east of La Palma, and the situation on the bridge was much the same as on the bridge of the '*Bonanza Express*' approaching Las Palmas - the paper charts were laid out.

Apart from the GPS signal failure, it was a typical late afternoon around La Palma, sunny and breezy.

The four main networks of GPS satellites – US (Navstar), EU (Galileo), Russian (Glonass) and Chinese (BeiDou) had all been jammed. Or, more precisely, their governments had turned on 'selective availability' – that is, deliberately degraded the signal of the satellites which passed over that region of the North Atlantic Ocean, as they passed. This was done by changing the time signal broadcast by the overflying satellites and is common during times of tension or during military exercises. Only the military GPS receivers of each country worked with their own network during such periods.

China had acted first and this had been noted by the US and Russia. The NSA, in response to the UK's tip-off, instructed the control centre in the Cheyenne Mountain complex to turn on selective availability for the Navstar satellite network over the Atlantic and Western Mediterranean Sea. Russia did not know what was happening, but followed suit very quickly with its Glonass satellites. The EU was much slower in its reaction as the Galileo network was not under a unified military command and control structure.

*

Steve moved quickly into the entrance of the tunnel, his desert boots crunching softly on the gravel surface. It appeared at first to be a cave, but after about thirty meters the downward sloping tunnel curved to his right. The residual daylight still reflected off the lightly coloured dry limestone rock wall. After another twenty meters his helmet had adjusted to the almost total darkness – the image intensifier had switched to IR. He held the pistol pointed at the ground a couple of meters ahead of him. As his other hand traced the roughly-hewn soft rock wall he could feel the claw marks left by the mechanical digger. The tunnel had been hewn in an arch shape and continued to slope down, straighter now and he reckoned it dropped at about one meter in twenty.

Every five meters or so he checked the walls and roof and he'd counted two hundred and sixty paces when the crunch under his feet stopped – he was on concrete. The GPS was useless here. By his fake Rolex watch it had taken him eight minutes and he'd had no reason over the last few days to doubt its accuracy. He kept close to the left hand side and noticed that the walls were now cement-lined. Then hands felt traces of mould and water, so he was now below the water table. He stumbled and bit his lip as his left ankle twisted in a water gutter at the side of the tunnel. He groaned – but thankfully it was not his weak ankle, the one that had failed him for SAS entry.

Slowly he became aware of light and of a humming sound. The image in his helmet visor was now of the tunnel clear in white LED light. Another fifty paces and he saw a steel door in the side of the tunnel. The decal on the door suggested danger of death – electrical. He crossed the tunnel and examined the door.

*

Much happened within that final critical period.

At the airport in Gran Canaria, the public announcement was read with the usual professional detachment:

'Due to operational restrictions, all flights are immediately grounded until further notice. Incoming flights are being diverted. We will provide further information when we receive it. In the meantime we advise passengers to contact their airline.'

In the departure lounge and check-in areas there was a loud and sustained groan followed by an excited chatter – this was simultaneous across all the airports in the Canary Islands.

At Las Palmas, Norwegian Air flight 1839 to Bergen was already rolling on full power and was told to abort take off. It was too late – they were past the V1 take-off velocity so a take-off abort was not an option. The take-off proceeded smoothly and they were instructed to 'go-around' after a short hold while a Ryanair flight on final approach landed.

The departure lounge at Las Palmas airport, Gran Canaria, looks out east across the main commercial runway. The Spanish Air Force Base, known as Gando, is clearly visible from the lounge, its runway beyond the commercial strip running in parallel and separated from the sea by the hangar area. The warplane hangars are clearly visible and as the passengers watched, a flight of four F/A-18 Hornets rolled out and started their taxi to the runway end.

Over the years many tourists have been entertained watching the F18s scream down the runway, their afterburners lit – night and day – for their exercises. Usually the take-off would be into the prevailing brisk north easterly breeze, with a sharp climbing turn to starboard over the peninsula of Punta de Gando. This day was, apparently, no different.

However, those few tourists with some knowledge of aviation matters who were watching from the windows of the departure lounge realised that this was more than a training exercise when the take-off angle approached 60 degrees and the afterburners stayed on through the climbing turn, their long tongues of flame burning prodigious amounts of fuel as the planes accelerated. Within minutes the watchers had located the air navigation warning on the web and put two and two together. The rumours spread quickly, morphing into hijack stories with terrorists involved.

In the cockpits of the F18s, the pilots were pumped up – the briefing had been, well, brief – 'Arm, fuel and get in the air'. It could hardly be called a 'scramble'. Weapons were in storage and no planes were held on armed standby. It took more than a precious thirty minutes to arm them with air to surface weapons. Mistakes were made and one plane took off with one of the weapons arming pins in place and one other failed its pre-flight check with a hydraulics fault.

As the three F18s of Raven flight made their turn the order came for them to head southwest at 1000 feet at full military power and then head 290 degrees for Punta Rasca at the southern end of La Palma some 60 miles further.

The sonic booms caused panic – and even one heart attack - on the beaches and golf courses at Maspalomas on the tip of

Gran Canaria as the F18s broke the sound barrier, holding at 1,000 feet.

The F18s were twenty miles out when target data came through, but there was still no order for weapons to go hot. The panic in the Spanish Ministry of Defence in Madrid was palpable. Although scenario plans were detailed and had been rehearsed following the Madrid metro bombings and the Rome incident, there was no scenario for such an incident as this. Satellite communications with the Spanish Prime Minister had broken down - he was on a flight to an EU meeting in Bratislava.

The final order to take offensive action and release weapons had to come from him or in extremis, his deputy, but the deputy PM was at a hotel with a lady – and could not be disturbed. Precious minutes were lost whilst his mistress untied him from the ornate brass bedstead. He threw on a bathrobe to hide his latex underwear and he then was finally able to answer the frantic knocking at the door by his aides.

Five thousand feet above the Raven flight of F18s, a Binter Canarias flight from Gran Canaria to La Palma was on final approach with flaps lowered and undercarriage down, about eight miles from the runway apron. It bucked as the rising sonic boom hit the aircraft. The passengers included a dozen or so tourists plus local business people and family visitors – thirty seven in total, plus three crew. The GPS system had failed, but the failure posed no danger at all. Then, a sécurité announcement was broadcast to all aircraft in the northwest Atlantic. Spanish air space around the western Canary Island group was closed - all incoming commercial flights were to divert to airports in mainland Spain.

"Control, Raven One. Target in sight ten miles, I repeat target in sight. Request authorise weapons tight."

"Raven One, Control. Negative weapons tight. No authorisation, repeat no authorisation. Weapons safe, acknowledge. Enter holding pattern angels one at five miles from target, loiter speed.'

"Control, Raven One. Roger Weapons safe. Reducing speed to loiter, angels one. Holding for weapons tight authorisation."

234

"One, Three. I have a problem – my HUD is reporting 'internal error', request RTB."

"Three, One. Copy that. RTB immediately."

The two remaining F18s screamed onward, with Antonio Mazar at the controls and Fernando Galves as his WSO – weapons systems officer. In Raven Two, Matias Garcia was backed up by his WSO, Diego Rodriguez.

*

They jumped in unison as the double bangs of the sonic boom reached them.

"What the hell was that?"

It was a rhetorical question. Peter didn't expect an answer from Tricia.

"I think that sound could have been a sonic boom. We used to hear them when we went to the Butlins holiday camp in Minehead when we were kids. Concorde used to fly down the Bristol Channel and go supersonic."

"You may be right. Look can you see those two planes out there?"

Tricia took the binoculars and fiddled with the focus after taking her sunglasses off.

Underground in the control centre in Sidi Bel Abbès, there was no panic.

"*Al-Mahdi*, the GPS signal on the ship has stopped. The autopilot has failed."

"Captain, what is going on, what do we do?"

"There is a navigational warning – here, look."

In the virtual reality bridge of the *Al-Rasul*, the captain pointed to the Navtex feed and they heard the transmission from Las Palmas port control.

"The dogs must suspect something, but how can that be?"

The AIS system on the electronic chart was also showing the navigational warning. "We need to go to the backup gyrocompass system. Wait – it looks as if that has failed too – it takes a correction signal from the GPS transmissions."

They watched as the captain's hand manipulated the autopilot controls in the virtual bridge, linked directly to the real ship via a high-bandwidth satellite link."

"Very, well, we will use the fluxgate compass input to the autopilot, and if that doesn't work I will steer the ship myself using the remote link. The only problem will be maintaining an accurate course as we have no position fixing system. I may miss the precise impact point."

"Is there nothing you can do?"

"Yes, I think there is. I can use the radar to get the exact range from the lighthouse at Punta de Lava, there – you see?"

Their eyes followed his hand as he pointed out of the virtual ridge window at the lighthouse seven miles away to the north.

"It may work. It is not possible to use all the old methods with this virtual bridge. We are at the required range from the lighthouse now. I have to steer the ship on an exact easterly course. There may be some current running down this side of the island."

"You must get it right."

"*Insha'Allah* I will do my best. It seems that the compass input to the autopilot is still working – that uses no outside signals. I will monitor the range with the radar."

On the chart plotter the captain/name aligned the electronic chart with the radar image. "There, I have put a marker on the radar image – we must hit that – it matches the impact point which you specified on the chart."

Ben-Zhair turned to Nassim Kateb.

"Will that target point work Nassim?"

"I am not a seaman, but it sounds logical – as long as the radar image is accurate."

"Can it be otherwise, Captain?"

"The image on the radar may be strongest from the high land behind the coast. There could be some difference. I am checking the water depths now, too, that will help."

"We have only a few minutes left to go."

"Jafa, is the weapon initiation proceeding as it should?"

Sharifi was not on the virtual bridge – he was in the weapon control room next door with the technicians.

"Yes, *Al-Mahdi*, all vital signs are as they should be."

"Control, Raven One. We see men on the deck of the target ship."

"Raven One, Control. Roger that. Continue to hold, we're receiving your images now. Weapons safe, repeat, weapon safe."

"Control, Raven One. Roger, weapons safe."

"Raven One, Control. Move into a loiter pattern over target at angels one."

"Control, Raven One. Roger that - holding pattern over target at angels one. Weeds three miles to the south."

The WSO looked at his targeting screen and confirmed that they could detect commercial traffic below 2,000 feet at 3 miles range. "Control, One. Roger weeds three miles south."

Raven flight moved in to circle their prey, with no authorisation to go weapons tight – the NATO brevity code for authorisation to fire at an identified hostile target.

As Maajid was climbing the ladder to the control cabin of Number One Derrick there was a monstrous rumble and he almost lost his footing as the ladder shook. It was the sound of the twenty huge generators starting up in the container stacks below him. Grimly he climbed upward and into the small control cabin.

He looked at the controls. As a junior officer he had learned the operating principles many years before, and nothing much had changed. The engine started immediately he turned the master switch and pushed the button.

Slowly he raised the derrick's jib out of its secure stowage chocks and swivelled it, gingerly lowering the main block to the first container. The chains were swinging wildly and the heavy pulley block hit one of the three technicians. The sickening, crushing thud was inaudible to him above the roar of the generators and he winced as the smashed body arced onto the side-deck. He held his breath as the other two managed to attach one of the chain hooks to the corner of a container before dancing away. This was not a job even for experienced seamen let alone nuclear technicians.

Underground at Sidi Bel Abbès, they heard the voice of Qasem Hamadani, Head of Security, from the room where Sharifi's team was monitoring the weapon's initiation sequence.

"There are men on deck it looks like Maajid and the technicians."

"They can do nothing" responded Jafa Sharifi. "The weapon is secure and the ship is locked down."

"Then why are they moving the derrick and attaching a chain to a container? Was the derrick not secured?"

"Yes of course it was."

"Then how can they move it?"

Captain Hindawi spoke. "The derricks – there are two as you can see – have donkey engines – that means that they can operate standalone."

"No-one told me!"

"By the beard of the Prophet, what can they do?" Ben-Zhair was shouting now."

"It is attached to one of the generator containers."

"Iqbal, launch the drones." Qasem Hamdani spoke with quite authority. Stop that crane and kill the men."

"*Aiwa* Qasem, drones away."

Hatches slid open on the roof of one of the cargo containers at the top of the stack above Hold 3. Two drones flew out, lifting and moving to the side deck of the ship and then tracking along its length, seeking the target.

"Qasem, drone one has infrared lock-on."

"Do it, but be careful not to damage the missile container."

Under the quadcopter military drone the small chain gun swivelled to follow the IR lock and started work on the remaining two technicians.

"Stop that derrick!"

Maajid moved to pull the 'Raise' lever with his right hand and then noticed the drone hovering alongside the ship, keeping pace at 16 knots. Then the two technicians collapsed as they reached the ladder, torn apart by the small calibre explosive shells from the drone.

Iqbal was shouting. "Qasem, it will not lock on through the glass cabin front."

"Fire it anyway."

The drone continued to hover and high above the deck Maajid watched in terrified fascination as the chain gun swung round in response to the command from Morocco. Then the glass in front of him shattered before his brain could register the flashes from beneath the drone.

In Sidi Bel Abbès they watched as Maajid slumped over the controls and the shattered glass showered the other bodies on the deck. The jib of the derrick continued to swing and snap tight against the hoisting chain attached to the container. Then it swung back as the ship gently rolled on its way to the target.

"Jafa!"

"All is well *Al-Mahdi*, all generators are operational and the capacitors are fully charged. We are cooling the lasers to operating temperature."

"*Al-Mahdi*, the tunnel entrance gate is opening."

"We are expecting no-one. Lock us down. Qasem – why was there no approach alarm?"

"We turned down the sensitivity as the wild dogs were setting it off at night."

"By the Beard of the Prophet, am I surrounded by idiots? This cannot be good!"

A disembodied voice came over the virtual bridge comms system as the lights flickered briefly. "Main power supply failure, standby backup generators operational."

"*Kha-ra!* Qasem, what defences do we have?"

Qasem paused. He had never heard ben-Zhair use such language.

"After the vehicle parking area there is a heavy blastproof steel door which leads to the elevators and stairwell."

"There is no other way in?"

"None, *Al-Mahdi*, other than the escape shaft into the University buildings. It is as you directed in your plan."

"By Allah, who are these people?"

Qasem spoke. "Let us look at the entrance camera footage."

"A camera? But it did not trigger an alarm. Why not Qasem? Where is the guard?"

"I do not know *Al-Mahdi*. Perhaps a fault in the circuit? Afwaz is not responding. He must be dead."

"By Allah, we have a dead guard, a working alarm which is turned down for dogs and a camera system which doesn't work at all. What in Heaven's name is going on?"

Koslov's words into his mike were in Russian but the Babelfish translation software announced them in Arabic over the Bluetooth bridge comms.

"*Al-Mahdi*, our radar is showing two aircraft circling the ship."

"Can we get them on a camera?"

Atop the antenna array on the highest part of the *Al-Rasul*, a camera pod swivelled and zoomed.

"What are they Yuri?"

"I think they are fighter aircraft, probably Spanish - F18s I think."

"They have only a few minutes before the detonation. Let us try out those very expensive Russian missiles we have on the ship and see how skilled you are."

He turned to the weapons console and nodded to Yuri Koslov.

A hatch in the shipping container atop Hold 5 on the *Al-Rasul* opened and a combined camera/radar antenna array slid smoothly upwards.

Babelfish broke the tension as it translated Koslov's words. "Point and shoot? We'll see." Koslov smiled grimly as his fingers danced over the control touchscreen. Koslov steered the camera onto one of the F18s three miles away and pressed 'Visual Lock' as it passed through the cross hairs. The guidance system's AI took over as he remotely armed the missiles in the shipping container. The six green arming lights turned to red on the touch screen in Sid Bel Abbès. "Ready, *Al-Mahdi*."

With a visual lock the F18 pilot would have no warning – it was a passive lock with the AI in the camera system directing the camera. The planes stayed below the mantle of cloud at the top of the island on the eastern perimeter of their hold pattern.

"Control, Raven One. We are picking up AA radar from the ship, no lock. Permission to go weapons tight."

"Raven One, Control. Negative weapons tight, acknowledge weapons safe."

"Control, Raven One. Roger weapons safe, standing by." The frustration was evident in his voice. They could not even use their weapons against a hostile target within the current ROE – rules of engagement.

"Raven One, Control. Incoming cruise missiles targeting the *Al-Rasul*, ETA ten minutes, acknowledge."

"Control, Raven One, roger that. Why can't we do the job?"

"Raven One, Control. Negative weapons tight, I say again, negative weapons tight. Acknowledge weapons safe."

"Control, Raven One. Mierde! Acknowledge weapons safe, standing by."

"Two, One. I have the IFF squawk from the cruise missiles. Tomahawks."

"Roger that One. At least something is working today. I also have it now. But who has sent them?"

The question floated. On the display in front of the WSOs, the 'interrogate friend or foe' light had come on identifying two radar targets on the targeting screen still 20 miles away running at 550 mph.

Then the others started to appear in line.

Steve opened his tool bag and fitted the compact hydraulic jack behind the padlock. It was a well-made 4 inch padlock, top of the range, six lever case hardened, and when he pumped the small handle the lock held firm. One more pump and the lock was undamaged but there was a metallic tearing sound as the weld of the hasp tore away from the steel doorframe. He waited and listened. There was no sound. He set to work on the second similar lock. This time the lock came apart and he pushed the door open.

He checked the room quickly then found a light switch, closing the door behind him. The wall facing him was covered with electrical switchgear. There were four heavy cables coming in – probably the feed from the university, he thought. The memory flashed - three Phase power – his Dad had taught him about that on his trawler. Steve cut the locks on the main switches and heaved the levers to Off. The lights flickered and came on again, along with a rumble. Steve cursed - standby generators, but he could see no other doors or switchgear.

Frustrated, he checked the walls – there was no sign of a fire alarm. That would have been too easy. He moved back out into the tunnel and keeping to the left hand side – with his good ankle next to the gutter – he eased forward towards the source of the light.

He counted another seventy five paces to where the tunnel opened into a parking area lit by fluorescent lights. There were several pick-up trucks, one minibus and two SUVs seemingly parked at random. Although he'd picked up some Arabic in the Yemen, he didn't waste time trying to decipher the legend on the minibus – there was a yellow silhouette of what appeared to be a mountain lion and beneath it some Arabic script and the words 'Université d'Oran. So, maybe twenty people or even more he thought, noticing three battered motor cycles. It would take too long to disable them all, so he moved on towards the far end where he could see a stainless steel elevator door. He stopped. Mountain lion? Christ, Ellie was out there and wounded. Couldn't lions smell blood? He checked his phone – no signal.

"Ellie can you hear me?" he whispered into his headset. No reply. He cursed Briggs and his boosted Bluetooth, knowing that was unfair.

The door seemed big enough to take a truck. He could not see any guards or other people as he sprinted down and examined the door. Then he saw a carefully concealed man-sized door in the corner near the elevator shaft. A fire escape? There were no handles, but there was a keypad. Like the elevator door it was very heavily engineered and looked to be blastproof. He clamped his smartphone to the electronic switchpad. The screen of his smartphone lit up as it clamped itself on. He cursed as he read the screen.

Unable to establish link with server

Steve didn't know how far underground he was, but estimated at least sixty meters allowing for the tunnel incline and the hill above. No way would a phone signal penetrate that. He put his hands on the door and leaned forward, pressing his head against the relatively cold stainless steel, trying to think of a way around the problem. Ellie had suggested an air shaft. He hadn't noticed any fans on the way down the tunnel – there must be a way of changing the air given that there were so many vehicles down here. Even terrorists had to breathe clean air. He sniffed - yes, it was clean although there was a slight tinge of two stroke fuel in it and a hint of diesel near the elevator.

He took out a cigarette lighter from the tool kit and flicking it on he could just see that there was movement of air inward from the tunnel. He looked around for the extractor vents and found them high in the corners near the elevator shaft. Then he noticed the tiny cameras in the corners – about ten feet above the ground. He pursed his lips as he thought about the likely number of people and his limited ammunition – and limited options.

From the container above Hold 4 on the *Al-Rasul*, the antenna array relayed a signal through a Russian satellite and an alarm sounded in an army command centre in the Russian controlled Ukraine. An anti-aircraft missile was hot. The control screen zoomed in on the coordinates on a map as a panicked Russian weapons controller ran into the room, dropping his mug of vodka-laced tea.

Andrei Nabukhov stared in disbelief at the screen. He had never heard of the Canary Islands but now his geography lesson had started. He touched the icon of an old red telephone handset on his screen as other members of his battery responded to the alarm on his screen and spoke into his headset.

"Yes Commander, a *Novyy Rassvet* is hot." A pause. "No, not in the Ukraine – it appears to be in the sea near some islands – wait – yes – in the Atlantic Ocean." A longer pause as the commander unloaded a string of expletives. The operator knew the phrase well, but never before had a commander told him to go fuck his grandmother.

He stuttered. "Y...Y...Yes, Sir, I am just checking. The serial number matches one of the missing pod of six." Another pause.

"Yes Sir, doing it now. It has now launched." He cursed again then after selecting the missile ID from the list he pushed the interlock icon with his left hand and the self-destruct icon with his right index finger.

"No response, Sir. It is not acknowledging the self-destruct command. Perhaps it is out of range? ... the range indicator does not go beyond 99 kilometers. Sorry Sir, I do not know whether it uses a satellite link or direct link. Yuri Koslov was the senior technician – he would know."

Igor Vasiliev, the missile battery commander was halfway through a lunch of zakuski – and half way through a bottle of vodka. He started to choke at the mention of the name Koslov. The previous unit commander responsible for the missing missile pod had been shot. There were plenty of rumours about the ultimate destination of what was said to be US$20 million but none had come his way and he was still drinking the cheapest vodka. He kicked his chair over as he headed for the control room.

Although Vasiliev didn't know it, Yuri Koslov - one of Nabukhov's former missile control comrades - was sitting in a leather-padded chair at an anti-aircraft missile control console, underground in Sidi Bel Abbès with Alexei Stepanov his former army colleague and lover alongside, watching.

Their journey with the missiles had started in the Crimea and taken them overland to Burgas in Bulgaria where they had boarded the ship which had delivered them to the *Yanbu Explorer* off Libya. Their bank accounts healthy - $500,000 could buy a lot of vodka.

Tricia adjusted the binoculars again.

"I can see men on the deck. There seems to be something flying around the ship. It looks like a helicopter but it's very small. Wait, I can see another. The ship doesn't seem to be slowing. There is a crane moving."

"Give me those binoculars."

"Here, I'm going to see if I can stream this onto Periscope. Oh dear, I forgot – there's no signal. I can still video it though."

Then they heard a stuttering sound and the crane swung lazily as the ship rolled.

"That sounded like gunfire."

"It must have been – I can see two men lying on the deck."

"Maybe the ship is out of control?"

"It still doesn't seem to be slowing. There are boxes on the deck."

"Those are shipping containers."

Peter Gillespie shook his head, wondering about the very different world his wife seemingly lived in.

Then there was a flash and burn as a missile left the ship and turned with a lengthening trail of white smoke, turning to acquire its target, heading for one of the F18s. Seconds later they heard the roar of its launch.

Tricia dropped the smartphone in surprise.

"Raven One, Two. Missile launch, repeat missile launch from ship. Countermeasures."

"Two, One. I have no lock warning."

"One, it's coming our way, roger no lock repeat no lock."

The F18s released chaff and flares as they moved away from each other, but their radar spoofers could not find a signal to spoof.

"Control, Raven One, SAM missile launch from ship, no lock, urgent request weapons tight and release authorisation."

"Raven One, negative weapons tight, stand by for further orders."

"Two, One. IR lock repeat IR lock, releasing countermeasures, starting evasive manoeuvres."

"Break left, break left!"

The shout came from Fernando Galves, Raven One's WSO – weapons systems officer.

"One, Two, de-louse me."

The pilot, Antonio Mazar, immediately rolled the F18 to port and pulled back sharply on the stick, stressing their bodies to 10G as they flight suits fought to prevent their blood draining to their lower bodies.

The WSO blacked out and did not regain consciousness.

"Two, One, commencing de-louse."

"What should we do?"

"Call the police I think."

"What's the number?"

"It's in the Rough Guide – here."

"Shit, there's no signal."

The Gillespies watched, speechless, as an F18 screamed close overhead under full emergency power, parallel to the southerly ridge of Cumbre Vieja at the innermost point of its holding circle. It was barely two hundred feet above their heads and well below the 6,400 feet of Cumbre Vieja itself. It turned sharply as the missile continued to close. Then the smart proximity fuse in the missile's warhead detonated. White hot titanium metal shards lacerated the F18's airframe, shredding the fly-by-wire harnesses and slicing through a ceramic-armoured fuel line. The JP54 fuel ignited and the critically damaged and burning F18 tore apart and started spiralling down into the banana plantation below. The momentum of the engines carried them in a parabolic arc offshore and into the sea. There was no sign of the pilot and navigator.

Their teeth rattled again as the second F18 screamed over them.

"Raven One, Control."

"Control, Raven Two. Raven One is down. SAM missile, no chutes. Repeat Raven One down, no chutes. Am hot–tailing out, awaiting weapons free authorisation."

Babelfish spoke. "*Al-Mahdi*, we have a kill."

There was a cheer in the bunker at Sidi Bel Abbès.

"Then let us have another, Koslov."

"Unfortunately it seems that the other coward has turned away, our weapon will not accept a visual lock. Wait, 'Radar lock possible, confirm active targeting.'"

"What are your orders *Al-Mahdi*?"

"What difference will it make?" Ben-Zhair nodded at the clock as a disembodied voice started a countdown, the ship driving forward towards Nassim Kateb's designated rocky outcrop within fifty meters of the shoreline.

They smiled – one of the technical team had recorded Donald Trump's voice print and it was being used for the final countdown. "Twenty seconds and counting." Ben-Zhair nodded. "For once the dog is telling the truth."

In the cockpit of Raven Two, Matias Garcia's heart rate jumped to almost 190 bpm. He had heard the squawk just as his WSO, Diego Rodriguez shouted. "Radar lock!"

"Control, Raven Two, we have radar lock."

"Raven Two, Control, weapons free authorised. Destroy the target."

The WSO completed the weapons selection and arming. The weapons console acknowledged the lock onto the radar signal from the ship.

"Matias, Rifle selected."

"Diego, Release weapon, countermeasures!"

"Rifle away!"

The AGM-88J AARGM home-on-jam anti-radar missile dropped from its pylon and screamed away from Raven Two, turning sharply onto the radar signal from the container above Hold 4 on the *Al-Rasul* and accelerating through the sound barrier to Mach 1.3. Simultaneously, the second *Novyy Rassvet* ('New Dawn') missile emerged from the container on the ship, turning and acquiring the extremely weak but sufficient radar signature bouncing back off Raven Two, along with radar jamming signals which its signal processing circuits filtered out. The electronics technology battle was underway.

In Raven Two, Matias rolled sharply away from the ship and pulled hard on the stick, climbing almost vertically at full emergency power. The G force was intolerable and both aircrew blacked out momentarily despite their pressure suits. Could they outrun the latest Russian missile technology?

The question was moot.

The airborne missiles passed one another at almost three times the speed of sound. Raven Two was now at 8,000 feet and travelling at almost 600 knots. The *Novyy Rassvet* missile turned into a smooth climb literally hot on the tail of Raven Two.

"*Al-Mahdi*, we have a missile launch from the F18 and two incoming targets which are identified as Tomahawk IV's. Wait, there are more – five echelons of two Tomahawk missiles, seven minutes from the ship."

"Koslov, you and Stepanov have full control of the anti-aircraft missiles – do as you have been trained. It is too late for them."

*

"I think it's going to hit." The fear in Tricia's voice was clear as she spoke the words slowly and distinctly. She was looking at the ship, whilst Peter's eyes were drawn to the missiles in flight – each heading in opposite directions and about to pass each other.

She watched in awe as the ship quickly slowed, skewing, as more than fifty thousand tons of steel met the rock and sand less than forty feet below. It drove onwards, its outer bottom hull ripping and filling with water, then the inner skin was tearing as the ship slowed. Inside, the rigidly built containment structure remained intact, the generators continued to run and the vacuum tubes remained solid. The decks and cargo stacks held firm – insurers mandated that such ships were designed to cope with such accidents.

Fifty meters outside Spanish airspace the first two cruise missiles self-destructed.

"What was that?"

Peter peered through the binoculars at two small clouds to the east. "It sounded like explosions. Far away, though."

They didn't see the others.

Peter held the binoculars. "It's stopped! It's only about fifty meters offshore. Maybe it's hit a rock or run into the shallows?"

From the Gillespies' vantage point the bow of the ship was clearly visible over the cliff edge and its thick cover of a banana plantation. They didn't know that the ship was hung up on an outcrop of harder igneous rock. This outcrop had been selected two years previously by Nassim Kateb to act as the initial conduit of the explosive shock wave. He planned that it would conduct the power of the weapon through a hard stratum into the softer rock which underlay this part of the island – at least before it all melted and turned into atoms and glass.

In Sidi bel Abbès, the voice of Jafa Sharifi was heard on the virtual bridge of the ship.

"All parameters are within limits – laser temperature, power bank levels, mirror alignment. Fuel pellet parameters are perfect!

Above it all, Trump's cloned voice droned on. "Counting down five seconds, four, three, two, one, trigger release. I love you all!"

Then the ship disappeared, as did the sea around it.

Less than a thousandth of a second later, the Gillespies' eyeballs exploded, their hair flashed into flames, clothes and skin incinerated, their bodies reduced to atoms, blasted up and over the instantly molten lava as the ridge of Cumbre Vieja took the full air and radiation blast of the nuclear explosion.

Raven Two and the missiles were instantly torn apart and reduced to atoms.

The nuclear blast wave punched along the edge of the island where the banana plantations had been an instant before. The town of Puerto Naos flashed aflame in the burst of radiation and was then flattened as the supersonic blast wave hit. The lighthouse disappeared. Lava, which last flowed in 1949, began to flow again, reheated by the huge energy of the sixty kiloton fusion detonation – and newly unleashed subterranean forces.

Four thousand feet up on the side of Cumbre Vieja, a small party of tourists was just reassembling at their tour bus after a walk across the lava fields – a bizarre moonscape dotted with pines and shrubs. The tour party was out of direct line of sight of the detonation but felt the ground tremble as the compression and shear waves travelling at more than a mile a second passed them, disturbing the sides of the volcano and shaking the island to its core. Two of them looked up at the sky which seemed to glow strangely despite the bright late afternoon light. Then the noise hit them – the so-called 'overpressure', hurting their eardrums which would surely have burst if they had been in direct line of sight of detonation.

They looked up in panic and following their instincts, they turned to scramble on to the minibus.

Within seconds the wind began to blow down the mountain as air was pulled in to feed the rising cloud which was just beginning to ascend from 'surface zero' – the point of explosion within the ship, just below sea level. The wind increased to a howl through the Canarian pine trees, raising a storm of black volcanic dust. The cinders rattled against the bus as it moved back on to the tarmac, the driver heading down the twisting road as the ground shook again.

Then, the white line on the road seemed to waver before his eyes and the bus started to snake. There were screams from the passengers as the driver struggled with the steering wheel.

"Madre de Dios!" the driver screamed as the asphalt slid sideways, taking the bus with it. The trees followed, along with a lava outcrop. Then, with an unnatural cacophony of sound, the island split along a curving arc from the southernmost tip along its spine and then west to a point just north of the already ruined and burning Puerto Naos.

Thirty cubic kilometers of the island were on the move, sliding down towards the Atlantic Ocean along with Nassim Kateb's network of sensors, people, cars, forests and houses.

The slide gathered pace and then the mountainside itself broke away, splitting along the 1949 fault line. The bus rolled and was overwhelmed by rock and ash as the slide gathered pace. The bus was four thousand feet above sea level – and going down fast, the passengers flattened under millions of tons of rock, with more than three hundred other vehicles, many falling off the high road and tumbling down into the rising mushroom and ash cloud. Hire cars, delivery trucks, a petrol tanker, family SUVs – the mountain was merciless as it slid inexorably, quickly gathering speed, into the Atlantic Ocean.

The movement of the earth was felt across the Canary Islands by the locals and the tourists, and by seismometers around the world. Even as it was happening alarms were being sounded in automated reaction to the initial wave pattern of a nuclear explosion. This was soon followed by the seismic wave pattern of the massive landslide.

The village of Las Indias was on the move. The spine of the island ridge split from halfway along the island to the very southern tip. The high villages of Fuencaliente and Los Canarios were on the westward, seaward side – and starting to move. Schools, shops, homes and cafés, restaurants and roads were all on the downward move.

Seconds after the nuclear explosion had created its own set of waves, the gigantic block of La Palma had started to slide down towards the Atlantic Ocean.

To the southern end of La Palma, north of Punta Fuencaliente, lay the monogenetic cinder cone of Teneguia, which had last seen action in 1971. It was a dormant volcano and scientists considered it unlikely to become active again.

But now it was awakening.

The top of the cone slid down towards the sea accelerating to almost 100 meters per second. Along with the cone slid the spine and the winery known as Bodega Teneguia. The volcanic vent underneath was uncovered just enough to allow the headless cone to spew. The outpouring of lava was irrelevant as there was nothing left to damage. The wines of Bodega Teneguia that were in shippers' stores, distribution depots and shops would appreciate in value over the years to come. Although they were very ordinary wines and did not keep well, they were unique, they were the last, there would be no more artisan wines from La Bodega Teneguia.

*

"You have an update, Sir William?"

Without preamble, 'C' launched into the update. "Our analysts have come up with a very grave scenario which might result from this attack. The PM has authorised me to inform you that the ship – the *Al-Rasul* - is believed to have a nuclear weapon aboard, similar to that used in the Rome attack. Our analysts believe that the ship is targeting a geological weakness in the island's structure. This could trigger a large landslip leading to a tsunami – and we all know what that means. The tsunami could threaten the coasts of the UK, Western Europe the Caribbean Islands and the US East Coast. There is a lot of data and analysis available – even a BBC documentary. I am sending through the papers and links now."

'C' looked around the table. Everyone was stunned.

"Prime Minister, Jonathan Tweedy, Director of the Atomic Weapons Establishment at Aldermaston is online to give us an update on the likely effects."

All eyes watched as Tweedy came on screen – his face and bluff northern voice had become all too familiar to them during events leading up to the Rome catastrophe.

"Prime Minister, All. I'll be brief. Near-surface nuclear weapons explosions have been studied at length. At the Baker test at Bikini Atoll way back in 1946, a twenty kilotons device at a depth of about sixty meters generated a series of surface waves which rolled outwards from the lagoon. The first wave was about thirty meters high at a distance of three hundred meters from the device location. However – and I stress this – these waves were fundamentally different to normal sea waves – including tsunamis. I would not see these specific waves as a threat, especially as the weapon is likely to be near or on the surface. I would add that we have only just started studying the Ward & Day material that Sir William has provided. It suggests that a major landslip at the island of La Palma could trigger a significant tsunami which could seriously threaten the UK, Europe, the Unites States and the Caribbean Islands. It could even cause widespread damage in Brazil. My initial view – and I am not a geologist – is that this is scientifically credible. Thank you, Prime Minister."

"Thank you, Jonathan." 'C' turned to the Prime Minister. "For information, Ward and Day are the authors of the original research paper on which this threat is based. We are attempting to co-opt the Executive Director of the National Oceanography Centre as I speak."

There had been panic in the National Oceanography Centre in Southampton as the PA tried to locate Professor Angela Somersby in response to a call from the Prime Minister's Office. Somersby closed her office door and opened her browser, astonished to be straight into the session – secure GCHQ communications software had wormed in and installed itself minutes before.

"Ah, good. I have Professor Somersby online now. Prime Minister."

The Cobra screen flashed.

You are alone Professor?"

"As requested."

"Good. Professor Somersby, this is the Cabinet Secretary speaking. You are online to a COBRA meeting chaired by the Prime Minister. Be aware that you are subject to the Official Secrets Act."

Somersby was breathless. "With respect, I signed that years ago."

The Prime Minister nodded to her Chief Scientific Advisor.

Somersby's black screen now changed from the text 'COBRA TOP SECRET to the live image of the Government's Chief Scientific Advisor. They knew each other well from many meetings on Climate Change policy.

"Professor Somersby, this is John Hopstead."

"Hello John."

"This is urgent and we've no time for niceties. Are you aware of a paper by Ward and Day relating to a possible tsunami originating at the island of La Palma?"

Somersby was silent for a few seconds as she mentally scanned years of scientific papers.

"Of course. It's an old paper and speculative in the extreme. Mostly discredited. They were trying to drum up research funding."

"Could a tsunami be triggered by a nuclear explosion on the island?"

The face on screen blanched visibly.

"Good God! Er…I don't know. I would need more information to make a judgement. Possibly, yes. It depends on the magnitude of the explosion and where it took place."

"Let us suppose that the worst happened and side of the island collapsed as they postulated. What is your opinion of the likely effects?"

"Ward and Day were geologists, not oceanographers, as far as I recall. Their wave modelling was very basic – we know a lot more now about tsunami propagation. However, I couldn't exclude the possibility of the most dire effects." 'Never say never' was always a good policy for a senior academic administrator and politicians.

"Professor Somersby, this is the Prime Minister. Please stay online and review the information we are sending you. We may have less than an hour before a tsunami might be triggered."

The PM turned to the Cabinet Secretary. "Sir John, send these papers through to the Spanish PM immediately. Make sure that there is no mention of any nuclear device.

There were a few sage nods around the table. This action could serve well in future discussions with Spain. Help was offered…and rejected. That would play well in the media…

Way back in 2001, two scientists - the geophysicists Steven Ward and Simon Day - had released a paper about the geology of the island of La Palma. The paper caused great controversy and led to a BBC documentary programme and newspaper headlines screaming 'Catastrophe'. Their work on the subject continued for several years, as did the arguments.

In the event, scientific consensus emerged that the event had a probability of 'once in ten thousand years.' That is not negligible and is the same as the earth being hit by a 100 meter diameter asteroid – which would cause significant devastation. Being struck by lightning is a 'one in a million chance'. Such odds should not be ignored, but frequently were and 310 people are killed each year by lightning in the U.S.A.

*

Less than two minutes after the explosion the island block settled on the 2,000 meter deep ocean bottom, the sea rushing in to fill the big hole the block had created in the surface as it sank. Just like dropping a brick into a bathtub, the initial wave built and rolled away as the block of island displaced the water. Then the sea rushed back in to cover the block. A dome of water grew and reached 700 meters in height within seconds – rather less than Ward and Day had predicted. No matter, this dome of water was the weapon that Nassim Kateb had proposed to ben-Zhair three years previously in Rabat:

"No-one has yet triggered a volcano, and perhaps we do not even need to do that, given enough power to disturb the rock of Cumbre Vieja and split the mountain along the 1949 rift line. And I think I now know the exact place to trigger that disturbance. Then, Allah will do the rest and we can send a tsunami to destroy half of the USA's economy, and who knows what else besides?

All we need is the trigger."

A lot had happened in the last three years, but the Cause of All Causes was beyond the imagination of most people.

The wavetrain was on its way. The peak height of the wave in the deep open ocean was little more than a meter, but with a wavelength of more than forty miles and a speed of well over four hundred miles an hour in the deep ocean, the energy contained in the wavepacket was huge.

Wave theory indicated that when the wave reached shallow water it would slow - and increase in height, dramatically, dangerously, unstoppably and fatally so, perhaps as high as 25 meters. Most people have seen videos of the 2004 Phuket and 2013 Japanese tsunamis. The magnifying effect of shallow water and the slow, inexorable creep of the water is truly terrifying – and unstoppable.

*

In the underground bunker at Sidi bel Abbès the ICIM team looked out through the virtual windows of the bridge of the ship, the images of those generated by the computer – there was no longer a bridge camera feed, no longer a ship on the wallscreen. There was a cheer as the local seismometer display panel showed the shock wave traces of the explosion. They had watched as Jafa brought the video feed up, replacing the view of the ship's bridge windows with a spectacular vista southwards across the island.

Hidden in rocky outcrops almost 7,000 feet above sea level at Los Muchachos, were two cameras. This high, northerly part of the island of La Palma is devoted to space research, with many astronomical observatories run by an international community of physicists. Jafa's concealed cameras were remotely controlled and now the cameras' irises re-opened after being automatically shut for the instant of the explosion lest the energy pulse would fry the delicate optical chips at their core, The real time video was transmitted up to the hijacked North Korean Kwangmyŏngsŏng-7 satellite and down to the antennae above the bunker. The scene was breath-taking and they watched in silent awe on the wallscreen as the disaster developed.

After the instant of the detonation a huge gas bubble had generated a shock wave which was followed by the formation of a spherical cloud. A chimney of water and seabed rock punched through the top of the cloud reaching almost to five thousand feet in height. Even the rising cloud could not obscure the full awe of the scene from the cameras as the southern half of the island started to slide with gathering speed into the sea.

Military monitoring satellites had observed the double flash and triggered alarms even before the seismic waves had been recorded. High power cameras had zoomed in from space in response to the feed of coordinates. When it comes to nuclear tests and explosions, no area of the world – even the Canary Islands – is unmonitored.

In 1979, the so-called Vela incident led the US to believe that a joint Israeli-South African nuclear weapons test had taken place in the South Atlantic. A US satellite had recorded the tell-tale double flash near the Prince Edward Islands off Antarctica. That nuclear test is still unverified – as far as the public knows. Since then, there are no areas of the earth's surface that are not monitored in such a way.

Nassim Kateb had read and studied the original 2001 paper by Ward and Day, he had seen the BBC documentary and other programs on YouTube and he had studied the full scientific debate. Over several years he carried out his own university research in La Palma and contributed his own findings to the debate with several published papers. The seed germinated and he eventually put the idea to ben-Zhair.

Kateb had also picked the target spot for the *Al-Rasul*. The ship had missed his exact target coordinates by less than a hundred meters, but that was of no consequence. It was close enough.

In their controversial paper, Ward and Day had predicted that between 150 and 500 cubic kilometers of rock (30-100 cubic miles) could slide into the Atlantic – that is about half the size of Long Island.

Within two minutes, the initial result of the collapse would be a dome of water half a mile high which would then generate a wavetrain – a tsunami - as it collapsed. This would be a classic tsunami scenario - in fact a megatsunami. That word was not an invention of Ward & Day.

They used accepted ocean wave theories to model the tsunami, and the results were frightening: coastal inundation from South America, through the Caribbean and up Florida and the East Coast of the USA. The United Kingdom too was threatened by significant inundation.

Since then, many people have seen the film of the effects of major tsunamis in Thailand and Japan, and they know that these events can be catastrophic. Predicting when a volcano will erupt or an earthquake will occur is a very inexact science. But triggering one is less so. Fracking (the extraction of gas from shale) is now an established technique, but during development of the process earth tremors were often a side-effect. It can be done.

For La Palma, the probability of a major landslide caused by a volcanic eruption along the rift of Cumbre Vieja was generally agreed to be once in ten thousand years. A natural event. But this was unnatural.

*

"Look, *Al-Mahdi*. It is the camera next to the main elevator shaft."

As they looked at one of the twelve camera images on the split screen, Baldwin shot out the camera dome. The image of his helmeted head disappeared.

"Who is that dog Qasem? How many are there?"

Qasem shouted orders. "Iqbal, Hossein – get down there now – and take two others with you."

Then another camera image disappeared.

"I think he is alone, *Al-Mahdi*."

"Let us hope so."

Steve rolled some C4 into a strip and pressed it down one side of the fire escape door, then attached a detonator and returned to the air grilles. The ventilation grilles were near the rock roof – ten feet up at least. He ran his fingers over the rock – soft limestone. Then, as he hammered a couple of pitons into the rock, the elevator began to rumble. Hanging single handed from the top piton he hooked the small grapnel onto the grille and let go with his other hand. He dropped until his right foot in the loop of the line went taught and the grille tore away from its fastenings and he landed awkwardly. He groaned - why did it always have to be on his weak ankle? He primed the detonator on the fire escape door for ten seconds and ran to the air duct.

Two seconds later and a smoke grenade was in the duct – and then the elevator doors started to open. With his back against the wall he pulled the pin on the second smoke grenade and held it trigger-ready – just as a sand coloured Humvee drove out of the elevator. Three men in the rear began firing out through the windows – and even the driver had a machine pistol in one hand out his window laying down short bursts at random. The other duct would have to wait. Steve fell to the floor and rolled towards the Humvee to get below the firing line and away from the blast. As a shell plucked at his trouser leg his smoke grenade arced in through a window of the Humvee. The Humvee slowed, wobbled and then stopped, the doors opening and the confused guards tumbling out beneath the orange cloud. Two, one...the C4 detonated ten meters away.

It had been simple and was over in less than ten seconds, despite the surprise of the Humvee. Steve checked the bodies, giving the *coupe de grace* to two of them. He shouldered one of the hot Uzis, fitting a fresh magazine and bagging another. He checked the picture on his phone against the dead faces - no match - then moved in to the elevator, cursing at the mix of weapons he carried.

The elevator was large enough to carry at least two Humvees – even a truck. Steve shot out the camera in the corner of the elevator car. The ceiling of the elevator was about ten feet up – unlike the films, it was not an option. He ran back out and cleared the bodies, then backed the Humvee into the shaft.

Now, which button to press?

The top button showed an image of a bed, below it another depicted a knife and fork. Another button depicted the shape of a ship, and the fourth a microwave antenna. He opted for the ship and hit the button for the floor above. Climbing back into the driver's seat of the Humvee he thought 'what's sauce for the goose is sauce for the gander'.

He cocked the warm Uzi and held it in his left hand outside the driver's window as the heavy elevator rumbled into motion.

 "They are returning, *Al-Mahdi*."

"Are you sure it is them Qasem? Where is the camera in the elevator."

"I think it is not working."

"Or he has destroyed it. Go, take the *jihadis,* their work is done here."

"Jafa, Hindawi and the rest of you, go with Qasem."

"But *Al-Mahdi*, I am not a soldier."

"Go Jafa, we are all soldiers for Allah. You are all trained *jihadis.*"

Qasem nodded – he had supervised their training himself, the previous year near Tabessa in eastern Algeria. He looked at Jafa. Despite his huge intellect and scientific skill with nuclear weapons technology, Jafa Sharifi was at heart a coward and had not performed well in training. When it came to combat he would be a liability and ben-Zhair had made his views plain to Qasem back on the ship, off Gibraltar.

"*Al-Mahdi*, I must protest. Suppose I am killed? Who will manage the nuclear technology?"

"There is no more nuclear technology – with Allah's help you have successfully deployed it all today against the infidels. Your technical team was on the ship with it. We now move to a new phase."

Ben-Zhair raised his pistol and at five feet there was no missing. One shot was sufficient. Qasem was disappointed – he had known that Jafa's shelf life was limited and had looked forward to doing the job himself.

Captain Hindawi and the others moved quickly to Qasem's side and took the weapons he passed out from the wallrack. He wiped a splash of blood off his arm as ben-Zhair spoke.

"Qasem – you know the evacuation plan. Capture that dog in the car park or elevator, wherever he is and then find out what he knows and if there are others. Then get Jamal and the other jihadis out. This bunker is obviously known – there will surely be others after him."

Qasem took two MP5s machine pistols off the wallrack for himself and led the team through out into the corridor.

With increasing alarm Koslov and Stepanov had been watching the scene play out from the missile console. They knew they were not considered to be *jihadis*, but infidels to be tolerated. Ben-Zhair grasped an MP5 for himself and after checking it turned to them. "You men did well – for Russians." The MP5 was steady as ben-Zhair's burst paid them off. He turned to Nassim Kateb, the weapon at his side pointing downwards.

"Nassim, your idea deserves full credit. With Allah's help we have brought it to life today. There has been nothing like it in the history of Islam, and even before that. You do know that you cannot go back to your post in Rabat?"

"Yes, of course, *Al-Mahdi*, and I am ready to serve Allah and the great cause in whatever way I can."

"That is a problem Nassim, and I have wondered what to do, what place you might have in the Caliphate. You can still serve the Caliphate. Come with me."

Steve did not know what to expect as he revved the engine of the Humvee. The two ton elevator door slid smoothly aside on well-oiled rails revealing a brightly lit dispersal area large enough to turn a truck in. His brain barely took in the stillages of equipment, food and plastic water tanks he floored the accelerator and drove straight at the four men about forty meters away running towards the elevator. He saw them split into two pairs and move to cover as they began firing.

No-one had shown them how to use a machine pistol properly. Their initial long bursts went high with the kick and a lucky couple hit the armoured windshield. With a very steady arm outside the window Steve let loose with three-shot bursts, the Uzi purring like a well-oiled sewing machine. He took out the two jihadis on the driver's side as he slewed the Humvee to the right and smashed into a pallet of electrical equipment.

Under the driving momentum of the two ton Humvee the pallet slid and crushed the other two men against another stillage. Steve threw the Humvee into reverse and accelerated hard, but there were no more shots coming his way. He opened the door and dived behind a pallet with a thousand litre water tank on it and then cautiously moved forward to clear the area. One man was dead with a chest wound, another cringing with a leg wound. Steve shot him as the *jihadi* raised his weapon.

The other two were crushed. He checked the picture on his phone and confirmed that none of them looked remotely like ben-Zhair. Steve jogged forward to the door at the end of the dispersal area. Then he paused and remembered Ellie. He called through his headset. No reply. He quickly texted 'All ok beware mountain lions x' on his phone and hoped it would go through when phone found a signal.

Qasem Hamadani was courageous but he was no fool and was sure that ben-Zhair had his own plan for escape - there were areas of the bunker to which even Qasem had no access. After dispatching Hindawi and the others to the dispersal area at the elevator, he headed down the stairs to the Electronics floor, only to find a corridor filled with Jamal's team choking on orange smoke. He led them down the stairs to the car park, through the door that Steve had been blown open. They ran to the University minibus.

"Jamal, you drive. You know where to go and what to do." Captain Hindawi climbed into the passenger seat while the other *jihadi* engineers and technicians occupied rear seats. The others piled into the Toyota trucks. Qasem mounted one of the motorcycles and followed the minibus and convoy up the tunnel.

Ben-Zhair moved to the end of the room which had served as the virtual bridge of the *Al-Rasul* and activated the keypad opening the door to a small stairwell, just a meter square.

"Nassim - wait for me in the stairwell – I will only be a few minutes."

Then, ben-Zhair took out his smartphone and checked the relay signal and encryption indicators. He speed-dialled 3.

It was late evening in the house outside Jakarta but the call was answered almost immediately.

"I was waiting for your call *Al-Mahdi*, as requested."

"I am just sending you another Announcement for release. It is truly an earth shattering event and with Allah's help we have succeeded. This Announcement is to be sent out immediately in the usual way through all the media channels we use. It is not to be called 'Announcement', but 'Message' – *al-Risala*." There is also a video feed. It is at the usual url. Publish the feed at the same time.

"It shall be done now *Al-Mahdi*."

"We will speak again soon."

"May Allah be with you."

The line dropped and Safi Hatta, the Head of Media for ICIM, retrieved the encrypted text of the Announcement. Ben-Zhair's obsession with security meant that this was the first Safi had heard of the plan in detail. He had managed all the previous Announcements, each one escalating the cause, the content available only at the last moment. He sat down on the rattan mat floor as read the details.

"By all that is Holy!"

After reading it again he scrambled to his desk and looked at the video feed, smiling with joy at the wonderful events. He immediately published the video link through an anonymiser. Then, he called his assistant to check the satellite antennae alignments and the fibre cable tapped into the main telecoms trunk which ran outside, accessed via a tunnel he had built from under his sleeping room.

Steve could smell the cordite before he reached the Bridge room and peered in cautiously through the open doorway. He could see a range of controls, displays and wall screens, with one dead man in the central area staring back at him and two more draped over chairs at a console. Now he could smell burning electronics.

'Bugger me' he thought in awe, recognising the layout of a ship's bridge and the familiar controls he had learned as part of the Royal Marines ship anti-hijack training. He was looking in from one of the bridge wing doors, but the forward view was the imagery being piped from the cameras at Los Muchachos. The image was of clouds of dust and smoke, and at the epicentre the spherical cloud was condensing into heavy rain. It was entrancing but a movement caught his eye and he saw a man at the other open bridge wing door forty feet away, apparently using his phone. Steve swung his Uzi to bear but man the slipped out through the door before the burst spent itself against against the steel door.

Ben-Zhair cursed as he and Nassim climbed the steps up to his sleeping quarters. It was clear that the facility was compromised and Qasem had failed to stop the intruder.

He would build another bunker complex, ready for the next phase of his grand strategy. He relished the challenge. Money would not be a problem, especially after this success.

In his quarters, ben-Zhair quickly changed his desert fatigues for a clean white dish-dash, fitted a keffiyeh to his head and checked himself in the mirror as he added a pair of black-framed spectacles. Then he located his briefcase and placed his smartphone inside and checked the pile of dollars along with the keys to the Mercedes SUV which was in the car park. He pocketed some other items and his small desk was clear. He looked at Nassim. He was dressed as he had been since ben-Zhair had arrived – in pressed slacks and a shirt, with sandals - his regular academic attire. He wore a set of *mas'bah* – prayer beads - around his neck. Ben-Zhair nodded in satisfaction.

Ben-Zhair took a last look around at the room before they entered the stairwell. "Let us go, Nassim. It is a long climb and I will brief you as we go."

After two stops to recover their breath they emerged into a locked service room off the main concourse in the Radio Astronomy Faculty of the University of Oran. Ben-Zhair concluded his briefing. "Do you remember the café in Annaba where we met last year, near the Plage Saint Cloud?"

"Certainly, *Al-Mahdi*."

"Good, then let us meet there again in two days time, after morning prayers."

"I understand."

Perhaps you really do, thought ben-Zhair, but that is unlikely. In the bunker two floors below, he had seen Kateb in a new light and a plan had quickly shaped in his mind.

Nassim was just another research fellow, and he, ben-Zhair, a visitor. No one paid them any attention as they walked out through the concourse.

Ellie had sat in almost total silence for the ten minutes that Steve had been gone when she heard a detonation and gunfire, then all went quiet again. Her phone vibrated and she checked the secure message from Barbary.

'Withdraw immediately, situation hot. Will arrange extraction from RV1.'

'Hot' – what a stupid thing to say – this had been a suicide mission from the start. She swore then wondered how on earth she could get the message to Steve – if he was still alive. Never before had she worried about anyone in the way that she worried about him. The options were not attractive and she was lost in thought when something caught her eye. She raised her pistol in the direction of the movement and then started in shock as a jerboa hopped past her and on into the brush. She didn't know it was a jerboa but she did know that it was the weirdest creature she'd ever seen.

Satisfied that she was not in danger of clinical shock she washed down some more painkiller then checked her weapons and stood unsteadily, groaning at the pain in her leg. Limping slowly, she moved towards the tunnel then stopped and listened. Yes, it was definitely an engine – getting louder - and the noise was from the tunnel. She turned and hobbled back to her hide, wincing from the pain. She heard the rumble as she dropped behind the rock, and when she looked was astonished to see a minibus emerge, followed by two trucks, travelling very fast along the track across the front of her position. As they passed a few feet away in clouds of dust and grit she raised her weapon and swivelled her body, shouting as her leg gave way under her without a shot fired. She was almost in tears. That was a real fuck up! Then, just as she got to her feet again she heard another engine. A motor cycle appeared from the tunnel and stopped at the entrance. She watched the man move to the left hand side of the tunnel portal. He put his hand into a cleft in the rock then stood back apparently using his smartphone. The phone chirped and Qasem nodded as the detonator acknowledgement signal came through. He turned towards the motorcycle.

Never before had Ellie killed anyone in cold blood, but Steve was in there somewhere. The range was about thirty meters and she loosed a burst from the machine pistol. It went high and Qasem dropped to the ground, scrabbling desperately for cover at the tunnel entrance.

Shots came back at her – he certainly knew what he was doing but Ellie couldn't see where he was concealed. Seconds later he broke cover and started to run away from the tunnel entrance, firing as he ran. A loud explosion cracked out and the tunnel entrance collapsed in a cloud of dust and rock, enveloping Qasem. His motorcycle stood, shuddered and collapsed under a hail of rocks as Ellie dropped instinctively, her ears hurting. Smaller stones were falling on her and rattling on her helmet. She stood up and shook herself off then moved forward cautiously. After a few minutes she located an arm protruding from the rubble. The body covered by limestone rubble – and there was no pulse in the wrist.

She could see no way into the tunnel. Tears came to her eyes. What the hell had happened to Steve?

The door was locked, and there was no more C4 in his kit. Then he felt the floor tremble and a distant percussion. He examined the keypad and cursed when he realised it was just the same as those on the elevator. He thought about the man he'd seen and thought he was a good match to the picture of ben-Zhair. Steve smiled. Ben-Zhair – if that's who he was - had been using a mobile phone. Maybe there was a cellphone relay in here? As he thought it, his helmet replayed a voicemail from Barbary. 'It's too bloody late pal, I'm in too deep now'.

"Ellie, are you there?" he spoke into the helmet.
"Yes."
"Barbary's telling us to pull out, it's too hot? Since when has he started caring? Anyway, it's too late, the device has been triggered. I'm on ben-Zhair's tail - I think. Keep a very low profile as there may be too many for you to take on – perhaps twenty. Do not try to engage with them, you will not stand a chance."
"It's too late. A busload of them got away, plus two trucks. I only got one of them, more by accident than design. He was the last one to come out."
"Only one?"
"Yes, I didn't expect a convoy."
"You'd be dead if you engaged with that many. It was a bad plan of mine."
"He blew the tunnel entrance."
"That figures. Got to go, I think that there's another way out."
"Roger that. Be careful. No mountain lions so far. Standing by."
He pressed the icon that Ellie had demonstrated then held his smartphone against the access pad. He felt the electromagnet engage. Then the screen read:

Seeking server connection path...
Connecting...

Analysing...

Yes! There was an hourglass on screen which turned every second as a counter ran up to 15 seconds.

Unlatching pulses operational...
Task completed.

There was a click.
'Gotcha'!
Steve pulled the door open and was confronted by a small lobby area about a meter square, with a spiral steel stairway fitted into a shaft in the solid rock. He looked up the stairwell and listened but could hear nothing. There was low level lighting and a service duct running up the shaft. He started climbing and within seconds the 'sent' acknowledgement came through. He'd counted eighty steps when he came to a door off the stairwell. Another keypad which took another thirty seconds to unlock. He was losing time but had to be sure he wasn't passing ben-Zhair. He crouched, his Uzi raised and ready as he pushed the door open, looking into very plain single bedroom with a small bathroom off. There was no-one there. He checked the drawers of the small desk and found a gun cleaning kit. There was a small empty wall cabinet, and an electric kettle on a tray with some green teabags and an earthenware mug. He opened the closet – there was a dish-dash, a western suit and some underwear on a shelf. At the bottom was a range of boots, trainers and sandals. The windowless room was bare of pictures and personal items, although there was a wallscreen facing the bed.

He saw aircon and wallscreen controllers on the small table next to the single bed with a rumpled bedcover in a garish purple-striped Moroccan design. A small refrigerator held some water and beers. Steve's mental clock was counting and was up to one hundred and forty seconds when he noticed the pile of worn fatigues beside the bed. He held them up and riffled through them. He sniffed the dark wet splashes on the shirt and nodded at the distinctly ferrous smell of fresh blood. Yes, they could have been worn by the man he saw.

The waste basket was empty. Steve entered the shower room.

He jumped and swore as he raised his pistol, then laughed when he realised the helmeted man was his own reflection. 'Relax man, relax.' The cabinet was empty. Then, he found some hairs in the plughole of the shower tray. He grimaced as he wrapped them in toilet tissue and put them in a pocket. He thought of Bryan in Malta. Now dead – but avenged. 'You taught me well matey'.

He started climbing quickly again and counted another twenty seconds before he reached another door. He was panting hard after climbing at four steps a second - eighty steps.

Steve emerged from the elevator into a small bare room lit by a single bulb and checked his watch – just under seven minutes since he'd seen ben Zhair. The room was no more than six feet square and lined with shelves of cleaning materials. He closed the door behind him and a bare white wall faced him. No one would know that the stairway was there. The other door to the service room had an access pad on the inside. Now that was strange…

He could hear voices and activity on the other side of the door and had no idea what to expect. Hostiles or not?

His helmet chimed softly and he heard Ellie's voice.

"Are you ok?"

"Just. I don't know where I am right now – close to the surface I think. Ben-Zhair is about seven minutes ahead of me. Are you ok?"

"Yes."

"Wait there for me as agreed. Got to go - be careful."

"You too."

The connection dropped. 'I wonder' he thought. Steve spoke to his helmet "Anthony, google earth."

Less than thirty seconds later he knew what to expect. Google Earth had placed him in the centre of the Radio Astronomy campus, which was no surprise. Google located a map view of the facility which placed him in the concourse, at the surface. He looked carefully at the layout on the display, trying to memorize the key points.

Then Steve checked the pistol in his waistband and replaced it, pulling his shirt down. He put the Uzi in his toolbag and slung his helmet over his arm. Then he dusted off his clothes as best he could, checked his toolbag and waited as his phone unlatched the door. The door opened outwards and holding it slightly he peered through the small gap. He could see ten or fifteen people, male and female, in both western and Arabic dress. The layout from Google maps had indicated that the entrance doors were to his right, with the main desk to his left. There seemed to be some kind of panic. Maybe they had felt the explosion when the tunnel entrance had blown? They would probably think it was an earthquake.

As nonchalantly as possible, Steve opened the door, stepped out into the concourse and closed the door. It was a panel in the wall, without handles or any sign that there was a room there. A few students looked at him as he walked across the concourse attempting to identify ben-Zhair – without really expecting to. The man was certainly no fool and would very probably be gone by now. He swallowed a couple of handfuls of water from the drinking fountain as he crossed the concourse, his eyes scanning the twenty or thirty people there – they looked like students, and they were chattering excitedly. He passed through the sliding doors. Out from the air-conditioned interior, the heat hit him like a wall as his eyes carefully swept the car park, the bright sunlight a pain until he put his motorcycle helmet on. He reckoned he was a minimum of five minutes behind ben-Zhair, and probably ten. The room search had taken too much time. Had he climbed faster than ben-Zhair? The door locks had been delays. It did not look good.

*

The Radio Astronomy campus sat near the top of the hill, with a commanding northerly view. Over the campus buildings Steve could see the very top of the hill, which bristled with a variety of antennae for radio astronomy research and communications.

The approach road to the campus meandered up the hill and Steve had a clear downward view for at least a mile or so, he reckoned. The road was clear. To his left he could see arrays of wire strung out on the open hillside, which he supposed were aerials for radio astronomy. He brought up Google Earth again in his helmet. He could see that the access road had a track joining it from the east – the track appeared to go round the hill and head south to the N95 – the route they had come in on. Ellie was somewhere off that track. Suddenly there was movement - the late afternoon sun glinted off a Mercedes SUV pulling out of the far end of the car park. He started moving as it joined the access road, heading down the hill. Could it be ben-Zhair? 'Fifty-fifty' he muttered to himself as he looked around for transport. All the scooters and motorbikes were locked. These days, even in Algeria, there were very few vehicles that could be hot-wired – and he was no expert anyway. He checked his smartphone again. There was a text icon 'transport'. Standing at the line of motor cycles, he pressed the icon.

The familiar hourglass showed then the screen cleared and a list of code numbers scrolled down the screen, then stopped. There was a beep. Four bikes along the row, the blinkers on a dusty Suzuki 125 started to flash. As he ran he put his helmet on and mounted the bike. 'Full of fuel too, this is my lucky day.'

He gunned the motorcycle out of the car park.

"Ellie, I'm out on a bike. I think ben-Zhair is in a silver Merc SUV, maybe a mile ahead."

"I'll call it in to Barbary."

"Scrub the RV, You'd better get out of there pronto - that bang will have been heard – they certainly felt it in the campus. Let's set a new RV at the beach. I don't know how long I'll be, but if I'm not there in twenty four hours you'd better arrange your extraction."

"I don't think I can ride a bike. The leg is stiffening up."

"Shit! Did you take any more tabs?"

"Yes."

Steve leaned into yet another corner and accelerated for the next. He couldn't see the Mercedes but was surely closing the distance.

They both heard a chime in their headsets, then Barbary' voice.

"Tiger One and Two. Listen very carefully. A nuclear weapon has been detonated in the Canary Islands. Capture or kill ben-Zhair at all costs. The US is now in on this and they may attack the bunker. Do you copy that?"

"Tiger Two here. Yes loud and clear. I saw the pictures here. The bunker has been blown."

"Barbary, the target is believed to be in a silver Mercedes SUV heading from the Radio Astronomy campus down to the A1 autoroute. Identity NOT positively confirmed. Am in pursuit will advise asap."

"Tiger One here. Roger that, I'll get on to it."

"Ellie, I'm coming to pick you up."

"Tiger Two, Barbary. Your orders are to get on that SUV. Leave Tiger One – we'll pick her up?"

"And exactly how will you do that?"

"I can't disclose that now, just follow orders!"

"Make your mind up Barbary. You just told her to pull out."

"Before I knew you had the acquired the target."

"Ellie, throw your helmet as far as you can, now!"

"What?"

"Just do it. I don't trust these fuckers. Wait for me. Anthony, sleep."

Steve braked hard and stopped, then removed his helmet and threw it into a dry gully. He accelerated downhill and swung hard right onto the dirt track. Would Barbary really top them? He didn't know, but wasn't taking any chances.

The shrubs tore at him as he slid round the bends on the track. Then he heard an explosion and groaned.

As he rounded the final twist in the track before the tunnel entrance, Ellie emerged from behind some bushes, with an Uzi in her right hand.

"It's ok, I talked to the helmet first."

"Mine's still active somewhere."

271

"I'll text Barbary later. They can test their satellite link – if they have one."

"You doubt it?"

"Not really."

"Better get rid of our Tigers too."

"You remember where the self-destruct button is?"

Her look said it all.

Thirty seconds later Ellie climbed onto the pillion and after adjusting their shoulder bags, Steve accelerated the Suzuki back along the track.

As they re-joined the campus access road they heard the two detonations behind them. At best, Steve estimated that ben-Zhair was now at least ten minutes ahead of them. It seemed hopeless. Where would he be heading?

They could see the junction with the A1 autoroute ahead. Right or left, that was the question in Steve's mind as he brought the Suzuki to a halt.

"We need to be smart here. Which way will he have gone? Will he take side roads?" They both looked at Google Earth.

"Call Barbary. We need help."

*

The Message

"Prime Minister, one moment."

"Yes, Sir William?"

"We need to reconvene immediately. ICIM have just published an Announcement. We have verified it as authentic. There is also live video footage on the web."

The PM had already digested the details before all the Cobra members were back in their seats less than ten minutes later. She was aghast at the video feed images. After bringing the meeting to order, the Cobra screens showed the text of the announcement:

AL-RISALA
Issued by ICIM Operations Command
Dated: 15 Ramaḍān, 23:40 A.H., Mecca time.

The Islamic Caliphate in the Maghreb has today carried out a successful nuclear explosion on the coast of the Spanish Island of La Palma.

As planned, this event has created a tsunami which is now travelling towards the coastlines of the United States and Europe.

You were warned, and now we have acted.

It is not too late to embrace the love of Allah.

Signed: ICIM Operations Command

End

"Those bloody Tomahawks might have stopped it!"

"I agree General Rushby, but it was Spain's call."

"Prime Minister, I will provide an unattributable press briefing making it clear that Spain was told in advance and we had missiles airborne which were destroyed at the insistence of the Spanish Prime Minister."

273

"Let's wait a couple of days before we do that, Foreign Secretary – it might be more advantageous just to threaten exposure. Let's not overplay our hand."

"Where are we with the media announcements?"

"The BBC and ITV are just going on air now Prime Minister. You need to get to the media suite – you're on in five minutes."

Their screens showed the BBC and Independent channels in split mode.

All programmes are interrupted for a News Flash
Please stand by for urgent Government news broadcast

*

The jockeying had started before the adjourned Cobra meeting reconvened. It was a turf war in reverse – after all, which minister or department dealt with waves? No minster was pushing for responsibility – the aim here was to avoid taking it on. Was it DEFRA – the Department for the Environment, Food and Rural affairs? They usually dealt with flood issues. Alternatively, should it be the Home Office – the news of a threatening tsunami was sure to cause public panic and dislocation across southern England? The Defence Minister sat back, relieved that this could not possibly end up on his desk.

The Prime Minister re-opened the meeting after a brief discussion with the Cabinet Secretary, who was usually the arbiter on matters of protocol and precedence.

"Colleagues, time is of the essence. I am limiting this meeting to thirty minutes as I believe we have less than two hours before a possible national disaster. The First Ministers of Scotland, Wales and Northern Ireland are listening in to this meeting, as are all Chief Constables, Metropolitan mayors and municipal mayors. In view of the wide audience, please avoid discussion of classified defence and intelligence matters. Now, firstly, the Secretary of State for Defence will provide a summary of what has happened, so far as this is a terrorist incident. Then the Secretary of State for the Environment will

274

give us a summary of the environmental threat. Then, we will hear from the Home Secretary about public and general internal security. Then the Chancellor will give us the Treasury's first impressions of economic impact after which we will discuss the actions arising and the public statement. Andrea, if you please."

"Indeed Prime Minister, colleagues. A nuclear explosion has taken place on the Canary Island of La Palma, instigated by the Islamic Caliphate in the Maghreb – you will have seen their announcement on line, updating on your RSS feed as we speak. That is public knowledge." There was a tremor in her voice as she continued – she had never been prepared for this type of defence issue - who had? "We had some advance knowledge and tried to prevent it but failed. The explosion was designed to trigger a landslip and has apparently succeeded. The result is a tsunami, also known - incorrectly - as a tidal wave. As I speak this tsunami is spreading outwards across the Atlantic with a possibility of an arm of it reaching the South Coast of England and other parts of Western Europe. Such a tsunami had been postulated and modelled some years ago. The potential consequences are of the utmost severity. We have mobilised all spare land forces to assist with public safety and security. Thank you."

"Secretary of State for the Environment, if you please."

Charles Kimble's image appeared on a hundred touchscreens across various locations in the country as the virtual COBRA meeting continued.

"We are still reviewing all the technical work of the key paper by Ward and Day, and the various US and British documentaries. A train of several waves – perhaps as many as twenty – could hit the south and west coasts of the UK. These could be up to seven meters high. Now, about the impact. In summary, there is a very real risk of coastal inundation across the south of England, with all coast areas below one hundred feet of elevation at risk. Loss of life would be substantial and on a scale we have never seen before – if the predictions are correct. We are working with the Met Office to determine the speed, direction and size of the wave using existing ocean data buoys and weather satellite images. We are not hopeful of

275

obtaining any useful data in the limited time we have left. It would be prudent to plan for the worst.

We are urgently reviewing our national flood defence plan as it relates to the South Coast and its estuaries. We need to issue urgent Flood Warnings to the public, and would recommend that they all be RED. We do not believe that there is any flooding threat beyond the South Coast, although some advisors are suggesting that the Bristol Channel coasts could be in danger. Apparently the Channel resonates to long waves such as tides and there is an outside chance that the Somerset Levels and areas up towards Gloucester could be inundated. An amber warning for those areas might be prudent. The BBC and other media channels are standing by. Announcements will also be made on Twitter and other social media. Thank you Prime Minister."

"Issue the warnings now."

"Yes Prime Minister." The Secretary of State spoke to an aide at her side. "It has been done."

"Good, Home Secretary?"

"Prime Minister, colleagues. The risks as we see them will be, one, significant loss of life. Two, damage to national infrastructure such as power and gas supplies, transport and distribution networks. There may be issues of public order and looting in larger coastal cities such as Southampton and Portsmouth. Clearly there would also be a national economic impact, including rebuilding and so on. We would recommend that the Riot Act is read in all threatened cities before the waves hit. That will give the police authority to take whatever steps are required without delay. That's it in a nutshell."

"Thank you. Chancellor?"

"Prime Minister, colleagues. You will appreciate that with less than an hour's notice we cannot possibly have a handle on the likely economic consequences. All I can say at this time is that we consider the cost to be, say, ten times that of the serious flooding in 2013-14 – the figures are on your screen now, then the best estimate for the total economic damages is thirteen hundred million pounds in England and Wales, with a range to take account of uncertainty of one to one point five billion. Damages in England accounted for ninety one percent and in

Wales for two percent - the rest was Scotland and Northern Ireland. So, let's say this event – if it occurs – could result in an impact of fifteen billion pounds. Frankly, I think even that could be a gross underestimate. That is all I can say at the moment, Prime Minister."

"Those numbers seem a bit small to me."

"We are still working on the figures, Prime Minister. In contrast, the total economic costs of Hurricane Katrina to Louisiana and Mississippi was estimated at one hundred and fifty billion US – say one hundred billion sterling, but it's difficult to compare. Of course the insurance companies could claim that this was terrorist act as a get-out from their responsibilities."

"There would be public uproar if that happened. Thank you Chancellor. Let's move on. We have dusted off the national emergency plans and not surprisingly there is no scenario for an event such as this, other than major nationwide flooding which does fall within our top ten strategic risks to the UK. The relevant plan is Emergency Plan HO17. You all have access to this.

I propose that plan HO17 is what we proceed with. The Home Secretary will be the Plan Director as specified. You all have designated roles within that plan, the chain of command and with actions to be undertaken. It does not require relocation of the Government, though local city and municipal offices in threatened areas may need to relocate.

Unless I receive information to the contrary, I will expect to announce a National State of Emergency at six p.m. – that is, in fifteen minutes time. Does anyone have anything they wish to add – principals only please? One moment. I am just receiving information that Lisbon is experiencing rising sea levels. There is clearly no time for comment. Please go about your duties immediately."

As she left the room the RSS feeds started running news flashes about a disaster in Portugal.

*

277

Washington

There was rage in the Oval Office.

"Are you absolutely sure?"

"Yes Mr President. It is authentic and the threat is credible. The media want a statement. There's total panic all down the East Coast. The markets are plummeting and the SEC is halting all trading. The dollar is in freefall."

"What, in the three minutes since this frigging announcement was released?"

"Yes Sir. The Secretary of Homeland Security, the Chairman of the Joint Chiefs, Director Calucci of the CIA, and the Secretaries of State and Defense have been summoned. Fortunately they are all in town today. The Director of the NSA will be on video. The meeting is scheduled to start in fifteen minutes time. Bill Templeton is finalising your video statement now. You are scheduled to broadcast live at one p.m. Everyone is ready in the Sit Room."

The President winced as his stomach complained when the high speed elevator accelerated down to the Situation Room. He steadied himself against the stainless steel walls of the pod.

The President's Chief of Staff announced his entry to the Sit Room and the meeting began with a review of the ICIM announcement followed by CIA and NSA summaries of the explosion and satellite images. Lastly came clips of the video from Los Muchachos.

The mood was an intensifying counterpoise of rage and shock.

"Secretary Lopez, what do we have in our scenario portfolio for this event?"

"There is no relevant plan with Defense, Mr. President. The tsunami would be considered a natural event."

"Mr. President, it falls under the US Continuity of Operations plan with FEMA, under my remit at Homeland Security."

"Secretary Schmidt?"

"Yes, Mr. President. FEMA is the Federal Emergency Management Agency. The agency has disaster relief plans and offers advice on preparing for hurricanes and flooding, tornadoes, volcanos, power outages, storms etc. Tsunamis would fall under 'flooding', I guess."

"Jesus H Christ – you guess?"

"We have a plan for a plan..." Schmidt grimaced as the President stared back at him.

"...Sir. NOAA says that based on the original research – which is disputed – New England has six hours, Chesapeake eight hours and Florida nine hours. Florida and the Bahamas are likely to be the worst affected. This is bad Mr President – potentially a lot worse than a nuclear bomb in the middle of New York."

"Who in hell is NOAA?"

"The National Oceanic and Atmospheric Administration."

"Aren't they the people who got climate change wrong?"

"They still believe that climate change is happening Mr President."

"Can I believe anything that they say? How the fuck can they administer an ocean?"

"We can trigger the FEMA ERT-N. FEMA has pre-recorded announcements and their Emergency Alert System links into all the broadcast TV and radio stations plus the online news channels, to advise people what to do. And there are sirens, just as we have here in Washington for extreme weather."

"What in hell is FEMA ERT-N?"

"FEMA's National Emergency Response Team."

"Can they mobilise in six hours?"

"They can respond quickly to earthquakes, Sir."

"Do it."

The elevator doors opened and Bill Templeton was waiting outside the Sit Room. He thrust the draft text of the Presidential Address into the President's hands.

"Six fucking hours! How can I go to the people and tell them about this? I cannot go to the people with no fucking plan!"

"It still needs some final editing Mr President."

"I'll bet it does. Where is the Chairman of the Joint Chiefs?"

"In the Situation Room Mr President, waiting for you."

The Sit Room held at least thirty people with all eyes examining the images on a huge wallscreen which depicted the Ward & Day colour images of the predicted tsunami propagation across the Atlantic. A tsunami had never made it on to the list of strategic threats to the United States. The President was announced and everyone stood to attention.

"Let's get on with this – I'm due on air in fifteen minutes. What have you got for me Chairman?"

"Mr President an ICIM nuclear bomb in the Canary Islands has triggered a tsunami."

"I know all that – just get to the solutions will you?"

"Mr President, there are no military solutions as far as we can establish. We are moving our capital ships and boats – that is submarines - out to sea from Norfolk and other East Coast naval bases, but time is short. All forces are on high alert in case of opportunism from other countries."

"If the worst comes to the worst, do we expect any opportunism from say Moscow or Beijing?" The President looked at the Secretary of State.

"Mr President, we are still assessing the situation, but certainly Putin is likely to take advantage. Our main concern is that North Korea will make a move into the South."

"If they try that then we flatten them. Period."

Next, the President turned to the head of the Fed.

"What about the markets?"

"Mr President, the dollar is in freefall, currently trading thirty eight percent down on the Asian exchanges. As to the markets, the SEC has gone through all the Circuit Breakers – they're at Level One now."

"Level One – that's eighteen fifty points down on the S&P 500?"

"Correct Mr. President."

"Jesus."

"And Rule 48 is in operation in all the New York and Chicago exchanges."

"What a disaster! And the tsunami hasn't even hit us yet."

"Mr President?"

Deck turned to Secretary Schmidt.

"We don't believe that Washington is threatened, but nevertheless I recommend that we move you to the Mount Weather Emergency Operations Centre, along with the State Governments of those threatened states. That will make it much easier to coordinate the response."

"Where's that?"

"The Blue Ridge Mountains, Virginia. It can accommodate two thousand people. It's really meant for you and the Federal Government, but it would make sense to use it for the governments of the affected States."

"Can we do that in six hours?"

"Probably not everyone, but we need to make the move so that state government can continue after the tsunami strikes, because it will likely take months to restore normality if the worst happens."

"Let's move on that. Now, Secretary, what about the physical damage and loss of life that's expected?"

The forecasts were terrifying. By extrapolating the loss of life in the Phuket and Japanese tsunami disasters, the estimate was upwards of a million dead in Florida alone. That was likely to be the worst hit state as it did not have any significant areas of high ground. But there were other states likely to take a significant hit. After another six minutes the President left the meeting in a state of high frustration and deep concern as he headed to the media suite adjacent to the Sit Room.

"Fellow Americans, it is with great sadness that I address you this afternoon. Many of you will already know that the East Coast of our great country faces the approach of a tsunami within hours. We cannot predict what the effects will be, but they are likely to be very serious. Many lives have already been lost in Europe and we send our condolences to the people there.

The first point that I want to make is that our country is strong – very strong – and will come through this event even stronger. So, I want to warn any foreign country that is considering a plan to take advantage of the situation – don't even think about it. We have the resources to respond in spades, and will do so without hesitation.

Secondly, trading has been suspended on all major exchanges until next Monday at the earliest.

Now, Fellow Americans, about your personal situations.

The National Oceanographic and Atmospheric Administration has told me that all low lying areas in all coastal States from Maine to Florida plus the US Virgin Islands and the Bahamas are under threat of inundation.

Please watch your local news channels for detailed guidance on what to do in your local area. It will not help to jam the roads or empty the supermarkets. Consider your neighbours, especially if they are incapacitated in some way. Be calm, listen to the advice, and plan. Above all, stay cool.

Finally, as I speak to you, our Armed Forces are undertaking several operations which will lead to the achievement of justice. You should know that we will find and destroy ICIM, the perpetrators of this heinous crime - you need have no doubt of that. Wherever they are, we will hunt them down – and we will never give in to terrorism.

That is all I have to say at the present time.

May God be with you all.

The Prime Minister closed her office door and took out the red smartphone. 'C' responded immediately.

"Do you have an update for me?"

"Yes Prime Minister, I was about to call you. Our people are at the control bunker in Algeria. The Serbian terrorist is dead, and we have gained entry. The operation is still in progress."

"How many is 'we'?"

"One inside and one outside, wounded, Ma'am."

"My God 'C', are you serious? Is that all the people we have on the ground there?"

"You insisted on complete deniability Ma'am – it was impossible to put a larger black team in given the time constraints."

"Shit!"

'C' looked askance at his smartphone.

"Ma'am?"

"Where precisely is this bunker?"

"Prime Minister, do you really need to know that?"

"I most certainly do."

'C' sighed, puzzled by the question.

"It is buried in a hill beneath the University of Oran Radio Astronomy Campus near a city called Sid Bel Abbès – that's in Algeria."

"I see. Completely deniable you said, and only two of our people?"

"Correct, Prime Minister."

"Very well, keep me posted."

'C' felt distinctly uneasy about this conversation and scratched his head in thought as he left the Prime Minister's office.

"Charles, I want a one to one with the US President ASAP – and I mean one to one. Absolutely secure. This is a Red Call." Chief of Staff, Charles Medwin got to work.

Ten minutes later, 'C' closed the door of his temporary office beneath 10 Downing Street and logged in to his tablet in response to the Hotline icon which had flashed on his phone. He watched the video feed live as the call unrolled. He was, after all, a keeper of secrets and to do that one first had to have access to the secrets.

"Prime Minister - Sarah."

"Mr President – Thomas - I will not waste your time at this critical moment for your country. We know the precise current location of Abu ben-Zhair, head of ICIM. We both know that he is the instigator of the terrible events in the Atlantic Ocean which now threatens your country. Our operation to terminate him has resulted in the deaths of our agents. Abu Ben-Zhair is still alive."

"Where is he now?"

"I will tell you that he is in Algeria, but before I provide more details Thomas, there are one or two things that I would like to clarify."

"Sure, Sarah. The price."

"I would not put it in such bald terms, Thomas, but it would be helpful if I could have your assurance that the trade negotiations between our countries are concluded rapidly – say within one month, and on the basis of the current Heads of Terms and the details so far agreed. Additionally, we want your agreement to our proposals on the stalling points of tariff free arrangements and barrier-free market access for all British goods and services."

"That's a big ask, Sarah."

"Oh, there's more too, but of course your ability to announce that within twenty four hours of the tsunami catastrophe the United States had located and destroyed the perpetrator of the event – well, that should play really well at a time of dire national emergency – and stabilise the markets too. Don't you think so, Thomas?"

Thomas Deck grimaced. Sarah Michelson was a hard bitch alright.

"I'll need proof of ben-Zhair's location."

"DNA may be difficult to obtain, but will you accept the assurances of our head of MI6?"

"If I get the nod from the Director of the CIA and the Secretary of Homeland Security when they see the data, then yes. Is the Algerian Government complicit in this?"

"Not as far as we know. They abhor ICIM as much as we do."

"Then we have a deal."

"Do I have your word on this, Thomas?"

"Yes, Sarah, you have my solemn word. A deal's a deal."

"Very well, then we are agreed, Thomas, subject to the other matters which are of a relatively minor nature which we can discuss later."

Neither of them were fools when it came to doing deals. Deals could always be undone, but for Sarah Michelson it was a big step forward.

'C' groaned. Our agents dead? Not yet they weren't. He knew what was coming and called Barbary.

"Get them out of there now and save the questions for later."

He'd done what he could. They were deniable – and that meant that the PM need never know. Then, his smartphone chirped – incoming Red Cedar. It had to be the PM. Political expediency ruled, as ever.

Fifteen minutes later C' had advised Al Calucci, his opposite number in the CIA, that an active operation was underway to capture ben-Zhair. The coordinates of the bunker were provided. It was agreed that the United States would be able to take full credit for his capture – or death. It was out of his hands now. He made no mention of agent deaths.

*

The Portuguese City of Lisbon had been lucky, protected by the shallow estuary of the River Tagus and other natural features. Indeed, the tsunami had turned and dissipated as it met an underwater mountain range 150 miles south west of the Portuguese coast. The seamounts of Hirondelle, Josephine, Gettysburg and Ormonde, together with the features known as the Ampère Bank, the Coral Patch and the Gorringe Ridge, are quite shallow as compared to the wavelength of a typical tsunami – depths are as shallow as 30 meters in places. As the La Palma tsunami met the underwater barrier the interaction created huge turbulence and freak waves. One monstrous freak wave capsized and sank the ferry *'Albayzin'* which was bound from Cadiz to Las Palmas. But there were gaps in the natural defences of the sea bottom in this area. Further north than Lisbon on the Portuguese coast lies the small fishing town of Nazaré. This town is noted for attracting surfers – an underwater canyon focuses the ocean swell close to the shore, and waves as high as a hundred feet are regularly surfed by the world's leading boardsmen – and women.

As the UK Prime Minister was adjourning the Cobra meeting in London, the Canhhao de Nazaré focused part of the rapidly spreading tsunami. Nazaré was being completely destroyed and more than four thousand lives were ending.

Further south, the commercially vital Algarve coastline escaped almost completely although the low lying islands off Faro and Olhão were swept clean.

Out in the Atlantic, 600 miles to the west, the tsunami continued relentlessly towards the Caribbean and US coastlines at almost 500 m.p.h.

The President addressed the Chairman of the Joint Chiefs of Staff directly.

"What are my options, Joe?"

General Joe Haines looked at Samuel Chilcott, the Secretary of State for Defense - his boss- who nodded, his lips a thin line.

"Mr. President, based on the objective of killing BZ these are…"

The wallscreens and embedded tablets in the table showed a list.

"…One, a cruise missile strike. It will take two hours to execute, and would need the cooperation of the Algerian Government. But there's also a university campus on top of the bunker."

"Fuck them. The whole US East Coast is open to destruction."

"It would be an act of war and a war crime to boot Mr. President."

Thomas Deck looked at the Secretary of State. "I don't care a damn. Next, Joe."

"A Seals attack. We have Naval Special Warfare Unit 10 in Rota, in Spain – the Sixth Fleet is too far away, off Syria. For the quickest route we'd need the cooperation of the Brits to refuel in Gibraltar. And of course, that of the Algerian Government."

"The Brits will be a big yes, but could we do it without Algerian cooperation?"

"It would be better if we had it. They have very potent air protection – Algeria is a wealthy country. They have practically the whole range of Russian SAMs including the latest tech Russian SAM20 long range missiles and the Russian Sukhoi 30MKA multi-role fighter. It would be 50/50 if we could get a chopper in and out – even our stealthiest."

"Shit. 50/50 is no way to go - yet. Next."

"A Predator drone strike. They only carry Hellfire missiles which really lack the punch for underground bunkers. We'd have to air launch one – we don't have any in Spain and the Sixth Fleet…"

"Yes you said, tied up off Syria. Next."

"That's it Mr. President. Anything else would take more than the six hours you stipulated. So a MOAB is out of the question."

"I only counted one real option there, Joe. The Seals. The first blows up a campus, the third has no punch and hits the campus anyway."

"We're working with limited information Mr. President and a very short time horizon."

"Yes, well the information question is something for the CIA and NSA later. I'll also want to know how come the Brits knew so much and got ten Tomahawks launched for that ship. We wouldn't be having this meeting if it wasn't for European fucking politics."

The President's secure smartphone chimed gently. He looked at it "Ladies and Gentlemen, I need to take this call, alone. Let's reconvene in five minutes."

The room emptied, with no-one showing their surprise that there were red-phone secrets that the President would keep from the National Security Council even at this time of dire national emergency.

"The UK Prime Minister has just told me that they have a bead on ben-Zhair and are *en-route* to a rendezvous near Oran in Algeria. They are saying that it's our pick-up. It seems that the bunker has been disabled. Joe, get a plan together. It should be easy for Chrissakes – he's being delivered for us. You have fifteen minutes. The coordinates will be coming through Langley."

"Yes Mr. President."

"And by the way will you stop calling this fucker BZ? You make him sound like some Phi Beta Kappa fraternity wonk.

He's a fucking terrorist, in a different league even to bin-Laden."

No one around the table had seen such rage from the Commander in Chief – or such a lack of spirit from the Chairman of the Joint Chiefs.

"Yes. I'm going to parade that bastard on TV myself. I may even shoot him there in full view of the world."

The President was known for his colourful language and extravagant statements, and no one around the table doubted that he was capable of such an act. The Director of the Secret Service made a note to brief her teams *very* carefully, so that the President's reputation for shooting from the hip did not turn into hard reality.

"Mr President." The President looked at Al Calucci, the Director of the CIA.

"Yes Al?"

"We're just picking up signs that the North Korean armed forces are moving to a higher state of readiness – the highest, we believe. There are signs of reserves being moved towards the 38th parallel.

"The motherfuckers! Sam, put the UN on notice of our intentions to bomb the fuck out of Pyongyang if that dumbfuck makes another move."

Secretary of State Chilcott blanched. The text of the announcement to the UN was ready – one of several that had been prepared months before.

"Joe, we have the military options ready don't we?"

"Yes Mr President."

"Good, await my orders."

Deck looked at his Chief of Staff. "What is it now?"

"The UK Prime Minister is on the line, Mr President."

"What, again? I just spoke to her."

"She says that she has more information for you – you really need to know. She said to say that it concerns North Korea."

"Shit. I have to take this. No, don't move, I'll take it in a side room." Deck wondered what the price would be this time.

Sidi Bel Abbès

Half an hour after the call to Barbary, Steve and Ellie were on their way again, and Steve was even more sure that he didn't belong in the connected world. The Mercedes SUV was headed northeast and was now about an hour ahead of them. It looked as if he was headed back to the heart of the Dangerous Corridor in eastern Algeria.

It had been good fortune that the vehicle was a rented Mercedes SUV. The Mercedes was a premium rental, and the Algerian rental company – Fig Tree Rentals in Annaba - had ensured that the SUV was fully sync'd with the 'Mercedes Me' service link. This automatically tracked the vehicle and provided remote diagnostics. The hack into the Mercedes site had been more challenging, but the automated software toolset cracked it within 15 minutes. Then, it was just a matter of trawling the database for a time and location match. Just one Mercedes Me vehicle had been at the campus this morning. After that its position was available to GCHQ in real time – and they piped a convenient locator to Ellie's smartphone. There was also the name of the driver and a mobile telephone number.

Ellie's phone was on speaker as Barbary spoke. "Here's the plan. It will be dark in a couple of hours – just after eight p.m. so you will have to act in daylight, unfortunately. He's currently moving at about sixty miles an hour. We're going to trigger a remote vehicle diagnostics warning through the Mercedes network, just before he reaches Bou Khadir – that's about 80 miles ahead of him now. His vehicle will tell him that there is a problem and advise him to wait at the Bou Khadir service station for an hour until Fig Tree Rentals delivers a replacement vehicle. That's where you take him. So, get going. We'll work up some more details as you go."

"And what if he gets impatient and calls Fig Tree directly?"

"We'll cover that – and get his phone number as well, although we're currently trying to obtain that by other means."

Half an hour later, Steve pulled into a service station and bought some sun glasses. There were no cycle goggles available in the shop to protect them from the dust and flies which were slowing down his progress. There were a couple of scarves too, and these would help. He added a keffiyeh and agal, then picked up a few bottles of water and fruit juice, together with some baguettes.

"Steve, my leg is getting worse. The painkillers are not working." Steve glanced down and could see fresh blood soaking through what remained of Ellie's trouser leg.

Ellie had told him that her leg was throbbing.

"You've had all the antibiotics but your temperature is still up. You need fluid too. Drink more water. I need to change the dressing. There's morphine in the first aid kit. I'd better call Barbary."

"I'm not taking morphine."

"You might have to."

"Not yet."

"Tiger Two here. One's wound is getting worse. She needs proper medical attention pronto."

"There's a private ambulance *en-route* to meet you.. This will be used to extract ben-Zhair. She will be in a doctor's care within a couple of hours from now. RV coordinates follow."

"One hour, that's all I'm waiting. Then I'm taking her to the nearest hospital, ben-Zhair or not."

"And what do you think that their reaction will be when they see a gunshot wound?"

"I don't care – at least she will get treatment."

"Don't be too sure of that. Have you ever been in an Algerian prison?"

An hour later, after another conversation with Barbary, Steve pulled the Suzuki into the service station, keeping well away from the apparently empty Mercedes SUV.

The driver had been startled when the SUV started speaking with a very pleasant female voice, then he cursed as he discovered 'A transmission problem', whatever that was. The Satnav showed a flashing 'spanner' icon on the road ahead which marked the service station. He acknowledged it as the destination and saw that it would take 45 mins to get there.

He parked the vehicle near the exit and facing out, although he couldn't go anywhere yet. His cold phone rang and a lady from Fig Tree told him that the replacement was on its way.

The coffee was good in the café and there was much excitement as the customers watched the news on Canal Algérie. The Announcement was analysed and graphics illustrated the tsunami on its way across the Atlantic. Clips of the Phuket and Tōhoku tsunamis were played. He was having difficulty sitting still in his corner seat – the temptation to stand up and cheer was almost overpowering. The ICIM had generated fear on a huge scale. There was pandemonium in the US and Europe. Another SMS update from Fig-Tree Rentals told him that they had been delayed with the replacement vehicle but should be with him shortly.

As he waited, he finally gave in to temptation and ordered an Algerian brandy. The US President was due to broadcast in fifteen minutes.

Steve had learned how to wear a *keffiyeh* in the Yemen, and had no difficulty fitting the *agal* headband which held it in place. He had parked the Suzuki out front of the café and scouted the truck park at the rear and the truckers entrance to the café. Then he'd walked through the café to get an idea of the layout. The French influence was still strong, even down to the chequered table cloths. He stopped at the bar to order coffee, then returned to Ellie who was out front.

"Here, I got you a coffee. It's good. A sandwich too. I can't remember when we last ate."

"This morning, a croissant."

"Ah yes."

"Mmm, this is great. You look like a real raghead trucker."

"Good, that's the way it should be. He's in there – at least I'm seventy percent sure that it's him. He looks younger than his photo, though."

"I'd better get final clearance from Barbary."

He answered immediately.

"Seventy percent is good enough given that it's all we've got. The vehicle rental was to a bogus company so it all looks as we'd expect. The plan is good so get on with it. The RV with the ambulance is set for eight thirty p.m. local time – don't be late."

"Roger that. There's probably half an hour of daylight left. We're ready."

"Let me know as soon as you've got him. Check the time – the text goes in five minutes, I say again five minutes from - now!"

"Got it. We're moving."

"Are you sure you're ok, Ellie?"

"Yes, I'm OK, Steve. Stop worrying, just a bit weak that's all."

"I should really change that dressing. Take some more antibiotics."

"Yes, yes, I will. Let's just get on with the plan and grab this bastard and then get to the RV. We don't have much time."

"Your phone will ring when he's on the move." He checked his pistol and put back in his waistband at the rear.

Steve walked back into the café through the front entrance and took a stool at the bar. There were a dozen or so customers, all glued to the CNN news channel on the wallscreen. The video from Los Muchachos was being played repeatedly. The clip showed planes and several explosions in the air and then a brief black screen – the caption said 'Instant of nuclear explosion' followed by the formation of the spherical cloud and the collapse of the south of the island into the sea.

It was absolutely magnetic to watch.

Steve felt his phone vibrate and then focused on ben-Zhair. The man who had planned the mayhem being shown on the TV looked at his phone. He nodded to himself and then moved to pay at the bar, carrying his attaché case.

The Spanish naval base in Rota in the Bay of Cadiz base was a frequent stopover point for US warships, with a convenient air force base nearby. The warning of the tsunami flashed from the Office of the Chief of Naval Operations in Washington had led to frantic activity at Rota, where there was currently only one US warship. There had been no time for the *USS Michael Murphy*, an *Arleigh-Burke* class destroyer to put to sea, so tugs had been used to lay beam anchors and pull the ship away from the quayside. This was precautionary – they had no way of knowing whether or not – and how seriously - the tsunami would hit the Bay of Cadiz.

In the event, the Bay of Cadiz had not been affected -the offshore reefs provided some protection and the vagaries of the hydrography further out in the Atlantic resulted in barely measureable effects along the coast near Cadiz. A hundred miles to the northwest, the low lying Algarve took some serious punches.

Barely had the moment of crisis passed than the destroyer received further orders from Naval Command and another set of frantic preparations began.

Steve followed ben-Zhair out of the café and across the car park to the Mercedes SUV where Ellie was standing in the gathering twilight, leaning against the vehicle. She smiled as she addressed him in French.

"Bonsoir Monsieur, je represente Figuier Location de Voiture. Vous avez un problem?"

"Oui. Ou est l'autre voiture?"

"Avec mon collège."

Steve closed in and tapped ben-Zhair's left shoulder. As he turned in surprise he met a solid right uppercut. Steve caught him as he fell against the SUV.

"That was the weakest part of the plan. Come on, let's get him round the other side."

They found ben-Zhair's car keys and in the light of the open passenger door Ellie rolled up the left sleeve of ben-Zhair's shirt. Within seconds the morphine injector was empty.

"I'm fading Steve."

Steve checked the GPS on the dashboard of the SUV.

"Eight minutes to the RV. Hang in there Ellie, talk to me, remind me about *Rubaiyat*."

"I'm finding it hard to think…"

James Marinero

It was dark now and the road they were following was definitely not fast and straight. Ellie groaned occasionally as the vehicle bumped over the poor surface and rolled on its suspension. In the rear seat, ben-Zhair was laid out. Barbary's doctor had said that the morphine dosage should be enough to keep ben-Zhair under control for at least an hour – if not unconscious then at least very happy and docile.

Ellie's smartphone spoke "You have arrived at your destination."

Once ben-Zhair had been subdued and they had started the SUV at the service station, Steve had struggled with the vehicle's GPS system which was set up in Arabic, so he'd had to switch to Ellie's smartphone for directions. That had kept her focused, but now she was slipping in and out of consciousness.

"Where's that bloody ambulance?"

Steve climbed out of the SUV and checked the coordinates. Right place, right time. He could see the sea ahead reflecting the setting new moon and the lights of shipping heading east from the Strait. He ran round and opened Ellie's door. She was now fully unconscious and her breathing was shallow, her pulse weak and fluttering. His phone vibrated.

"Tiger One, extraction in thirty seconds. Don't do anything stupid – and don't give away any secrets. Not even code names. The password is 'convocation' Got it?"

"Convocation. Yes. Get a fucking move on – Ellie's very weak, she needs immediate attention." Steve looked up and turned his head, listening, suspicious of Barbary, frantic about Ellie. Moving closer to the Mercedes he crouched, pistol in hand.

Suddenly he was surrounded by men in black – very big men. The bullhorn voice was almost painful in his ears. "Throw your weapons down and lay flat on the floor hands behind your head. We will use deadly force!"

There was a whirring sound which grew stronger and then he was blinded by intense light as a stealth helicopter rose from behind the dunes. Sand was swirling and visibility was almost zero.

Steve complied, but Ellie was still in the passenger seat.

294

More black-clad figures dropped from the helo and swarmed over Steve who shouted "Convocation, convocation, convocation!" They helped him to his feet.

"Convocation acknowledged, sir. I'm leading this Seal Team. Call me Rufus." They were shouting in the maelstrom.

"The woman in the car is one of us, she needs a doctor immediately."

"Where is the target?"

"In the rear seat, he's had morphine to subdue him. For Christ's sake get a doctor to the woman."

"A medic is attending to her now, Sir."

Steve moved towards the Mercedes but Rufus grabbed his arm. Like all his team, Rufus was one of the physically biggest men Steve had ever seen. He dragged Steve to the US Navy Seahawk MH60S, instinctively but unnecessarily ducking under the spinning blades. Steve could see a stretcher being loaded. A Seal carried ben-Zhair's briefcase in a large Ziploc bag.

"Ten seconds" he barely heard Rufus say into his comms mike.

Strong arms pulled Steve aboard as the Seahawk started to lift, and he was strapped into a seat and given a headset. The cabin was dark and he could just make out one stretcher. It was very cramped – this MH-60S was a Block 2 Mines Countermeasure variant anti-submarine helo which had been rapidly reconfigured for this interdiction – and these guys were huge and heavy.

"All accounted for. Cleared for lift-off."

The Seahawk lifted, banked and turned in one smooth movement, accelerating quickly to a hundred and fifty six knots.

Steve didn't hear the detonation of the incendiary charge in the Mercedes SUV or see the 3,100 degrees Centigrade bright magnesium flash below.

"RV site sanitized" someone said over the comms.

Steve looked around the dark cabin.

"Where is my wife Rufus?"

"Your wife sir?"

"Yes, the lady in the fucking car!"

"Oh, I see. I didn't realise that she was your wife, sir. I'm very sorry, she didn't make it sir. The medic pronounced her dead at the scene. We had to leave her body – we're overloaded anyway."

"What the hell! She's dead? You left her?"

"Yes, sir."

"And if she'd been alive?"

"She wasn't sir."

"What's happened to her body then? Is it just lying there for the Arabs to look at?"

"No sir, everything at the RV was destroyed by fire. No traces, no evidence. Completely sanitized."

Steve was speechless. He held his helmeted head in his hands and turned inwards, incapable of crying. Ellie dead, Ellie 'sanitized'. He had lost friends and family before but this was pain like he'd never felt and he began to sob quietly.

The Seals had been drawn from Naval Special Warfare Unit 10 (NSWU-10) in Rota, Spain. The Seahawk had left the *USS Michael Murphy* and vectored across Andalucia and the Mediterranean to the rendezvous near Cape Figalo, a distance of some 260 miles. With a range of 245 miles and no in-flight re-refuelling tanker available, the helo would have to land – and soon, even though it carried one of the optional two extra internal fuel tanks.

Steve lost track of time – his mind had retreated to the helm of his old boat Adèle, at sea on a starlit night. He could feel the easy motion of the boat, hear the chuckle of the sea against her hull as she lifted and swooped over the waves. It was his way of coping with the anguish, a meditation. Then he felt his straps tighten as the Seahawk slowed and they touched down, bringing him back to a reality he didn't want. The engines quickly spooled down and he looked out to see the familiar shape of *HMS Bulwark's* superstructure lit by floodlights. The helo was quickly strapped down by men on the ship's flight deck and then seamen began pulling out and connecting a fuel hose to the Seahawk. The helo rolled gently with the ship.

"What happens now, am I getting off here?"

"Sir, we have orders to take you with us – we're headed for the airbase at Rota. You will be debriefed there."

"I'm not going to Rota. I want to go to Gibraltar."

"It's not optional, Sir – I have my orders. Your government has agreed."

"I bet they fucking have."

Steve looked at his smartphone. Not even a satellite signal – the Seahawk was well and truly blacked out. Then he felt the helo's engine wind up and they were climbing away again, headed north-westwards. He was too numb to feel anything and just started to plan, to think about anything but Ellie. The trouble was that all his plans had involved her. His brain cycled through the events, her words, her actions – and her fading away rapidly in that last half hour. He could have done things differently - he *should* have done things differently. He could have taken her to a hospital. But he had not. She had not wanted him to – they were after all, just following orders. Orders, fucking orders and now she was dead.

The helo began to climb higher and the ride became rougher as they flew through the night turbulence over the mountains of Andalucia. Minutes later they were descending and then down on the ground, under the arclights at the edge of the airbase at Rota.

As Steve was removing his helmet the inert form of ben-Zhair was unloaded and by the time they reached a building at the side of a hangar, the stretchered ben-Zhair was being loaded on to a grey-painted executive jet, a Seal carrying the briefcase. The plane started rolling within seconds.

Rufus was accompanied by two other Seals as he led him through the door and into an office suite. There were several men seated there, none of them in uniform.

One man stood and moved towards him, his hand outstretched.

Steve moved quickly "Barbary, you fucking bastard!" but the Seals were quicker and he was pushed down into a chair.

"Hold on. Let's calm down. Do we really need to tie you up?"

Steve shook his head.

"I'm really sorry to hear about the loss. We did all we could. Here, have a drink." On the table stood a jug of coffee and a bottle of Veterano Spanish brandy. Barbary pushed a mug of coffee towards Steve, adding a generous slug of brandy.

"That's it. I'm done." Steve put his hand on the table and exposed a piece of toilet tissue.

"What's that?"

"Ben-Zhair's hair, I think. From the shower tray in the bunker."

Just then they heard the scream of the two Rolls-Royce engines as the grey Gulfstream took off for its non-stop flight to Andrews Air Force Base in Washington D.C.

Rufus looked up and said "Shit!" then reached for the tissue paper but Barbary had got there first.

"Lieutenant, we only agreed to provide the prisoner. If you want anything else you'll have to take it up with your commander. Your countrymen here…" Barbary nodded to the other civilians "…will agree."

One of the other civilians spoke. "Leave it with us Lieutenant."

"On whose authority?"

"Your Commander-in-Chief. You did a good job and you may leave us now and return to base."

"You are not in my chain of command."

"Maybe not, but your orders are on the way." Lieutenant Rufus Payne considered the situation and nodded. "We'll wait outside pending further orders."

Shortly afterwards the men in the room heard the Seahawk take off for the two mile flight back to the *USS Michael Murphy*.

After the debrief started Barbary deflected some questions from the two CIA men on the grounds of operational security and lack of authorisation. This led to calls to Washington and London and eventually some very tight ground rules were established, much to the dissatisfaction of the CIA operatives. Steve then described events from the moment they had approached the bunker under the campus until the moment of lift-off from the RV.

Within an hour the debrief lasted was over.

Barbary drove Steve to a hotel. Nothing was said.

"You're free to return to Gibraltar now, Baldwin. Good luck."

*

Within 10 minutes of the landslip, the initial energy of the tsunami wavetrain had spread over 600 miles as the wave radiated out into the broad Atlantic, with the South America, the low islands of the Caribbean, Florida and the US East Coast in its path. Western Europe was in its path too, with Portugal being hit hardest and first.

Within two hours the tsunami was meeting the shallows of the continental shelf to the southwest of the UK and France. The shelf extends out more than 160 miles from Lands End and with depths in the main of less than 150 meters or so, its dragging effect on the tsunami was significant.

The English Channel experienced some small effects – a strong spring ebb tide flowing westwards caused many freak waves as it interacted with the faltering tsunami, and the westerly gale which was blowing. Several lives were lost in an early season offshore sailing race.

Other than that the English Channel was unaffected, as were the Irish Sea and Bristol Channel. France too escaped serious effects, but some ships were damaged in the Bay of Biscay. This area is noted for freak waves - the edge of the continental shelf is very steep here, compounding the effects on high seas resulting from strong westerly weather.

The sea bottom in the Atlantic Ocean is marked by the world's longest mountain range – the Mid-Atlantic Ridge, extending from North East Greenland down almost to Antarctica. In parts it extends above the sea surface – Iceland and the Azores archipelago form part of the ridge, but mostly its depth in the north Atlantic is of the order of 1000-2000 meters – a mile or so. By the time the tsunami encountered the Ridge, the huge potential energy of the initial water dome would be dissipated along a 4,000 mile wavefront.

Mitigation

Bengt Jacobsen jumped with fright as a Minuteman III missile launched from its underground silo with a huge roar, just a mile away. Bengt was a farmer inspecting the green shoots of his recently planted wheat crop in the late evening sunlight. Just outside White Sulphur Springs in Montana, he watched in awe – and fear - as the local cluster of buried silos disgorged their deadly contents skyward. The arcs of white smoke from the three-stage solid fuel rocket motors carved their way upward as the missiles leaned under the control of their inertial guidance systems and turned onto a heading just east of south. It was a pretty but deadly picture as the trails formed an almost surreal arch in the blue sky. This local cluster of missile silos was ranged around Malmstrom Air Force Base. The land on which the silos were buried had been his family's land, land which his father had leased to the US Government in perpetuity way back in the 1960s. Since boyhood he'd hoped to God that he would never see the day that the ground opened in anger, but now the day had come.

A few seconds later and a few hundred miles nearer the target line, the missiles from the silos around Minot AFB in North Dakota and Francis E Warren AFB in Wyoming were aloft, their trails carving the evening sky.

Bengt ran back to his truck and heard a newscaster on the radio announce an imminent broadcast by the President. Bengt punched his home number on his cellphone. "Ingrid, get into the tornado shelter, I think we're at war. I just saw a spread of Minutemen missiles launch from the silos. I'm heading straight back and should be with you in half an hour. Tell the ranch hands what's happening so that they can get home. Phone the kids too. The President is on the TV in five minutes."

*

There had been a buzz in the air as the President motioned everyone in the White House Sit Room to sit down just after 6 p.m. Washington time.

"What have you got Joe?"

"It seems we've come up with a potential way to defend ourselves against the tsunami, Mr President. There is a theoretical research paper on the use of acoustic gravity waves to mitigate the effects of a tsunami by some guy called Usama Kadri. I stress the word theoretical."

"Come on Joe, Is this a trick? Another guy called Usama?"

"He's genuine, Sir, we checked."

"Ok then, acoustic whatever - speak English will you?"

"I'll try to simplify it Sir. If we can generate a wavetrain to work against the tsunami, then we could reduce its amplitude – I mean size – and disperse its energy. We'd need a lot of energy over a huge area to do that. The research paper talks about an earthquake, but that's out of the question."

"It wasn't for ben-Zhair!"

"Yes Sir, but that was a unique set of geological circumstances. We don't have much time and my team are still working the math, but we figure we have a chance within the three hours left if we use our biggest fusion bombs, deployed in a line facing the tsunami, at maybe a hundred feet below sea level, in the open ocean. We're monitoring the tsunami propagation using satellite laser altimetry and specialist software which France has provided. We estimate three hours now till it starts to hit the Bahamas."

"Can we get the bombs in place in time?"

"We'll use LGM-30G Minuteman III missiles sir. We're preparing target coordinates as I speak – we would aim to have simultaneous detonations so that our generated wavetrain interferes with the tsunami as it passes over the Mid-Atlantic Ridge, where the water is shallower. Obviously, we will have to notify Russia, China, the UK and France in advance to avoid any misunderstandings. Also, there would be environmental consequences. For example, the UK and Western Europe would be subject to some fallout."

"That can't be as bad as losing our whole East Coast."

"Yes Sir. I emphasise that time is of the essence. Missile flight time would be of the order of twenty minutes from our Mid-West silos. We have one warhead per missile – that's a START treaty limitation. I am recommending we use one hundred missiles of the five hundred we have in service. At a spacing of twenty five miles that will cover a two thousand five hundred mile tsunami wavefront and hopefully shield the coast from New York down to the Florida Cays. We will aim for simultaneous detonations which mean that we'll have staggered launch times from our silos in Montana, North Dakota and Nebraska. We'll need to advise shipping and aircraft to avoid a one hundred mile wide zone."

"There are bound to be casualties at sea, but we have no choice."

"Yes Sir."

"Move it forward as quickly as you can, I will speak to Putin and the others. We'll need to provide them with target locations – arrange that as soon as you have them. We don't want to start World War Three."

"Yes Mr President. At the appropriate time we'll need the nuclear launch codes from you."

"Of course. I'm not going anywhere without the football."

"Mr President, I really must emphasise that this is a shot in the dark. The paper is theoretical. It might have no effect at all. And I will need you orders in writing, Sir."

Deck looked around the hushed Sit Room. "I assume that you're all behind me on this one. There is no other option. A hundred missiles is a very small price if it works."

There was a nod of assent from every single person in the huge room, but their eyes showed gleams of hope for the first time that afternoon.

"My Chief of Staff will arrange the formal orders. I will announce our plan to the people once the missiles are airborne. FEMA will continue with the Emergency Response Plan already underway." Deck turned to his Chief of Staff. "You'd better get my statement drafted. I hope it's going to alleviate some of the panic we've got on the streets."

*

Bengt Jacobsen floored the accelerator and barrelled along the straight track across the prairie a long dust plume behind him in the evening air. His ranch was over fifteen miles away and he made it in fifteen minutes – no mean feat on a prairie farm service track.

When he ran into the house, Ingrid was seated in the kitchen. There was a tumbler and a bottle of Jim Beam bourbon on the table.

"Why aren't you in the shelter? Did you call the kids?" The questions tumbled out.

*

The President and his team had been hard at work talking to the Kremlin, Beijing, London and Paris to inform them of the planned missile launches and the target line in mid-Atlantic. All French, Russian and Chinese tracking stations went to an immediate state of highest alert – any deviations from the declared trajectories would be viewed very seriously. The British and French also raised their alert status to the maximum. With over 8,100 miles range – not disputed but believed to be higher – a Minuteman III guidance malfunction could put all of Europe and even the Middle East in danger of a strike. It would only take a 1% failure rate to result in 1 missile going awry.

The European governments were also concerned about the anticipated nuclear fallout, but there was nothing that they could do or say that would sway the US Government. Thirty minutes notice was all they got.

Minutes later the satellite images of the simultaneous nuclear explosions were watched across the world. It was chilling, but it was effective. The 2,500 miles long line of thermonuclear warheads had done their work, but not without loss of life on seven cargo ships.

Only two missiles had failed to detonate. As a result of guidance system failures, they had been destroyed in flight by command from NORAD deep beneath Cheyenne Mountain. At sea an urgent US Navy operation was started as they raced to recover the two warheads before the Russian Navy got to the sites.

By the time the tsunami reached the US coast of Florida its energy was dispersed along 8,000 miles and its impact was much less severe than the worst of the dire news channel prognostications. Florida was hit the hardest with damage and loss of life surpassing that of Hurricane Katrina in the Gulf of Mexico. Despite the Ward and Day mathematical model of the tsunami's effect, which forecast waves of 25 meters height hitting the coast of Florida, for example, the eventual result was of lesser consequence.

But disappointment is relative – mathematical models are not always accurate in their predictions, and in this case they didn't need to be. Huge panic and terror had brought much of the US East Coast to a standstill, and the effects on the internet and international commerce had been unprecedented in their scale. And the US had used 20% of its nuclear strike capacity to prevent an even worse catastrophe.

*

Ingrid poured the bourbon and smiled.

"Sit down and sip, Benny. It's all OK. The missiles are aimed at that tsunami wave, out in the Atlantic Ocean – you know, like we heard about earlier. We are not at war. The President just finished his announcement on the TV. They don't know if it will work or not, but as he said 'it's the best shot we've got'. He said that there were a hundred missiles and they aimed to create a huge set of waves to flatten the tsunami."

"Thank the Good Lord for that, Ingy. I was real scared out there – I thought we were at war. Never thought I'd see the day they launched those missiles. The ground was shaking and I was real scared."

He picked up the bottle of bourbon and started pouring another shot.

*

Prime Minister Sarah Michelson had thought long and hard about releasing the information to Washington and to gain the most benefit required that she used the utmost finesse. She believed that she'd played the hand perfectly. Deck's closing words to her had been:

"If this turns out to be correct – and I note that you have put heavy caveats on it – then you can just name your price."

A result. 'C' would not be happy, but then he never was. *She* was the Prime Minister, after all.

In Washington the evening had turned into night – a cold and frosty starlit spring night and still the first day of Ramadan, although it was now the 16th May in Mecca. Deck returned to the Situation Room after speaking with the British Prime Minister. His face was puce in colour. His personal doctor, in a side room, was monitoring the President's vitals and sent a secure SMS to the President's Chief of Staff, expressing concern about blood pressure. This was no time for a heart attack.

"I never imagined it could get any worse, but it just has. I have just been told that the Brits are sixty percent confident that BZ's..." he held his hand up acknowledging the usage of the abbreviation "...originated in North Korea and were sold to Iran. The first was used in Rome." There was a huge clamour and Deck waved for silence. "Ben-Zhair stole them from Iran. There were only two, and they were based on a public technical design from Stanford, right here in the US – a peaceful design it seems. A fucking own goal."

Sam Chilcott tried to speak. "Wait Sam. The Brits *could* be playing a clever game and are way off a hundred percent confidence anyway. She's been drip feeding me. I've done enough negotiating to know that she may be holding something back – certainly she would not give away any sources, even if she herself knew them - not yet anyway. We can work on that. What we need to do *right now* is check this, any way we can. I am going to call Ben Liebowitz and see what he has to say."

"Mr President?"

"Yes Sam?"

"If Israel knew about this they would already have hit Iran."

"I realise that. He's not stupid, he'll want to check the facts himself."

"He's got an election coming up in six months."

"Good point but let's set him on the trail anyway. Get your Middle East people at State prepared. Right, Joe, have we got joint strike scenarios for Iran and North Korea?"

"Not simultaneously – that's never ever been contemplated, but we can weld two together and generate a range of combined options."

"Well you'd better contemplate it now! And factor in possible action from the Israelis. If they will not act against Iran then we'll go it alone. Pyongyang is on the move and that will be our strike priority. Send my Chief hourly updates. We reconvene in three hours. All of you - get to work. Meeting adjourned."

Deck's Chief of Staff passed him a post-it note. He scanned it and then crumpled it and put it in his pocket. No fucking doctors, not now.

He walked to the washroom and thought that it had been a bad afternoon. The night to come would surely be worse. The strategic problems that the US had faced for years and failed to solve had now come to a head simultaneously. Russia had yet to tip its hand, but Putin would make a move – that was a certainty.

Deck would have to resign soon, but he wanted to be remembered as the President who had staunchly defended US interests during the most unpredictable conjunction of major world events in history. That would be his legacy.

The only problem was that the country did not deserve that dumbfuck Vice President he was stuck with. He hadn't figured the solution to that yet. Six months was all he had left and he knew that the pancreatic cancer could not be beaten. Only four people knew right now – and that four did not include his wife. He looked at himself in the mirror, smoothed his hair and smiled grimly. 'President Thomas Deck, are you ready to rock and roll?'

*

Epilogue

Over the Atlantic, the man in the stretcher on the grey Gulfstream slowly came to his senses. He felt the doctor check him but continued to feign unconsciousness. He conjured up an image of the gate of Heaven, said a prayer, and bit down hard on his rear molar.

'C' and the Prime Minister were in her office at 10 Downing Street.

"Let me get this straight. We have a sample of DNA – maybe contaminated – which we believe came from ben-Zhair?."

'C' nodded. "Hair follicles."

"And the Americans have a body, supposedly that of ben-Zhair, who committed suicide on the plane extracting him to Washington?"

"Yes Ma'am, cyanide in his tooth, and compromising papers in the lining of his briefcase, we've been told. They included outline plans for a new, non-nuclear phase of the *jihad* – targeting Russia and the Far East."

"And the DNA sample we have?"

"It does not match that of the body, Ma'am, although it matches one of two sets on the briefcase. The CIA sent us both sets."

"And the CIA does not know that our sample doesn't match the body's DNA?"

"Not yet, Ma'am. I've stalled them citing equipment issues, but I can't hold out any longer."

"Can we er...'*fix*' the sample?"

"I thought you might say that. Yes we can, it's only a dataset after analysis. We will send them data which matches the body. Just copy the set on the briefcase that doesn't match the hair."

"Good, let's do that. I'd hate Deck to think I'd sold him a dud, especially now that he's gone public on the 'execution of the mastermind.' "

"Very well, Ma'am."

"Who *was* the man who committed suicide?"

"We don't know."

"And the real ben-Zhair?"

"We're still looking. You don't need to know anything else Prime Minister."

"Thank you 'C'. Now, about the situation in Iran and North Korea. Thomas Deck is on the warpath. Then we'll have the Cobra meeting about the nuclear fallout coming our way."

*

The drizzle was compounding Steve's intense misery as he walked back to Marina Bay, passing the security box at the stern of the *Sunborn Gibraltar.*

"Steve old mate, where have you been?"

"Hi Liam. I went away for a few days."

"Anywhere interesting?"

"Not really, just along the Spanish coast to a quiet hotel."

"So, where is your beautiful lady today then?"

"She's dead."

"Dead?"

"Yes Liam, dead."

"Oh, Christ in Heaven, I'm so sorry, Steve. Are you sure, I mean – oh fuck I don't know what to say."

"There's nothing you can say."

"I didn't know. That's a bloody shock. How?" The look on pain Liam's face betrayed his genuine emotion.

"No reason you should have. It was a car accident in Spain. I don't really want to talk about it, thanks."

"Blimey. The world is going to hell in a handcart. A nuclear bomb in the Canaries, a tsunami in the Atlantic, Israel attacking Iran and now it looks like war in Korea. And now Ellie. Jesus Christ, what a shock. Why didn't you call me?"

"What for Liam? It wouldn't change a thing would it? Not a fucking thing. So just can it, right?"

"Hey, steady mate. I'm just trying to help, you know,"

"Yes, sorry, I know you are, but you can't."

"Tell you what, let's get really tanked tonight."

"Thanks Liam, but I need to be alone for a while."

"Fair enough, mate, but drinking alone is not a good idea. I should know."

"I've had plenty of practice myself. Anyway, I'll be moving on soon - I'm going to take *Rubaiyat* round the coast, maybe to Cadiz or up to the Algarve. Spend a few months up that way, sorting myself out. I've had enough of Gib."

"I don't know what it'll be like up there – the eastern Algarve got hit by the tsunami."

"Did it? I haven't seen the news for a couple of days."

"Yeh, along the low lying bits. It even inundated Faro airport but that's on marsh anyway. They were expecting a major disaster in the US too, but it seems they got off fairly lightly. Can't predict these things can you?"

"No."

"Well, if you need some crew, I'm right here."

"Thanks again, but I've got to get used to handling her myself."

"Ok, mate. Well you know where I am – you've got my numbers and email address."

"Thanks, Liam I'll see you around."

Steve turned and headed down the quay to *Rubaiyat*. The sooner he was away from Gib the better it would be all round. Then he'd do his serious drinking alone.

His smartphone vibrated. He looked at it - Barbary. He dropped the phone into the water at the quayside and walked on.

*

References and Further Reading

The Baker Test at Bikini Atoll:
https://en.wikipedia.org/wiki/Underwater_explosion

Callisto Hacking Group:
http://www.independent.co.uk/news/uk/home-news/hacking-foreign-office-data-callisto-group-phishing-scam-cyber-security-a7684296.html

Cause of all Causes:
Ḥamīd Al-Dīn Al-Kirmānī: Ismaili Thought in the Age of Al-Ḥākim. *Paul E. Walker.* Pub: I B Tauris & Co Ltd, 1999.

Charles's Hole in T'Wall Bar:
http://www.yourgibraltartv.com/blog/10935-jan-22-iconic-hole-in-t-wall-pub-to-close-after-40-years

Chinese Remainder Theorem:
https://en.wikipedia.org/wiki/Chinese_remainder_theorem

Cumbre Vieja Collapse:
https://en.wikipedia.org/wiki/Cumbre_Vieja

Doomsday Scenario:
http://www.geo.arizona.edu/~andyf/LaPalma/doomsday.html

Guoanbu:
http://intellibriefs.blogspot.com/2008/03/chinese-secret-service-from-mao-to.html

[The] Hacking Team:
https://nakedsecurity.sophos.com/2016/04/19/how-hacking-team-got-hacked/
https://en.wikipedia.org/wiki/Hacking_Team

Mercedes Me:
https://www.mercedes-benz.com/en/mercedes-me/connectivity/

Krypton Fluoride Lasers for Nuclear Fusion Implosion:
http://www.ncbi.nlm.nih.gov/pubmed/26560597

Laser Pumped Fusion Research:
http://www.scientificamerican.com/article/high-powered-lasers-deliver-fusion-energy-breakthrough/

http://www.nature.com/nature/journal/v506/n7488/full/nature13008.html

Level 3 Communications:
https://en.wikipedia.org/wiki/Level_3_Communications

Lightning Strike Probability:
http://www.lightningsafety.noaa.gov/odds.shtml

Megatsunami, Ward & Day original research paper:
http://onlinelibrary.wiley.com/doi/10.1029/2001GL013110/pdf

Megatsunami:
http://guardianlv.com/2014/04/east-us-destined-for-future-mega-tsunami/

Megatsunami La Palma:
http://www.drgeorgepc.com/TsunamiMegaEvaluation.html

New Canary Island?
http://www.bbc.co.uk/news/magazine-15917740

Nazaré Surf:
https://www.youtube.com/watch?v=D1L9Pm4qrf8

North Korea Hydrogen Bomb Test, 2016:
http://www.bbc.co.uk/news/world-asia-17823706

North Korean Satellite:
https://en.wikipedia.org/wiki/Kwangmy%C5%8Fngs%C5%8Fng-4

North Korea Submarine Launched Ballistic Missile test 2015:
http://www.reuters.com/article/us-northkorea-missile-idUSKBN0UK02P20160106

North Korean Ballistic Missile/Satellite Launch 2016:
http://edition.cnn.com/2016/02/08/asia/north-korea-rocket-launch/

Nuclear Fusion Bomb Design:
https://en.wikipedia.org/wiki/Thermonuclear_weapon

Nuclear warheads – miniature:
https://en.wikipedia.org/wiki/Davy_Crockett_(nuclear_device)

Protector Drone:
http://www.janes.com/article/55008/uk-to-double-top-end-uav-fleet-with-new-protector-platform

Radon as an earthquake predictor:
http://physicsworld.com/cws/article/news/2010/mar/18/a-radon-detector-for-earthquake-prediction

http://www.geo.mtu.edu/volcanoes/santamaria/volgas.html

Risk:
'Risk – The Science and Politics of Fear', Dan Gardner. Virgin Books, 2009.

RSA Encryption:
https://simple.wikipedia.org/wiki/RSA_(algorithm)

Tempora:
https://en.wikipedia.org/wiki/Tempora

https://www.theguardian.com/uk/2013/jun/21/gchq-cables-secret-world-communications-nsa

Tsunami Mitigation
http://www.heliyon.com/article/e00234/

U.S. Seals Naval Special Warfare Group TWO:

https://navyseals.com/nsw/structure/

The Vela Incident:
https://en.wikipedia.org/wiki/Vela_Incident

http://www.jpost.com/Israel-News/US-suspected-Israeli-South-African-nuclear-test-474765

War on Terror:
'Unconquerable Nation: Knowing our Enemy, Strengthening Ourselves' (Brian Michael Jenkins. RAND, 2006)

Author's Notes

'Cause of All Causes' completes the Magreb Trilogy. The idea for this book came to me many years ago, and blending it in with the first two books in the trilogy and with topical news has been very enjoyable. Writing topical novels is an interesting process because the ground is continually shifting, and the last year has been outstanding in that regard.

Some aspects of cryptography (at least as far as I can begin to understand it) have been tailored for the purposes of the story. For those with a deeper interest I have provided reference links. Invention I have kept to a minimum – most technologies mentioned in this book do exist.

Some minor details of geography have been changed for the convenience of the story. As to the precise way in which a tsunami originating in La Palma would propagate, be refracted and its energy dissipated, then that is a mixture of Ward & Day's ideas and my own speculation. The paper on using acoustic waves to mitigate a tsunami is very recent research.

My thanks as always go to Rosy Jensen for her keen eye and encouragement. The errors, as always, are my own.

And finally, a big *thank you* for taking the time to read this book. I try to write to entertain and inform. If you have enjoyed it (or not) then a review on Amazon or Goodreads would be much appreciated. Your feedback is always welcome – email me! And check out my free book offer!

James Marinero, May 2017
Grenada, West Indies
james@jamesmarinero.com
http://jamesmarinero.blogspot.com
Twitter: @jamesmarinero

Join my Readers List and get a Free Thriller Book*
at:

www.jamesmarinero.com/free-book

Marinero's skill at describing people with a few deft strokes is remarkable. The action is fast, furious and believable. This is a must read for lovers of complex geopolitical thrillers: - Lee Holz, author of The Bowin Novels

Make no mistake, our society is under threat...

In this terrorism thriller, Steve Baldwin has sailed to Crete in his search for a quiet life, still licking his wounds after a near-fatal assignment in the Red Sea. The Royal Marines had been his family, but now he tangles with Helena, a Greek waitress who is far from what she seems, so Baldwin sets sail again.

In Malta, he is coerced by MI6 into the pursuit of a psychopathic female specializing in assassinations, with whom he shares some painful, bloody history. Can he ever escape these two clever, dangerous and demanding women - one of whom he is ordered to kill?

Malta, with its Crusader history, is a key target for terrorists. Abu ben-Zhair, the cold and calculating Islamist master planner, is upping the terrorism stakes and religion is just a lever in his lust for power.

The chase - and the women - are more complex than Baldwin could ever have imagined.

*Free Books offered change from time to time and may vary from that illustrated here.

About the Author

James Marinero grew up in West Wales and has at various times been a chef, a milkman, maths lecturer and private tutor. He spent over 30 years in IT as a consultant and project manager and ran his own computer business for several years.

He has been passionately involved with boats and the sea for over fifty years and is now achieving a lifelong ambition to write novels and entertain readers. He spends much of his writing time on his boat, which he has sailed extensively in the Atlantic and as far as Brazil. He is a qualified open water diver.

During his various careers he has worked in the Middle East, Russia, Scandinavia, the US, Kazakhstan and much of Europe.

His personal interests, career, education and travel background have equipped him well to write adventure and techno-thriller novels.

When he is not on his boat he lives on the Hampshire coast.

Coming Soon from James Marinero

The Theory of Dreams

Also by James Marinero

Fiction:

Gate of Tears
(featuring Steve Baldwin)

Sicilian Channel
(The Maghreb Terror Trilogy Book 1 featuring Steve Baldwin)

Sword of Allah
(The Maghreb Terror Trilogy Book 2 featuring Steve Baldwin)

Non Fiction:

Susan's Brother

www.jamesmarinero.com
james@jamesmarinero.com
http://jamesmarinero.blogspot.com
Twitter: @jamesmarinero